BREAKING EVEN

By Elizabeth Fackler from Tom Doherty Associates

BREAKING EVEN

ELIZABETH FACKLER

A Tom Doherty Associates Book
New York

BREAKING EVEN

Copyright © 1998 by Elizabeth Fackler

This book is printed on acid-free paper.

A Forge Book
Published by Tom Doherty Associates, Inc.
175 Fifth Avenue
New York, NY 10010

Forge® is a registered trademark of Tom Doherty Associates, Inc.

Library of Congress Cataloging-in-Publication Data

Fackler, Elizabeth.
    Breaking even / Elizabeth Fackler. —1st ed.
      p.   cm.
    "A Tom Doherty Associates book."
    ISBN 0-312-85911-2 (acid-free paper)
    I. Title.
PS3556.A28B74   1998
813'.54—dc21   98-5717
                                     CIP

First Edition: July 1998

Printed in the United States of America

0 9 8 7 6 5 4 3 2 1

To Michael

Hekuba's Price

★ Autumn 1883 ★

1

★

Hekuba and Heaven were sisters, though one was the color of richly creamed coffee and the other was ebony. At sixteen, Heaven was fine-boned, her delicate features surrounded by sumptuous curls that fell halfway down her back. Her waist and hips were tiny, her breasts firm and round, her feet as graceful as an antelope's. Hekuba was tall and lean with barely any breasts and feet like shovels. Her hair was so kinky she kept it short and covered by colorful kerchiefs she wore knotted at the nape of her neck. Her nose was straight and prominent, her lips curved and full. She rarely smiled.

Heaven nearly always smiled, her dark eyes laughing. From an early age she had been trained as a courtesan, first educated in a Catholic convent, then instructed in the carnal art of pleasing gentlemen, successfully disregarding the contradiction between those schools. Despite the cream of her complexion, she was stained with the sin of being Negro, and the nuns had taught that black folk weren't allowed in the upper echelons of the hereafter. Heaven reasoned that since no degree of piety could make her white enough, neither could any amount of sin make her blacker.

Although slavery had been illegal in the United States for twenty years, neither she nor Hekuba complained. Recognizing that freedom guaranteed poverty to people of color, they preferred being kept in style. When the man from the West bought Heaven, he agreed to take Hekuba, too, thinking such a thin woman wouldn't eat much and a loyal servant was always welcome.

His name was Raul Ortega and he owned the pueblo of Sulphur Springs in the southeast corner of Arizona Territory. It wasn't much of a town, no more than a collection of adobe buildings around the springs that attracted travelers. Ortega sold lodging and meals in his hotel, guns and ammunition in his store, horses at his livery, liquor in his cantina, and pleasure in his brothel. He kept half a dozen young women for the amusement of his patrons, but Heaven was for his eyes alone.

His origins were humble, and the delicate Creole girl from New Orleans was his pride. She spoke French and English as well as Castilian Spanish, which lisped from her lips with charm. Only when he was sure their children would not be as dark as Hekuba did Ortega plan to marry Heaven. Though he took his pleasure every night, a year had passed with no sign of a child when the posse rode into his pueblo tracking thieves.

Ortega knew the jefe of the posse. In that region of scant law enforcement, he also knew the value of earning such a man's gratitude, so he gave the jefe his Heaven for the night. Then Ortega stayed away from the cantina, not wanting to watch her with another man. When the jefe and his compañero rode out in the early hours after midnight, Ortega walked into the saloon to see Heaven still at the table. Feeling dread that his gift hadn't pleased the jefe, Ortega asked Cipriano, who managed the cantina, "Has she not left this room?"

Cipriano shook his head. "He never touched her."

Ortega could scarcely believe that. "¿Está en lo cierto?" he demanded.

Cipriano nodded. "He talked to her with pleasure. And later

he went outside and left her with his compañero, but neither of them touched her."

Ortega felt offended. He had offered his prize and she had been refused. Suspecting it was neither her beauty nor her charm the man had declined but the consequence of owing him a favor, Ortega walked across the room and stared down at her. "Why didn't he want you?" he asked gruffly.

She raised her eyes, fearful of the consequences of her failure. "He told his friend," she answered softly, "that he was faithful to his wife."

Ortega grunted. Even if he had known the jefe was married, he would never have expected the man to honor those vows. He appraised the woman, searching in vain for flaws. She was wearing her best frock, her hair was clean, and despite spending many hours in the smoky cantina, she still emitted a flowery fragrance. The reason was as he suspected: Seth Strummar wished to remain free of obligation to Raul Ortega. "Go to bed," he told the woman.

Keeping her gaze on the floor, she left the cantina with a semblance of chagrin. Once outside, however, she forgot Ortega's disappointment and ran to his home, through the rooms connected like boxcars on a train to the last chamber where her sister slept. Leaping onto the feather bed, Heaven laughed as she tickled Hekuba awake.

"What is it?" Hekuba asked drowsily.

"I am in love!" Heaven declared.

Hekuba's mind cleared with sudden dread. "With whom?"

"His name is Joaquín Ascarate." Heaven sighed. "Isn't that a beautiful name?"

"Do not let Ortega suspect your feelings," Hekuba warned. "He will cut out your lover's heart and make you eat it."

Heaven laughed again. "He cannot," she said. "My caballero is too much man."

"Huh," Hekuba said. "Where is he from, your precious Joaquín Ascarate who is so much man?"

"He lives in Tejoe and is the compañero of Seth Strummar."

"And who is he?"

"An important man. Last night Ortega gave me to him but Señor Strummar was not interested. After a time, he left me alone with Joaquín. We talked and talked, Hekuba, and I have never known such pleasure in a man's company, such grace and gentleness in his eyes, such love in his soul."

"What did you talk of?"

"Everything!" Then she whispered more somberly, "He told me he was raised in a brothel and had watched his mother die of a carnal disease. His eyes held such sorrow when he told me this. He touched my cheek and said he would save me from such a fate." She sighed soulfully as she hugged herself. "When I told him Ortega had promised to marry me, Joaquín said such a promise from a man who would share me with others is less than I deserve. He said he would marry me and keep me to himself always."

"Huh," Hekuba said again. "Men always say that."

"But this one is different. He will return and keep his promise."

"He is already gone?" she asked with fresh suspicion.

Heaven nodded. "They were chasing thieves. Joaquín said when it was done, he would return and buy me from Ortega."

"Did you tell him you had a sister?" Hekuba asked, worried at being left with Ortega's wrath.

"Yes, and that I would not be happy leaving you behind, so he said he would take you, too." She grinned with triumph.

"Huh," Hekuba said. "Promises are easy on the tongue."

"If you had met him," Heaven argued, "you would not doubt his word."

"I doubt all promises," she answered. "Do you remember what Ortega said of this town? How sweet the spring was, how soft the shade of the cottonwoods, how gentle the breeze from the desert? Look at what it is: the water smells of sulphur, the trees are twigs, and the winds are hot and full of dust. Such is the promise of a man."

"Not my Joaquín," Heaven said. "You will see."

Hekuba rose and walked to the window, looking across the desert at the moon setting below the distant peaks. "I hope you are right," she murmured.

Autumn brought only a lessening of heat. Travel on the road increased and Ortega's business kept him busy, so Heaven had hours alone to dream of the handsome caballero who would rescue her. Weeks passed, however, without his arrival. Each night as she lay beneath Ortega, she willed her body to reject his seed, to hold her womb in readiness solely for her beloved. Yet so many days passed that when she looked into Hekuba's eyes, she saw a reflection of her own growing sorrow.

Hekuba felt weary with disappointment. If Heaven gave Ortega a child no darker than a Mexican, then he would marry her and Sulphur Springs would be their home forever. The prospect was bleak. Yet if the child were dark or Heaven failed to conceive, Ortega would sell her and there was no guarantee the new man would take Hekuba, too. What would become of her then was a fate she dared not contemplate.

In the afternoon of a late October day, she was alone in the cantina gathering whiskey to take to Ortega's parlor. She was kneeling on the floor behind the bar, arranging the six bottles snug in a crate, when she heard horses stop outside. Slowly she stood up and watched two men walk in. One was tall and fair, with pale eyes that met hers with curiosity. The other was Mexican, slight and dressed in black. He was smiling as he approached her.

"Are you Hekuba?" he asked in a gentle voice.

She nodded.

"I am Joaquín Ascarate," he said. He watched her eyes flare with recognition and he laughed softly. "Has Heaven told you of me?"

She nodded again, feeling fear now. Both of the men wore guns and their cartridge belts were fully loaded, as if they were habitually in need of many bullets. And though their clothes were clean and well tailored, she doubted if they had enough money to buy such an expensive woman from a man with no inclination to sell. If they meant to steal Heaven, it was unlikely they would burden themselves with her, too.

"Think we could have a drink?" the tall one asked with a smile.

Hekuba noted the soft drawl in his voice, marking him as a Texan. He was at least ten years older than his friend and seemed amused at the romance that had brought them back to such an insignificant place as Sulphur Springs. "What would you like?" she asked, dropping her gaze.

"Whiskey'll do," he said.

She put the glasses on the bar and poured from a bottle of Ortega's most expensive Kentucky bourbon. "Is there anything else you wish, señores?" she asked.

"What's 'Hekuba' mean?" the tall one asked.

She had never seen such eyes before, as gray as gunmetal and changeable as the sky. Their humor made her bold. "It is the name of an ancient queen," she replied, raising her head higher. "What does 'Seth Strummar' mean?"

"It's the name of an outlaw," he answered, winking at her as he lifted his glass. She watched him drink the shot of whiskey in one swallow.

"Would you like another?" she asked.

He nodded and watched her pour. She looked at Joaquín Ascarate's glass, but it was still full.

"Is Ortega around?" he asked.

"I will find him," she said.

Walking into the bright sunlight, she felt her hopes fade. What future could an outlaw offer her sister, even the compañero of an outlaw? Perhaps comfort, perhaps even wealth, but both would be as short-lived as he. With a heavy heart, Hekuba found the patrón in the corral watching Oso shoe a horse. She told Ortega that two men in the cantina had asked to speak with him, then watched him walk away as she listened to Oso work behind her.

"What do you know of this man, Seth Strummar?" she asked the blacksmith.

He looked up from his work. "Is he here?"

She nodded.

Oso dropped the hoof he had been filing flat and looked toward the cantina. "He's about the most famous outlaw still alive in these parts."

"A thief, then," she said.

"Was once. I heard he's retired."

"So no longer dangerous?" she asked with fresh hope.

Oso chuckled. "His reputation's built on killin' more'n stealin'."

"Has he killed many?" she whispered.

"More'n two dozen, is what they say. That don't sound believable, does it? But I know for a fact he killed two men just last month."

"Why did he kill them?"

"One was a bounty hunter who tracked him to Tejoe. The other a bank robber, one of them he was chasin' when he came through here leadin' the posse."

"How can an outlaw lead a posse?" she asked.

Oso shrugged. "He did his crimes in Texas and has been livin' clean in Arizona."

"In Tejoe?"

He nodded.

"Is it a nice town?"

"Better'n Sulphur Springs," he said, going back to work.

Hekuba listened to the rhythmic grating of the file, then asked, "What do you know of his compañero?"

Oso scraped the file a few more times, then let the hoof drop from between his knees and stood up straight again. "They're two of a kind," he said, "though rumor has it Ascarate started out to be a priest." He looked down the road toward the cantina. "Wonder what they came back for?" he asked rhetorically. Tossing the file into the dust where it clanked against his other tools, he walked into the stable and pumped the bellows on the fire.

Hekuba stood in the corral feeling the warm wind lift her skirts and caress the bare skin of her legs, then she walked through the open gate and up the road to the patrón's home. When she found Heaven bathing in the tub, Hekuba urged, "Hurry. Your caballero has come."

2

★

 Hekuba was in the yard brushing Heaven's damp hair when Ortega returned. He stood in the doorway and watched them. Although he regretted parting with his Heaven, he reasoned the sacrifice would bind the outlaw to him with obligation. Then, too, Heaven had failed to conceive, and Ortega wanted sons to care for him when he was old. He thought maybe God was telling him to seek a wife from his own people and leave the heathens to themselves.

Slowly he walked into the sun and stood looking down at the beauty he no longer owned. "I have loved you as if you were white," he said.

A succulent smile played on Heaven's lips, though she kept her eyes veiled behind her lashes. "I have loved you the best I could," she answered.

"I have sold you," he said.

She stood up. "May I ask, señor, to whom you have sold me?"

"His name is Joaquín Ascarate. He says he will treat you well."

With more happiness than Ortega had ever seen on her face,

she looked at her sister. Hekuba did not smile, and he suspected she understood better than the beauty what was happening.

"Pack your things," he said. "They wish to leave now."

"And my sister?" Heaven asked, her dark eyes dancing.

Ortega frowned, knowing she had never felt such joy thinking of him. "The other one bought Hekuba."

Suddenly Heaven's joy was clouded. "You promised we would not be parted," she whispered.

"They, too, promised that," he said. "Ascarate didn't bring enough money for both of you." He laughed bitterly. "He thought you would come cheap, but I demanded fifteen hundred American dollars."

She gasped, amazed at the amount.

"I made a good profit," Ortega said. He turned to go, then looked back at Heaven standing in the sun. Though he wanted to tell her he would miss her, at least to wish her good luck in her new life, he walked away saying nothing.

Hekuba and Heaven, carrying their belongings packed in two valises, left the house they had lived in for a year and walked down the street to the cantina where four horses were tied. One was a sorrel glistening red in the fading light of sunset, the other as black as midnight. Beside them were two bays with sidesaddles. Neither of the women had ever been on a horse and they eyed the bays with trepidation.

"Our first adventure," Heaven whispered.

"Let's hope it is the most difficult of what lies before us," Hekuba answered.

When the women entered the cantina, the men were still drinking at the bar. Heaven's caballero smiled and came forward eagerly. The outlaw watched them leave together, then looked at Hekuba, letting his gaze slide down her body and rise again to her face. He did not smile. Thinking he was unhappy with his purchase, she raised her head higher beneath his scrutiny. He finished his whiskey, took a coin from his vest pocket, and slid it across the bar toward Cipriano, who also didn't smile. No one said good-bye or wished them luck. Hekuba walked out and watched the Mexican lift her sister onto the smaller of the bays, noting that the man was gentle and his eyes shone with love, not lust.

"Need a hand?" the outlaw asked softly from behind her.

She hadn't heard him coming and she whirled around to look up at him. He clasped her waist and easily lifted her into the saddle. Then she was looking down at him, though his face was hidden by the brim of his hat. When he handed her the reins, their eyes met again, both of them aware that he owned her now. "I will try to please you," she murmured.

He chuckled, then moved away and swung onto the sorrel. As they followed behind Heaven and her caballero leading the way north, Hekuba was keenly aware of the man riding beside her, so close she could have touched him. "Are you taking us to Tejoe?" she asked.

He nodded, a playful light in his pale eyes.

She wanted to like him but remembered what she had heard about his killing so many, and she knew such a man would not always be playful.

"Should've bought you a hat," he said.

She touched her kerchief. "I never wear one."

"The sun'll boil your brains tomorrow," he said.

"There are many places in the world as hot as this desert," she answered, "where people wear no hats."

"Where might they be?" he asked pleasantly.

"In Africa and the Holy Land."

He thought about that, then asked, "Do they wear robes, like in the Bible?"

She nodded.

"Reckon your scarf'll be okay, then," he said. "Being as you're from Africa. Ain't you?"

"My mother's mother was stolen from the Gold Coast," she agreed.

"And your father?"

"Was also a slave, but I never met him and know nothing of his people."

"Never thought slaves did," he said.

"You are Texan," she said.

"Was once."

"Did your family own slaves?"

He shook his head.

"My sister's father was a Spanish nobleman," she said.

"That makes her Creole," he said. "But you're just a solid nigra."

"Just," she said.

He smiled. "Well, I'm just a solid sonofabitch, so don't worry about it."

"I never have," she said.

He laughed with soft surprise, then said, "You ain't ever been on a horse either."

"No," she said. "Am I doing something wrong?"

"If that horse should spook right now," he said, the remnant of his Southern accent barely a hint in his voice, "even if you managed to keep your seat, you wouldn't have any control."

She studied the way he held his reins, and pulled the slack out of hers in imitation. "Is this better?" she asked.

"Good enough," he said. "That animal ain't gonna spook for anything short of a rattler. It's about the sorriest horse I've ever seen."

Impulsively she asked, "Am I the sorriest woman you have ever seen?"

"Not by a long shot," he answered, his gray eyes warm. "But I bought you for your sister, so don't worry about that either."

She had never met anyone who used his eyes the way he did. Both penetrating and playful, they teased with fun above a core of steel that she suspected could turn deadly in a flash, though maybe that was because she knew his reputation. Carefully she asked, "Is there something I should worry about?"

He looked ahead at his compañero and Heaven. "Well," he drawled, "Joaquín's gonna marry Heaven before we get home. I tried to talk him out of it, said he should get to know her first, but it's not them that need to get used to the idea. You'll be the only people of color in Tejoe and not likely to be entirely welcome." He looked across at her, his eyes suddenly so cool they glinted like metal. "You ever handle a gun?"

She shook her head.

"Tomorrow I'll give you a lesson," he said.

"Will the people of Tejoe threaten us?"

"Heaven can pass for white. But you'll have to mind your p's and q's not to raise their hackles. Since I don't live in town, I'd feel better knowing Joaquín had some kind of backup."

"Isn't there somewhere else you could put me?"

He smiled. "Don't think my wife would appreciate my showing up with a woman I'd bought and paid for, so I can't take you home. And I can't see putting you in the wilderness by yourself. You wouldn't like that."

"Perhaps I would like it more than living with people who feel no welcome for me."

"They'll get used to you," he said. "It'll be enough."

"As long as I can handle a gun?"

"It's a healthy skill to own," he said.

They spoke no more, riding north through the twilight. At full dark, they camped in an arroyo sheltering them from the wind. It was warm enough that they didn't build a fire. Neither did they have supper. The men gave the women their bedrolls and stretched out on their saddle blankets a short distance away. Hekuba and Heaven settled down in the makeshift bed, both of them aching from their first hours on horseback. Before they went to sleep, Hekuba whispered, "Are you still happy with your caballero?"

"Very." Heaven sighed. "He is a good man."

"He is an outlaw, did you know that?"

"The other one is," she answered. "My Joaquín is not."

Hekuba lay awake long after her sister had fallen asleep, watching the stars slowly move across the black sky and wondering what their life would be like living in a town of white people. She thought, too, of what the outlaw had said about not taking them home because his wife wouldn't like it. Despite the way his gaze lingered on her body, maybe he really had bought her only for her sister and wouldn't claim any rights. She was so plain no man had ever shown interest in making such a claim, so she didn't guess he felt tempted. Yet when she remembered him saying she wasn't the sorriest woman he had seen, Hekuba smiled because that was as close to a compliment as she had ever received.

When she awoke in the morning, the men were not there. Quickly she woke Heaven and they walked down the arroyo to where it turned so they could do their business without fear of interruption. When they returned to the camp, the men were still gone. For one brief moment Hekuba thought she and her sister had been abandoned. Then she saw the four horses saddled and waiting, and she chided herself for her foolishness. On the blankets lay a canteen of water and a small, clean towel that hadn't been there before.

Heaven laughed. "Isn't my Joaquín thoughtful, Hekuba?"

"Yes," she said, wondering if it hadn't been the outlaw's wife who anticipated their feminine needs.

"Pour it for me, Hekuba," Heaven said, her tone not presumptuous only because she was accustomed to being served by her sister.

Hekuba poured water into Heaven's cupped hands and watched her wash the delicate face that inspired men to pay fifteen hundred dollars to possess her. Heaven dried her beautiful face, then sat on the blankets and rummaged in her valise for her brush, running it through her tangled curls until they shone in the sun. Kneeling in the sand, Hekuba washed her own face. She ran her hand through her short bristly curls, then shook out a clean kerchief and tied it on her head. With the last of the water she rinsed her mouth and spit into the sand, rejecting her envy of Heaven's beauty with the sour taste of sleep. She had just finished rolling the blankets and brushing them free of sand when the men returned.

The outlaw stayed by the horses, pulling the cinch tight on his sorrel, as Joaquín approached the women. He smiled with eyes only for Heaven. "Buenos días. It's a beautiful morning, isn't it?"

"Yes." Heaven laughed.

Joaquín turned to Hekuba. "Seth said he will give you a shooting lesson before we leave. Pay attention to what he tells you. There is no better teacher in the country."

Heaven asked coyly, "Will you not teach me to shoot, Joaquín?"

"For the moment, I would rather our time together be more quiet." He held out his hand. "Would you like to go for a walk?"

She took his hand, smiling up at him. Hekuba watched them with envy, seeing Joaquín's arm slide around Heaven's waist and how she leaned close, as if even an inch were too much distance between them. When Hekuba looked at the outlaw, he slid his rifle from its scabbard and carried it over.

"Ready for your lesson?" he asked with an amused smile.

She nodded.

He scanned the arroyo in the direction opposite from where the others had gone, then studied her face without a hint of the avoidance she was accustomed to seeing in men's eyes. "Sleep okay?" he asked.

"Fine," she said. "Thank you for asking."

He chuckled. "You've been to school, haven't you, Hekuba?"

"Yes," she admitted warily.

"You talk like a schoolmarm," he said, opening the rifle and emptying the bullets into his palm. He pocketed half of them, then said, "What we have here is a Winchester forty-four forty. This is how you load it."

She watched him fit the bullets into the slot and slide it shut, meeting her eyes. She felt her heart beat faster, having him so near. He emptied the rifle again, then handed it and the bullets to her. "You do it."

She succeeded without dropping any, though she felt clumsy after his expertise.

"Close the magazine," he said.

"Where the bullets are?" she asked.

"That's right," he said. "Now push the lever away from yourself to cock it."

"Which lever?" she asked.

He took the rifle back and cocked it fast, the noise sharp in the quiet. Hekuba was amazed at the smoothness of his action, obviously perfected by years of practice. Then he uncocked the gun and handed it to her. "You do it," he said.

She pushed the lever as far as it would go. "Should I bring it back?"

"You ever hear the expression 'half-cocked'?" he asked.

"Yes. It means entering a situation without adequate preparation for its danger."

"That's where you've got the rifle," he said.

She returned the lever to fit tight beneath the metal circle under the trigger.

"Hold the stock against your shoulder," he said. "You know what the stock is?"

She met his eyes, feeling a prick of anger. The truth was she didn't know what the stock was, but she had seen men fire a rifle so she raised it into position.

"Now sight down the barrel," he said.

She did, squinting through one eye.

He reached over and settled the stock higher on her shoulder. "Not your arm," he said. "If you hold it there you'll end up with a bruise bigger'n Africa. Keep it high and hold it firm. See the notch at the end of the barrel?"

"Yes," she said.

"Line it up with what you're aiming at."

"What shall I aim at?"

He looked down the arroyo again. "See that dark spot in the curve of the bank?"

"Yes," she said.

"Try to hit the center of it."

She adjusted her aim. "Now what?"

"Pull the trigger," he said.

As the explosion shattered the silence, the shock of the recoil knocked her feet out from under her. She sat down hard, losing her grip on the rifle so it flew from her hands and landed a yard away.

He walked over and picked it up, barely repressing a smile. "It's best to keep the gun out of the dust," he said.

"I'm sorry," she said, standing up and brushing off her skirt.

"Try it again," he said, handing her the gun.

She raised it and squinted down the barrel.

"You have to cock it each time," he said.

"Oh," she said, embarrassed at her ignorance. She pushed the lever away and returned it, then held the stock tight on her shoulder, planting her feet firmly on the ground.

He moved to stand behind her. His right arm held her waist as if he was afraid she'd fall again, while his other hand adjusted hers on the barrel, sliding it further toward the sight as he pressed his cheek close to hers, his whiskers prickly on her skin. In a near whisper, he said, "Make yourself one with the gun, Hekuba. Put yourself inside it and will the bullet to go where you want. Don't forget to aim, though. Willing it alone won't get you much."

She could feel his body the entire length of hers, faintly smell the sweat on his shirt and, to her surprise, a delicate fragrance of whiskey on his breath.

"When you feel your concentration's steady," he said, "squeeze the trigger like it'll break if you touch it too hard."

The explosion threw her against him, and his arms closed around her waist, holding her up.

"Not too bad," he said, peering through the smoke as he stepped away from her. "You only missed by a coupla feet. Try it again."

She cocked the rifle with trembling hands.

"Ain't nothing to be afraid of," he said. "A gun ain't evil in its own right."

"I am not afraid of the gun, Mr. Strummar," she answered.

After a moment's hesitation, he said softly, "Call me Seth."

She planted her feet firmly, sighted carefully, and lightly touched the trigger, determined to impress him. This time she absorbed the shock, feeling it jar the entire length of her spine but keeping her feet. She looked through the smoke at the target.

"That was worse," he said. "Try it again."

She cocked the gun, took careful aim, and managed to keep her feet, watching the bullet disappear with a puff of dust at the edge of the dark spot.

"All right!" He laughed. "Do it again."

She waited for the smoke to clear, then fired and watched the puff of dust escape from the edge of the target.

"You're pulling right," he said. "Bear left."

She cocked and fired. The puff appeared two feet left of the target.

"You still got one bullet," he said.

She cocked the gun and concentrated on the target, fired, and saw the bullet hit an inch into the circle. Lowering the rifle, she met his eyes with pride.

"You'll get better," he said.

"I hit half of them!" she protested.

"Yeah, but that spot's twice as big as a man's chest, and it ain't moving or shooting back. Let's see you load again."

She opened the magazine and shook the empties into her palm.

They were hot and she dropped them, then watched him take the other bullets from his pocket and hand them to her. Carefully she reloaded and slid the magazine closed. She raised the rifle, but he stepped forward and took it from her.

"We'll work on it some more another time," he said. "You can spook most people just knowing that much."

"Thank you for the lesson," she said, regretting it was finished so soon.

He laughed and walked over to his horse, slid the rifle into its scabbard, then yelled up the arroyo, "Hey, Joaquín! That priest is waiting." He turned around and caught her watching him, and he smiled as he walked toward her again. "We'll be in Tejoe tonight," he said. "Guess I'll take my rights before we get there."

Gently he clasped her shoulders and kissed her mouth. She simply stood and let it happen. He straightened up again, studying her face. "Either you don't like me or you ain't ever been kissed," he said.

"That was my first," she whispered.

He chuckled and gave her another. "Now you've had two," he said.

She smiled. "One more and it will be the same as my bullets that hit."

His arms went around her waist and pulled her close as he kissed her. This time his tongue came inside her mouth and she tasted whiskey, warm and sweet. For the first time she felt herself responding to a man's touch, and the desire kindled within her took her breath away. When he broke the kiss, he smiled and said, "We're gonna have fun teaching you to shoot, Hekuba."

Then he took her hand, led her to the horse, lifted her into the saddle, and gave her the reins just as the others came back.

The four of them resumed their journey north. At noon they stopped in a small tendejon in the middle of nowhere. Seth lifted Hekuba down, then led the horses to the trough. As he stood watching them drink, she followed Joaquín and Heaven into the coolness of the restaurant. Several men sitting at different tables looked up at the new arrivals.

Joaquín held a chair for Heaven. When he did the same for Hekuba, she felt suffused with gratitude because such courtesy had never before been extended to her. Heaven smiled happily and Hekuba, too, was beginning to share her joy in more than a vicarious way. When she looked at the proprietor, however, her good mood vanished.

He had advanced toward their table, then stopped and spread his feet to straddle more ground. "We don't serve niggers," he said with belligerence.

Joaquín stood up just as Seth stepped through the door carrying his rifle. "She's with me," Seth said, meeting the proprietor's eyes.

Hekuba watched the man's face blanch, but still he argued. "Goddamn, Strummar. I got nothin' against you, but when word gets out it'll ruin my business."

Seth let his gaze move around the other men. "Any of you object to my friend eating here?" he asked lightly.

No one said a word.

He looked back at the proprietor. "I don't hear nothing."

"I'll hear plenty," the man grumbled.

Seth jerked his rifle by the lever and the weapon cocked loudly in the silence then snapped back so he was holding it with his finger on the trigger.

"All right!" the man said.

Joining them at the table, Seth sat with his back to the wall and leaned the rifle, still cocked, in the corner behind him. Slowly Joaquín sat back down, watching Seth.

"I can eat outside," Hekuba whispered.

Seth's gray eyes met hers. "Ain't necessary," he said. "Those fellows'll tell he was forced into it, so you won't do any harm eating with us. And it's hot outside."

"Yes," she said. "Thank you."

He looked at Joaquín. "You ready for this?"

"I hadn't anticipated it," Joaquín admitted.

"Yeah, well, I saw plenty of it in Texas and folks can get down-right ugly before they figure out we ain't changing our minds."

"It is their minds that need changing," Joaquín said.

Seth smiled with affection. "You ain't ever gonna give up on saving the world, are you?"

Joaquín shrugged. "All I want is for Heaven's sister to be with us. That doesn't seem a lot to ask."

"Maybe not," Seth said, "but it might be a good idea if you introduce Hekuba as your servant."

"Heaven will be my wife," Joaquín answered. "If our children are as black as Hekuba, I will not call them servants."

Seth chuckled. "If your kids turn out to be pickaninnies, Joaquín, I'll defend 'em too."

"Gracias," he said.

Heaven laughed and said to Hekuba, "I told you my Joaquín is a caballero."

Hekuba smiled at her and her caballero, but when she met Seth's eyes, an understanding the others didn't share passed between them.

The proprietor brought their food, not meeting anyone's eyes.

3

★

The mission of San Xavier du Bac was called the White Dove of the Desert. From miles away it glistened in the sun like a shining emblem, a mammoth cathedral that had stood for over a hundred years as the epitome of holiness in the barren desert of heathens. As they approached, however, Hekuba saw evidence of its antiquity in the many patches of brown adobe crumbling beneath its white façade, and she realized that the church of the conquistadores had been declining for decades. That Joaquín was a descendent of those conquistadores made her doubt his strength to prevail, and she kept close to Seth.

She sensed that he felt as uncomfortable as she did inside the sanctuary. They followed the bridal couple to the altar and witnessed the ceremony in silence, Seth holding his friend's gunbelt as Joaquín knelt with Heaven in front of the priest. Only when he had regained his feet did Hekuba sense any gladness from Seth. Even so, he strode quickly from the church. She followed the newlyweds out, then watched as Seth returned his friend's gun. After Joaquín buckled it on, Seth held out his hand and said, "A favor returned. I'm glad I lived to see the day."

Shaking Seth's hand, Joaquín laughed. "I also am glad."

Seth turned to the bride and bent low to kiss her cheek. "Welcome to the family," he said.

Hekuba was impressed with the depth of friendship between the men. Contrary to her original misgivings, she now believed in Seth's power, outlaw or not, and she felt reassured of Heaven's happiness because Seth held her husband as kin. Hekuba stepped forward to hug her sister, wishing Seth would kiss her as he had the bride, but he was already moving back to the horses, apparently impatient to be home with his wife.

Tejoe was considerably larger than Sulphur Springs. As they rode through the dark streets, Hekuba saw many stores, a bank, and several restaurants. When she looked right at the crossroads, she saw one entire block of saloons. The music coming from them reminded her of New Orleans, though here the instruments were more rustic and the few lyrics she caught struck her as crude. They rode on through town and out the other end, where small homes were scattered in the desert. In front of one they stopped.

The house was so new that leftover adobes were still scattered in the yard. Seth lifted her down with a smile. "See you around," he said, swinging back on his horse and loping away. She turned to watch Joaquín carry Heaven across the threshold. Hekuba waited a moment in the darkness before walking inside.

A kerosene lantern had been lit and she saw a long room that was empty except for a small table under the lamp and a stone hearth dominating the far wall. She could hear Heaven's laughter as she happily followed her husband on a tour of the house, which was built in a square, the four rooms connected and all of them opening onto an inner patio. Hekuba walked onto the patio and stood alone, listening to their voices. She thought of Seth going home to his wife, of how he would kiss her in the joy of reunion, and she felt forlorn listening to the delight in her sister's voice.

Heaven opened a door onto the patio. "There you are! Come see your room."

Hekuba walked into the room where she would spend her future nights. It was furnished only with a feather bed covered by a blue quilt emblazoned with a white star. She smiled at Heaven's husband, then curtsied low before him. "You are generous, señor. In all ways, I will strive to please you."

He laughed softly. "You can start by not bowing to me, Hekuba. And by calling me Joaquín."

"As you wish," she murmured.

"Heaven and I will bring supper back," he said. "Is there something special you'd like?"

She met the dark eyes of this man who had changed her life, again surprised at his solicitude.

"I know what she likes," Heaven said. "Let me wash my face, Joaquín, before I show it for the first time in Tejoe."

He watched her go with so much love that Hekuba thought they could conquer whatever obstacles the town placed in their path. Still she had no wish to add to their burden, so when she was alone with Joaquín she said, "Mr. Strummar is right. We should say I am Heaven's servant."

Joaquín shook his head. "Seth is from Texas, and most Texans hate anyone who isn't like them. I think the people of Tejoe will be better than that."

She frowned, then asked, "Is his home nearby?"

"Not far. Soon we'll visit so you and Heaven can meet his family."

"And what of your family, Joaquín? Do they live nearby?"

"I have none anywhere, except you and Heaven. Seth has a wife, children, and Esperanza."

"Is Esperanza a sister?"

"A good friend who lives with us." He laughed at his mistake. "I mean with them. I live here now."

"Does she take care of the children?"

He smiled. "Among other things."

"How many children?"

"Two, and one on the way."

She nodded, displeased to learn Seth's wife was pregnant.

Heaven came back and walked out on Joaquín's arm, leaving Hekuba alone. She walked through the door Heaven had left open and found herself in the master bedroom. As in her room, the only furniture was a brass feather bed ready for sleeping. Unlike in her room, however, a simple wooden cross hung above the bed. She shivered, reminded of the cathedral and its decrepit strength. Then she smiled to think Seth had chosen a former priest for his compañero yet had felt as uneasy in the sacred sanctuary as she had. Their estrangement from Christianity was a bond they shared, and she hoped to nurture it by providing a heathen balance within the piety of Joaquín's home.

The next room was the kitchen. It was furnished with a stove and a hand pump over a sink in the counter, a table larger than the one in the parlor, this one with chairs. She walked on into the parlor, opened the front door and stepped into the yard, then looked up at the sky.

To the west it was lit with a dim glow above the town; to the east was only darkness beneath a myriad of stars. It was in that direction Seth had ridden, and she wondered how far he had to travel and if he came to town often. Since his wife was carrying a child, perhaps he would seek pleasure elsewhere during her confinement. But when Hekuba turned and caught her reflection in the window, she scoffed at her aspiration. Such a man would not lack opportunities for dalliance. If he sought the company of another woman, it would not be black Hekuba. Yet remembering his kisses, she felt encouraged to hope.

She walked back through the parlor and patio and into her own room, then closed the door to her sister's bridal chamber. Hekuba had never expected to be a bride. Always before she had felt content to live in her sister's shadow, but Seth had awakened inside

her a desire for more, even if all she could hope for were the pleasures of a concubine. If she should bear Seth a child, surely Joaquín
would extend his generosity to the offspring of his friend. Then
Hekuba would own more than sisterly love—she would be a
mother and possess living proof that once she, too, had been loved
as a woman.

Swaddled in such dreams, she sat in the darkness of her room
until she heard them return. When they called for her to join them,
she answered that she wasn't hungry and stayed alone, listening to
the soft murmur of their conversation drifting across the patio
from the kitchen. After a while, they extinguished the lamp in the
parlor and she listened to them move through the darkness to their
chamber and close its door. Hekuba felt thankful that the thick-
ness of the adobe walls allowed no sound to penetrate them. Not
because she minded listening to her sister receive love—she had
done that often in the past—but now she hoped to receive it herself, and she knew she wouldn't want anyone sharing her pleasure
with Seth.

In the morning, Joaquín took Heaven and Hekuba shopping.
Heads turned as they walked down the street, then crossed the
portal and entered Engle's Emporium. After introducing Heaven
to the proprietor, Joaquín turned to Hekuba and introduced her
as Miss Free, his wife's sister. Hekuba felt the reception chill. She
stayed by the door, not allowing herself to look at the merchandise as she listened to Joaquín request that an account be opened
for them. Anything they wish, he said, could be charged to the account and he would pay the bill. She looked up to watch the per-
plexity on the merchant's face as he weighed his profit against her
blackness. Finally he answered that he guessed it would be all
right.

"I am glad, Señor Engle," Joaquín said, "that you consider my
money acceptable."

"It isn't that and you know it," the merchant muttered, glancing at Hekuba still by the door.

She wished there was some way to hide her blackness, a paint she could put on her face, a drug to bleach her skin from inside. But even if she were to discover such a remedy, it was too late now. A drop of black blood was enough to condemn her in the merchant's mind, no less so for Heaven. With a few murmured words to his wife, Joaquín left them alone.

Heaven said, "Come pick out the material for curtains in your room, Hekuba."

She moved woodenly to the display of cloth, scanning the bolts for a pattern she liked. "This," she said, indicating a gay print of yellow with blue flowers.

"That's lovely," Heaven agreed. "I think this peach velvet will be nice for the parlor, don't you?"

Hekuba nodded. She would have approved any choice, only wanting to escape the cold eyes she felt all around her. She looked up and met the gaze of a white woman standing by the thread. The woman turned away. Across the room two others watched her without friendliness, and this time it was Hekuba who turned away.

"What do you think of this green for my room?" Heaven asked. "Do you like it?"

Again Hekuba nodded, feeling she had lost her tongue before the faces of hostility around her. "I wish to go home now," she whispered to her sister.

"Not yet," Heaven protested. "We have to look at the catalog to order furniture. And Joaquín said we might each have a new frock."

The thought of wearing a new dress the next time she saw Seth gave Hekuba the courage to follow her sister to the counter where the catalog lay open. The woman who was buying thread accepted her change from the clerk, then smiled at Heaven.

"I'm Mrs. Clancy," she said. "Welcome to Tejoe, Mrs. Ascarate."

"Thank you," Heaven answered with pleasure. "How kind of you to welcome us."

"Will we be seeing you in church?"

"Joaquín and I will attend Our Lady of Sorrows."

Mrs. Clancy looked pained. "Of course," she said. "Mr. Strummar and his family occasionally join us, but your husband never has and now I know why. It's odd I never suspected he's of another faith." She laughed at her mistake. "Please tell your husband how pleased we are that he's brought his bride to our town. We owe him and Mr. Strummar a great deal, and I know I'm not alone in appreciating their presence." She looked pointedly at the two women watching from the far end of the counter.

"I'm so pleased you said hello, Mrs. Clancy," Heaven replied, giving the woman a small curtsey.

"I'm sorry your charming beauty won't grace our church socials," Mrs. Clancy said. "We must work at bringing the churches together in civic affairs." She smiled again at Heaven. "Good day, Mrs. Ascarate."

Heaven watched her leave, then whispered to Hekuba, "Wasn't that nice?"

"Yes," Hekuba answered with a quiet sigh. Her sister hadn't even noticed that the lady had failed to acknowledge her by so much as a glance. "I'll see you at home."

Hekuba turned and walked out. Feeling too many eyes follow her along the street, she looked in desperation for someplace to hide. Spying a dressmaker's shop, she quickly stepped through the door.

After a moment, a middle-aged Spanish woman wearing spectacles emerged from behind a curtain. She studied Hekuba warily a moment, then asked with polite formality if she could be of assistance. Hekuba introduced herself and explained that she had come to town with Mrs. Joaquín Ascarate and wished to order a dress. She finished by saying that Mr. Ascarate would pay the bill.

The woman smiled. "Señor Ascarate is married?"

"His wife is at Engle's Emporium ordering furniture and curtains for the house," Hekuba said, thinking the woman could send down for Heaven's approval if she doubted her word.

The woman *tched*. "Don't let her buy frocks at Engle's. You showed good taste, Miss Free, in coming here. I make the best dresses in the territory, and I guarantee no other woman within a hundred miles will have anything similar to a gown ordered from me. Just take a look at the material while I find my pattern book." The woman smiled again and returned behind the curtain.

Hekuba searched through the bolts of material for something she thought would please Seth. From behind the curtain she could hear the seamstress instructing someone to run to the emporium and find out if Señor Ascarate really would pay the bill. Hekuba thought Joaquín had been right to think the merchants of Tejoe were not averse to his money.

She discovered a soft wool the color of the purple thistles she had seen in the mountains they crossed riding north. Hekuba remembered watching Seth pick one of the flowers and smell it as they were waiting for their horses to rest. She smiled, then turned to watch her sister come through the door.

"Home, indeed!" Heaven scolded playfully. "As usual, your wisdom is greater than mine."

Hekuba laughed. "Greater than a man's when it comes to choosing frocks."

"Come look at the patterns," the seamstress called happily. "They are the latest styles from Boston."

Hekuba made her selection and left Heaven ordering more than the one gift her husband had offered. Knowing that she had no concept of money, neither where it came from nor how difficult it was to replenish, Hekuba smiled at her sister's childishness. For a brief moment she felt happy, walking home. Then she again became aware of eyes following her progress. She held her head high and kept her dignified pace, though she wanted to run from their rudeness. Finally she reached the house and escaped into its privacy. She went to her room and sat on the bed, staring through the open door at the bare dirt of the patio as she wondered if she would ever garner the courage to step foot outside again.

When Heaven returned with Joaquín, they called her into the kitchen. They had brought lunch from a café, and Hekuba ate in silence while they discussed their plans for the house, Joaquín echoing Heaven's enthusiasm with approval of everything she said. Finally he asked, "Is there anything you wish, Hekuba?"

"I would like a wall around our house," she said, "so we may move in the yard without being seen."

"I'll have one built," he answered. "Six feet high, will that be enough?"

"Thank you," she said.

Heaven laughed happily. "We can plant flowers inside and create a paradise in the middle of this desert."

"It is already paradise," Joaquín said. "You alone make it so."

"Excuse me," Hekuba murmured, standing up. "I feel tired and will rest in my room."

"We are going to the cabinetmaker to see the chiffonnier he is making for us," Heaven called after her. "Wouldn't you like to come?"

Hekuba turned back and smiled at them. "Thank you, no. Have a good time."

She walked away, feeling their attention already on each other again. Crossing the patio to her room, she closed the door and lay down on her bed, not knowing what else to do. Though she didn't believe in Joaquín's God, she wished for some power to petition for a cure of her loneliness. She knew her ancestors in Africa had possessed a religion but it had been lost to her, and she could not accept the faith of a people who considered her too inferior to share their eternity.

Two days later, Heaven and Joaquín went riding in the desert and left Hekuba alone. It was late afternoon and the men building the adobe wall had already gone. She had washed Heaven's new china and was arranging it in the hutch that had been delivered only that morning, when she heard a knock on the front door. As she walked across the still-bare parlor, she saw Seth's sorrel through the window and felt her heart quicken in anticipation. Taking a deep breath, she opened the door.

He took his hat off and smiled at her. "Afternoon," he said, his gray eyes quick with fun.

"Come in, Seth," she said, stepping back and opening the door wider.

"I saw Joaquín and Heaven on their way out of town and thought you might be lonely."

"Your visit is always welcome," she demurred.

He tossed his hat on the table. "Don't suppose you have any whiskey?"

She shook her head. "Next time you come, I will be certain we do."

"Joaquín hasn't much of a thirst so I'll bring it myself," he said, looking around. "Nothing's changed in here, but I like the wall he's putting up outside."

"The rest of the house has changed," she said. "Would you like to see it?"

"Sure," he said, letting his gaze drift down her body.

She felt sorry she was wearing the same dress he had seen before. "I have another frock," she said, "but I didn't know you were coming."

He smiled. "Didn't come to see your frock. What were you doing?"

"Washing Heaven's new china," she answered, leading him into the kitchen.

He walked across to the hutch and studied the dishes arranged inside, then turned around and smiled again. "What else is new?"

She led him into Heaven's room to show off the new chiffonnier. "It is solid oak," she said, "and nicely worked, don't you think?"

"Yeah," he said, taking her elbow and guiding her on.

They crossed into her room and he closed the door, then stood studying what she had done. Besides the blue and yellow curtains, she now had a trunk for her clothes and a small vanity with a wash pitcher below a mirror. He moved to the window and checked the view between the curtains lifting in the breeze. "Bluebonnets," he said, referring to the flowers in the print as he turned back to her with a smile.

"Are they?" she asked. "I didn't know their name."

"They only grow in Texas," he said.

"Like you?"

He chuckled, coming closer. "I don't own you, Hekuba. Joaquín paid back the money I spent buying you."

She felt herself tremble inside at his being so near. "Money is not the only way to own someone," she said.

He reached up and gently pulled her kerchief off, tossed it to fall on the trunk, then touched her hair. "It's softer'n it looks."

"So am I," she answered boldly.

He moved away to sit on the edge of her bed, leaning back on his elbows as he watched her with frank curiosity. "You think you look hard?"

"It's difficult to imagine how white people see me," she said. "By their aversion, I can only suspect they find my visage discomfiting."

"I think you're beautiful, Hekuba. What do you think of that?"

"What do you think of it?" she whispered.

"I don't know," he answered. "It would sure simplify things if I didn't."

"I don't understand," she murmured.

"You belong to Joaquín, and I've always tried hard not to mess in his private affairs."

"Is he under your power?"

Seth frowned. "Why do you ask that?"

"Your words imply he is, and you are striving not to exert undue influence."

Seth shrugged and stood up. She admired his grace as he moved to the open patio door. Staring into the falling dusk, he said, "We were partners until a month ago. Now we're just friends."

"I don't understand," she said again. "Partners in business?"

He shook his head, then laughed, a soft sound of self-deprecation, as he turned to face her. "Maybe. The business of staying alive."

She watched him in silence.

"It's a long story," he said. "I'll tell it to you sometime." The sunset was fiery in the sky behind him, catching red highlights in the sandy color of his hair. "How old are you, Hekuba?"

"Twenty," she said. "How old are you?"

"I'll be thirty-five in January. If I make it."

"Is there a reason you won't?"

"A thousand of 'em. That's the dollars Texas'll pay to the man who kills me."

"Why?" she asked.

"I was a desperado when I was young," he said, moving toward her. "I did a lot of bad things."

"Such as?" she asked lightly, though her heart was pounding.

"Robbed a lot of banks, killed a lot of men," he answered, so close now she could catch the scent of whiskey on his breath. "Raped a few women."

"Not seduced?" she whispered.

"Raped," he said.

"Is that what you like?"

"Was once. Now I like it when the woman wants me."

"What would convince you?"

"A smile, when I'm standing so close and she knows I'm thinking about it."

Hekuba smiled.

He laughed softly deep in his throat, then reached behind himself and closed the door, not breaking the hold of his eyes on hers. "I ain't ever wanted a woman like I want you. Why do you think that is?"

"Why do you think?" she asked.

"Reckon it's 'cause anyone who can move through a world that hates her and still stand up straight strikes a chord of sympathy in me."

"You understand about moving through such a world," she said.

He nodded. "Will you take your dress off?"

She unbuttoned it and let it fall, so she stood before him in her shimmy.

"That, too," he said.

She pulled it over her head and dropped it on the floor. Then, without being asked, she stepped out of her drawers and faced him naked. "I am black all over," she said.

"I'd be disappointed if you weren't."

"Why?"

" 'Cause it's pretty," he teased. "And it matches my heart."

She laughed. "You're playing with me."

He nodded, suddenly solemn. "If you don't want it, say so now and I'll go on down to Blue's and find satisfaction there."

"Do you not find it with your wife?"

He frowned. "A seductress ain't supposed to mention a man's wife."

"I am not a seductress," she replied with astonishment, then added more softly, "Only a woman who wants honesty between herself and a man."

"You're wrong on the first count, but I'll grant you the second: I love Rico and I'll never leave her." He paused to let that settle in, then said, "She asked me to promise fidelity and I did, but now that she's pregnant her desire ain't up to mine. In a few more months she won't be wanting any at all. Last time I spent my hunger on Esperanza. This time, I'd like to spend it on you."

"I would like that," Hekuba said.

"You're apt to get pregnant," he warned.

"I would also like that."

He laughed gently. "Would you?"

"I am a woman," she said.

"No argument." He smiled, unbuckling his gunbelt and taking a step back to hang it on the headpost of her bed, then sitting down and pulling off his boots and socks. He stood up again, watching her as he unbuttoned his shirt. He took it off and hung it on the chair, unbuckled his belt, unbuttoned his trousers, stepped out of them, and tossed them aside. Naked, he held out his hands as if belittling himself as he said, "A pale Texan."

She thought him awesome, his body lean and carved with muscles, his sex powerful between his thighs. "I am a virgin," she whispered.

"I can handle that," he said. "Can you?"

She shook her head. "I wish it were no longer so."

He gestured toward the bed with a smile. "Allow me."

Awkwardly she approached, hesitant and unsure of herself.

He took her in his arms, lifted her off her feet, and settled her on the bed beneath him. "Just close your eyes and it'll be over before you know it."

"I hope not," she whispered against his shoulder.

"I'll take my time," he said, then kissed her as his hands explored her body.

Although she had never been touched by a man before, he was adept at arousing her ardor, and she lost herself in the catapult of sensations he elicited. When finally he pushed himself inside her, the pain was quick, the blood hot. He came and quickly withdrew, kissing the tears from her eyes. "It'll get better," he promised.

"I cannot imagine anything better," she answered.

He hid his face in the darkness between her breasts. Seeing his pale flesh next to hers, she raised her hand to touch his hair, so fine and soft. On his cheek, the beginning stubble of whiskers caught the remnant of sunset falling through the window, and she touched them too, feeling them prickle her fingertips. Then she ran her palm across the hard curve of his shoulder to the steely firmness of his arm, marveling at the strength of his muscles though he lay relaxed and at ease. Feeling his semen seep out between her thighs, she squeezed tight to hold it inside, not wanting to lose any part of him.

As if he sensed her possessiveness, he moved away to lie on his belly beside her, then sighed deeply, holding his head in his hands. Finally he said, "Joaquín ain't gonna be happy about this."

"Why should he care?" she asked, thinking nothing could mar the happiness she felt.

"He cares about everything," Seth answered. He got up and stepped into his pants, crossed the room as he buttoned them, then opened the door and looked into the darkness, lit now by a lamp from the kitchen.

Hekuba admired how the light shimmered on his skin. When she threw the covers off to get up, she saw the stain of blood. "I have ruined the sheet," she said.

He turned around with a surprised laugh. "Little blood never ruined anything."

She met his eyes, so kind and soft, so different from when she had first met him, and again when he had defended her right to eat in the tendejon. She realized he was two men, and she was privileged to know them both. Lifting her drawers from the floor, she stepped into them, then dropped her shimmy over her head, pulled on her dress, and buttoned it closed. He was sitting on the bed, tugging on his boots. His shirt was on but still unbuttoned, and she glanced at his gun on her bedpost, wishing it could always be there. Watching her, he stood up and buttoned his shirt, tucked it in, then buckled on his gunbelt. Already he was gone, she could see it in his eyes, and she dropped her gaze lest he read her desire as a demand.

When they walked into the kitchen, Joaquín was sitting at the table with anger in his eyes. Heaven was washing apples in the sink. She gave Hekuba a mischievous smile, then returned to her work. Hekuba took a towel from a drawer and began polishing the bright red fruit. She looked over her shoulder and saw the two men staring at each other.

"Ain't you gonna invite me to sit down?" Seth asked.

Joaquín pushed a chair from beneath the table with his foot.

Seth pulled the chair out and straddled it backward, giving his friend a teasing smile.

Hekuba turned her attention to the apples, feeling apprehensive as she listened to the sullen silence behind her. When all the apples had been polished, Heaven arranged them in a bowl and placed it between the men.

Joaquín nodded at the glossy red fruit. "Sometimes things that appear sweet," he said to his friend, "leave a bitter aftertaste."

"Nothing whiskey won't cure," Seth answered. "Think I'll go see Blue. Want to come?"

Joaquín shook his head.

Seth stood up and looked at Hekuba. "Walk me out?" he asked.

She followed him into the parlor and watched him take his hat from the table and tug it low above his eyes, then open the door and stare at his sorrel inside the half-built wall. Finally he looked at her and smiled. "See you around," he said, leaving without touching her again. She watched him mount his horse and ride away, then she returned to the kitchen. Joaquín was alone with the bowl of shiny apples.

"Sit down, Hekuba," he said.

She obeyed him, keeping her gaze on her hands in her lap. "I have displeased you," she said with regret for that fact alone.

He took a long time to answer. Finally he said, "I had hoped to have something free of Seth, but he won't let me."

She considered his words a long moment, then asked, "Are you saying that what happened between us has only to do with you and nothing with me?"

Again there was a silence before he asked gently, "Do you think your beauty overpowered his resistence?"

The truth of her inferiority hammered in her heart, but she raised her head higher. "I suppose his wife is very beautiful."

"Yes," Joaquín said. "Her hair is the color of sunlight and her eyes as blue as the sky, her features delicate and her figure perfect when she isn't carrying his child. Also, there are a dozen girls in Blue's saloon chosen for their beauty. If that is what Seth was seeking, he wouldn't have come here."

She had to concede the logic of his argument, yet couldn't bring herself to abandon hope. "Perhaps he was seeking something else."

Joaquín nodded. "A right to this house independent of me. He knew you wouldn't refuse him."

She faltered before his anger. "You have been good to me," she murmured. "I feel ashamed."

"That's why I'm sorry it happened," he said. "Seth is incapable of shame. His selfishness has burdened only you."

"It is a burden I welcomed," she argued.

"And will welcome again?"

She met Joaquín's dark eyes, defying their pain for the sake of her happiness. "I cannot refuse him."

"Then he has won," Joaquín said, bitterness beneath the kindness in his voice.

"If I leave your home," she countered, "his victory will be over me, not you."

"Except that Heaven will lose her sister."

"I'm sorry," she whispered. "I want something for myself."

"You think that's what Seth is?"

"The pleasure he gave is mine."

Joaquín sighed deeply. "It's my fault. When we met him in

the desert, I should've known he'd come here, and I should've come home to prevent this."

She held his eyes across the bowl of fruit glimmering like fresh blood in the lamplight. "You have been friends many years. Do not let me come between you."

"Heaven is the one who came between us," he said. "Seth can't accept that my loyalty is no longer completely his."

Carefully she asked, "Is it so impossible his wanting me has nothing to do with you?"

"I don't wish to be unkind," he said softly, "but why would he want you, Hekuba?"

Tears stung her eyes. "I asked the same question of myself," she admitted, "I told myself that such a man could not want me."

"Will you refuse him if he asks again?"

She knew she could not. "As long as I am in your home, I will abide by your wishes," she answered. "Tomorrow I will seek another place to live."

"What he wanted from you was access to my home."

She felt trapped, suspecting Joaquín was right. Then she remembered Seth saying she was beautiful and that he had never wanted a woman as much as he wanted her. She could not believe those were lies intended merely to seduce her. "If I leave and you are right," she said, "I will return strong enough to refuse him." She waited a moment, then asked, "Will you take me back?"

"That's Heaven's decision. Do you think she will?"

Hekuba shrugged. "She has never been without me. Perhaps she will learn she likes it better."

"So you are risking everything when you have no chance to be more than his whore."

Again tears stung with his words.

Gently he asked, "What will you do when you find yourself pregnant?"

"If I am blessed with his child," she answered bravely, "at least I will have something of my own."

"Do you think this town will allow you to stay and raise his child here?"

She knew Joaquín was saying that if she left his home she was also leaving his protection, and she remembered the hostility of the people on the street. To stand alone against them would take more courage than she felt certain she possessed. Then she remembered Seth saying he admired her courage, and she answered, "I will give them no choice."

Again Joaquín sighed. "Tomorrow I'll help you find a job and another place to live. Then we will see how much honor he has." He stood up and left her alone.

Hekuba looked at the bowl of apples in front of her. Selecting the best one, she took a bite and savored the tart flavor on her tongue. Joaquín's anger and the loss of her sister's companionship were next to nothing compared with the succulence of what she had gained.

4

★

 Her new job was working for a woman named Amy in her café. Hekuba stayed in the kitchen, helping to prepare food and wash dishes out of sight of the customers. Amy was blonde and pink-cheeked, and Hekuba could not look at her without thinking of Seth's wife. Each day, from before dawn until long after sunset, Hekuba worked in the kitchen listening to the white woman chatter while she herself said no more than was necessary to perform her tasks. When Amy went home, Hekuba cleaned the tables and the floor; then she, too, went home, walking a mile to the one-room casita Joaquín had rented for her. From his own home he had allowed her to take the furnishings of her room. She hung the yellow curtains on her only window and often touched the bluebonnets as if they were a gift from Seth, though they were not.

For a month she lived and worked aching with loneliness, not having seen the man for whom she had sacrificed so much. One night near the café's closing time, Blue Rivers sat talking with Amy at a table near the kitchen door. They were alone in the café, and Hekuba could hear them from where she worked scouring the stove. She was only half-listening until Blue said, "Seth hasn't come to town for a month, so I rode out to the homestead to find out why. You know what I found?"

There was a demurred denial from Amy.

"He was so drunk he couldn't stand straight. He's leaving himself defenseless when he's like that, and Joaquín ain't there to protect him anymore. Seth's sleeping in the room in the stable, and Rico's at her wit's end trying to figure out what's wrong."

"Did you talk to him?" Amy asked softly.

"I tried, but all he said was he felt better drunk and it was nobody else's damn business. Esperanza told me that when she tried to take his bottle away, Seth hit her. Can you imagine that? So she stays clear of him now. Lobo's the only one he'll let come near."

"Poor Rico," Amy murmured.

"Yeah. There she is, getting bigger every day and all twisted into knots worrying about Seth. Esperanza told me Rico spends most of her time crying in bed, alone of course. The pump broke, and when Esperanza told him a workman was coming to fix it, Seth said he'd kill any man he didn't know who set foot on the place. So they're toting water from the well now. The only time Seth sees Rico is when he goes into the house for more whiskey. He says if he has to ride to town to get some, he won't be back, so the women make sure he's got a good supply. That's all he wants of them. Killed a deer and jerked it himself, and it's about all he's been eating. Esperanza said he hasn't even changed his clothes, and you know how fussy he is about having a clean shirt. He doesn't seem to care about anything but how much whiskey's in his bottle." Blue sighed. "Something happened between him and Joaquín, but I can't get a word out of either one of them what it was."

"Joaquín fell in love," Amy said.

"So what? Seth's got a woman. Why shouldn't he?"

"If Joaquín had taken Heaven to live at the homestead, I don't think there would be a problem," she said.

"Maybe you're right," he answered. "But Seth should've known Joaquín would break free eventually."

"Is he still living on Seth's money?

"That's not a question I feel inclined to ask," Blue said.

"He must've spent close to a thousand dollars building and furnishing that house for Heaven. Seems to me he should be needing some kind of income by now."

"Hasn't said anything."

"Don't you think that's why he asked me to give Hekuba a job? Because he can't afford to support two women?"

"I don't know. How's she doing?"

"She's a hard worker and nearly silent as a post. I've got no complaints. But I wonder why she couldn't work for me and live with them, too."

"That's a good question. If Joaquín didn't want her around, he should've left her in Sulphur Springs. Nobody would've guessed Heaven's part black if they hadn't shown up with the sister."

"Maybe the problem between Seth and Joaquín has something to do with Hekuba."

There was a long silence, then Blue said, "She's as ugly as the day is long."

"I don't think so," Amy replied.

"Yeah, well, you ain't Seth. He's always had an eye for women and I ain't ever seen him with a homely one. Look at Rico, for chrissake. She takes my breath away, even though I've known her for years now. Why would Seth risk losing Joaquín over Hekuba?"

"I don't know," Amy said. "What do you think will happen?"

"I think one of these days Seth'll be gone."

"Will he leave Rico pregnant and with two children besides, one of them not even hers?"

"He'll take Lobo if he goes, and leave her enough money to get by. In Seth's mind, that's always justified everything he ever did to women, that he paid them for it."

Amy sighed. "Is there anything we can do?"

"Not that I can see. Why don't you close up and let me walk you home?"

"All right. Let me tell Hekuba."

Hekuba hurried to the back door, eased it open and stepped outside. She turned around and came back in, smiling as if she hadn't heard their conversation. Amy took her shawl from the hook and told Hekuba to lock up and she would see her in the morning. Hekuba gave no answer, listening to her leave through the front door with Blue.

As Hekuba cleaned the café, she kept wishing she could help Seth. But the deal she had made with Joaquín was that she would wait for Seth to come to her. Even if she broke that contract and rode out to the homestead, she didn't know what she could say. If she meant anything to Seth, he would have come before now. She had gambled with her pride and lost, and she felt like a fool for having been taken in by a man's seductive lies simply because she had never heard them before.

Perhaps she should return and contribute her earnings to Joaquín's household. He had spent fifteen hundred dollars to buy his wife, and another thousand to house her. Without an income, he must be pinched for money, and Hekuba felt partly responsible. Without her sister, Heaven's bride price wouldn't have been so high. And then again, Joaquín had paid the first month's rent on Hekuba's casita. Walking toward it through the cold November night, she felt heavy with remorse.

The next day, after the breakfast rush, she asked Amy if she might have an hour off. Amy readily agreed and Hekuba walked through town toward her sister's house. Her dress was the same brown wool of her shawl, a hue that looked golden against the darkness of her skin, and her kerchief was red. She held her head high as she walked along the portal, watching people get out of her way.

Except for the help she gave Amy, Hekuba felt she had no impact on Tejoe. Her casita had been built by a Negro named Adam Noah. After he abandoned the house, the bank bought it for back taxes, and no one cared that she lived there since none of the white people would have deigned to inhabit it. She often thought she may as well be a ghost, walking apparently unobserved between her home and work in the dark.

Now, however, she walked in broad daylight, and the people did notice. Most of them merely stepped out of her path. A few men snickered, but only after she'd passed them and didn't have to respond. She walked with more pride than she felt, holding herself erect and her head high, as if she were the ancient queen whose name she carried.

From a good distance away she saw the house of her sister. The completed wall made it a snug compound closed away from the world. When Hekuba pushed the gate open and saw the sunny courtyard, she felt forlorn to think that this had once been her home. Knowing she had lost it because of foolish pride, she knocked like a supplicant.

Heaven opened the door. In the moment before a smile of welcome eclipsed it, Hekuba saw sorrow on her sister's face. They hugged each other, then Heaven took Hekuba's hand and led her inside. The parlor was furnished now with a settee and chairs, the windows covered with draperies sewn from the peach velvet Heaven chose at Engel's Emporium. Though that had happened only a month ago, it seemed an event from the distant past to Hekuba. Heaven led her sister into the kitchen and set the coffeepot to heat on the stove before she smiled again and said, "Sit down, Hekuba. I'm so glad you came to see me."

"Is Joaquín here?" she asked in lieu of a greeting.

Heaven shook her head. "He left early this morning." She frowned. "He didn't say where he was going."

"You didn't ask?"

"I ask him no questions."

The severity of that hung between them. Hekuba whispered, "Have you displeased him?"

"He says not."

"What money are you living on?"

"I don't know."

"But you have enough?"

"He buys whatever I ask. Since the house is finished, I have no need to purchase anything but food."

Hekuba took a deep breath, then asked, "Have you seen Seth?"

Again, Heaven shook her head.

"Has Joaquín spoken of him?"

"No," Heaven said. The coffee simmered behind her. She turned around and filled two cups, then carried them to the table and sat down across from her sister. "Why did you leave us?"

"I wanted to pay my own way. I told you so then."

"You never mentioned wanting that before," Heaven argued.

"Perhaps I felt lonely watching your happiness with Joaquín."

"Does Seth visit you in your casita?"

"No," she said.

"Then how can it be a cure for loneliness?"

"It is not," she said.

"Do you wish to return? Is that why you've come today?"

All morning Hekuba had thought that was what she wanted, but now she found herself shaking her head. "I came to see how you are." She gave her sister a teasing smile. "Are you still happy with your caballero?"

Heaven looked down to hide her tears. "Yes," she whispered.

"Then why do you cry?" Hekuba asked gently.

"I do not think he is happy with me."

"Has he told you this?"

"No. He insists he loves me the same, but when I ask why you were banished, he says it was your choice. When I ask why Seth doesn't visit, he says he is busy at home. Always his answers are not answers. Other than that, our words are few."

"Does he leave you alone every day?"

Heaven nodded.

"And you don't know where he goes?"

"Once I asked and he told me not to worry about it."

Hekuba remembered Seth's teasing about things worth worry on their ride from Sulphur Springs. She wished she could return to that time and behave differently, but remembering the fun in his eyes, the warm strength of his body as he taught her how to handle his weapon, and the desire his kisses of reward had aroused within her, she knew she could not have responded otherwise if she were a hundred years wiser and more experienced in the ways of men. "It's my fault," she told her sister, "for allowing Seth to seduce me."

"Why should Joaquín care if his friend finds pleasure with you?"

"He said it had nothing to do with me, that Seth acted only to stake a claim on this house."

"Joaquín told you that?" Heaven whispered.

Hekuba nodded.

Heaven stood up and walked to the window, staring out at the bare dirt of the yard where next spring she would plant flowers. As if nestling seeds in that resistant soil, she said carefully, "When Joaquín and Seth first came to Sulphur Springs, Ortega gave me to Seth but he declined my favors, saying he was faithful to his wife. I have thought of that often this last month, wondering why he declined me yet took you at his first opportunity." She faced her sister with an apologetic smile. "No other man has ever before chosen you over me, so I decided Seth, in the wisdom of his superior age, knew from the beginning that Joaquín and I were meant for each other, and also that his possessing me would stain my virtue in Joaquín's eyes in a way that Ortega could not. Obviously Seth's choice in that situation had nothing to do with his wife, yet if he was so protective of Joaquín's pride in regard to me, why would he then take you as an act against Joaquín? I think my husband is wrong. Seth is an unusual man, and you are an unusual woman. I believe the desire bringing him to your bed was no less genuine than the one bringing Joaquín to mine."

Hekuba felt a rush of relief. But there was a flaw in her sister's logic that she could not fail to question. "Then why has he stayed away from me this last month?"

"Because of Joaquín's anger," Heaven answered. "Men are arrogant creatures who must be guided through the heart's realm without feeling the reins of our leadership. If you spend more time with us, Joaquín will learn that your charms are exactly those a man such as Seth admires, and perhaps he will come to accept that Seth sought your love to fulfill a need within himself, not to discourage one within Joaquín."

Hekuba nodded. "Your wisdom humbles me, Heaven."

She smiled. "I have been trained to understand the needs of men. Will you join us for Sunday supper? Please say you will come, Hekuba."

Believing Heaven was right and the path to Seth's heart lay in earning the friendship of Joaquín, Hekuba promised, "I will come."

She left her sister's home to return to work. Walking through the bright sun, she felt a new optimism even while she pulled her shawl close against the chill of winter. Though Joaquín had been wrong about Seth's motive for wanting her, it was his anger that was now keeping Seth away. The power of their friendship meant Hekuba could not have one while displeasing the other. When she saw Seth's sorrel tied in front of Amy's café, Hekuba told herself she must abide by the deal she'd made and let Seth prove Joaquín wrong. Slipping in through the kitchen door, she resumed work without showing herself to anyone in the dining room.

The dirty dishes had accumulated in her absence and she busied herself washing them, trying not to listen for his voice. She never heard it, and after a while Amy came into the kitchen and said the café was empty. Hekuba said nothing, biting back his name from crossing her tongue. All afternoon she worked industriously preparing food for the dinner hour. When it had come and gone, Amy told her the floor was clean enough and need not be mopped that night, and that she herself would close the café.

Hekuba took her shawl and walked home, chiding herself for allowing her foolish heart to hope merely because she had seen a red horse tied to the rail. There must be many sorrels in the world. Surely if Seth had been in the café, he would at least have come into the kitchen to say hello. All the way home she bit back tears as she had bitten back his name, telling herself he would not come until she had made peace with Joaquín.

Her casita sat alone at the edge of town. As she crossed the stretch of desert leading home, she saw a horse tied to the pillar of her small portal. The night was dark and she couldn't discern the animal's color, yet again, as if her heart refused to admit defeat, she hoped it was a sorrel.

When she came close, she saw a man on the bench under her portal. Though he sat in shadow, she knew it was Seth with a certainty she could neither credit to her senses nor deny. Restraining her joy, she stopped in the yard as they watched each other in the moonless starlight. Finally she allowed her feet to move toward him, then stopped again beside his horse, who nickered at her presence.

His voice soft and gentle and hungry with longing, Seth asked, "Ain't you gonna invite me in?"

"I should not," she answered.

He stood up, the starlight catching on the bullets in his belt. "Does that mean you won't?"

She moved again, taking the key from her purse and opening the door. She walked inside, turned around, and saw him still watching her from the portal. "Come in, Seth," she said.

He chuckled and stepped inside her home, closing the door and leaving them in darkness. With trembling fingers she lit a lamp, then studied him in the light. She could see no difference, as if a month of hard drinking had passed him by without effect.

He took his hat off and tossed it to catch on a hook by the door, then smiled at her. "Do you have anything for me?" he asked, the teasing light in his eyes again.

"What would you like?" she replied.

"The same as I had last time."

"Last time you deflowered a foolish virgin. No such woman lives here."

He grunted, then glanced around the room, his eyes settling for a moment on the curtains of bluebonnets. He looked at her again when he asked, "Did Joaquín kick you out because of me?"

"We made a bet," she said, "that you would not visit me if I did not live in his home. No one has won yet."

Seth smiled. "My being here must've turned the trick for one of you."

"I heard you have been so drunk all month you could not stand straight."

"Who told you that?"

"I overheard Blue Rivers tell Miss Amy."

"Blue," Seth scoffed. "He's so drunk most of the time he couldn't tell if a man was standing straight or not."

"I see him every day, but have never seen him drunk."

"Are you working for him now?"

She shook her head. "For Miss Amy."

"I was there earlier. She didn't mention it."

"Is there a reason she should?"

"Guess not," he answered, looking at her bed. "Reckon I made a mistake."

"Is that an apology?"

His eyes were cool. "Should it be?"

She shrugged. "Joaquín is the one who needs to hear it."

"What happened between you and me ain't got nothing to do with him."

"He does not believe that," she said, wanting desperately to believe it for herself.

"Don't you want me?" he asked with a pained smile.

"Almost more than anything."

"What do you want more?"

"My sister's happiness."

"Let's go see Joaquín and find out what's standing in the way."

"All right," she said.

She extinguished the lamp while Seth took his hat from the hook and preceded her out. He lifted her onto his horse, then stepped into the stirrup and swung up behind. She looked at him as he gathered the reins, their faces so close she could feel the warmth of his breath. He kissed her mouth, a long, lingering kiss that filled her with heat. "Please," she murmured.

"Please, what?" he teased.

"Wait," was all she could say.

He reined his horse and held her with his arm as he cantered around the edge of town to Joaquín's house, where he swung down and lifted her to her feet beside him. She thought he might kiss her again, but he only gave her a sardonic smile as he opened the gate and let her pass through in front of him. As she waited for him to tie his reins to the rail, she saw that a light was burning in Heaven's kitchen. Seth entered the front door without knocking and held Hekuba's elbow as they crossed the parlor to stop on the threshold of the kitchen.

Joaquín was at the table with a blonde woman, who was crying. When she jerked around to look at them, Hekuba was stunned by the woman's beauty, the sky blue of her eyes, the porcelain of her complexion, the gold of her hair falling in tangled curls down her back. The woman jumped up and ran to Seth, crying against his coat as she moaned, "I thought you'd left me."

Hekuba watched the pain on his face. Slowly his arms rose to hold his wife as he murmured into the yellow of her hair, "I'm right here, Rico."

"Yes," she answered, smiling up at him. She wiped her tears with a lace handkerchief, then noticed Hekuba for the first time.

Rico gave her a smile. "You must be Heaven's sister," she said, taking a few steps closer. "I'm Rico Strummar."

"How do you do," Hekuba murmured.

"I'm sorry to make such a scene in your kitchen," Rico apologized, giving Seth a look of longing. "I panicked when he left without saying a word to anyone, though Lord knows I should be used to his independent ways by now." She faltered, reaching a hand to the back of a chair to steady herself.

Hekuba let her gaze drop to Rico's stomach, round and prominent beneath her loose dress of a fine gray wool, the same shade as Seth's eyes when he smiled.

"Sit down, Rico," Joaquín said, standing quickly and guiding her into the chair.

"I'm sorry," she said again, looking up at Seth, confusion on her face.

Joaquín's eyes were sharp with anger as he looked at his friend; then they softened on Hekuba. "Come in," he said with studied irony, since they were already there. "Would you like me to call Heaven?"

"It's you we came to see," Seth said.

Rico looked back and forth between them, then at Hekuba again. "Don't you live here?" she asked.

Hekuba shook her head.

Rico studied her husband for a long moment in which no one spoke. "Where have you been?" she asked in a pleading tone. "I went to Blue's first but he hadn't seen you."

"I don't like you going into saloons, Rico," he said gruffly.

Fresh tears fell on her cheeks, but she said with defiance, "You met me in a saloon, Seth."

"I thought you were glad to leave 'em behind."

"I was only looking for you," she whispered.

"You should have tried Hekuba's house. That's where I was."

Rico glanced at her so quickly Hekuba could see that Seth's wife didn't suspect them. Hekuba retreated to the shadow of a corner as Rico asked, "Is something wrong?" She looked back and forth between Seth and Joaquín, but neither answered her.

"Reckon I should take you home," Seth finally said.

"All I want, Seth," she whispered, "is to be home with you."

"We've been there together the last month," he said.

"Not quite together," she answered, tears trembling on her lashes again.

"You think you could make it out the door without crying?"

She whimpered as if he had slapped her, but managed to blink back her tears as she stood up. Looking at Hekuba, she murmured, "Please forgive me."

Joaquín lifted a heavy dark cloak from another chair and settled it gently on Rico's shoulders, then met Seth's eyes with anger.

Seth looked at Hekuba. "Another time," he said, sliding his arm around Rico's waist. She leaned on him as they walked from the room.

Hekuba stayed in the corner, listening to his horse being led around the corner of the house, then the creak of buggy wheels. Finally she raised her gaze from the floor and met Joaquín's eyes.

He sighed deeply, no longer angry. "Sit down, Hekuba," he said. "Would you like something to drink?"

She shook her head, not moving.

He crossed to a cupboard and took out a bottle of whiskey, poured some into a glass and carried it to the table, sat down and sipped a moment, then gave her a melancholy smile. "So he visited you."

She nodded.

"Why did he bring you here?"

"We came to ask what was preventing my sister's happiness," she said softly.

"He just left," Joaquín said.

"Why should Seth have anything to do with Heaven?"

"I don't think I could explain it," he said, lifting his glass and watching her over the rim as he took another sip.

She turned to go, murmuring, "Good night."

"Wait," he called when she was halfway across the parlor. He caught up with her and lifted his jacket from the coat tree by the door. "I'll walk you," he said, giving her a small smile as he settled his hat on his head.

"It's not necessary," she demurred.

"I need the air," he answered, opening the door.

He held her elbow as they crossed the courtyard and walked onto the road, then he put his hands in his pockets.

After a while, she said, "Rico is a beautiful woman."

"You didn't see her at her best," he said.

"She was still lovely."

"Yes," he agreed. "Seth puts her through hell."

"Loving a man gives him that power," she said.

"How do you like hell?" he joked.

She was silent, and after a moment he said, "I'm sorry. I didn't mean to make light of your feelings."

She glanced across at him, responding to his kindness. "Rico never suspected us."

Joaquín shrugged. "She works hard at trusting him."

"That wasn't why," Hekuba said. "But it was evident he loves her very much."

"With Seth," Joaquín answered bitterly, "it is sometimes difficult to tell the difference between love and hostility."

They had reached her casita and he stopped on the road. "Are you all right, Hekuba," he asked, "living here alone?"

"Yes," she said.

He looked away for a long moment. "Perhaps I made a mistake and should have kept you home. I didn't expect him to do this."

"Do what?" she asked softly.

"Take it out on Rico," he said. "Everyone is suffering because of my selfishness."

"Yours, Joaquín?"

He nodded. "I wanted to have something independent of Seth. By trying to achieve it, I hurt not only him but his family and even you and Heaven. I gained nothing. You saw how he walked into my home tonight as if he lived there. He will not allow me to shut him out, and it is not something I really want. I wanted to make a gesture to prove that what is mine is not his. But, like all lies, it ricocheted with pain. Perhaps someday I will be wise enough to understand what I'm doing before I've done it."

She studied him in the starlight, a slight man not much taller than she, his hair and eyes just as black, his skin halfway between the darkness of hers and the paleness of Seth's, as he himself was between them, also between Seth and Rico, a pillar of kindness opposed to the pain of loving Seth, a suffering Joaquín shared with the women. "You judge yourself too harshly," Hekuba murmured.

He shrugged. "Perhaps not hard enough. If you wish to return to your sister's home, I will welcome you as much as she will."

Hekuba looked at the tiny casita, dark before them. "This is my home," she said.

Joaquín nodded, as if he understood. "Heaven says you are coming for Sunday dinner. I'll see you then."

She watched him walk away, then went into her house alone. She undressed in the dark and slid under the covers to stare at the black reality of her life.

Rico hadn't suspected Seth of even seeing Hekuba as a woman. Not as Joaquín said, because Rico was trying hard to trust him, but because she knew her husband well and such a man would not desire a woman such as Hekuba. As encouraging as Heaven's argument had been, Hekuba did not believe her sister's understanding of Seth was superior to his wife's. He would not leave the golden-haired Rico's bed for the pleasures of Hekuba's, not even in dalliance. So Joaquín had been right in seeing Seth's motives aimed at him, untouched by desire for her.

*　*　*

In the morning, Hekuba washed her face then forced herself to look at her reflection in the mirror. Her nose was too strong, her lips too full, her skin a damning black. And though her complexion was clear, her teeth white, and her eyes vibrant with health, they were not attributes to compete with Rico's beauty. Hekuba was thin, without the voluptuous breasts she had seen filling Rico's dress; her feet were not dainty, her hands not delicate. She was a mule of a woman, and though she might strive to comport herself with dignity, her countenance was beyond her power to change.

Her only clean dress was the same blue as Rico's eyes. Suppressing tears, Hekuba buttoned it, then splashed cold water on her face and walked out. When she turned from locking the door, she saw a man sitting a pinto horse in the distance. Feeling uneasy at the way the man watched her, she hurried away. The early light of dawn barely tinged the sky as she walked through town to Amy's. She unlocked the kitchen door and entered the cold, dark room. Kneeling before the stove still wearing her shawl, she started the fire. In a few minutes the strong blaze began to thaw the chill from the air, and she removed her shawl and rolled up her sleeves to work.

When Amy came in, her cheeks were pink from the cold. She stood shivering by the stove, rubbing her palms together over the grate as she smiled at Hekuba, rolling out biscuits. "I'm amazed I ever got along without you," Amy said. "You've made my life so much easier, I'm going to give you a raise."

Hekuba stopped work and stared at her.

Amy nodded. "An extra fifty cents a day, just because it's so pleasant to come in and find the stove already hot."

"You are too generous, Miss Amy," Hekuba answered. "I am grateful for what I have."

Amy laughed. "Then be grateful for a little more. If not for your help, I wouldn't have so much time to talk with Mr. Rivers, and that's a blessing I thank God for every day."

"Thank you for your kindness," Hekuba said, cutting out the biscuits.

As Amy watched her lay them in the baking pan, she asked, "Do you like Mr. Rivers?"

Hekuba looked up with surprise that her employer would solicit her opinion. "He is a gentleman," she said.

"There are many in this town who wouldn't agree with you."

Hekuba slid the pan of biscuits into the oven.

"I'll tell you a secret," Amy said, coming closer, "if you promise not to breathe a word."

"I talk to no one," she demurred, uncomfortable with the white woman's proximity.

Amy didn't notice. "I think Blue Rivers will soon propose marriage," she announced.

Hekuba smiled. "How wonderful for you," she said sincerely.

"Sometimes I am deliriously happy," Amy said, hugging herself. Then a frown fell across her face. "Other times, I ask myself if accepting the proposal of a man who owns a saloon and was once an outlaw will be making a wise choice."

"You love him, that makes it wise," Hekuba answered.

Amy shrugged. "On his own account, I think Blue Rivers is a fine man, though admittedly disreputable in some circles." She poured herself a cup of coffee, then stood near the stove sipping it as she watched Hekuba take a ham from the pantry and slice it at the counter. "He killed a man in Texas. Did you know that?"

Hekuba shook her head, glancing up before returning to her work.

"He's told me all about it and I believe he was justified, if a quarrel over poker can ever be completely that. But the man *was* cheating, and he *did* draw on Blue first."

"In such a circumstance," Hekuba murmured, "any man would defend himself."

"Yes. He was brought to trial, though, and sentenced to be hung."

Hekuba looked up, the knife poised in midair above the ham.

Amy nodded. "Seth broke him out of jail."

Hekuba smiled. "Mr. Rivers is fortunate to have Mr. Strummar as a friend."

Amy frowned and sipped her coffee. "Seth brought him here and set him up in business. Blue owns the saloon free and clear now, but he says his debt to Seth can never be repaid, and that's what worries me, Hekuba: to be the wife of a man beholden to an outlaw. Wouldn't that worry you?"

"No," she said. "If I loved a man and he loved me, I would follow my heart and accept whatever came."

Amy thought about that, then smiled kindly. "I hope someday you find such a man."

"There are no men of color in Tejoe," Hekuba answered.

"Joaquín chose a woman of color," Amy said.

"Heaven can pass for white. Joaquín should have left me in Sulphur Springs."

"I'm glad he didn't," Amy said, setting her cup aside and tying on an apron. "Without your help, I couldn't have played the coquette with Mr. Rivers and wouldn't now be contemplating the difficulties of being his wife."

Hekuba concentrated on slicing the ham to camouflage the envy she felt.

"Perhaps with your increase in income," Amy said, "you can buy yourself a new frock. You wear clothes so well."

Hekuba stared in disbelief of the compliment.

"You're so tall and willowy," the petite, well-curved Amy said. "And I wish I had a bosom as small as yours. Oh, I know men like large bosoms, but really, what good are they except to catch a man's eye and suckle his children? If I were a spinster like you, I'd just as soon be flat as a board."

She blushed as Blue opened the door and came into the kitchen. "Did I interrupt something?" he asked with a grin.

"I was just telling Hekuba what a fine figure she has," Amy hurried to say.

Blue surveyed Hekuba's figure. "It has the clean lines of nothing extra," he said diplomatically, though lust flickered in his blue eyes.

If Hekuba could have blushed, she would have.

Blue chuckled and said, "You've embarrassed her, Amy. That ain't the way to keep good help."

"Oh, sit down, Blue," she said, still embarrassed herself. "Hekuba and I understand each other fine."

He hung his hat and coat by the door, then sat down at the kitchen table. "You'll never guess what happened last night."

Hekuba looked over her shoulder to watch Amy set a cup of coffee in front of him. His hand slid up the outside of Amy's skirt to fondle her bottom with familiarity before he saw Hekuba watching and took his hand away.

"Are you going to tell us?" Amy asked, sitting down across from him. "Or keep us waiting in suspense?"

"The town council met last night," he said. "Tom Beck came into my place afterwards and told me all about it. Apparently the meeting was a hot one."

Hekuba pulled the skillet from the back of the stove and filled it with slices of ham as Amy asked, "What was the topic of discussion?"

"Who they want for sheriff," Blue said with a chuckle.

Hekuba cracked eggs into another skillet of melted butter.

"Well, who was it?" Amy asked.

Blue laughed. "They're gonna offer the job to Joaquín."

"You can't be serious!" Amy whispered.

"Beck told me they argued back and forth a good while before taking the vote. It was unanimous."

"Do you think he'll accept?" Amy asked.

Hekuba carefully flipped the eggs over-easy in the skillet.

"Would solve his money problems," Blue said.

"But what will Seth say?"

"Reckon he'll have a few choice words on the subject." He chuckled again. "To think Seth Strummar trained the new sheriff of Tejoe. It's a good joke, if nothing else."

"Maybe Joaquín will refuse," Amy said.

"Maybe," he agreed.

Hekuba pulled the pan of biscuits from the oven. She piled half a dozen on a plate, then took up Blue's ham and eggs and carried both plates to the table. As she was setting them in front of him, Amy said, "Seth was here last night."

"Did Rico find him then?" Blue asked, breaking the yolks with a fork.

"I didn't see Rico," Amy said.

Hekuba moved back to the stove and scraped out the skillets in readiness for customers.

"She came into the saloon looking for him," Blue said. "First time she's done that. But I ain't seen him since the last time I was out at the homestead. She told me Seth sobered up, then rode off without a word to anybody. She was certain he'd left her for good." There was a pause as Blue chewed and swallowed. "I told her he wouldn't do that without at least letting her know, and I offered to drive her home, but she said she'd stop by Joaquín's first so I figured he'd take care of her." Blue paused to sip his coffee, then said, "I did find out what Joaquín's been doing for money. Beck told me he's been breaking broncs for Howard Tate." Blue chuckled. "Now there's a hard way to make a living. I figure after getting thrown and stomped all day, the sheriff's job is gonna look real soft."

"So you think he'll take it?" Amy asked.

"I wouldn't make a bet on anything Joaquín or Seth is likely to do. If someone had told me a while back something was gonna come between 'em, I would've bet my saloon against it. So I'm just watching from the sidelines here on out."

The fluttering of flames in the stove and the quiet clinks of

Blue's cutlery were the only sounds as Hekuba began mixing another batch of biscuits.

"If Joaquín was sheriff," Amy asked softly, "isn't there a chance he might have to arrest Seth someday?"

"I sure would hate to see that happen," Blue answered. "I'd lose one or the other of my best friends, maybe both of 'em. But as long as Seth stays clean in Arizona, that problem shouldn't come up."

"And if he doesn't?" Amy asked.

"Then Joaquín'll have a hard decision to make. My guess is he'd turn in his badge 'fore he'd go against Seth, but like I said, I ain't placing any bets on this round."

5

★

That was Saturday, and Hekuba worked late into the evening. When Amy finally closed the café, Nib Carey was there to escort her home. Nib worked for Blue, who didn't like Amy walking alone through town on a Saturday night, but no one thought Hekuba needed protection. Every night, Saturday or not, she walked through the shadowed alleys without fear.

This night, however, she was aware of a horseman following her. He kept his distance but she could see he rode the same pinto she'd noticed outside her home that morning. The horse was nearly all white except for two black spots over its eyes like a bandit's mask, so she knew she wasn't mistaken in thinking it was the same man. When she quickened her pace, the horseman hung back, not crowding her but obviously following. At home, she unlocked her door, then looked at him again.

Slowly he ambled his horse into her yard. He was a big man, broad and muscular, and as he came closer she saw that his skin was as black as hers. He swung down and took off his hat. "Doan mean to spook ya none, ma'am," he drawled. "Mah name's Adam

Noah and dat's mah house ya livin' in." Under the moonlight he looked to be in his midthirties and handsome.

"I'm sorry, Mr. Noah," she said warily. "This house was bought by the bank for taxes. I'm renting it now."

"Taxes?" he asked with disbelief. "Dey got taxes in da terr'-tory now?"

She nodded. "If you want your house back, you'll have to make arrangements with Mr. Clancy at the bank."

"It be nigh on three years since I seen it. Reckon I could come in and look it over befo' I decide?"

She considered, noting the gun on his hip, and that his coat was tucked behind the butt of his pistol as if he habitually kept it there.

"I won't harm ya none," he said softly.

She went in and lit the lamp, then looked at him again through the open door. He tied his horse to the portal and stepped inside, letting his gaze scan the room.

"Ya got it fixed up purty," he said. "Nevah look dis good when it be mine." He studied the ceiling. "Dey fix da roof? I could nevah keep it from leakin'."

"It hasn't rained since I've been here," she said.

He looked at her with the same frank assessment he'd used to study the house. "How long dat be?"

"Six weeks," she said.

"Ya jus' missed da rainy season den. Comes nigh 'bout July, big ol' dunderstorms crashin' into da mountains." He looked at the floor. "Ya couldn't tell dat rain be settin' on da flo'boards?"

She shook her head.

"Guess dey fix it den. Prob'ly charge me fo' da work, if I was to buy it back."

"Do you intend to do that, Mr. Noah?" she asked with trepidation.

"Doan know. Wasn't no other colored folk here befo'. How many dey be now?"

"Only my sister and I," she said.

He grinned. "Where ya learn to talk like white folk?"

"I was educated in New Orleans," she answered.

"Taught ya good, din't dey?" He cast his gaze down her body then smiled into her eyes again. "Yo' sister be livin' in dis house too?"

Hekuba shook her head. "She lives with her husband."

Noah puzzled over that, then asked, "Her husband be white?"

"Mexican," she said.

"How come ya ain't livin' wif dem?"

"I chose not to. If you'll excuse me, Mr. Noah, I've worked hard today and am not in the mood for company."

He didn't move. "Where ya be workin'?"

"Amy's Café."

"Mightn't I call on ya dere tomorrah?"

"Tomorrow's Sunday. The café is closed."

"How 'bout Monday, den?"

"I'm not in the mood to receive callers," she said, then added merely for politeness, "Thank you kindly, Mr. Noah."

He smiled. "Seems to me yo' mood need improvin'."

She didn't answer.

"If I was to eat at da café, it wouldn't 'zactly be callin' on ya, would it?"

"People of color aren't allowed in the café," she said.

"Only in da kitchen?" He laughed. "Tejoe ain't changed since I be heah las'. Why ya be workin' in a place dat won't let ya sit wif da cust'mers?"

"It's a job," she said.

He nodded. "Mightn't ya tell me yo' name?"

"Hekuba Free."

"Yo' daddy be a slave, takin' a name like dat."

"That's right," she said.

"And yo' sister's daddy be da mas'er?"

She shook her head. "A Spaniard."

"So she be Creole and ya be black. She got herself a husband and ya got yo'self a job. Life sho' doan be fair, do it?"

"I have no complaints," she said.

"Huh," he said. "I reckon dat a lie, but I be lettin' it pass. Will ya tell me one mo' thang fo' I go?"

"If I can," she said, relieved he was leaving.

"I heah tell Seth Strummar be livin' round heah. Dat be true?" His eyes had changed. They were sharp now with a cruel hunger.

"I've never heard of him," she said.

"I seen 'im heah last night, Miss Free. I seen 'im put ya on his hoss and kiss ya. Wasn't it Strummar done dat?"

"Please leave," she said.

"I be goin'," he said. Then he laughed, though it didn't touch his eyes. "Next time ya see Seth, tell 'im a ghost done show up to say howdy-do." He laughed again as he walked out, and she could hear him laughing as he rode away.

She closed and locked the door, then leaned against it studying her humble home, the tiny kitchen around the hearth, the battered hutch she had painted yellow to disguise its scars, the leather-topped trunk for her clothes, the feather bed with its dark blue quilt and single white star in the middle, the yellow curtains decorated with bluebonnets. Other than her clothes, the house was the first thing she had ever possessed all to herself. She wondered what it would cost to buy it, and if she could beat Adam Noah to the bank and claim it first.

With that thought, she felt confirmed in her decision not to return to Heaven's home and live under the protection of Heaven's husband. Independence was lonely, but Hekuba felt a satisfaction at making her own way in the world. Even though being scullery maid in another woman's café wasn't a position of prominence, it offered more autonomy than living off the generosity of her sister's husband.

When she remembered the cruel gleam in Adam Noah's eyes, however, Hekuba felt afraid of opposing him. He had built this house and still thought he had a claim to it. The banker might think so too, especially if Noah had the money to buy it back, cash in hand. All she could offer was a small weekly payment, the increase in her wages. Perhaps if Joaquín accepted the job as sheriff, he could influence the banker's decision. She was also ostensibly Seth's friend, if only through kinship with her brother-in-law, and Seth's reputation might intimidate the banker into accepting her proposition. She remembered Adam Noah had claimed to know Seth, too. A ghost from Seth's past, is what Noah had said, his eyes gleaming with a cruel light. She shivered, remembering that.

After heating water on the stove, she washed her dresses and hung them near the fire to dry, then went to bed. As she lay in the dark before sleep, she tried to decide which dress she should wear to Heaven's for Sunday dinner. Hekuba had brought three nice dresses with her, brown, blue, and black, and the one Joaquín had bought her was the soft purple of thistle blossoms. Thinking it might be politic to wear his gift while soliciting his advice on buying the house, she decided on the purple.

In the morning, she ironed the dress carefully, then stitched a new lace collar on it. When she surveyed herself in the tiny mirror, she could see only her shoulders draped with the ivory collar, her dark neck and face, and her short, bristly hair. Among her collection of simple, gold earrings, she had one pair of amethyst studs which her sister had given her. They had been a gift from Raul Ortega, and Heaven hadn't wanted to wear them for Joaquín. The purple amethysts matched Hekuba's dress and glimmered in her earlobes like regal stars. Remembering that Seth disliked her kerchiefs, she left her head bare. In her best black shawl, she walked the distance around the edge of town to Heaven's home.

Heaven wore a dress of pink satin beneath her voluminous apron, and her ebony curls were tied away from her perfect face with a pink satin ribbon. She hugged Hekuba and led her into the kitchen, fragrant with turkey roasting in the oven. The counter, however, was chaos. Eggs teetered in precarious perches and the pitcher of milk was cracked and leaking, creating a paste of scattered flour. In a bowl was a coagulated lump of dough.

Hekuba laughed. "What are you making?"

"Biscuits," Heaven answered contritely. "I wish they had taught cooking in our convent."

"It would have been more useful than painting flowers on china," Hekuba agreed. "I've learned to make biscuits at the café. Let's clean this up and start over, shall we?"

Heaven sighed, rummaging in the bottom of the hutch for another pitcher. "I have potatoes boiled, too," she said, standing up, holding the empty pitcher. "But they're already done, and the bird won't be finished for hours yet."

Hekuba smiled. "We can heat them again, then mash them. How does that sound?"

"Thank you, Hekuba," Heaven said, giving her another hug. "I'm afraid Joaquín's tolerance of my cooking has gone beyond amusement. Yesterday he asked if I could make enchiladas and I had to ask what they were. He'll never be happy with me if I don't learn to please him at the table."

"You'll learn," Hekuba said. "Perhaps you can come to the café and watch what we do."

"Could I?" Heaven asked eagerly. "The days are so long here alone."

"I don't think Miss Amy would mind, and since Joaquín would benefit, I doubt that he would object."

Heaven smiled. "He's so sweet. Last night I burnt the beans but intended to serve them anyway, not having anything else prepared. As soon as he walked into the house he said, 'You've burnt the beans.' I burst into tears, so he took me to supper at the hotel. Everyone was watching us and I felt so grand. It was a sumptuous ending to a rather sorry beginning of our evening."

"Where is he now?"

"Outside tending his horse. He pampers that animal as much as he does me."

"Perhaps it serves him as well," Hekuba teased.

Heaven laughed. "Or better, you mean."

They finished cleaning the counter, piling the eggs back into the basket and pouring the milk into the new pitcher. "We should wait until the bird is nearly done before mixing the biscuits," Hekuba advised. "Have you anything for dessert?"

Heaven shook her head with chagrin. "I had planned to serve apples, but I dropped them the other day, and now they're all brown and bruised."

"We could bake them in a pie. How does that sound?"

"Delicious!"

"It won't take long to prepare and can cook alongside the turkey. Cut out the worst spots and slice what's left very thin, then sprinkle them with a cup of sugar while I make the crust. You have flour on your face. Perhaps you should wash it."

Heaven's hand flew to her cheek. "I'll only be a moment," she said, hurrying from the room.

Hekuba took her shawl from the hook and walked out to the stable. She found Joaquín checking over the hooves of his horse. He smiled at her, then continued working the tip of his knife around the inner lip of each of the horse's shoes. Waiting until he had finished, she watched him return the knife to its sheath on his belt before she said, "I thought I would take Heaven to the café next week and give her a few cooking lessons, if you have no objection."

He laughed easily. "If she could learn not to burn beans, we would at least not starve to death."

"I'm sure she has other talents," Hekuba said, dropping her gaze. She heard his gentle laughter again and met his eyes. "I've come to see you alone, Joaquín, to ask your advice."

"Sit down," he said, nodding at a wooden, lidded box.

She settled herself on it and watched him survey the desert beyond the corral as if he were searching for anything amiss. As usual, he was dressed in black and wore a gunbelt fully loaded with cartridges. She wondered if he put it on as habitually as his clothes. The hour was still early and he hadn't left home, yet the weapon was there. Finally he returned his gaze to her, apparently satisfied that the world hadn't changed since the last time he looked at it. Leaning his shoulder against the doorjamb, he waited for her to speak.

She sat up straighter and said, "I would like to purchase the casita where I live. Do you think the bank will sell it to me?"

He thought a moment, then answered, "I guess that means you'd rather not live with us."

"I prefer being on my own," she said softly.

He nodded. "The casita will cost two hundred dollars. Are you asking for the money?"

"I would like to make small payments from my wages, to the bank if possible. Otherwise, perhaps you could pay the bank and I could pay you."

"I wouldn't accept money from you, Hekuba."

"You expect me to accept it from you. I see no difference."

He studied her a moment. "If Amy closed her café and you lost your job, what would you do?"

"There are other jobs."

"Yes, but under another employer, you may not feel so satisfied with your independence."

"All problems have remedies," she said.

He looked away again, at the desert stretching empty beyond the corral. "Are you happy living in Tejoe?"

"I think I can be content," she said.

"Alone?" he asked, meeting her eyes.

"I have you and Heaven."

"And Seth?"

She hesitated only a moment before saying firmly, "He is not mine."

"Do you believe he never will be?"

"I never aspired to possess him, Joaquín." He was silent so long she asked, "Do you wish you had left me behind?"

He shook his head. "I am thinking, though, that another town might suit us better."

"What would you hope to find somewhere else?"

"Other people of color," he said.

"So you will lower yourself to us, rather than raise us to you?"

"I don't see it that way," he said. "Only that I wish to join a community and it doesn't seem possible here."

She looked at her hands in her lap, thinking he hadn't yet learned of the town's intention to offer him the sheriff's job. "Perhaps you underestimate the tolerance of this community."

"It isn't only you," he said. "I came here to be with Seth. After our partnership was broken, I thought I could establish ties independent of him without threatening the sanctuary he's built for himself. But look what happened when I did that."

"What happened?" she murmured, afraid he would chastise her again for her intransigence.

"I nearly destroyed his home. Without his family, Seth will lose the gains I worked so hard to help him achieve."

"I see no destruction of his home," she said. "The other night when Rico came looking for him, he responded to her need, and his deep love for her was evident. Perhaps what you perceive as destruction has been only a difficult passage that has been transcended."

"Perhaps," he said with a melancholy smile. "We'll know more after today. They're coming to supper."

"All of them?" she whispered.

He nodded. "The awkwardness you and I are now anticipating is why I was angry with Seth. He created it by taking advantage of your innocence."

"It was my fault," she murmured.

"No, it was his. Rico is high-strung, especially when carrying a child. Yet Seth tortures her with his infidelities when she needs most to feel secure. If he helped her feel strong she could please him, but he doesn't help her, he tests her constantly. I suspect it's because he's hoping her failure will give him an excuse to leave and become the outlaw he was when we met."

"Your expectations for him aside," Hekuba said, confused at the depth of Joaquín's involvement, "I don't believe he would abandon his wife."

"They aren't married," he said with a bitter smile. "He has a wife and child in Texas."

She stared at him in stunned surprise.

"He also abandoned Lobo's mother," Joaquín said, his voice carrying a tinge of gloating at Hekuba's reaction. "Seth has spent his life leaving women behind. Apparently it's a habit that is difficult to break."

"But he took Lobo from his mother," she argued. "Surely that shows some sense of responsibility."

Joaquín shrugged. "He only did it because I promised to help him raise Lobo. Seth thinks I have now broken my promise."

"Because you have a wife of your own?"

"Not only that. When I met Seth I had intended to be a priest. After watching him achieve vengeance for the sake of a woman we both cared deeply about, I set my ambition aside to follow him, thinking to save the soul of one man would be worth more than serving a church I thought he had proved wrong. I was content with our progress until another woman, acting in our interest, was killed. Seth took her death in stride, but his indifference shocked me into seeing I had lost my original intention beneath his dominance. So I broke our pact and decided to stand on my own. That resolution led me to take a wife and build this house where I could live independent of Seth, thinking I could free myself of carrying the weight of his sins and still be his friend." Joaquín paused to give her a melancholy smile. "But I brought Miss Free into my home, and Seth used her to mock my illusion of achievement."

"I'm sorry," she murmured, understanding now how deeply Joaquín *was* involved.

He shook his head. "The fault isn't yours. It's mine for abandoning him before I had completed what I set out to do."

"And what was that?"

"Bring him to God," he answered simply.

"Do you mean your goal was to make him a Catholic?" she asked, barely disguising her disdain.

Again he shook his head. "The liturgy doesn't matter. What Seth needs is expiation of his sins. Without it, he can only ride the repercussions of his past. That path does not lead to justice."

"What is justice?" she scoffed.

Joaquín smiled with patience. "A balanced scale."

"Those are just words, Joaquín," she answered, more brusquely than she would have wished. "I have never seen justice in this world."

"Neither have I," he said. "Perhaps it exists only in the mind of God."

"Then how can we mortals presume to seek it?"

"It is the essence of honor," he answered.

She stood up. "Your philosophy is too ethereal for a mere woman, Joaquín. Our needs are more basic. Will you consider my request pertaining to the house?"

He nodded. "We have no need to hurry."

She thought of Adam Noah but decided against pressing for speed. "Thank you," she said. "I will help Heaven in the kitchen." As she walked away, Hekuba told herself Joaquín seemed especially suited to being a lawman. He would justify his acts with theology and temper them with mercy, yet crucify criminals with his mistaken notion of God's redemption beyond the veil of death.

6

★

 The apple pie was cooling in the window, the biscuits browning in the oven, and Hekuba was mashing potatoes when the guests arrived. She listened to the hubbub of greetings as she whipped the potatoes smooth. The voices from the parlor were soft with the intimacy of friendship, Seth's laughing, the women cooing over each other, a Spanish accent from one, Joaquín modestly silent as they complimented his home.

"Hekuba," Heaven called. "Come say hello."

"In a moment," she answered. "I must finish this first."

A rotund Mexican woman came into the kitchen. Her sleek black hair was wound into a bun on her neck, her face creased with age yet still pretty. "I am Esperanza," she announced with a smile. "May I help you?"

"Thank you, I've just finished," Hekuba said, covering the bowl and setting it on top of the oven to stay warm. She washed and dried her hands, then took off her apron.

Esperanza smiled again. "Such a pretty dress. And your earrings are beautiful."

"A gift from my sister," Hekuba answered. "I am pleased to meet you."

"Ah sí?" She laughed. "You have heard of the tyrant who rules the homestead with her sharp tongue?"

"I hadn't heard that," Hekuba replied.

Rico came in. "Hello, Hekuba. My, it smells good in here."

Rico's dress was blue and Hekuba congratulated herself for not wearing her own dress of the same color. "You look lovely, Mrs. Strummar," she said.

"Please call me Rico. We're almost kin."

"As you wish," Hekuba murmured.

A boy ran into the room. Seven or eight years old, his hair was a few shades paler than Seth's and his eyes the same gray, though the boy's shone with emotion. He stopped and stared with so much curiosity that Hekuba suspected he had never seen a black person before.

"This is Heaven's sister, Hekuba," Rico told him. "This is Lobo, the terror of our family."

He frowned at his stepmother, then smiled at Hekuba. "Pleased to meet'cha," he said.

"The pleasure is mine," she responded.

He laughed, the sound arrogant with confidence, and Hekuba thought to have such a child would be worth any sacrifice.

"Come meet our daughter," Rico said, offering her hand.

It was so soft she obviously did little labor, and Hekuba again felt like a mule of a woman as she allowed Rico to lead her into the parlor. A toddler sat on the cushion of the settee. Her dress was red velvet, her long curls blond, her eyes blue and open wide. Hekuba thought she would never be done with seeing yellow hair and blue eyes in the women around her, but she smiled at the child as Rico said, "This is Elena. Elena, this is Heaven's sister, Hekuba."

The child studied the black woman standing before her, then raised her arms to Rico. "Mama?" Elena wailed, tears suddenly spilling from her eyes.

Rico lifted her daughter in her arms and held the child above the roundness of her belly. "Hush, Elena," she soothed.

"I'm scared," the child whimpered.

"No reason," Rico said, hugging her close.

Hekuba looked at Seth. In a black suit and a blindingly white shirt, he was leaning nonchalantly with one elbow on the mantle. As he gave her a rakish smile, Hekuba felt awed at the power of his charm. Before she knew she would do it, she curtsied low in front of him.

He laughed softly. "Did you see that, Esperanza?" he asked in a teasing voice. "Hekuba bowed to me."

"I see it," she huffed. "She will learn better, no?"

"I kinda liked it," he said, his eyes warm on Hekuba.

"You would," Esperanza retorted. "But you mustn't do it, Hekuba," she said with solemn warning. "It will go to his head and he will be even more impossible to live with than now."

"I can't imagine that," Hekuba whispered.

"If you're ready for an adventure," Joaquín said quickly, "come sit down. Heaven's meals are often surprising."

"So is her sister," Esperanza muttered, her dark eyes piercing into Hekuba's.

Hekuba retreated to the kitchen while Joaquín led his guests to the patio. He had placed a plank on sawhorses for a table, covered now with a white tablecloth and all the crockery in the house. Hekuba kept her eyes on her tasks while she helped Heaven carry the food from the kitchen, then they sat down on opposite sides of Joaquín, with Esperanza between Hekuba and Lobo, who sat across from Rico, wife and son flanking Seth, who faced Joaquín. Elena sat in a high chair they must have brought with them, positioned between Rico and Heaven. Hekuba barely listened to the conversation, which was carried by the women and revolved around the best opportunities for shopping in Tejoe. She watched Elena eating applesauce with a tiny silver spoon.

The golden-haired girl seemed thrice-blessed, possessing a

cherubic countenance, a beautiful mother, and a powerful father. Hekuba knew that even if her wish were granted, the child she and Seth produced would not bask in the sun of Elena's blessings. As if feeling Hekuba's envy, Elena clutched her silver spoon and shook it at Hekuba, then brought her tiny fist down hard on the tray of her chair.

"Goodness, Elena," Rico admonished. "You've upset your applesauce." With a few quick flicks of her napkin, Rico wiped the tray clean and righted the bowl, then both mother and child looked at Hekuba.

Rico smiled. "They're a nuisance at this age."

"She's a beautiful child," Hekuba said.

"Thank you," Rico answered. Elena stuck out her tongue but her mother didn't notice, looking over her head to listen to Heaven ask Esperanza for her green chile recipe. Rico laughed and said, "Joaquín likes it so hot none of the rest of us can bear it. Except Seth, of course." She gave her husband a teasing smile. "Sometimes I think he's half Mexican, at least in his stomach."

"What's the other half?" he asked with humor.

"Pickled in alcohol," Esperanza muttered.

Seth laughed. "Reckon you're right. You got any whiskey, Joaquín?"

"I will bring it," Hekuba said, rising and walking away from the sudden silence. She carried the nearly full bottle to the table and set the whiskey before him.

"Thanks," he said softly.

She knew from his smile that her eyes were hungry with longing, and Hekuba retreated again to the kitchen lest everyone see her helplessness before him. She began washing dishes.

Heaven came in with a stack of plates cleared from the table. "Come sit down, Hekuba," she said. "We can do these later."

"In a minute," she answered.

Heaven carried the pie to her guests, and Hekuba listened to them congratulate her on the culinary feat, noticing that Heaven failed to mention she hadn't made the pie. But when she heard Seth decline dessert, Hekuba no longer cared that she wasn't given credit. She continued to clean the kitchen, listening to their conversation drift through the open door, insignificant topics interspersed with the babbling of the toddler. Occasionally Lobo's young voice rose above the others with a strident question, and Hekuba noted it was always his father who answered him. Other than that, Seth was silent. When she could find no further excuse to dally in the kitchen, Hekuba returned to her place at the table, noticing that the whiskey was half gone.

Esperanza was sitting in the shade with Elena asleep on her lap, and Rico and Heaven were talking softly together near Joaquín. Lobo was standing at his father's side, restless and impatient. Hekuba was aware of Seth's eyes on her as she sat down across from Rico and Heaven. A silence fell. Feeling compelled to fill it, she said, "I met an acquaintance of yours the other night, Seth. He asked me to say hello."

"Who was it?" he asked, pouring himself more whiskey.

"Adam Noah," she said.

Seth's eyes glinted like knifes. "Where'd you see him?"

"He came to my house, which was once his," she explained, "and said he would ask the banker about buying it back."

"Was he friendly?" Seth asked in a low voice.

"Too much so," she said, looking at her hands in her lap.

His voice sharpened with anger when he asked, "Did he hurt you?"

She shook her head, quickly meeting his eyes. "It was only that I didn't care for his company."

Seth sipped his whiskey, watching her.

"Who is he?" Rico asked with a quiver of fear in her voice.

"A ghost," Seth said.

"That's what Mr. Noah told me," Hekuba murmured. "That he was a ghost from your past."

Seth nodded. "I thought he was dead."

"Who is he?" Joaquín asked, commanding an answer.

Seth poured himself more whiskey and set the bottle down, then said quietly, "He rode with me and Allister about a hundred years ago."

"What does he want?" Rico wailed.

"Maybe just to see the house he built," Seth said with a smile.

Joaquín asked, "Why didn't you mention knowing him when I rented the house?"

Seth shrugged. "There must be more'n one Adam Noah in the world. And, like I said, I thought he was dead."

"Will it never end?" Rico cried. "Men showing up to kill you!"

"Nobody's mentioned that," he said gently.

"Has he reason to?" Joaquín asked.

Seth gave him a mocking smile. "That ain't your concern, Joaquín. You have a family now." He winked at his son. "And I have Lobo."

The boy's pleased laughter was the only sound until Hekuba said, "I didn't mean to upset everyone. Mr. Noah asked me to pass along his greeting, and I thought I should."

"I'm glad you did," Seth said. "I'll be expecting him now."

"What does he want?" Rico wailed again.

"Take it easy," Seth said.

"Tell me the truth!" she demanded. "Has he reason to hurt you?"

"Guess he could see it that way," Seth admitted.

"Will you tell us?" Joaquín asked.

Seth shook his head. "It ain't your concern."

"Do you think," Joaquín asked with strained patience, "that because I no longer live at your home, I won't help you?"

"I think you won't be there if I need you," Seth answered.

"You're wrong," Joaquín said.

Seth finished his whiskey, then stood up and smiled at Hekuba. "You ready for another shooting lesson?"

She looked at no one as she rose in obedience.

Lobo asked, "Can I come?"

"You don't need any more lessons," Seth said.

He took Hekuba's elbow and guided her from the patio through the parlor to the courtyard, where a pair of matched chestnuts stood harnessed to a carriage. He reached inside the buggy and lifted a Winchester from the floor, then led Hekuba out the gate and into the desert, where they stopped and met each other's eyes. "Tell me his exact words," Seth said.

"That was all," she replied. "Except . . ."

He waited a moment, then prodded her. "Except what?"

"He must have been watching the house for several days. He saw you kiss me that night on your horse."

Seth looked away. "Try to hit that saguaro over there," he said, cocking the Winchester and handing it to her.

She was trembling too much to sight on the cactus until his arms came around her, adjusting her grip. "No reason to be frightened, Hekuba," he said, his cheek close to hers. "Besides, it's usually when you're scared that you need to shoot straight, so you best learn to control it."

"Yes," she whispered.

"Move your hand up a little. That's better." He stepped away from her. "Let's see you hit it."

She pulled the trigger.

"Too high," he said.

She cocked the gun and tried again, scoring a hit.

"Do it again," he said.

She fired and missed.

"Too far to the right," he said.

"How can you see a bullet that misses?" she asked, her cheek against the stock of his weapon.

"I can see where you're pointing the rifle. If you shoot now, you'll be too low."

She adjusted the sight and pulled the trigger, scoring a hit.

"Keep going," he said.

She hit twice more, then lowered the gun and turned to face him. "What should I do if Mr. Noah comes again?"

"Stay away from him."

"Is he dangerous?"

"You don't need me to tell you that, Hekuba."

"No," she said.

"Why don't you move back in with Heaven and Joaquín?"

"I like my casita," she said. "Do you think the bank would favor my offer to buy it over Mr. Noah's?"

"It ain't the bank's house." Seth smiled. "I bought it last week."

She stared at him for a long moment. "If I had known that, I wouldn't have allowed him in to look at it."

Seth smiled again. "We'll have to see more of each other so I can keep you up to date."

With all of her fortitude she answered, "I have no wish to hurt your family or mine."

"You have a touch of lavender in your eyes," he said softly. "Those earrings bring it out."

"Don't, Seth," she moaned.

"Yeah, I'm a sonofabitch." He laughed. "Let's go back. I'll collect my kisses later."

"No," she said.

"No, what? You won't go back, or you don't want my kisses?"

"Rico needs you so badly, Seth."

"I know it. But that ain't what I need."

"Maybe it is," she murmured.

He took the rifle and dropped the empties on the ground, then reloaded from his belt, raised the gun, and fired, shooting and re-cocking so fast it sounded like one long explosion. She watched the arm of the saguaro fall into the dust with a thud. He emptied and reloaded again, then met her eyes. "Until you can shoot like that, I think we should keep up our lessons."

"Why am I in danger?"

"You're connected to me," he answered wryly. "That's why Joaquín didn't take his bride to my home."

"He didn't take her sister there either," she pointed out.

"But she's living in my house just the same." Seth smiled sardonically. "Since Adam Noah has already seen us kissing, he knows I care for you. He doesn't know how much, but when he figures it out, he'll know I'd take a risk to protect you. I'll feel better knowing you can help me do that."

"If you don't visit me again, Mr. Noah will think we're only connected because of Joaquín."

"But I will visit you, unless you tell me right now you don't want me to."

"I don't want you to," she whispered.

"Because of Joaquín?"

"And Heaven and Rico."

"That's three against two," Seth conceded.

"And Lobo and Elena and the child Rico's carrying."

"You left out Esperanza."

"Her, too, then."

"How about Blue and Amy? Let's see, there must be five hundred people living in Tejoe. Why don't you throw them in? Then there's my wife and child in Austin, and a coupla thousand people between here and there. Why don't we just throw the whole world against us and see what happens?"

"The world is against us, Seth."

He laughed. "I've never run from a fight."

"What are you fighting for?" she retorted in frustration. "The pleasures of my bed? You could have the same from a hundred women."

"Guess that ain't it then."

"What is?" she asked helplessly.

"Maybe I'm in love with you."

"I can't believe it!" she cried.

"Why?"

"Look at me!"

He smiled. "I can't keep my eyes off you."

"Oh, Seth! We can't hurt everyone who cares for us."

"If I visit you nights, who's to know?"

"Adam Noah," she reminded him.

"Yeah, well, he likely won't be around long."

"No," she moaned. "Do you think I could love you with blood on your hands, knowing it had been shed for me?"

"I'm dripping with blood, Hekuba. A little more ain't gonna change nothing. Besides, he came here looking for me, not you." He touched her cheek and smiled into her eyes. "If I come to your door, will you turn me away?"

"You know I couldn't."

"Then let's stop arguing," he said. "Especially since we can't kiss and make up in plain view of God and Joaquín."

"You'll do what you want, won't you," she said.

Seth laughed. "Always have. Come on. I feel the need for some more of your brother-in-law's fine whiskey."

"You drink too much," she said, letting him guide her back toward the house.

He slid the rifle onto the floor of the buggy, then looked down at her. "If you want to get rid of me, nagging's a surefire way to do it."

"I don't want to be rid of you," she whispered.

He smiled and opened the door, then gestured for her to precede him. Everyone watched them return. Seth stopped on the threshold, but Hekuba moved into the kitchen to busy herself washing the dessert plates. As she worked at cleaning the white china, she heard Seth say, "Reckon it's time we went home."

Rico came into the kitchen, carrying a lace handkerchief. "Dinner was delicious," she said with a smile. "Heaven told me you cooked most of it." She looked out the open door to the patio and said, "I was so hoping Seth and Joaquín would make peace today, but they're staring at each other as if they're enemies."

"It will come," Hekuba assured her.

Rico dabbed at her eyes. "I'm sorry. It seems I'm always crying when you see me."

Guiltily, Hekuba said, "Women are usually emotional when carrying a child."

Rico shook her head. "It's not that. Seth is . . ." She stopped and looked down a moment, then smiled bravely and was about to speak again when Seth called her name from the parlor. "I'm coming!" she answered with an edge of bewilderment. She took a step closer and kissed Hekuba's cheek. "I hope we can be friends."

"I would like that, too," she answered, surprised at the gesture of affection.

"I can see why Seth likes you." Rico smiled. "You radiate strength, while I so often feel weak."

"I'm sure it's because of your condition," Hekuba said.

"Rico!" Seth called.

She gave Hekuba a last hug and hurried into the parlor saying, "Goodness, Seth, what's your hurry?"

Esperanza came in from the patio, carrying Elena, still asleep. "I am glad we met," Esperanza said with a frown. "We will see more of each other."

Watching the Mexican woman trundle from the room, Hekuba felt keenly aware of a threat in her words. Then the front door closed and the house was silent. Hekuba stood immobile, listening to the carriage drive away. When the gate closed behind it, she felt abandoned. Heaven was clearing the table. Hekuba started to go help, but Joaquín suddenly blocked the door.

"Why did you mention Adam Noah at the table?" he asked, obviously angry though striving to speak softly. "It would have been better to tell me or Seth in private rather than frighten Rico."

"I had no way of knowing she would be frightened," Hekuba answered defensively. "Neither did I suspect I would have a chance to tell Seth privately."

"Will you see him again?"

"I told him no."

He studied her, then asked, "Did he agree?"

She shook her head.

Muttering a curse beneath his breath, Joaquín looked away for a moment, then met her eyes again. "I want you to move back in with us."

"And live under your forbearance? No, thank you," she replied.

"Perhaps Adam Noah will buy his house and you will be forced to do as I wish."

"Seth told me he bought the house last week."

"Seth did?"

She nodded.

"So he's keeping you," he said in disgust, "without asking anyone's permission."

"I'm still paying rent to the bank."

"You're paying rent to Seth if he owns the house. Usually the man pays the woman for such an arrangement."

She stared into the face of his condemnation. Then, without another word, Hekuba walked into the parlor, lifted her shawl from the hook, and left.

7

★

 Heaven came running after her. "What happened, Hekuba?" she asked tearfully.

"Nothing," she answered, not breaking her stride.

Heaven planted herself in her sister's path. She hadn't taken time to fetch a shawl and the evening breeze lifted the skirt of her pink satin dress as she moaned with pitiful confusion, "Oh, Hekuba."

"Go back to Joaquín," she ordered curtly. "He needs you more than I."

"You have been my best friend all my life. Must I choose between you and my husband?"

"I will not submit to his rule, but it is where you belong."

"Without you?" she whispered.

"It is usual that brides leave their families."

"Joaquín paid a lot of money to keep us together," she argued.

"Perhaps someday I can repay his generosity, but I belong to no one."

"Not even your sister who loves you?"

"Go back to your husband, Heaven. Make him happy and ensure your future. I will take care of myself."

"Do you think you can stand alone without a man?" she scoffed. "You are strong, Hekuba, but no woman is that strong."

"I have never had a man," she answered.

"Because you lived under mine!"

"It is no longer so."

Tears ran down Heaven's cheeks as she studied her sister. Finally she said, "You will always be welcome in our home. I hope someday you choose to return." Then she spun away and ran back to Joaquín.

Hekuba watched her a moment before resuming her walk home. The sunlight was fading and the evening promised to be cold. But as she shivered beneath her shawl, she knew it was from more than the wind. She and Seth had already hurt everyone who loved them, yet Hekuba knew only that she would sacrifice all she had for his love. When she came in sight of her casita, the pinto was tied to her portal. Slowly she approached, seeing Adam Noah sitting on the bench.

He stood up and smiled as she came near. "I was hopin' ya'd have suppah with me, Miss Free."

"I've just come from eating. Thank you just the same," she said, unlocking her door and going inside, turning to close it in his face.

He stopped it with the flat of his palm. "Did 'ya be tellin' Seth hello fo' me?"

She nodded.

"What he be sayin' back?"

"That he thought you were dead."

Noah snickered. "Hopin' I was dead is mo' like it."

"Why would he?"

"If ya be lettin' me in, I tell ya 'bout it."

She stepped back outside, pulled the door closed, and sat on the bench under the portal. "I can listen here, Mr. Noah."

"Dat be all raht," he said, then paced back and forth in front of her. As before, she noted his coat was tucked behind the butt of his pistol. When he stopped, he planted his feet wide and asked, "Seth be tellin' ya we rode together?"

She nodded.

"It was da las' job he pull wif Allister, and we rob a bank in Goliad. Ya know wheah dat is?"

She shook her head.

"In Texas. I be wif Seth and Allister only a short time when we pull dat job. Da other men, dey don't like ridin' wif a nigra and dey complain 'bout it, but Seth he takes mah part, says I a good gun and mah bullets jus' as deadly as a white man's. Seth he from Texas hisself so he be growin' up wif folks dat hate nigras, but he a pariah so he un'erstand how it feel to be hated by ever'one. Ya be knowin' dat word 'pariah'?"

She nodded again.

"Thangs went wrong on dat job. We kills a sheriff, white a'course, and it be mah bullet dat kills 'im. I know I be lynched and prob'ly worse if dey catch me, so soon's a chance come, I ask fo' mah share of da money, figgerin' on makin' fo' Mexico fast. But da first chance dat come be when da posse dey trap us in a swamp." He paused, his brow furrowed with remembering. "It be hell in dat swamp. Da skeeters be eatin' us 'live and we gots no food and even da water be bad. We decides to split up, all goin' dif'rent ways and leavin' our hosses so da posse think we still dere. Befo' I leave I ask fo' mah money. Allister, he says he done lef' it when we stops to rest da hosses. I tell 'im dat wasn't da deal, and I draw down on 'im, but Seth he jabs a pistol in mah back to defend Allister. I say I got a raht to dat money since I da one kill fo' it, and Seth he agrees but he backs Allister and says dey don't be havin' it but dat we should meet in Matamo'os and he'd give me mah share."

Again he stopped, watching her carefully. "I believe Seth. I trust 'im, so I say dat be all raht and I run through da swamp and get away. But I los' ever'thang, Miss Free. Mah hoss and saddle, even mah spurs. Come time to be meetin' in Matamo'os, dey be no

sign of Seth no' Allister. I heah da law be scourin' da country good
fo' me so I stay down in Mexico. When I fin'ly come back, I hunt
fo' da men dat rode on dat job, and after a while I find Tom Doheny in San 'Tonio. He be raht su'prised to see me. He says dey
done lynch a po' boy in Goliad, thinkin' he be me, so dat why Seth
be thinkin' I dead. Doheny, he tells me nobody on dat job gots da
money, and he ain't be seein' Seth fo' a long spell. I nevah did find
Seth, but I heah after a time dat Allister be dead and Seth, he lef'
Texas. So I come heah and I be workin' as a gun fo' da owner of a
mine, den dat fella drop dead of a heart 'tack and 'bout da same
time, I heah Seth be in El Paso. I strike out fo' dere, but by da time
I get dere, he gone. I keep lookin' and I keep hearin', but ever'time
I think I find 'im, he gone befo' I get dere. Not dis time. And since
he don't share dat loot wif da others, I figger Seth he be owin' me
'bout five thousand dollars." He studied her a moment, then asked,
"What ya think of dat story, Miss Free?"

She considered, then said, "If it's true, I think Seth will pay
what he owes."

Adam Noah laughed. "Not wifout me forcin' his hand, I don't
'spect."

"Is that what you intend to do?"

"Dat money be mine. And since a po' boy done pay da price fo'
mah crime, it free and clear. But I done give up on findin' it and I
come home to retire heah in Tejoe. 'Magine mah su'prise to find
out Seth be heah all along."

"Yes," she said, thinking fast. "Why don't you let me talk with
Seth and tell him what it is you want? Perhaps this can be settled
peacefully and you can be friends again."

He laughed harshly. "Seth be knowin' what I want. But I 'pect
ya be wantin' to talk to 'im anyway. I'll come back tomorrah night
and find out what he say. If he wants to settle peacefu', he be heah.
If not, I be lookin' fo' 'im wif mah gun. Ya be tellin' 'im dat, Miss
Free?"

"Yes," she said.

"See ya tomorrah night, den," he said.

She watched him mount his horse and ride away, wondering how she could get word to Seth that she needed to see him. The obvious person to go to was Joaquín, but Hekuba had no wish to speak with him again. She locked her door and walked through town to the bawdy district.

Hekuba had occasionally worked in Ortega's cantina in Sulphur Springs, so she entered the Blue Rivers Saloon with only mild trepidation. She approached the bartender, introduced herself, and asked to see Mr. Rivers. The bartender told her to wait and walked upstairs. After a moment Blue appeared on the balcony, frowning down at her. He hesitated, as if knowing she wouldn't come with anything but bad news, then he descended the stairs, scanning the floor of his establishment with a proprietary pride. When he approached, he took her elbow and led her out on the boardwalk to talk.

"I need to see Seth," she began bluntly. "Do you know where I can find him?"

Blue studied her a long moment. "Why don't you ask Joaquín?"

"He's not home," she lied.

"He's prob'ly out at Seth's."

"I don't think so," she said. "Seth and his family were with us for supper today."

"Why didn't you tell him what you need to say then?" he asked with suspicion.

"I didn't know it then, Mr. Rivers," she replied, striving for patience. "Will you be seeing him tonight?"

"Hadn't planned on it. But if it's important, I can ride out there."

"It's important," she said.

"That you see Seth tonight," he said.

"Or in the morning. Tomorrow night will be too late."

Again he studied her in silence. "All right," he finally said. "I'll ride out and tell him."

"Thank you," she said. Walking away she could feel his eyes following her until she turned the corner.

After waiting several hours in her casita, she decided Seth wasn't coming. She had just changed into her nightgown when she heard a horse outside. Peering from behind the curtain, she saw him tying his sorrel to the same pillar where Adam Noah's horse had been tied. Quickly she pulled her wrapper on and opened the door.

He smiled at her as he came in, saying softly, "Hope I didn't wake you."

She shook her head. "Please sit down, Seth."

He took off his hat and tossed it onto the hook, then sat at the table, watching her. She sat across from him and told him Adam Noah's story, unable to read his reaction in the gray sheen of his eyes. When she finished, he stood up and extinguished the lamp, then walked over to the window and looked out for a moment. Finally he turned around and said, "I'm sorry you're in the middle of this, Hekuba."

"Will you give him the money?"

"Allister and I never went back for it. Unless someone accidentally stumbled across it, it's still stashed somewhere south of Goliad."

"You don't even know where?"

Seth shook his head. "We all lost on that job, Noah as well as the rest of us."

"What will you do?"

"Meet him tomorrow night and explain the situation."

"And if he won't accept your explanation?"

"Then I'll deal with his gun. Ain't that what he said?"

Dismayed at his calm, she asked, "Isn't your life worth more than five thousand dollars?"

He shrugged. "Maybe I'd rather be dead than broke."

"How can you say that?" she whispered.

He laughed gently, looking devilishly handsome in the moonlight. "It's always been my consolation that I wouldn't leave Rico and the children penniless."

"I'm sure they'd rather have you than money."

"Fortunately, they don't have anything to say about it."

"So you intend to refuse Mr. Noah?"

"Yeah. But I won't do it here. When he shows up, send him to Blue's."

"Then just sit here and wait to learn which one of you is still alive?"

"Noah and I were friends once. Maybe it won't come to that."

"How do you know?"

"I don't." He laughed. "Anything can happen."

"How can you laugh!" she cried.

"To tell you the truth, I never expected to live this long. If Adam Noah is the man who finally brings me down, least it won't be the law."

"If you hadn't given Joaquín the money to buy Heaven and me, you would have some of what Mr. Noah wants."

"I told you Joaquín paid me back."

"Where did his money come from? Wasn't it yours?"

He shrugged again. "Originally it belonged to people in Texas. When Joaquín and I first hooked up, I gave him five thousand for saving my life, which he did more'n once."

"Can't you give Mr. Noah five thousand for the same reason?"

"That would make me a coward. I'd rather be dead."

When she lowered her face to hide her tears, he came around the table, pulled her to her feet, and held her close, kissing her neck.

"Please," she moaned.

"Please, what?" he answered, untying her wrapper.

"Don't," she pleaded.

"I may be dead tomorrow, Hekuba," he coaxed. "Won't you let me die a happy man?"

"Don't joke," she said.

"I ain't." He dropped her wrapper and unbuttoned her night-gown where it closed high on her neck. "Let me see you," he said, tugging the gown up and pulling it off. "Let me love you," he murmured, bending low to kiss her breasts.

She allowed him to lead her to bed, then sat on the edge watching him undress until he stood before her naked.

"A condemned man," he teased, "asks permission to enter your sanctuary."

She laughed despite herself, standing to embrace him. He kissed her, tossed the covers out of the way, and pulled her onto the bed. Entwined in the moonlight falling through the bluebonnets covering her window, he was pale and powerful, she dark and receptive. As he moved within her, he murmured her name over and over as if it were a litany of salvation.

"I am not," she whispered to his praise. "I cannot," she answered his requests.

"Yes," he said, again and again, until her affirmations echoed him with passion.

In the morning, she awoke to meet his eyes. He fondled her breasts, leaned low to kiss them, then lay back and said, "I think last night was the first time I've fucked a woman sober."

She smiled. "How was it?"

"You tell me."

"I loved it."

"Me, too," he said, sliding his hand down to nestle between her thighs. "Let's do it again."

"I'll be late for work."

"I'll tell Amy I kept you."

"You will not!" she protested, but they both knew she would relish his claiming her in public.

When finally they left the house, he walked her to the café, leading his horse along behind. Blue was at the kitchen table as they came in together, and Amy was working at the stove.

"Don't get mad at her, Amy," Seth said. "It's my fault she's late."

Hekuba turned away to hang her shawl on the peg, hearing a heavy silence. When she turned around again, Seth winked at her from where he was sitting at the table. Blue and Amy kept their eyes to themselves. Hekuba busied herself at the counter, mixing biscuits for the breakfast crowd already filling the dining room. From the clock on the wall, she saw that it was already seven and the café had been open an hour.

When Amy left the kitchen to wait on customers, Seth got up to pour himself a cup of coffee, then sat down again across from Blue, both of them silent. Hekuba worked diligently to make up for lost time. Finally a lull came, and Seth asked if he might have breakfast, too. She cooked him ham and eggs and gave him the last of the biscuits, then began washing dishes. Still the men said nothing, and she wished Blue would leave if he only meant to stare at her back all morning.

Seth had finished eating and she had just poured both men fresh coffee when Joaquín came in from the café. He stood facing the men, letting them get a good look at what had changed.

Finally Seth said, "If my eyes ain't deceiving me, Joaquín, that's a badge on your coat."

In a quiet voice he answered, "I was riding to tell you when I saw Lobo on his way to school and he said you weren't home."

"I spent the night with Hekuba," Seth said, his voice flat. "Is that against the law?"

Joaquín looked at her, still holding the coffeepot. Then he looked at Blue, then finally back at Seth. "I have no wish to oppose you. I hope I never have to make that choice."

"You will," Seth said. "I'm meeting Adam Noah tonight. When I kill him, are you gonna try'n arrest me for shedding blood in your jurisdiction?"

Joaquín squared his shoulders. "Since you have told me your intention, I can't call it self-defense, can I?"

Slowly Seth stood up. "You can call it anything you damn well please."

"Wait a minute," Blue said, standing too.

"I always thought lawmen," Seth said, his voice like ice, "were killers who'd lost their nerve. But I never thought of you as a killer, Joaquín."

"Neither have I lost my nerve," he said.

"I can see that. But if you try'n arrest me, you won't succeed. I guarantee it."

"Wait a minute," Blue said again. "We can work this out."

"Reckon not," Seth said. Then he laughed bitterly, still watching only Joaquín. "Why is it two men who've ridden together a lot of years can't part company without a fight?"

"I have no wish to fight you," Joaquín answered.

"Pinning a star on your coat made you my enemy. It was your choice, not mine."

"It will be yours if you break the law in Tejoe."

"Maybe you better fill me in on the laws. I've never cared much what they are."

"You know them well enough. If you kill Adam Noah after threatening his death in front of witnesses, I will have to arrest you."

"Make sure your gun's carrying a full load."

"It only takes one bullet."

Seth snorted with scorn. "You kill me with one bullet and you'll be the luckiest goddamn lawman in history."

"The unluckiest," Joaquín said. "But I will honor my oath."

Seth nodded. "Are you gonna get out of my way or do you want to do it now?"

Joaquín stepped aside and Seth strode out, slamming the door. Joaquín walked out through the café.

"Jesus," Blue said, meeting Hekuba's eyes.

Amy came in with a tray of dirty dishes. She looked back and forth between them, then asked, "What happened?"

"I must ask for the day off," Hekuba said, taking her shawl and leaving without waiting for an answer.

She walked home through the bright, cold sunlight, closed and locked the door of her casita, then fell on the bed, smelling the scent of Seth and sex from their night together. She told herself she should act to prevent what was coming. If she had any money she would pay Noah off, but there was no chance of that. Yet there must be another solution, if only she could find it. Some way to eliminate this stranger whose presence threatened to irrevocably destroy the friendship between Seth and Joaquín. Finally she stumbled onto a plan: When Adam Noah came that evening, she wouldn't send him to Blue's as Seth had asked, she would take him into the desert and kill him herself. Seth would think Noah's courage had failed and he had run. Joaquín would know only that Noah had disappeared. The problem would vanish.

Hekuba walked to her sister's house but didn't let Heaven see her. Quietly she eased the gate open and crossed through the parlor and patio to the master bedroom, where she knew Joaquín kept a loaded pistol in the bedside table. Taking the weapon, she eased through the back gate and into the stable, where she took a shovel from the tack room. Then she walked far into the desert, to a bare space marked by a single saguaro. Behind it, in a shallow depression in the land, she labored to dig a grave. The ground was hard and the work difficult. She was drenched with sweat before she had dug a long trough barely two feet deep. Deciding it would be adequate, she left the shovel beside the grave and returned home. She bathed and dressed in fresh clothes, tucked the pistol in the garter of her stocking, and sat down to wait for Adam Noah.

Slowly the light fell from the sky. Steeling her resolution for what lay ahead, she kept comparing the love between Seth and Joaquín when she had first met them with their anger as they faced each other in the café. She felt determined to restore the former and banish the latter, believing it was hers to do because she had been the one to fracture their friendship. Remembering Rico's tears and Lobo's insouciance, she knew they would be destroyed by Seth's death, no less than Heaven if Joaquín died, and Hekuba told herself she was acting to protect the women and children from harm. When Adam Noah arrived in the red light of dusk, she opened the door with a bewitching smile.

"Dat da first time I seen ya smile," he said, still sitting his horse. "Ya be a mighty purty woman, Miss Free."

"Thank you, Mr. Noah," she said. "Seth asked me to take you to where he wants to meet."

Noah frowned. "Wheah dat be?"

"Out in the desert," she said.

Noah studied her, calculating. "Dat all raht," he finally said.

"Will you let me ride on your horse?" she asked sweetly.

"I be pleased," he said, swinging down and holding out his hand.

She let him lift her into the saddle, then he swung up behind, smiled, and said, "I tempted to kiss ya like Seth done da othah night."

She hid her face, and he laughed softly. "Mebbe after dis is ovah, ya be feelin' dif'rent 'bout dat."

"Maybe," she whispered.

He turned his horse and followed her directions to the saguaro standing alone in the wilderness. Before they came in view of the open grave lurking behind a slight rise in the earth, she told him to stop.

"Seth not heah," he said.

"He asked that we wait," she answered.

Noah swung down and lifted her beside him, then turned and studied the land between them and town, fading into twilight. Before she could allow herself to hesitate, Hekuba lifted her skirts and pulled the pistol from her garter. She raised the gun with both hands and took aim at his back, a scant stretch away. Her finger barely touched the trigger, but the explosion shattered the silence as Noah staggered forward under the impact of the bullet. She realized she'd pulled right and had barely winged his shoulder. The wound wasn't fatal. As he began turning to face her, he reached for his own gun. She pulled the trigger as fast as she could, all four of her bullets piercing the right side of his back. Though her gun was empty, she kept pulling the trigger, watching him fall as the echoes thundered across the emptiness and ricocheted off the distant mountains, rolling back again and again until finally she was left in the silence of solitude.

Five bullets holes pierced Noah's body, blood oozing from the torn shreds of his coat to stain the sand with his death. She dropped her gun and took hold of his boots, struggling to drag his weight across the rise of earth and into the grave. He landed on his back and she stared into his eyes, open with surprise. Quickly she picked up the shovel and threw dirt on his face, then frantically worked to cover the corpse and fill the hollow around it, tamp the dirt, and smooth it over. She tossed sand until the grave looked the same as the desert around it. Dropping the shovel, she retrieved Joaquín's gun, nestled it in her garter again, and started home.

The clomping from behind made her whirl around to see Noah's horse following her, the black spots around its eyes making it look like a harlequin of mockery. She yelled at it and clapped her hands, but the horse only shied a few steps and stared at her in confusion. Kneeling, she picked up stones and threw them at the animal until it galloped away, dragging its reins. She repeatedly looked back over her shoulder to be certain it was gone as she continued her trek home. Again she bathed and dressed in fresh clothes, then sat down to wait for Seth.

It was nine o'clock before she heard the approach of a horse. For a frightened moment she sat immobile, afraid it was Noah's pinto returning to condemn her. Finally she forced herself to rise and peer from behind the curtain of bluebonnets. When she saw Seth tying his reins to the portal, she flung open the door and threw herself into his arms, feeling his strength enclose her in the solace of safety.

Finally he broke their embrace, led her inside, and closed the door. He lit the lamp, then studied her a moment before he said, "Noah didn't show. Was he here?"

She shook her head.

"You sure he said tonight?"

She nodded, unable to speak.

"What's the matter, Hekuba?" he asked softly.

"Nothing," she managed to say.

"You're lying," he said.

"I was frightened, is all."

He studied her a while longer, then blew out the lamp, opened the door, and stared into the desert. "Doesn't make sense."

"Maybe he lost his nerve," she said.

"Adam Noah was never short on nerve."

"That was years ago," she argued. "He could have changed."

Seth closed the door and faced her again in the dark. "Reckon I should go home."

"Don't leave me," she sobbed, clinging to him with need.

His arms encircled her and held her tight. "He's been here, hasn't he, Hekuba?"

"No," she said, her face against his shirt.

"Did he hurt you?"

She shook her head. "I haven't seen him."

"Then what's got you so spooked?"

"I was afraid!" she cried, meeting his eyes. "Waiting can be as terrifying as anything that happens, waiting and thinking, hoping and dreading. I was afraid."

He smiled. "No reason to be afraid of a ghost. It seems that's all he was."

Tears spilled down her cheeks. "Don't leave me alone tonight, Seth," she pleaded.

"I ain't been home since yesterday," he said, watching her carefully.

She stepped out of his embrace and turned her back to wipe her tears, thinking she had planned only how to execute the deed, not how to assuage her fear after it was done.

From behind her, Seth said, "Let me take you to your sister's for the night."

She shook her head.

"Because of what happened between me and Joaquín?" When she didn't answer, he said, "We've quarreled before. Reckon I was taken by surprise, seeing him behind a badge. We'll work it out. Now that Noah's gone, there's no bone to fight over."

"Is that true?" she whispered, grasping at the hope that what she had done was right after all.

"Don't see why it shouldn't be," he said, then asked pointedly, "Do you?"

"No," she said, struggling to dam her tears.

Softly he said, "I don't like leaving you alone when you're upset."

"I'm not upset," she said.

"The hell you ain't." He turned her around to face him again, looking so deeply into her eyes that she felt certain he could read the truth. "You sure you didn't tell him to meet me someplace else, thinking he'd give up?"

She shook her head.

"He won't, if that's what you did."

"I didn't," she insisted.

Seth nodded. "I'm taking you to your sister's, so don't argue. You want to bring a nightgown or go without?"

"I'll take a few things," she said, not moving.

"I'll wait outside," he said, giving her a sardonic smile, "or I might be tempted to spend another night here and maybe forget where I live."

She managed to smile back, then watched him walk out. The emptiness of her casita spurred her to action. She lit the lamp and packed what she needed, bundling Joaquín's pistol in the folds of her nightgown, thinking this would give her a chance to replace the gun before he realized it was gone. With a sudden jolt she re-membered the shovel left by the grave. She shuddered, knowing she had to retrieve it, and with the horror of that thought she blew out the lamp and fled to Seth's side. He lifted her onto his horse and swung up behind, then stole a quick kiss. She clung to him with a sob.

"I wish you'd tell me what happened," he said.

"Nothing happened," she whispered. "I was only terrified with waiting."

"You're a poor liar, Hekuba," he answered, reining his horse around. "But it'll come out when you least expect it. It always does."

She buried her face between the sides of his open coat. Listen-ing to his heartbeat keep cadence with the hoofbeats, she told her-self Seth was alive and returning to his friend because of what she had done, and the terror she felt was a small price to pay for that victory.

8

★

Joaquín opened the door, his pleasure thinly camou-
flaged by a smile of sarcastic surprise above the silver
star on his lapel.

Seth laughed gently and said, "Hekuba ain't feeling well so I
brought her home."

"Come in," Joaquín said, opening the door wider.

Heaven laid her embroidery aside and quickly crossed the parlor to hug Hekuba. "Would you like to lie down?"

Hekuba nodded and let her sister take her valise and lead her
into the spare room. She sat down on the new bed and watched
Heaven lift the glass chimney off the lamp and reach for a match.
"I don't need light," Hekuba said.

Heaven replaced the chimney and turned to look at her with
concern. "Are you ill?"

Hekuba shook her head.

"You don't look well, Hekuba."

She shrugged. "I would like to sleep now."

"Of course," Heaven answered. "I'll start some coffee for the
men and come back and check on you."

"Please don't," she said. "I'll be asleep."

"As you wish," Heaven said, hurt at the rebuff. "Are you sure you're all right?"

"I'm fine," she lied, forcing a smile to give credence to her words.

As soon as Heaven was gone, Hekuba hurried to her valise and found the cold metal of the gun within the folds of her nightgown. Opening the door into the master bedroom, she stood a moment peering into its darkness before she walked across to the bedside table, slid open the drawer, and replaced the pistol where she had found it. Quickly she returned to the spare room and closed the door.

Her heart was beating so fast she felt faint. Quietly she opened the door to the patio, then she sat down on the floor and leaned her head against the wall as she breathed deeply of the cool night air. She could see Heaven moving about the brightly lit kitchen, and through the open door to the parlor, she could hear the men talking.

"Reckon I owe you an apology," Seth said.

"Do you?" Joaquín teased, pleasure evident in his voice.

"It's gonna take a while to get used to that star on your chest, Joaquín. You can't expect me to overturn habits I've carried all my life in the blink of an eye."

"No," he said. "But it has not made me your enemy."

Hekuba heard liquid gurgling from a bottle, then Seth asked, "What happens if you have to choose between me and your oath of office?"

"You have lived here three years without breaking any laws," Joaquín answered.

"You're forgetting extradition. The states are moving in that direction."

"Arizona is still a territory."

"So far," Seth said.

After a moment, Joaquín asked, "What happened with Adam Noah?"

"He never showed."

"What was he after?"

"Money we stole ten years ago. Allister hid it before we made the split and we never went back for it. Noah thinks I owe him his share."

"Can't you tell him where it is?"

"I didn't see Allister hide it. I don't know where it is."

"A lot of money, I suppose."

"If I paid him, I'd have to get a job." Seth laughed. "I don't hanker to pin on a star and there ain't much else my talents are good for."

"That was exactly my problem," Joaquín said. "I was breaking broomtails for Howard Tate, but a few weeks of that convinced me to find another way to make a living."

Seth laughed again. "It's a young man's game, that's for sure."

Hekuba tried to take comfort in the soft pleasure of their voices. With a few kind words their friendship was restored to its old rapport. If only she could be so easily repaired, forget the echoes of the gun ricocheting across the desert, the ugliness of Adam Noah's body with five bullet holes oozing blood, the surprise on his face as she had last seen it in the grave. If she hadn't interceded, maybe Noah would have accepted Seth's explanation and returned to Texas to search for the money. Maybe she was as peripheral to Seth's life as Joaquín assumed she was, and her deed had accomplished only this agony of guilt she must bear alone.

She heard Seth say, "This is beautiful work. Heaven's an artist."

"Yes," Joaquín agreed. "They taught embroidery and painting in her fancy school. I wish they had included a course in homemaking. She's getting better at ironing my shirts, but I doubt she'll ever be as good as Esperanza."

"Not to pick at a sore, Joaquín, but you could still be living with us."

"The time has passed when I felt comfortable living off your money," he said. "Besides, from what you said, it's running low."

"A tad," Seth admitted. "When I planned for my future, I hadn't counted on such a large family."

"Yet you are courting more."

"We could raise horses, you and me."

"It wouldn't work."

"Why not?"

"Rico is good at closing her eyes to many things, but I doubt even she will be able to ignore that Hekuba's child is yours."

"She ain't pregnant yet."

"How do you know?"

Hekuba could hear one of them pouring more whiskey.

Joaquín said, "I will take care of her and the child if it comes, but I hope it doesn't. I envisioned Hekuba as another Esperanza in my home, not as a threat to yours."

Seth was silent.

"Is she a threat to Rico?" Joaquín asked.

"I don't want to hurt anyone," Seth said.

"Then put your feelings for Hekuba aside."

"Don't think I can."

"Why not?"

"She haunts me when I'm not with her, and when I am, I feel like it's where I belong."

Hekuba hugged herself, the joy of hearing Seth's declaration poisoned by the fear that she could never again meet his eyes without seeing Adam Noah staring blindly from the grave.

Softly Joaquín asked, "What do you see when you look at Hekuba?"

Seth chuckled. "An ancient queen with a crown of pride."

"She is proud," Joaquín agreed. "But no beauty."

"She is to me."

Joaquín sighed. "If not for Rico, I would welcome your love of Hekuba. But Rico will not go away, Seth, any more than Elena and the child she is carrying. Will you abandon them, as you did Johanna and Esther?"

"No," Seth said.

"Yet you will continue to sleep with Hekuba?"

"Reckon."

"Do you think it's to anyone's benefit to make her your mistress?"

"I can't help that I love her."

"It's possible to love a woman without taking her to bed."

Seth laughed. "Maybe for you."

"It's no joke, Seth. You say you won't abandon Rico, but by continuing to see Hekuba, you will kill the love you share with each of them."

"That's my talent, ain't it?" he answered bitterly.

"One you keep alive by failing to curb your lust. Do you think I never felt desire for Johanna? When I was taking her to Austin, many nights she cried in despair, tempting me to offer the love you denied her. I resisted those yearnings for the sake of our friendship."

"Well, you're a better man, Joaquín," Seth said.

"Only because I keep my eyes open to the consequences of my actions. You turn your back, as if not seeing the suffering you inflict means it will not exist. Perhaps it doesn't for you, but how do you think Rico is feeling right now?"

"Not good."

"Doesn't that bother you?"

"Yeah, it does."

"And Hekuba? Do you think she is joyous in your love? Is that why you brought her here tonight, because she is so happy you chose not to leave her alone?"

"Adam Noah spooked her," Seth argued.

"Who is Adam Noah to her?"

"Nobody," he admitted.

Hearing a coyote howl across the emptiness of the desert, Hekuba shivered, sitting on the floor in the dark.

Seth said, "I'll just say good night to her and be on my way."

She knew she should get up, but she couldn't move. Listening to him come in, she saw the light slash across the room only to disappear again as he closed the door. He reached down and lifted her to her feet, then held her close. "You gonna be all right?" he asked.

"I am only all right when you hold me," she said.

"Then why are you crying?"

"Because you are leaving."

He picked her up and carried her to the bed, laid her on top of the covers, and sat down beside her. "This ain't good, Hekuba. You're crying and Rico's crying and I feel like I'm in hell. Can you see any way out of it?"

"No," she said.

"Me, either," he said.

"What will we do?"

"Maybe I should tell Rico the truth. Maybe she can accept it if it's out in the open."

"Don't, Seth," Hekuba pleaded.

"I've never lied to her. If she asks, I'll tell her."

"What good will that do?"

"It'll be better'n living a lie," he said.

She thought of her lie about Adam Noah, and a confession perched on the tip of her tongue. She bit it back. "Perhaps your love for me will pass and you can be happy with Rico again. If so, why should we hurt her now?"

"One of you is gonna be hurt."

"I can bear it. She can't."

"That's why I love you more," he said, touching her cheek.

She kissed the palm of his hand. "I can thrive on the scraps of your love."

"You have more'n that."

"Go home to Rico and tell her you love her. It is not a lie. By making her strong, we can survive."

He traced her lips with his finger, then raised his hand to the tight curls of her hair. "Maybe I should become a Mormon, then I could keep you both."

"The Mormons would not allow you to have a black wife. They consider us inferior."

"I didn't know that," he said. "Doesn't seem very Christian."

"It was Christians who made us slaves," she answered.

He snorted. "I can't imagine a world more hypocritical than this one."

"So what difference does it make if we ease our way with small lies, as long as the truth is alive in our hearts?"

"Small lies have a habit of ricocheting," he said.

"Be good to Rico," she whispered. "Your goodness will ricochet instead of our lies."

"Maybe," he said, leaning to kiss her with passion. Reluctantly he broke away from her and walked to the door. Turning back, he asked, "Will you go to work tomorrow?"

"Yes," she said.

"I'll be there to walk you home."

She felt dread at the thought of returning to Adam Noah's house, then reminded herself that Seth owned it now. "Please," she said.

She lay alone, listening to him leave and to the hoofbeats of his horse fading into the distance. After a while she heard Joaquín and Heaven close the house for the night and go into their room. Hekuba waited until enough time had passed for them to find sleep after love, then she rose and walked into the desert to retrieve the shovel.

The moon was bright, illuminating the way, but she walked with leaden feet toward the place of her crime. From a distance, coyotes howled. Though she shivered hearing their mournful song, she told herself they were far away and would not harm her. As she came nearer, however, their yips grew louder and she could hear growls from deep in their throats. When she crested the rise in the land and looked down at the grave, she saw with horror that they had dug up the corpse. The wild dogs stopped to stare at her a moment, then returned to their grisly feast. Appalled, she watched a coyote drag an arm from the grave and carry it into the shadow of the saguaro. When the dog squatted on its haunches and grinned at her with gore hanging from its teeth, she fled, abandoning the shovel.

Across the barren desert she ran, her hope for escape doomed. In the morning, vultures would circle the sky above the uncovered corpse, attracting attention. Her crime would be discovered, and it would fall on Joaquín to arrest the perpetrator. With agony, Hekuba eased open the gate in the wall around her sister's home. As quietly as she could, she hurried through the courtyard to the latrine, went inside and closed the door, then stood trembling as she tried to stifle her tears before returning to the house.

When she finally emerged, she saw her brother-in-law watching her from across the yard. Resolutely she raised her head higher and walked into the house. His eyes followed her, but he remained silent.

9

★

Blue came for breakfast in the café as usual, but now he and Amy shared looks in silence. Feeling their eyes on her back, Hekuba forced her hands to work. The day eked by, each moment laden with the expectation of Joaquín walking in wearing the star of authority. During the dinner hour, Hekuba had to fry steaks. The blood bubbling to their surface reminded her of Adam Noah's oozing through the bullet holes in his coat, and she strove to staunch her nausea. Finally, when Amy was closing the café, it was Seth who walked through the door.

Hekuba felt a moment's happiness seeing his smile. He hung his hat on a hook and stood leaning against the wall, waiting for her to finish. While she was mopping the day's accumulation of dust from the floor of the dining room, she heard the kitchen door open, and her heart stopped, then beat again when she recognized Blue's voice.

"I was hoping to find you here," he said.

"Why's that?" Seth asked.

"Didn't you hear they found Noah's corpse out in the desert?"

Now Hekuba froze in body and mind, waiting for Seth's reply.

"I just rode in," he finally said.

"The grave was too shallow and coyotes dug it up," Blue said.

"Where?" Seth asked.

Blue waited a moment before he asked, "Don't you know?"

"No, I don't," Seth said.

"It was about two miles southeast of town." There was a pause, then Blue said, "I haven't seen Joaquín all day. Have you?"

"No," Seth said.

Hekuba pushed her mop into the last corner, wrung the mop out, carried the bucket to the front door, and threw the dirty water into the street. She closed and locked the door, then walked into the kitchen, forcing herself to smile at the men. "Hello, Mr. Rivers," she said lightly, as if she hadn't heard their conversation.

"Evenin', Hekuba," he answered without a smile.

Seth's eyes were ferocious meeting hers, and she quickly turned away. Carefully she washed her hands in the basin, threw the water into the alley, then lifted her shawl from its peg. Seth opened the door and they walked into the darkness together. She listened to his boots on the hard, rocky soil, the soft jangle of his spurs, the clomping of his horse following behind.

When they were inside her casita and she had lit the lamp, she turned to face him and saw her burden reflected in his eyes.

"It wasn't necessary," he said.

"It's done," she answered.

"Nowhere near."

They stared at each other across the fluttering flame of the lamp. Finally he asked, "Did he attack you?"

"No," she said.

"You can say he did and they'll call it self-defense."

"I shot him in the back," she said.

His eyes darkened to a deep slate that made her feel cold. He asked, "What gun did you use?"

"A pistol I took from Joaquín's room. I put it back."

"Did you reload it?"

She shook her head, stunned at her negligence.

"Why didn't you tell me last night?"

"What good would it have done?"

"At least we could've buried the body so it wouldn't be found. Think hard, Hekuba: did you leave anything behind to connect you with what happened?"

"The shovel," she said. "I went back for it last night, but coyotes were there and I ran away without it."

"Where'd you get the shovel?"

"From Joaquín's stable."

"If you were trying to frame him, you did a damn good job."

"I wasn't," she whispered.

"You reckon he'll believe that?"

"Why would I hurt him?"

"He won't think it was you."

The truth of his words struck her with panic. "I'll confess," she moaned.

"The hell you will. Just keep quiet and we'll play it as it falls."

A horse approached slowly, as if dreading to come near.

"That'll be him," Seth said.

"Then it's over," she said.

"It's only beginning. Keep quiet, no matter what happens. Promise me, Hekuba."

"What will he do?" she whispered.

"The only evidence against me is a threat. That ain't proof of guilt."

"Do you expect me to let you be arrested?"

"We'll play it as it falls," he said again.

She shook her head, blinking back tears as they heard the horse stop outside. When she opened the door, she nearly fell to her knees and begged mercy from the anger in Joaquín's eyes. He brushed past her and stood opposite to Seth.

"You know why I'm here," Joaquín said with baffled fury.

"Reckon," Seth said.

"I can't believe you!" Joaquín shouted. "Coming to my house last night, talking as if we were friends while all the time you were lying! Have you no honor?"

"I didn't do it," Seth said.

Joaquín made an inarticulate sound of disgust. "I arrest you for the murder of Adam Noah. Will you surrender?"

Only the flame fluttering in the lamp made a sound in the room.

Finally Seth asked, "Hasn't it occurred to you that you might be wrong?"

Joaquín shook his head. "You killed him with my gun and buried him with my shovel, in a grave a child would have dug so there was no chance of escaping notice. Am I wrong to think you were acting against me?"

"I've never shot a man in the back."

"If you didn't do it," Joaquín mocked, "how do you know he was shot in the back?"

Hekuba moaned, but neither of them looked at her.

"Give me your gun," Joaquín said.

A moment of eternity slowly slid into the past before Seth drew his weapon with his left hand and handed it over.

"No!" Hekuba cried.

His eyes on Joaquín, Seth muttered, "Stay out of it, Hekuba." Then he said to the sheriff, "Let's go."

She stood stunned with remorse, watching through the open door as they mounted their horses and disappeared in the night.

A week passed, days and nights of tortured loneliness, before Hekuba heard Seth's name again. She was working alone in the café's kitchen, with Blue sitting at the table behind her, when he suddenly broke the silence.

"Have you read the editorial in this morning's paper?" he asked with an edge of anger.

"No," she said, not looking at him.

"I'll read it to you," he said. Before she could protest, he began: "By the modern miracle of telegraphy, the arrest of Seth Strummar has been relayed throughout the nation. The State of Texas has petitioned his extradition, but the Honorable William Safford, Governor of this Territory, has boasted that Arizona won the honor of hanging the most cold-blooded killer the Southwest has ever known. An ironic sweetness to the story is that the arresting officer was none other than Joaquín Ascarate, former compañero of the outlaw. It was Sheriff Ascarate's first official act, and by performing his duty without bias of friendship, he has justified the faith the citizens of Tejoe placed in him when they appointed him their sheriff."

Hekuba listened immobile, her hands frozen above the pie crust she had been rolling out.

Blue continued reading: "Strummar's career has been unsurpassed in the annals of murder, beginning with his first killing when he was only seventeen. Within a year of shedding first blood, he joined forces with the deadly cutthroat, Ben Allister, and together they inflicted a reign of terror on the citizens and a plague of loss on the banks of Texas. In 1870, the two desperados were frolicking in an Austin saloon when the Rangers attempted to arrest them. Strummar killed one of the Rangers before he and Allister escaped, and it is rumored that he killed another Ranger here in the Dragoon Mountains of Arizona. The number of men who have fallen before Strummar's gun is unknown, but estimates range as high as two dozen and he has never been heard to contradict that number. In 1875, Allister was shot to death by his own wife. Strummar hanged her in vengeance then disappeared. He was reported seen in scattered pueblos around the Southwest, and everywhere he rode, blood accumulated in his tracks. So long did he escape the retribution of the law that a legend grew proclaiming him immortal. He is heralded in ballads sung in cantinas on both sides of the Mexican border as a glorified dealer of death. His most recent crime, however, was an especially dastardly one: He murdered by shooting in the back a former comrade in banditry who came to collect his share of the spoils Strummar had kept for himself. So dies the stuff of legend."

Carefully Hekuba pushed the rolling pin across the pie crust again.

Behind her, Blue said, "Seth's never shot a man in the back. And if he had killed Adam Noah, his body would never have been found."

Hekuba turned to face him. "So you think someone else did it?"

"Damn straight," he said.

"Who?" she whispered.

"I don't know. The motive's the stickler. Seth's the only one who has one. When he left my place that night, he said he was going to your house. Did he show up?"

"Yes," she said.

"Could you give him an alibi?"

She was silent.

"How long was he there, Hekuba?" Blue asked sharply.

"Only a few minutes. He took me to my sister's house."

"And left right away?"

"After an hour or so."

"Rico said he didn't get home until three-thirty. Plenty of time to meet Noah in the desert and kill him, except that ain't what happened. Do you know what did?"

She shook her head. "How is Rico?"

"Torn up. Lobo's threatening to kill Joaquín if he hangs Seth, but I don't think he'll have to, I think just the doing of it would kill Joaquín. It ain't gonna come to that, though. I'll break Seth out if he's found guilty."

"If he isn't, will he be released?"

"Hell, no. Like the paper said, Texas is howling for the privilege of hanging him."

"Then what are you waiting for?" she asked.

"He told me not to. Said he wants to be cleared of this charge so he won't be known as a backshooter."

"Will he be cleared?"

"It ain't likely unless we can find the killer. This town has wanted Seth's blood ever since he got here. They've forgotten all the good he's done them. The hotels are already filling up with reporters for the trial, and the good citizens are gloating over the money they're making. It turns my stomach."

"Mr. Rivers," she began, the confession on the tip of her tongue.

Amy came through the door with a tray of dirty dishes. "That pie should have been in the oven an hour ago," she complained.

"I'm sorry," Hekuba murmured, returning to work.

Behind her Blue said, "I've found a buyer for my saloon, Amy."

There was a silence, then Amy asked, "I guess that means you're leaving."

"I'll go with Seth," he said. "I owe him that."

"Our happiness?" she cried. "Is that fair, Blue?"

"No," he said, his chair scraping loudly as he stood up. "But no matter what happens now, Seth can't stay in Tejoe or even the territory. He'll be on the run again and I'll be with him. There ain't room in that situation for a wife."

Blue walked out, slamming the door. Amy sank into a chair and buried her face in her lap as she cried. Feeling numb, Hekuba washed the flour from her hands, dried them on her apron, then took it off and reached for her shawl. Without a word, she opened the door.

"Where are you going?" Amy cried. "If you leave now, Hekuba, don't come back!"

She gave no answer, closing the door and forcing herself to walk toward the jail. The street was crowded with strangers, ghouls come to gloat over tragedy. She threaded her way among them, unseen by most: a tall, thin black woman with a kerchief on her head. From a block away, she saw Nib Carey standing in front of the jail with a shotgun. He watched her approach, then stood aside as she opened the door and walked into the sheriff's office.

Joaquín sat behind the desk, holding his head in his hands. Seth lay on the bunk in the first cell. Both of them stood up, appraising her as she stopped in the middle of the room.

"What are you doing here, Hekuba?" Joaquín asked with worn patience.

She looked at Seth.

"Don't," he said.

"I must," she answered, then turned her eyes on Joaquín. "I killed Adam Noah."

Joaquín grimaced with scorn. "Why would you?"

"To protect Seth."

Joaquín sighed. "No one will believe you, Hekuba, any more than I do."

"It's the truth!"

"Give it up," he said. "You'll help no one by lying." He walked out, closing the door and leaving them alone.

She looked at Seth caged in the cell. "I've destroyed you," she mourned.

He shook his head. "My whole life has been leading up to this. I'm sorry I drug you into it."

"I killed him," she argued.

"Because I loved you. I wish it was otherwise, but I've made a habit of pulling people I love into the dirt."

"Mr. Rivers told me he intends to free you."

"You think Joaquín's gonna let him? You think I want 'em killing each other?" He shook his head. "It ain't gonna happen, Hekuba. Forget your part. This is mine and I'll carry it."

"I can't accept that," she whispered.

"Ain't yours to accept or deny. Reckon it's justice that Joaquín's the one to deliver me to the law since I stole him from the church in the first place. You see, this is a closed circle, Hekuba, and you're outside of it."

"You're wrong," she said. "I'm in the middle."

"Maybe," he conceded. "But once the wheel's turning, the hub can't stop it."

"Something can," she insisted.

He smiled with melancholy. "In this case, it's likely to be the trap of a gallows."

The door opened and Lobo ran past her to reach through the bars for his father. Seth knelt down and smiled at him. "You been going to school?" he asked softly.

"No!" the boy cried. "I'm gonna kill Joaquín. I swear it, Seth."

"Hush," he said. "I don't want that."

Hekuba forced herself to turn around and look at Rico. Her belly was ponderous beneath her skirt, her eyes red with tears, her face thin and grieved. She smiled bravely. "Hello, Hekuba. It's been a long time since I've seen you."

"I'm sorry, Mrs. Strummar," she said. Momentarily blinded by tears, Hekuba pushed through the door and hurried down the street. She was nearly a block away before she realized she'd seen Esperanza in the carriage outside the jail. Hekuba returned and petitioned, "May I speak with you, Esperanza?"

The woman barely looked at her.

Hekuba climbed into the carriage anyway, desperate to explain. She began bluntly: "This is my fault."

"I know that," Esperanza answered curtly.

"You know?" Hekuba whispered.

"Both Rico and I have known from the first. We have watched Seth wander for years, and we love him beyond any pleasure he might have found in your bed. Yet because of his lust, he sacrificed all of us to protect you. Don't expect sympathy from me."

Hekuba reeled away from the woman's hatred, stumbling out of the carriage to fall in the dirt of the road. When she looked up, Esperanza wasn't even watching her. With a cry of despair, Hekuba gained her feet and ran through the crowd to the silence of her home.

10

★

 On the day of the trial, fifty reporters crammed into the courtroom, leaving little room for anyone else. Hekuba was standing outside when Seth was brought across from the jail. He was handcuffed, walking beside Joaquín, and they were flanked by Nib Carey and Blue Rivers, both wearing badges and carrying rifles. Seth scanned the crowd, then met her eyes and gave her a brief smile before he disappeared inside.

Joaquín was the first to testify. In a voice heavy with regret, he stated that the defendant had threatened to kill the deceased, that he had access to the gun and shovel used in the crime, that no one else in Tejoe was known to be acquainted with the deceased or to have any motive to murder him, and that when accused of the crime, the defendant denied shooting the deceased in the back, thereby confessing to knowledge of where the fatal wounds had been inflicted.

The coroner was called and testified that the deceased had met his death as a result of five bullets from a Colt's .41 fired into his back from close range on the night of November 23, 1883. Henry Downing, a local gambler, testified that on the night in question the defendant had cut short a poker game and left the Blue Rivers Saloon at eight-thirty, saying he had an appointment to keep. Maurice Engle, owner of Engle's Emporium, testified he had been returning from a business trip to Tombstone and had seen the defendant on the road three miles east of Tejoe at two-thirty on the morning of the twenty-fourth. The prosecution rested.

Judge Hunnicutt frowned down at the prosecutor sent from Phoenix for this one important case. "You realize, Mr. Hally, that this is all circumstantial evidence."

"I do," the prosecutor gloated. "But given the defendant's reputation, I consider it more than adequate."

Hunnicutt looked at Edwin Stark. "Are you ready to proceed with the defense?"

"I am, Your Honor." He stood up. "I call Miss Hekuba Free."

A hush fell over the crowd, a quiet so silent her footsteps echoed like gunshots as she walked from the back of the room. Passing the defense table, she heard the attorney whisper, "She's our only chance, Seth."

She took her place and looked at all the white faces watching her; then she met Seth's eyes, cold with warning.

Stark approached. "Just tell us, Miss Free, everything you know of what happened on the night in question."

She looked only at him as she spoke, struggling to keep her voice under control. "Mr. Noah came to my house the night before and asked that I arrange a meeting between himself and Mr. Strummar. When I gave that message to Mr. Strummar, he asked that I send Mr. Noah to the Blue Rivers Saloon the following night. I promised I would, but before meeting Mr. Noah to tell him what Mr. Strummar had said, I went to Mr. Ascarate's house and took a pistol from where I knew he kept it and also a shovel from his stable. I walked into the desert, dug a grave, then returned home. When Mr. Noah arrived, I told him Mr. Strummar had asked me to take him, Mr. Noah, to a meeting place in the desert. I rode with Mr. Noah, directing him to the place I had earlier dug the grave.

When we had dismounted, Mr. Noah turned his back. I pulled the pistol and shot him five times."

The courtroom was silent for a long moment, then Stark asked, "Why did you kill Adam Noah, Miss Free?"

"He told me he had come to Tejoe to kill Mr. Strummar. I acted to protect Mr. Strummar."

"Why didn't you come forward before now?"

"I did!" she asserted, her voice strident beneath suppressed tears. "I told the sheriff, but he refused to believe me."

Gently Stark asked, "Why?"

She looked at Seth, the coolness of his eyes nearly camouflaging his pain, then at Rico behind him, her face pale above her ponderous belly, at Esperanza beside her staring with hatred, then at Joaquín watching with sorrow. "He knows I am in love with Mr. Strummar," she answered, her voice barely above a whisper, "and thought I was lying to protect him."

"Can you tell us, Miss Free, why this court shouldn't draw the same conclusion?"

She raised her head, tears falling across her cheeks as she said with determination, "I tend to pull right when I shoot. My first bullet creased his right shoulder. As he was turning to face me, I emptied the gun and the rest of the bullets struck the right side of his back. I replaced the gun that night in Mr. Ascarate's home, but neglected to reload it. I also neglected to return the shovel to his stable. After I had buried the body and gone home, I realized I had left the shovel by the grave, so I returned to retrieve it." Her voice broke. She swallowed her tears and said, "Coyotes had dug up the corpse. I saw one dog carry an arm a short distance away."

Judge Hunnicutt frowned from the bench. "Sheriff Ascarate, has she accurately described the fatal wounds in the deceased?"

Joaquín stood up, meeting Seth's eyes with torment. "Yes," he said.

"And was the corpse missing an arm?"

Still he stared at Seth as he answered softly, "Yes."

"Do you now believe the witness is speaking the truth by confessing she herself committed the crime?"

Joaquín looked at the judge. "Yes."

Hunnicutt sighed. "Miss Free, I remand you into the custody of Sheriff Ascarate to be held for sentencing. The jury is dismissed and all charges against Seth Strummar in the township of Tejoe are dropped. The prisoner is remanded into the custody of the officers from Texas for extradition."

The reporters ran for the telegraph office, the judge left the courtroom, and Hekuba stood up meeting Seth's eyes. He shook his head at her, then turned his back to speak a few quiet words to Rico. She was crying, unable to gain her feet. Esperanza sat beside her, staring with hatred at Hekuba.

Joaquín came forward and took hold of her arm, guiding her from the witness stand and across to the defense table. With Blue and Nib protecting them, Hekuba walked beside Seth to the jail. Neither they nor their escorts spoke. Joaquín led her into the far cell, then nailed a tarp so it hung over the bars to give her privacy. She sat on the bunk, listening to the hammer, staring at the floor, then heard the iron door close and lock as Joaquín left without speaking. From the dim silence of her cell, she listened to the Texans tell him they would leave with their prisoner in the morning.

Slowly the light fell from the sky. She could feel Seth's presence beyond the curtain and across the empty cell between them, but no one spoke. Finally she heard the front door open, letting in the noise from the street. Then the door closed and two sets of footsteps crossed the office. She sat on her bunk and listened as the door to Seth's cell whined open, then she heard footsteps retreating to the front door. Again it opened and closed, leaving her with the muffled sounds of a child sobbing.

"Hush," Seth said gently. "Can't you give me a smile to remember, Lobo?"

The child sniffled.

"That's better," Seth said. "You're gonna have to be a man without me."

"I can't," Lobo whimpered.

"Sure, you can. You're already halfway there. And you won't find a better teacher'n Joaquín."

"I don't believe that!" Lobo answered with defiance.

"You will," Seth said. "He only did what he had to. That's what a man does."

"But Texas will hang you, Seth!"

"No sense crying 'til it happens."

"Won't Blue help you escape, like you did for him?"

"I told him not to. Not much chance of success, with six Rangers taking me by train. Anyway, I didn't save him so he could die returning the favor."

"There must be something I can do," the child argued.

"Take care of Rico. Will you promise?"

"Yes," he whimpered.

"It'll give me comfort, knowing you're looking after her."

"She's waiting outside."

"Yeah," he said. "Give me a hug."

There was a long moment of silence, then Seth said, "I've always been proud of you, Lobo. Don't let me down."

"I won't," he said.

"So long, then."

"Good-bye, Seth," he said, his voice breaking.

Lobo's footsteps ran to the front door. It opened, letting in noise, then closed, shutting it out. Hekuba heard a woman's footsteps, then Seth asking softly, "Do I have to say good-bye to everybody crying?"

"Oh, Seth," Rico moaned. "How can I live without you?"

"Better'n with me, most likely."

"It's not true."

"Tell me you'll be all right, Rico."

"I'll survive," she said, "for the sake of our children."

"I'll write you when I get to Austin."

"Yes, please," she whispered.

Hekuba listened to the rustle of their clothing as they embraced, and she pictured Rico's face buried in Seth's shirt, his face in the golden abundance of her hair.

"I've given you a lot of grief," Seth said.

"More love than anything," Rico answered. "I'll wait for you, Seth."

"Wait for what?" he scoffed.

"Maybe you'll escape, or maybe they'll only send you to prison."

"Don't count on it."

"No matter how many years pass, I'll never give up on seeing you again."

"If I get loose I'll come back, otherwise we'll have to wait for Joaquín's hereafter."

"Kiss me," she sobbed.

Another silence fell on Hekuba's tortured ears, then Seth said, "Go along now. Take care of yourself."

Again the front door opened and closed. Heavy footsteps crossed the floor.

Seth chuckled. "Least you ain't crying, Esperanza."

"I have cried," she said.

Seth's bunk complained, and Hekuba pictured them sitting together, two old friends sharing their last moments.

"Who would have thought," Esperanza asked, "after all you've lived through it would come to this, and by Joaquín's hand?"

"Should've expected it," Seth said.

"Sí, you trained him, but not for this."

"It's more'n that. He started out to save my soul, remember?"

"I don't like his method," she said.

"It's the expiation of sin through suffering. I asked for it, taking on a priest for my partner."

"Oh Seth," she moaned. "You joke about everything."

"Ain't no joke," he said.

"No," she agreed. "You will come back to us, will you not?"

"If they don't kill me."

"Don't let them. Crawl and beg, but stay alive, Seth."

"I don't call that alive."

"We will love you no matter how they change you."

"You know what they do to men in prison, Esperanza, and they'll see me as a special challenge. Don't reckon I'll survive their whip even if I escape the gallows."

She sobbed.

"I didn't say that to make you cry. I need you to see the truth, it's the only way you can help Rico. Will you do that for me?"

"Yes," she said.

" 'Attagirl," he said. "She needs you now more'n I do."

Hekuba heard her stand up.

"You've been a good friend, Esperanza," Seth said. "Ramon was a fool to let you go."

"I have been happier living in your shadow than in his sun," she answered.

Her heavy footsteps trudged from the room, the front door opened and closed, lighter footsteps returned, the door to Seth's cell whined closed and the key turned in the lock, then the footsteps retreated. Again the noise from the street was let in and shut out, leaving only silence.

"Hekuba?" Seth called.

She lifted the curtain and faced him through the empty cell.

"About ten miles south of Goliad, on the road to Mexico, is a limestone canyon heading east. Half a mile into it there's a cedar tree growing out of a crevice. Under the roots of that tree is a pair of saddlebags full of money. You'll need it when you get out of prison."

Astonished, she asked, "You mean you could have given him the money all along?"

Seth shrugged. "Maybe. If I felt I could've trusted him to share it with me." He smiled. "But I never got the chance to find out."

"So this was all for nothing," she whispered.

"Helluva lot of nothing," he answered.

"Oh Seth," she sobbed. "Do you regret loving me?"

"Can't see any sense in regretting pleasure, can you?"

"No," she said. "I will always cherish the time we had together."

"I hope that's true and you don't end up hating me before this is over."

"Never," she vowed.

"Yeah, well, that's a long time." He smiled, then turned away to stare out his window into the falling darkness.

In the morning, she watched the transfer of custody. The six Rangers were jubilant, Joaquín solemn, as Seth was shackled hand and foot. While the Rangers picked up their rifles, Joaquín shook Seth's manacled hand and whispered, "Buena suerte, compadre."

Seth laughed, a sorrowful sound of self-deprecation. "My luck left with your loyalty, Joaquín."

Hekuba watched Seth walk from the jail accompanied by the clatter of chains and surrounded by an armed guard. Joaquín stood staring after them, then went out the back door and left her alone.

The next day she was taken to the courtroom for sentencing. Nib Carey escorted her; the sheriff had declined the duty. Judge Hunnicutt called the murder a crime of passion and sentenced Hekuba to one year in the territorial prison at Yuma. Her sister didn't come to say good-bye, but Joaquín was there to see her off. He led her from the cell and manacled her hands together in front, then stood meeting her eyes.

"Now do you wish you had left me behind, Joaquín?" she asked through her tears.

Morosely he studied her a long moment before answering. "If

I hadn't taken Seth with me when I went back for Heaven, he might never have met you. Because I wanted him to share my happiness, I destroyed him."

"It was I who did that," she argued.

Joaquín shook his head. "Without Seth, I wouldn't have been able to pay your price. But that was only money. How could I have foreseen what you would cost, Hekuba?"

Hoping to lighten his burden, she said, "Seth told me it's right that you were the one to deliver him to justice. Can you believe that, Joaquín?" He was silent and she sobbed into his face of grief, "Tell me you can, so I may bear the weight of what I've done."

"I've given up on finding justice," he said, moving away from her as Nib Carey came in from outside.

It was Carey who took her in a buggy to Benson, then escorted her on the train west to Yuma. As she sat by the window watching the desert grow more desolate, she felt Seth's child stir in her womb, and Hekuba smiled.

Joaquín's Penance

★ Spring 1897 ★

11

★

The cantina was in the poorest part of Nogales, a ramshackle adobe sunk into the ground. Joaquín descended the three steps from the door and saw that the room was long and narrow as a grave, and so dark anything could be lurking in the far recesses of shadow. His boots echoing on the wooden floor, he walked across to the bar. The keep was a skinny man. His bald head shone beneath a kerosene lantern, its low wick providing the only source of light in the room.

"I heard Seth Strummar is here," Joaquín said softly.

The man's eyes sharpened with hostility but he merely shrugged.

Joaquín petitioned, "I am a friend and would like to see him."

Again the man shrugged.

"Is he here?" Joaquín asked.

"No hablo inglés," the man said.

Joaquín started over in Spanish. He had barely begun when he felt the barrel of a pistol in his back.

"Who's asking?" a gruff voice demanded.

"Joaquín Ascarate," he said, looking over his shoulder at an American who had seemingly come out of nowhere. He was dirty with dark, mean eyes.

"What d'ya want?" he asked.

"I am a friend and bring news of his family."

The man sniggered. "I'm Nick Ryan. And if there's one thing I know about Seth, he don't like surprises."

"Just tell him who's asking," Joaquín said.

The American jerked his head at a Mexican in the shadows, a burly man wearing a huge sombrero that hid his face in the dark beneath its brim. "Tell him, Fierro," Ryan said.

Fierro moved across the room and knocked on a door, then opened it and disappeared inside. After a moment he came back and nodded at the American with the gun.

"Keep your hands clear of your shooter," Ryan said, wagging his pistol toward the door.

Joaquín crossed the room, hesitated in front of the closed door a moment, then took a deep breath and pushed through.

Seth sat at a table with a half-empty bottle of whiskey in front of him and a woman beside him, asleep with her head on her folded arms. He looked nearly the same, though the thirteen years since Joaquín had last seen him were etched in his face. The room was only slightly more palatable than the cantina, lit by another kerosene lantern hung from the ceiling. The dim light revealed a bed against the far wall, nothing else. After watching Joaquín for a long moment of silence, Seth leaned close to the woman and spoke softly in Spanish, telling her to wake up.

She murmured a protest, then sat straight with a frown, shaking the tangle of black hair out of her face. "Ay, Seth," she crooned in a husky voice. "¿Tienes hambre, no?"

He shook his head. "Dejanos," he said, nodding at Joaquín.

She looked at him then, her black eyes narrowing with suspicion. "¿Quién es?"

"Un amigo mío," Seth said, meeting his friend's eyes without a trace of a smile.

When she stood up, her dress fell open to reveal an unlaced camisole, her breasts threatening to escape. She looked down at Seth as she laced the garment, tied the ribbons in a bow, and buttoned her dress over it.

Seth watched her hands, then met her eyes. In the playful smile he gave her, Joaquín saw a glimmer of the man he had known. "No vayas lejos," Seth said softly.

"No, hombre," she murmured, then turned and walked out, brushing past Joaquín with a moist fragrance of sweat and sex.

The two men stared at each other for another long moment before Seth said in a tone of indifference, "If you're gonna stay, shut the door."

Joaquín did, then watched him fill a glass with whiskey.

"Want a drink?"

He shook his head.

"How about a seat?" Seth asked. "Or are you gonna stand there staring like the wrath of Jehovah?"

Joaquín pulled out a chair and sat down.

Seth sipped the whiskey, watching him.

"Rico asked me to find you," Joaquín said.

"Is that the only reason you're here?"

He nodded.

"You like what you see?"

He shook his head.

"Then get out," Seth said, emptying the glass of whiskey.

"She needs you," Joaquín said.

A knock sounded on the door. Without looking away from Joaquín, Seth called, "Pasa."

The American leaned in. "Escalante's here."

"Tell him to wait," Seth said.

Ryan looked at Joaquín, then closed the door.

"Got business coming down," Seth said. "Is she in trouble?"

"She has been since you left."

"That wasn't exactly my choice," he retorted with an edge. "Was it?"

Joaquín shrugged.

"Out of your jurisdiction, ain't you?" he taunted.

"Yes," he said. "Why haven't you come home?"

"I am home," Seth answered, standing up and walking across to the window. He looked the same as Joaquín had always seen him, tall and lean, dressed simply in well-tailored clothes and quality boots, a Colt's .44 in a belt fully loaded with cartridges between the gun and a sheathed bowie knife. When he swung open a wooden shutter and looked out at another cantina, brightly lit across the wide, dusty street, a sudden eruption of mariachi music and shouted laughter penetrated the glass.

"After we read in the newspapers of your pardon," Joaquín said, "I wrote Johanna and she wrote back, saying it was true but you hadn't even stopped to see them when you were released from prison, that you bought a horse and headed south, that's all any-one knew. Finally I heard you were here."

Seth turned around, his gray eyes hard. "Why do you care where I am?"

Joaquín stood up. "I have suffered much for what I did, Seth. But it's over now. You're a free man. Why live in México as if you were still a fugitive?"

"Maybe I like it here," he said. "I'm running a damn smart scheme and got everything I need. Coupla men I can trust," he paused to smile, again striking Joaquín with a memory of better times, "long as I don't turn my back, a hot woman in my bed, plenty of money." He shrugged with the old smile of self-mockery that tore at Joaquín's heart. "What're you offering?"

"Love," he said. "Not only of a good woman, but two children who have yet to know their father. Also compadres you can trust even when you do turn your back, not like these who will kill you as soon as it's to their advantage."

Seth laughed bitterly. "Did Lobo ever forgive you?"

Joaquín shook his head. "He has been gone a few years now. No one has heard from him."

Seth turned around and stared out the window again. "How's your wife?"

"Fine," Joaquín said.

"Any children?"

"We have a son."

"And her sister?"

"She died in prison."

Seth was silent.

"What good did it do you to survive," Joaquín asked, "if this is how you choose to live?"

Seth folded his arms on the crossbar of the window, hiding his face in their darkness as he mumbled, "It's all dead."

Appalled at the defeat in his friend's voice, Joaquín argued, "You are not dead yet. There is still time to live."

The doors in the cantina across the street opened and the gay mariachi music filled the room. Seth lifted his head and stared outside, then chuckled with irony. "Someone just got married."

"A good omen for new beginnings," Joaquín said.

Seth looked over his shoulder and asked, "Ain't I ever gonna be rid of you trying to make a man out of a border rat?"

Joaquín caught just a hint of the old challenge. Softly he asked, "You remember when you married Johanna? How the priest at first refused to do it? Do you know how I convinced him?"

Seth hid his face in the darkness of his folded arms.

"I vowed to bring you to God," Joaquín said. "Only then would the priest allow you into the sanctuary."

Seth said nothing.

"I have not given up."

"That's your problem," Seth said.

Suddenly gunfire erupted from the fiesta across the street. A bullet shattered the window pane and Seth lurched backward, then fell to the floor.

Joaquín snuffed the lantern, dropped to his hands and knees, and crawled across to where Seth had fallen. He moaned as Joaquín explored his shirt and found the wound just below his ribs. If the bullet was lead, Seth was gone. If steel, he had a chance. Joaquín reached up and swung the shutter closed, cutting off the light and softening the music, then rolled Seth onto his side to find the exit wound, small and neat. "Steel," Joaquín said. "You are still alive."

"Thank God," Seth mocked, then groaned, clutching Joaquín's arm with a tremor of pain.

The door opened, throwing light across the floor as Fierro came in. Seeing only his silhouette advancing toward them, Joaquín was about to ask for help when he saw the barrel of Fierro's gun come down. It struck Joaquín's head, knocking him out.

Feeling pain throb inside his skull, Joaquín became aware of the music again, then of lamplight flickering on the ceiling. He sat up and rubbed the top of his head, saw two men bent over Seth, who was lying on the bed as they tried to staunch the flow of blood, and another man beyond the table, the American who had held a gun on him before, doing it again.

"Get up," Ryan said.

Joaquín did, knowing by the absence of weight on his hip that his gun was gone. "The shot came through the window," he said.

Fierro stood up from the bed and glared at the closed shutters. "There's no hole in the wood, pendejo. Do you think we're stupid?"

"I closed the shutter," Joaquín said. "Look at the glass on the floor."

"Maybe I will later," Fierro said, drawing his gun. "Right now I think I'll shoot you."

Joaquín looked at Seth unconscious on the bed, one man still working to stop the flow of blood. Glancing back and forth between the two men staring at him with guns in their hands, Joaquín said, "I am his friend."

Fierro shouted out the door, "Raul!"

A boy dressed in ragged white trousers and the loose smock of a peon ran into the room.

"Open the shutters," Fierro barked, jerking his head toward the window.

The boy ran across and flung open the shutters, revealing the bright lights from the fiesta distorted through the jagged edges of broken glass.

Fierro glared at Joaquín as if the broken glass proved nothing.

The man tending Seth said, "I've stopped the bleeding. If we can keep him still, he's got a chance."

"Gracias a Dios," Joaquín whispered.

Fierro wagged his pistol toward the door. "We will keep you out of trouble until Seth tells us what happened."

Joaquín turned around just as the woman came in. She stared at him with horror, then ran to the bed, whimpering comforting words in Spanish.

"Move, hombre," Fierro growled.

Joaquín walked out in front of the pistol, then stopped in the saloon and looked at his captor.

"Keep going," Fierro said, nodding toward a back door.

They walked out and followed a dark alley behind three adobe buildings, then entered a dusty warehouse. At the end of the aisle was an empty corn bin reaching to the rafters, its door and walls slatted wood. Fierro shoved Joaquín inside and locked the door with a padlock and chain. Meeting his eyes through the slats, Fierro said, "If Seth dies, so do you." Then he turned and strode out, leaving Joaquín alone.

On both sides of him were identical corn bins. Thirty feet above was a roof with starlight shining through its cracks. Joaquín began climbing the slatted walls until he could catch hold of the crossbeam. Swinging his feet, he kicked a hole in the roof, careless of noise, then hoisted himself up with his arms and swung astride the beam, poking his head through the hole as he looked around.

Fierro stood on the balcony of the next building, his rifle aimed at Joaquín's eyes. They stared at each other a moment, then Fierro snarled, "Get back in your cage or I will shoot you."

Joaquín swung off the beam and descended to the floor of the corn bin, arriving in a shower of dust. The warehouse door opened and the kid came in carrying a lantern and a new Springfield rifle. He set the lantern on the floor just outside the corn bin, then cradled the rifle as he studied Joaquín.

Joaquín smiled. "You are Raul, no? I am Joaquín Ascarate."

Raul's dark eyes flickered with recognition.

"Have you heard of me?" Joaquín asked.

Raul shrugged.

"I am a friend of Seth's," Joaquín said, guessing the kid's age to be twelve or thirteen. He had a smooth, whipped-chocolate complexion, lanky black hair cropped straight across at his collar, and eyes sharp with doubt.

"If you are truly his friend," he asked, "why did you shoot him?"

"I didn't," Joaquín said.

"Why do they say you did?"

"I was there."

"Espero que viva," the kid murmured.

"Yo, también."

They stared at each other a moment longer, then Raul asked, "Are you hungry? I could bring you something to eat."

"Water would be good," Joaquín said.

The kid turned and walked away. Joaquín stood in the center of the corn bin listening to the music from the distant fiesta.

Magdalena sat on the edge of Seth's bed, watching his eyes open heavily. "Am I still alive," he asked, "or did they kill you too?"

"We are both alive," she answered.

"Too bad," he said. "Killed at a wedding, we'd've been bound for eternity."

She smiled, wiping the sweat from his forehead with the flounce of her petticoat. "Would you like that?"

He slid his hand between her thighs. "Yes," he said.

She laughed deep in her throat. "Do you know this Joaquín Ascarate?"

Seth's eyes cooled with warning. "Who's asking?"

"He's here. Don't you remember?"

"Joaquín's here?"

She nodded, watching him look away to veil his thoughts. "He was in the room when you were shot. Santiago and Nick think he did it. Did he?"

Seth shook his head.

"Are you sure?"

He met her eyes. "Where is he?"

"In the warehouse." She hesitated, then plunged ahead. "What of the run, Seth? Should Escalante go alone?"

"Hell, no!" he said roughly, half sitting up.

"Lie down!" she cried, seeing fresh blood stain the bandage she had tied beneath his ribs.

He fell back against the pillow. "Escalante's working for the buyers," he said under his breath. "He won't give jackshit for our side."

"Who, then?" she asked urgently, afraid he would pass out before telling her.

He smiled slyly. "Send Joaquín. Get his word to serve our purpose. Make it a condition of his freedom."

"¿Estás seguro?" she whispered.

He nodded.

"Santiago and Nick won't like it," she argued.

"Joaquín'll come through for us. Tell them I said so."

"Bueno," she said, standing up. "I will be back."

"Bring more whiskey," he said.

The door to the warehouse opened and Joaquín watched the woman come in, a slender silhouette in a full skirt against the darkness outside. Raul turned to face her as Joaquín stood up from where he'd been squatting against the wall. She stopped outside the slatted door and stared at him, her nostrils flaring beneath the high thrust of her cheekbones as if she found his scent offensive. "Seth has said you will go in his place and serve our purpose in exchange for your freedom. Will you?"

Angry that Seth would put a condition on his release, Joaquín asked coldly, "What is your purpose?"

"It is only yours to say yes or no, señor," she retorted.

"If I say no, you will kill me?"

"With pleasure," she said.

"Then I say yes."

She spun and ran back down the aisle and out of the warehouse. Joaquín looked at Raul. "What is it they want me to do?"

"Deliver the goods. Fierro has too much fight to trade and Ryan speaks no Spanish. Also, it is the most dangerous part and Seth always goes alone. That is why he is jefe."

"What will I be delivering?" Joaquín asked warily.

"Guns," the kid said with pride. "To the bandidos in the Sierra Madre."

"Sonofabitch," Joaquín muttered. "For how much money?"

"Much," Raul said.

"They expect me to carry guns to bandits hundreds of miles into México and return alone with a lot of money?"

Raul shrugged. "Seth does it. If you are truly Joaquín Ascarate, it will be no problem."

* * *

It was midnight when Fierro escorted Joaquín down the alley to a stable, Raul following silently behind. Three horses stood saddled, Joaquín's among them, and a packtrain of loaded mules filled the aisle, their noses in feedbags. Ryan was standing off to one side with the woman and the other man who had been in Seth's room. Joaquín recognized his own gun in the other man's belt. They all stared at each other with mutual distrust in a silence broken only by the munching of the mules.

"You understand the deal?" Ryan finally asked.

Joaquín looked at the packtrain, quickly counting seven animals heavily loaded. "Where?" he asked.

"Escalante knows," Ryan said, jerking his head at the other man. "He'll take you to the buyers, then bring you back far as Casas Grandes. It's your choice whether you come the rest of the way through Mexico or the States. Seth does both, depending on the climate, and I ain't talking rain."

"Can I see Seth?" Joaquín asked.

"No," Fierro growled. "You give your word to us. It is us who will find and kill you if you fail."

"I give my word to do my best," Joaquín said. "But you know as well as I it's a risky business."

"I have made the trip before," Escalante said. "We should have no problems."

"How is Seth?" Joaquín asked, looking at the woman.

She shrugged.

"He told us you didn't shoot him," Fierro said with undaunted hostility. "He also said we should trust you, but myself, I don't believe it."

Escalante stepped forward to hand Joaquín his gun. Joaquín opened the cylinder and saw it was empty.

"Jus' leave it that way for now," Ryan said. "We want you back here in two weeks with our five thousand dollars."

"If you don't come," Fierro warned, "we will look for you. If we find only your corpse," he shrugged with a grin, "such is the fate of bandidos, but we will have either our money or your corpse, hombre, make no mistake."

Joaquín looked away from the threat to watch Escalante tighten the cinch of his saddle. The woman untied the reins of another horse and swung up, her red skirt flying in a graceful arc as she kicked her leg over. Joaquín looked at Ryan. "The woman is going with us?"

He nodded. "Her name's Magdalena."

Joaquín looked at her again. She was dressed in a sturdy jacket, a man's shirt, and high leather boots under her skirt, all dark so as not to catch light. Her hat was as black as her hair falling in a braid down the center of her back, and her eyes rested no more kindly on him than they had from the start.

"I don't want her," he said.

"Tough shit," Ryan jeered. "Seth says she's going."

"Why?" he demanded.

From astride his horse Escalante said, "She's a good gun. Vamanos."

Raul began taking the feedbags off the mules, moving fast down the line as he tossed the bags against the wall. Escalante leaned from his saddle to catch the lead rope, then reined his horse out the door. Joaquín watched the mules file past, followed by Magdalena, not looking at him. When she was gone, his own horse stood alone tethered to the wall.

Ryan said, "We jus' let our merchandise ride out with only a woman seeing to our int'rest. If you ain't going, one of us is, after we kill you."

Joaquín holstered his empty gun, walked across and untied his reins, looked at the two men and the boy watching him, then swung on and trotted after the others. He rode past the woman and mules to fall in beside Escalante. They shared an appraising look as Joaquín pulled his pistol and loaded it from cartridges on his belt,

noting it was now half empty. "I hope we have plenty of ammunition, amigo," he said wryly.

Escalante grinned. "Two thousand rounds on the mules. I think
it will be enough."

12

★

 As they rode through the sleeping pueblo, Joaquín kept quiet though he was simmering with anger. By forcing this deal, Seth had acted as if they were partners again and the thirteen years in between hadn't happened. Joaquín stifled his rage, promising himself he would succeed so he could fling the money in Seth's face as the insult it was, then go home to tell Rico that she and the children were better off alone. With a cold wave of insight, he realized Seth probably intended this deal as a lesson to teach exactly that; but Joaquín didn't care to learn Seth's lessons anymore; he only wanted to prove Seth wrong. He looked over at Escalante. "How far are we going?"

"Five days into the mountains." He smiled. "There will be a big fiesta when we arrive."

"Who're we meeting?"

He smiled apologetically. "You should trust me, since I must return the favor on nothing more than Seth's saying so."

Joaquín nodded. "Is there likely to be trouble between here and there?"

The Mexican shrugged. "Our cargo would be welcomed by many, but only the bandidos can afford to pay."

"What of the Rurales?"

He laughed. "They also would like our cargo, but they would not pay, so it is best if we avoid them."

"If we don't, will they take the cargo and let us go?"

"No, hombre. In such a case, you would be wise to let them kill you."

As the town was left behind, the road led across the starlit desert with the distant mountains a dark ridge on the horizon. Joaquín had never been in the western part of Mexico before. At the age of seventeen he had traveled north from Mexico City on the Camino Real and crossed the Rio Bravo into El Paso. Except for a brief time hiding out when Seth had been wounded, Joaquín had felt no desire to return to his country, and he felt none now.

For hours they rode in a silence broken only by the plodding of the many hooves, the creaking of the packs, the snorts and sighs of the animals. When the sky lightened into the gray before dawn, Escalante turned off the road and followed a faint trail into the desert. The land sloped downward, and soon they were winding into a gully that widened into an arroyo towering overhead on both sides.

Escalante pushed on, riding through the rosy sunrise and into the yellow light of morning. At the other end of the arroyo, they crossed a dry lake bed. By that time the sun was high and the pale sand shimmered with heat waves. Across the expanse, Joaquín saw a smudge of greenery. An hour later he could make out a corral shaded by cottonwoods and a scattering of adobe hovels. After a while he saw an animal in the corral, which he gradually determined to be a burro. As the packtrain ambled into the yard, the donkey brayed an alarm. A wiry old man came out of one of the buildings and watched from the shade of the portal.

Escalante rode up to the corral, opened the gate, and sat his horse, watching the mules plod in. The burro shied against the fence, still braying. Joaquín reined up, taking in the old man and the chickens loose in the yard, a garden with corn stalks three feet high and squash vines rampant and lush. A young man came to the door, buckling on a gunbelt. He pushed past the viejo and walked toward the corral, eyeing Joaquín warily. The woman reined her horse alongside Joaquín's. Although she looked tired after their long ride, her eyes were sharp and she held her rifle across the pommel of her saddle.

The young man was talking with Escalante now, who listened a moment, then dismounted. "Let's go eat," he said to Joaquín. "Ignacio will tend the animals."

Joaquín swung down and handed his reins to Ignacio, who was watching Magdalena. She, too, dismounted and carried her rifle toward the house. Joaquín followed her and Escalante inside. In the dim, cool interior, the viejo shook Escalante's hand with welcome. After Escalante explained that Seth had sent Joaquín in his place, the old man said, " 'Sta bien. But what of Magdalena?"

Escalante shrugged.

The old man gave a toothless grin. "Perhaps Seth sent her as a present for me and Ignacio, no?"

"She belongs to Joaquín on this trip," Escalante said.

The old man laughed, meeting Joaquín's eyes with admiration. "Seth must think you are muy hombre to handle his job and his woman, too."

Joaquín said nothing, glancing at Magdalena behind him with her rifle. She kept her gaze on the floor.

"Andale pues," the viejo said, beckoning them into the kitchen. "Come in, sit down."

Joaquín sat with his back to the wall, watching Magdalena take the chair next to his without looking at him. Escalante sat down facing them as the old man brought cups of thick, boiled coffee. He gave the first to the woman, but she didn't look at him either until he said, "Hiraldo was here yesterday asking when you were expected."

Joaquín watched her eyes flare with danger at the news.

"We left late," Escalante said, slurping coffee, "because of Seth being hurt."

"Is the wound bad?" the viejo asked sorrowfully.

Escalante shrugged. "As long as he keeps it clean, he should be on his feet when we get back." He smiled snidely at Magdalena. "Knowing Seth, I am sure he has a good nurse tending him day and night."

She turned her head away with disdain.

The viejo served them spicy chile beans and cold tortillas. While they were eating, Ignacio came in and sat down at the table. The old man put a full bowl in front of him, too, then retreated to stand before the stove. As he shoveled the beans into his mouth with a rolled tortilla, Ignacio said, "Hiraldo was here yesterday."

"Who is he?" Joaquín asked.

Escalante watched the woman when he said, "Hiraldo once rode with Seth, but he made a mistake and was cut out. Is that not right, Magdalena?"

She shrugged.

"What does he want with us?" Joaquín asked her.

She glanced at him, though her eyes were veiled, and said softly, "Hiraldo thinks he has money coming because he helped arrange this shipment. We took a vote and disagreed."

Joaquín looked at the men. Escalante was concentrating on his beans, but Ignacio warned, "He is someone you should watch out for, hombre."

"He would be smarter to make his move on our way back," Joaquín said.

"If all he wants is money," Escalante agreed.

"What else would he want?" Joaquín asked.

Escalante cleaned his bowl with a tortilla, then chewed and swallowed it before he said, "An introduction to the bandidos."

"To take over the business?" Joaquín asked.

Escalante shook his head. "To ride with them."

"Then he shouldn't be any threat," Joaquín said.

"Except to get in with the bandidos you must offer a contribution. Your cargo would do the trick."

"Would these men buy it from him, knowing he had stolen it from us? Wouldn't that be risking their arrangement with Seth?"

"His arrangement is to deliver the goods. You do that and they will buy them. But if they can get them cheaper, or free, they will do that, too. Wouldn't you?"

Joaquín shook his head. "I would never buy stolen goods."

Everyone stared at him, even the woman.

Escalante laughed. "You are selling stolen goods."

Silently Joaquín cursed Seth, then asked with feigned calm, "Who were they stolen from?"

"The American cavalry. What difference does it make?"

"I like to know my enemies," he replied tersely.

Ignacio grinned. "Your enemies are the governments of the United States and Mexico, the hacendados who own this country and hate the bandidos, the rival bandidos who want these guns for themselves, and Hiraldo Fuentes, who is one mean hombre."

Joaquín felt a fresh assault of anger that Seth had demanded he do this. He stood up and asked between his teeth, "When are we leaving?"

"Sunset," Escalante said. "Six hours from now."

Joaquín looked at the old man. "Where can I sleep?"

"I will show you," Magdalena said, rising too and walking out.

He looked at the men, all watching the woman leave.

Ignacio grinned again. "I have heard she is hot," he whispered with a wink.

Joaquín followed her with no anticipation of pleasure. They left the house and walked across the yard and into a hut. Stopping on the threshold, he watched her turn down the one bed. "Is there another place I can sleep?" he asked without grace.

She stood up straight and answered, "I gave my word to Seth that I would never leave your side."

Joaquín looked at the corral full of horses and mules, the little burro pressed up against the fence, outweighed and outnumbered. He sighed and stepped inside the room.

There was no window, no furniture other than the bed. She lit a candle stuck into a niche dug out of the adobe wall. "Lock the door," she said with impatience.

He turned around and lifted the crossbar off the floor, fit it into place, then looked at her again.

She was halfway undressed, her skirt and jacket hanging on hooks along the wall. She unbuttoned her shirt and hung it, too, then sat down on the bed to tug off her boots. He watched her stand up, pull her shimmy over her head, hang it on her shirt, then face him naked. "What would you like?" she asked.

"To be out of this," he said.

She shrugged and got into bed, sliding under the covers as she watched him approach. He unbuckled his gunbelt and hung it on the bedstead, took off his boots, then lay down on top of the covers and stared at the thatched ceiling.

Leaning from the bed, she blew out the candle. The covers rustled as she settled herself. After a few minutes he heard her breathing change and knew she was asleep. He thought maybe she would be grateful that he'd left her alone, maybe even like him a little more because of it. He knew he needed an ally.

Carrying weapons stolen from the U.S. Army wasn't a healthy thing to do, but since he was in Mexico they couldn't touch him. The Rurales were something else. They wouldn't take kindly to gringos arming bandits. That Seth and Escalante had pulled it off before probably meant their route had been cleared by bribes. So the main trouble spots were likely to be other bandits or Hiraldo Fuentes. A man with a grudge would sometimes sacrifice life itself to get revenge.

Joaquín understood the feeling well. He wanted nothing more

at that moment than to hit Seth with all he had. That his friend would put him in this position—the man whose life he had saved more than once, and whom he had found again by leaving both their families unprotected—riled Joaquín until he felt like a pillar of bricks on the bed.

Magdalena moaned and rolled over to face him. Her hand came out from under the covers and began unbuttoning his trousers. He reached down and stopped her.

"Ay, Joaquín," she murmured, kissing his cheek. "Give it to me so you will be fresh when we rise, eh?"

Between the coercion of her kisses and the tenderness of her hands, she drew him beneath the covers into the wet succulence of her comfort. He succumbed violently, expelling his anger into her body. She was a match for his wrath, coaxing all the bad feelings out of him until he lay drenched with sweat thinking only of her beauty beneath him as he buried his face in the tangled storm of her hair.

"Is not so bad, Joaquín," she whispered. "The bandidos know we are coming and protect us. Is later, carrying the money back to Nogales, where trouble comes."

He raised his head and looked down at her, though it was so dark he could barely make out the glimmer of her eyes. "What about Hiraldo Fuentes?"

"I know him well," she answered, "and do not believe he will cross Seth."

Joaquín rolled off her to sigh into the darkness above him. "How long have you known Seth?"

"Since he first came to Nogales. I have been his woman a few months now."

"Doesn't it bother you," he mocked, "that your man shares his woman with others?"

"Seth is more than my man," she answered solemnly. "He is jefe. I am proud to be favored, but if he takes another, I will still follow him."

"What do you gain by following him?"

"Life," she said.

"Weren't you alive before?"

"Yes, by the grace of another jefe. He died."

Joaquín thought about that, then asked, "Could you imagine living without a jefe?"

"Only by working with others can a person survive. Seth is a gringo but his courage feeds us."

"Do you mean admiring his courage feeds your own?"

"No," she said with scorn. "He makes money so we can eat. I have five sisters and two brothers, all young, and a mother who is old. Raul has nine younger brothers and sisters. Though he is only twelve he is the man of his family. Fierro has a wife and children, widowed sisters-in-law with their children, and several viejos in his home. Ryan's woman also has much family. And there is Ramona, the vieja who washes Seth's clothes and cooks his meals. Fifty people in Nogales eat because of Seth."

Joaquín thought of the five he himself supported, and even then his wages were so meager that their luxuries were bought with the remnants of Seth's bank account. Overwhelmed at the thought of being responsible for so many, Joaquín felt some of his anger at the jefe dissipate. That made him think of Rico, however, who was hoping he would bring her husband home. "If Seth were gone," he said softly, "you would find another jefe."

"We would look," she said with vigor. "Fierro would try, but his blood is too hot and he would not live long. Ryan will go when Seth does, he is a follower, nada más. Raul, if given time, will do. Seth has taken him under his wing and it is Raul's good fortune to be taught by a great jefe."

"What is it exactly," Joaquín asked with keen interest, "that makes a great jefe?"

She thought a moment, then asked, "Did you know the word macho comes from mules?"

"No," he said.

"They are half-breeds between horses and burros, taking something from both but losing much. Whether male or female, mules produce no young. Did you know this?"

"Yes," he answered slowly, not following her logic.

"One time in a million births, a male mule overcomes the cruelty of his breeding and is born with a hard-on. He can still fuck, and he sires horses that carry no trace of the burro. Such males are called machos, and only such a man becomes a great jefe."

Joaquín smiled, appreciating how aptly his friend fit that description. "But still," he argued, "with a labor force of fifty people, it seems you could do something legal to make money."

"The gachupínes take it all," she answered bitterly. "In México, if you are neither slave nor bandido, you starve."

Joaquín nodded, remembering the gachupínes he had seen in his youth in Mexico City, the blue-eyed Spaniards who owned the wealth of the country. "That is why I left," he said.

Her laughter mocked him. "You are here now, hermano. Perhaps you will not leave again, eh?"

"Don't call me hermano," he joked to discount her words. "If I were your brother, we would be committing an even greater sin than we are."

"It is not a sin," she replied, "to give each other comfort."

"I am married," he said. "It is a sin for me."

Again she laughed, this time gaily. "We are going to hell anyway, Joaquíto. What difference does one more sin make?"

"Do you truly believe in hell?"

"¿Quién sabes? If heaven and hell are a lie, we have only the pleasures of life." She touched him with familiarity again. "If tomorrow we die, why should we not be well fucked, eh?"

Unable to think of an answer, he covered her again with his sin until, finally, he was able to sleep.

They were both awakened by Escalante pounding on the door and yelling, "Vamanos!"

* * *

As Joaquín was saddling his horse, the old man came over. "Do not trust Escalante," he said softly. "He tried to leave, and only the guns of Ignacio and I persuaded him to rest while you were sleeping." He grinned at Joaquín's surprise. "If it happened that you were sleeping with such a woman in your bed."

"Gracias, viejo," Joaquín answered, holding out his hand.

The old man nodded, shaking with him. "Tell Seth how I helped him, eh? Tell him I am loyal always."

"I will," Joaquín promised, not failing to notice the loyalty had nothing to do with him.

"Qué te vayas bien," the old man said, stepping back and giving him room to mount.

Joaquín swung onto his horse and trotted to the head of the packtrain, deliberately keeping his eyes veiled though watching Escalante carefully. At the edge of the yard Joaquín turned back to wave but the viejo and Ignacio had already gone inside.

The desert stretched empty, the cactus throwing long shadows from the setting sun. On the horizon, the mountains looked bloody. As he watched the sunlight darken into twilight, he heard a mule sigh wearily at the prospect of another night of hard labor.

Comparing his sheriff's job to this task he was attempting in Seth's stead, Joaquín felt a lawman's begrudging admiration for Seth's criminal achievements. He reassured himself by thinking that even as a youth he had recognized Seth's abilities and willingly followed him. Joaquín's goal, however, had never been to become a bandit but to persuade Seth to leave the outlaw life behind. He had succeeded until his decision that they were equals compelled him to break free; then his freedom had led to Seth's incarceration. Now it seemed they were back at the beginning, only instead of Joaquín raising Seth to good citizenship, Seth had pulled Joaquín into criminality.

He reined his horse back by Magdalena. She gave him a smile, which he returned, but he wondered how she judged him compared to Seth. They had shared a woman once before. When they'd first met in El Paso, Joaquín had deliberately sought out Seth's whore under the guise of emulating him by sharing his lover. The woman had been violent in bed, and when Seth learned of the liaison, he'd advised Joaquín to seek a more gentle teacher. Now Joaquín burned with embarrassment to think what that woman must have thought of his performance.

Magdalena was apparently adept at reading men. She gave him a saucy grin and said, "Tonight we will be camping in the mountains. I hope you keep me warm, Joaquín."

He laughed, thinking that among his other attributes, Seth was adept at picking women.

At midnight they stopped in the rocky foothills by a spring dripping from a cliff into a sandy pool. The animals drank deeply as the people refilled their canteens, meeting each other's eyes occasionally but saying nothing. They neither unsaddled nor unloaded the packs, and within an hour they were moving southeast again, feeling a chill as they climbed into the mountains. Only the cadence of hooves on the stony ground, the sighing of the animals' fatigue, the snorting of dust from their nostrils, and the creaking of their burden accompanied their ascent into the mountains.

By sunrise the packtrain was halfway to the crest. The desert swept below in a great slope of dust and sand, cholla and prickly pear. Ahead Joaquín could see the pines, twisted and gnarled at this altitude but rising to great heights in the high country above. Escalante kept the animals moving until they reached a box canyon with a stream flowing through it, where he declared they would camp.

He and Joaquín worked nearly an hour to unpack the mules, the long wooden boxes heavy and cumbersome. Joaquín saw they were marked as property of the U.S. Army and stamped with their contents: one dozen Springfield "Trapdoor" Repeating Rifles. The smaller boxes each held five hundred rounds of .45-70 black powder ammunition. Joaquín grimaced when he saw the caliber, realizing they wouldn't fit his .44-40 Winchester, then shook his head at Seth's audacity.

He had been out of prison for only a year, pardoned after serving twelve years of a life sentence, which had been commuted by the governor from the original order of execution. Surely, if the legislators and good citizens who had petitioned for Seth's pardon knew what he was doing with his freedom, they would regret their mercy. Joaquín had sworn to uphold the law, and he acknowledged with more than a trace of bitter humor that his oath had been successfully undermined within hours of his reunion with Seth.

By the time the men had settled all the animals for the night, Magdalena had a cold supper ready. They had foregone a fire, not wanting to attract attention with smoke, and they sat in the chill of the evening, eating methodically, then leaning back in their blankets and eyeing each other with a somnolent wariness.

After a time, Escalante said, "I will take first guard."

" 'Sta bien," Joaquín agreed, watching the Mexican walk away from their camp. Magdalena rose and carried her blankets across to his, then lay down beside him, unbuttoned his trousers, and took him in her mouth. He let her do all the work, keeping his ears pinned to any change in the forest around them. When she had finished, his spine felt warm and his eyes drowsed heavily.

"Go to sleep," she murmured. "I will watch and call you when he returns."

Joaquín felt misgivings but gave in to his weariness. His deep sleep seemed to last only a moment when he felt her hand on his arm and heard her whisper, "He is coming now." Then she was gone, leaving a chill where her body had sheltered him from the cold.

Meeting Joaquín's eyes, Escalante asked, "Do you never sleep?" He laughed. "Since you are awake anyway, it is your turn to watch." He lay down and rolled himself in his blankets.

Joaquín stood up, looking across at Magdalena. She too was

rolled in her blankets, already asleep. He took his rifle as he walked to the promontory overlooking their ascent, the desert below shimmering in the heat waves of noon. Sixty miles across that barren expanse, Seth lay badly wounded.

Remembering back over the years of their friendship, Joaquín wanted to say he now understood all those times Seth had played with women despite Joaquín's argument against it. He now knew Seth had been relieving his tension for the sake of survival, and that a woman's loyalty could provide all the protection a man needed, enough to cover him so he could rest. He also wanted to say he knew Seth wasn't shirking duty by providing for strangers instead of kin, and admit that the task Seth had chosen was more challenging than his own job as sheriff.

Joaquín felt perplexed comparing his life to Seth's. Seth was an outlaw and he a sheriff, yet whose virtue was brighter remained an enigma. He wished for time to talk it through, and hopefully, as he had so often in the past, find enough of an answer in the strength of their friendship. At this moment, however, Seth was possibly dying. Joaquín yearned to be with him, to make amends, if it were at all possible, for delivering him to the law. The best way to do that, assuming Seth survived, would be to take him home. But first Joaquín must complete this trip into the mountains and return to Nogales. Impatiently, he waited for the sun to drop below the horizon, then he walked back to camp and woke Escalante.

Without a word, they repacked the mules, saddled their horses, and continued their ascent into the Sierra Madre. In starlight, they followed the faint trail winding through the mountains. Joaquín saw no evidence anywhere that they were not alone in the vast wilderness. At midnight they stopped in a meadow by a small trickle of water. The climb had been hard on the animals, Escalante explained, and there was no more water for another day's journey. They unpacked the mules and hobbled them to graze on the grass, then ate cold tortillas and salted venison, again not risking a fire.

When Escalante took his rifle into the forest to stand first guard, Joaquín looked at Magdalena.

Again she joined him without being summoned, and again he lost himself in the pleasures of her body. For long moments he forgot to listen. He would catch himself and jerk away from her, scanning the forest around them, seeing no one, hearing nothing. She would smile and hold her arms to entice him back. As he surrendered to her respite, striving to keep his mind alert to the approach of danger, he again felt an affinity for how Seth had always lived: divided in his attention, seeking comfort while protecting himself, no matter how many compadres had sworn to do it. Joaquín came with a great sigh of relief, then nestled the woman in his blankets, meeting her eyes with a silent demand that she tell him again he could trust her.

"Do not worry," she promised. "I will watch and wake you when it's time."

He fell asleep believing her, then awoke alone in his blankets with a rifle in his face.

13

The man behind the rifle wore the gray uniform of a Rurale. Beside him stood another wearing a plumed hat.

"¿Como se llama?" the man with the feather asked.

"Joaquín Ascarate," he answered, quickly glancing around. Magdalena and Escalante were gone, though the mules and horses still grazed in the meadow, the packs undisturbed except for one long box, which had been opened. He could see the uncovered rifles shining in the bright light of morning.

"To whom do you carry weapons?" Feather Hat asked.

Joaquín knew only that he was speaking to an officer of the Mexican army of Porfirio Díaz. He shrugged.

The gunbarrel hit his head hard. When he came to, his hands were tied behind his back and to his ankles. The soldier had built a fire and was cooking coffee for the officer, who sat on Magdalena's blankets watching him. Joaquín felt the stiffness of crusted blood on the side of his face. He moved, trying to ease the pull of the ropes numbing his hands and feet, but he only tightened the knots and made his head ache more, so he lay still. "Is it a crime, señor," he asked, "to carry merchandise into Sonora?"

"It is a crime to sell guns to bandidos," the officer replied with a gleam in his dark eyes. "I do not think your merchandise is intended for the army."

"It could be," Joaquín said. "I was hired merely to care for the animals."

"And you never asked what they carried?" he scoffed. "If that is so, you are stupid. If not, you are a liar. Which is the truth?"

"They paid me well not to ask," he said.

Feather Hat smiled. "I hope your family has the money already. If not, it is unlikely they will see it."

The soldier filled a cup and handed it to the officer, who took it without thanks, still watching Joaquín as he blew on the coffee to cool it. The soldier squatted nearby and picked up his rifle again.

"What will you do with me?" Joaquín asked.

"Kill you," Feather Hat said.

Joaquín scouted through his mind for possibilities of escape, but bound as he was he could think of none, so he asked, "Why haven't you already?"

The officer laughed, looking at his soldier, who laughed, too. "There is time for other things," Feather Hat said. "I never like to kill a man too quickly."

Joaquín could smell the coffee. "May I have something to drink? I am very thirsty."

The officer slowly emptied his cup on the ground, then held it out to the soldier, who refilled it and gave it back. "Perhaps," Feather Hat said, "if you could remember who was to receive your shipment, you might have some water."

"They never told me," Joaquín said. "I was to learn when we got there."

"Where?"

"The mountains, that's all I know."

"You know too little, hombre," the officer said. "And you wear American clothes. Are you not an expatriate?"

"I was born in México City," Joaquín admitted, "but I am an American now."

"From where?" Feather Hat asked without interest.

"Arizona. I came here looking for a friend and fell among strangers who threatened my life. They promised to let me live if I helped with the mules. It seemed an easy thing compared to dying."

"How does it seem now?" Feather Hat teased.

"Like a mistake," Joaquín said.

The soldier laughed but the officer stood up and walked away from the fire. Then Joaquín heard many horses, and he twisted around to see a troop of soldiers arriving. He quickly estimated thirty riders, and noted that their leader also wore a plume. He and Feather Hat talked a while, glancing occasionally at Joaquín, though he was too far away to catch their words. He looked at the soldier holding the rifle across his lap. "Who is he?" he asked.

"Colonel Gonzalo is the officer on the horse," the soldier said. "The one who captured you is Capitán Calero. He will take you to Tonichi and execute you by firing squad, unless you can prove you are American."

"And if I can?"

"Then you will be forced to work in the mines, señor," the soldier said. "Myself, I would prefer the firing squad."

"What if I can tell him what he wants to know?" Joaquín asked, hoping for time.

The soldier shrugged. "That you will goes without saying. No one denies him long."

Joaquín watched the soldiers dismount and begin catching the mules and loading the packs. All three horses were still there so he didn't think Escalante and Magdalena had gone far. He wondered if they were watching and if they would help him, but the forest seemed empty.

In half an hour the soldier cut the rope from Joaquín's ankles and told him to get up. He stumbled. His feet were numb and his head hurt so badly he nearly fainted. Another man led a horse over, and the two soldiers pushed Joaquín into the saddle, his hands still tied behind his back. As the soldiers mounted their own horses, Joaquín watched Colonel Gonzalo ride away with half of the troop. Capitán Calero led the other half with the packtrain and their prisoner back down the trail Joaquín had ascended the day before.

For hours they ambled along, leaving the mountains behind as they entered the desert. Joaquín swooned in the saddle, drifting in and out of consciousness, using all of his strength to stay on the horse. Finally they reached a small adobe presidio, rode in through the gate, and stopped in the dusty compound. The mules kept moving to the corral at the far end, but most of the soldiers sat their horses watching Joaquín. Two dismounted and came toward him, then pulled him from his horse and dragged him to a post embedded in the middle of the yard.

His hands were untied but only for the time it took the soldiers to shackle his wrists to the top of the post. He looked for the officers and saw them disappear inside a building, then heard a bullwhip crack in the air behind him. The burly man holding it grinned beneath his dark beard as he approached his work. Joaquín looked at the soldiers, still sitting their horses, their faces shuttered with indifference. The one who had been with Calero walked over and advised Joaquín to tell all he knew or suffer much.

"I know nothing," Joaquín said.

The soldier nodded and Joaquín heard the whip slicing through the air before it lashed his back. He gasped with pain, struggling for the dignity of suffering in silence, but as the whip fell again and again he heard himself screaming. Finally the soldier's voice came as if from a great distance, asking if he wouldn't spare himself. Joaquín could only shake his head in bewilderment that this was happening to him. The whip plied its torment again, until he succumbed to the mercy of unconsciousness.

When he came to, the plaza was deserted, the moon just beginning to edge into the dark sky. He thought he felt bugs crawling in the wounds on his back, but he couldn't be sure it wasn't the oozing of blood. His hands were numb, his arms aching with his weight. When he struggled to gain his feet and ease the pressure off the shackles, his movement broke open a scab on his back and he felt blood flow thick and hot, proving that what he had felt before was bugs. In fury he lunged at the chain holding the shackles, but it held. He could do no more than lean against the post and wait.

For brief snatches he slept, for longer stretches he stood in agony. The night seemed interminable. Finally he saw a rosy glow above the horizon, but what the day held for him he couldn't guess. Gradually men started moving around the compound, though none came near. He could hear flies buzzing about his back. When he imagined them laying eggs that would grow into maggots, he nearly went mad, raging against the shackles with the remnant of his strength. Then he commenced yelling, cursing all Rurales and the stupid befeathered officers who had been born of less than women. Finally his throat refused to emit sound and he suffered in silence until he again passed out.

The shock of cold water on his back revived him. He jerked awake to meet the eyes of Calero.

"Did you enjoy your sleep?" the officer asked pleasantly.

Joaquín just stared at him.

Calero smiled. "In such circumstances, it is usually more enjoyable than being awake."

Forcing his tongue to work, Joaquín managed to ask, "Am I charged with a crime?"

Calero laughed with ridicule. "Do you think I need permission to kill you?" he scoffed. "If so, you are mistaken."

"I am American," Joaquín said.

Calero shrugged. "You look méxicano to me. True, your clothes are those of a gringo, but Joaquín Ascarate is not a gringo name, and you yourself told me you were born in México."

"A long time ago," he whispered.

"Perhaps it is something you wish never happened?" Calero teased. "Perhaps you wish you were never born anywhere, eh? But you have come home, Joaquín Ascarate, and this is what happens to men who sell guns to bandidos in México."

"I have heard that in México the Rurales are bandidos."

Calero smiled coldly. "I should whip you for that, but I have decided to keep you alive one more day. Spend your last hours thinking hard, Joaquín Ascarate. If you do not remember names and places by sunrise tomorrow, you will be shot."

Joaquín listened to the officer walking away on the hard, stony ground. Behind him he could hear horses drinking from the trough, and the sound of the water dripping from their mouths tortured him. He held to his sanity, honing it from within to survive.

Sometime later, he couldn't guess how long, soldiers took him down and tied his hands behind, then dragged him into a cell. They threw him on the dirt and closed the door, leaving him in darkness. He slept. When he awoke it was to the chittering of mice and the prick of their tiny claws as they fed on his back. He leapt to his feet and kicked at the rodents scattering around him as he bellowed with outrage. When his cell was again so quiet he felt himself alone, he dropped down to sit in the dirt and lean his head in his lap.

He tried to conjure up an image of his wife smiling with love, or of their son laughing in play, but he was unable to see them in the darkness of his mind. He tried to summon a vision of Rico and the homestead, but remembered only her sorrow since losing Seth. Too clearly Joaquín remembered his last meeting with Lobo, then nineteen, and how the boy's eyes had burned with hatred for the man who had arrested his father. Though Joaquín reminded himself it was Seth's fault he was in a Mexican prison with his back whipped to shreds, he still longed for his friend, as he had from the moment he'd surrendered custody to the Texas Rangers. He had wished Seth luck and Seth had laughed, saying his luck had left with Joaquín's loyalty. Perhaps now Joaquín's luck was also gone.

The door opened and light flooded his cell. He sat up to squint at the men standing in the door. One was Capitán Calero and the other was the soldier with the whip. Joaquín couldn't take his eyes off the black snake coiled in the man's hand.

Calero asked kindly, "How is your memory today, Señor Ascarate?"

"I cannot tell what I don't know," he managed to whisper.

The capitán turned his back and the soldier unwound the whip, snaking it across the dirt as if he needed to test its strength. Joaquín saw and heard it in the air before he felt it cut into his shoulders. He rolled this way and that across the floor to escape, but the lash always found him. He could do no more than hold himself in a tight ball of silent endurance as the pain consumed his mind. When he could think again, he realized the whip had been idle for several minutes. He met the eyes of the officer watching with indifference.

"Still nothing to say?" Calero asked as if bored.

Joaquín remained silent.

"Shoot him," Calero said, turning smartly on his heel and leaving the cell.

More soldiers came in and dragged Joaquín across the yard to an adobe wall where another post stood, this one with shackles waist high. As the rope was cut from his wrists and they were locked into the shackles, he strove to stay on his feet and focus on the firing squad coming toward him, five men with rifles and downcast eyes.

Behind them, the presidio's gate opened and a horseman rode in. Joaquín shook his head, thinking to clear his vision, but it stayed the same. Escalante met his eyes as the firing squad formed a ragged line in front of him.

The sergeant drew his sword and raised it high, where it quivered in the sunlight. "Listo," he drawled.

The soldiers stood at attention.

"Apunto," the sergeant said.

The soldiers raised their rifles.

Watching Escalante talk with Calero, Joaquín prayed for salvation as he heard the sergeant take in breath to give the final command.

"Alto!" Calero shouted from the other end of the compound. The sergeant's head swiveled around, his sword still high, the rifles still aimed at Joaquín's heart.

"Bring the prisoner to my quarters," the capitán ordered.

Joaquín felt himself slump with relief as he exhaled a prayer of thanks to the Virgin of Guadalupe for her mercy. The soldiers took him off the post, dragging him across the yard and through the door of the comandante's oficina. When they let go, Joaquín fell to the floor. Summoning the strength to stand up again, he tried to focus on Escalante in a corner.

"Would you like some water?" Calero asked in a friendly tone.

Joaquín nodded. The capitán filled a glass and handed it over. Joaquín drank eagerly, then dropped the glass and leaned with his hands on his knees as the water came back up.

Calero looked at the mess on his floor and laughed. "Why didn't you tell me you work for Señor Seth? We could have avoided this unpleasantness."

Joaquín stared at him with hatred.

"You cannot blame us, Joaquín Ascarate," the Rurale said. "We do not like gringos selling arms to bandidos, unless of course they buy from us the right to do so." He smiled at Escalante. "You will tell Seth it was an honest mistake."

Escalante shrugged.

Calero studied him, then finally said, "I will let you both go for only the ammunition."

"We have already paid you," Escalante protested.

"Yes, but it will seem odd now if I let you go with all of the shipment, no? Especially as my men do not have such fine weapons. The soldiers will think better of me if when they next meet, the bandidos are short of bullets." He shot a look of disdain at Joaquín, then said to Escalante, "You should tell Seth not to hire such stupid segundos, eh? We caught him asleep in the sunshine."

"We had been traveling all night," Escalante said.

"But you were not there sleeping, were you?" He shifted his smile to Joaquín. "You are lucky, hombre. Another moment and the mistake would have been irrevocable."

Joaquín said nothing.

Escalante came to stand near. "Can you walk?"

Joaquín nodded and followed him onto the plaza. Soldiers were already at work repacking the mules. When a horse was led to him, Joaquín pulled himself into the saddle, then followed Escalante leading five mules loaded with boxes of rifles. The water had revived Joaquín enough that he noticed the presidio had just gained two thousand rounds of ammunition. He wondered what the bandits would say to receiving guns without bullets, then decided he wouldn't be there to hear their complaints.

As soon as the fort was out of sight, he reined his horse to a stop. "I am going north," he said.

Escalante gave him a patient smile. "How far do you think you would get without a gun?"

"Give me one from the shipment," he answered.

Escalante shook his head. "You still would have no bullets. You should come to the hacienda and let your wounds be tended. If you still wish to ride north in the morning, no one will stop you."

"Where were you when the Rurales came?" he asked testily.

"Watching from the trees. There was nothing I could do."

"You could have told them the same thing you did today."

"Colonel Gonzalo was there. We made no deal with him, only Calero. It took me so long to get back because I had to walk to the hacienda for a horse." He smiled again. "Magdalena is there. She is a good nurse and I think you need care, Joaquín. You'll feel better tomorrow."

Without waiting, he turned his horse and rode on, leading the mules. Joaquín let his horse fall in behind, suspecting that Escalante was right and he would not survive to leave Mexico without a weapon, to say nothing of food and medicine for his back.

The Hacienda de los Fuentes was a crumbling collection of low adobe buildings around a fountain in the center of a walled plaza. The gate opened without Escalante requesting permission to enter, and half a dozen charros stood in the yard watching the two horsemen and five mules plod in.

Joaquín scanned the men, seeing the same indifference he had seen in the eyes of the soldiers. Several moved, but only to unload the mules. Wearily Joaquín slid to the ground and stood leaning against his saddle. After a moment, a soft voice whispered beside him, "Ven aca."

He looked up to see Magdalena, her face full of sorrow. She tugged gently at his hand, then led him across the yard and through a door into a room, cool and dark, furnished only with a cornhusk mattress on the dirt floor. "Lie down," she said. "I will bring water."

He listened to her footsteps hurry away as he dropped to his knees, then he crawled to lie face down on the mattress. Thinking he should turn over to be ready for trouble, he remembered he had no weapon. After a moment, the woman returned and closed the door, shutting out the sounds from the plaza. Striking a match, she lit a candle, then knelt beside him with a bowl of water. He moved first to drink, lowering his head over the bowl as if he were an animal. He drank slowly, raised his head and waited, then drank again before lying back on the mattress, cradling his head in his folded arms.

She tore away the shreds of his shirt and tossed them aside, then dunked a cloth in the water and began gently cleaning his wounds.

He closed his eyes until she said softly, "Now you will be scarred as Seth is."

Joaquín opened his eyes, staring at the candlelight flickering on the raw adobe wall. "Was Seth whipped in prison?"

"Many times," she said.

"For what?"

"Trying to escape." She blew on Joaquín's back to dry it. "One night, when he was drinking more than usual, he told me about it. He said that under law they could not give him more than thirty-nine lashes, but they always gave him that many, except for once they gave him twenty. The first time, he heard someone tell the man who was whipping him not to hit so many times in the same place, but after that he tried not to listen when it happened. When they were done, they put him in a hole half the size of a grave. He could neither stand nor lie down. They kept him there three days without food or water; then when they let him out, they took him back to work. That was when he was given only twenty, the time he fainted in the sun after coming out of the hole and being told to break rocks as usual. He fainted and they whipped him for shirking his work."

Joaquín closed his eyes in remorse.

"He never gave up trying to escape," she said. "But it was impossible without help, and every time he took another prisoner into his plan, the man revealed it to the guards so he would receive an early release. Each time Seth was whipped the full amount of the law. He told me that even when news of his pardon came, the warden whipped him as a reminder of what was waiting if he should be sent back to prison. Seth said he was sick when he left, so he didn't visit his father who had gone to great trouble to secure his pardon. Although Seth didn't say so, I know he was too proud to face his father beaten." She paused, then warned, "This will hurt."

Joaquín almost laughed to think anything could hurt more than her words. When he looked over his shoulder and saw her lifting a bottle of tequila, he braced himself but still was not prepared for the pain. In his agony he thought he whispered Seth's name. Magdalena blew on his back to dry the alcohol, and under her cooling breath, he passed out.

When he awoke, the candle was only a nub barely burning on the floor. He looked for the woman and saw her sitting in a corner with her knees drawn up under her skirt. He couldn't guess what she saw in him; in her he saw his only ally. Softly she asked, "¿Tienes hambre?"

"Por favor," he said.

She rose and walked out, the strumming of a guitar floating in for the moment the door was open. When she returned, he could smell the supper she brought. The aroma gave him strength to sit up and raise his hands for the bowl. It held a thick caldillo of goat meat and a bent tin spoon. He ate quickly, then accepted the coffee she offered. It was sweet with sugar and tepid with milk. He watched her over the rim of the cup as he drank.

"You will be all right," she said. "I am sorry it happened. We could do nothing. Escalante caught me in the forest and was taking his pleasure when the soldiers came. By the time he was finished, it was too late to help you."

Joaquín said nothing, sipping his coffee as he watched her.

"Do you forgive me for failing you, Joaquín?"

"It's over now," he said.

She gave him a smile. "Tomorrow we will continue our journey, if you feel well enough."

"I am not going," he said.

"You must," she whispered. "I cannot ride into the camp of bandidos alone."

He shrugged, then winced as the movement tore at the scabs on his back. "The Rurales kept half the shipment," he pointed out angrily.

"Escalante will get it back," she said.

"How?"

"Calero only kept it to save face. Escalante will pay him again and everything will go on as before." She risked a teasing smile. "Welcome back to México, hermano."

"Why does anyone stay?" he muttered.

She laughed softly. "In the corrida, the bull is driven into the ring and tortured until he dies. Such is life, no?"

He pulled himself to his feet, holding on against the dizziness that threatened to dump him in the dirt. "I need to go outside," he said.

Her skirt rustled as she stood up. "I will take you."

When she opened the door, the guitar music struck him with a melancholy memory of his childhood. Magdalena picked up her rifle from where it leaned against the wall and carried it by her knee as they crossed the courtyard. Several men watched them from the shadows. Softly he asked, "Can you get me a gun?"

"There are none extra here," she said.

He looked at her rifle, wanting to ask for it. The way she clutched it tightly, however, made him suspect her loyalty didn't extend any further than her faith in him to protect her. Telling himself he shouldn't trust her either, Joaquín went into the latrine and shut the door.

When he came out, she was standing some distance away, looking north into the desert. She turned to watch him approach and he gave her a smile. "Were you thinking of Seth?" he asked.

She nodded, her dark eyes flashing with fire. "I doubt that he is thinking of me. Perhaps of you, eh?"

Joaquín shrugged, and again winced as pain tore down his back. "I am thinking," he said with a chuckle of self-mockery, "of how I wouldn't be here if I hadn't searched for him."

She laughed. "Perhaps in the future you will—how do gringos say it?—leave well enough alone, no?"

"What is well enough?" he asked, resting his arm across her shoulders as they walked back to the plaza.

She gave him a kiss on his naked chest and whispered, "For me it is a man in my bed." Her breath felt warm on his skin.

"Any man?" he asked, thinking of Escalante.

"Almost any is better than none. I cannot always be the jefe's woman."

"Why not?"

"A jefe deserves a young woman, no?"

He thought of Rico, who had already passed her fortieth birthday, though to Joaquín's eyes she was still beautiful. Magdalena led him to sit on a bench under the portal. Leaning his elbows on his knees, he studied the compound occupied by charros, who looked away rather than meet his eyes. "How do you find being Seth's woman?" he asked. "Is he good to you?"

She snorted in disdain. "He enjoys tormenting women with his games, to make us laugh or cry while he is only playing." She shrugged, giving him a sad smile. "But then, if I was his wife, perhaps he would not treat me so."

"He already has two wives," Joaquín said. "He was the same with them."

"Two still alive?" she asked archly.

He nodded.

"They have his niños, I suppose."

Again he nodded.

"Does he send them money?"

He shook his head. "The first was rich in her own right, the second he left ten thousand dollars to when he went to prison."

"Ten thousand American dollars?" she whispered.

"Do you think it was enough?"

"With such riches I could live forever."

"It's only twice the profit he'll make on this one deal," Joaquín pointed out.

"But not all for him," she answered. "Seth keeps very little for himself. Sometimes I wonder why he takes such risk for so little gain."

Joaquín smiled. "Maybe he is the bull in the corrida, wanting only to gore the tormentors before he dies."

"And who are you, Joaquín?" she asked softly. "Are you one of the picadors or the matador?"

He looked away, listening to the sad song of the guitar in the shadows. "Once I was clown, diverting the bull while the matador moved in for the kill. Now perhaps I am only the mule who drags the carcass from the ring."

"Fool them all," she whispered. "Do your work before he dies."

He looked at her sharply, a dark beauty holding a rifle and petitioning him to take away the jefe she depended on for life.

Suddenly she laughed, a ferocious sound of doomed gaiety. "I will find you a shirt," she said, standing up. "Will you wait here?"

He nodded and watched her walk away, marveling at the loyalty Seth inspired in women, that she would petition for his deliverance knowing it would be her loss. He wondered what she and the other fifty people in Nogales would do if Seth left. Not starve, Joaquín felt certain of that. They would find another jefe and go on as they always had, suffering under the whims of fate but managing to survive. As Rico would, also Seth's children, Elena and Jesse and even Lobo, wherever he was.

Joaquín realized he was the one who needed Seth home. Only by restoring what had been before could he hope to right the wrong of having delivered his friend to a legal system that tortured its felons. His best chance of achieving that was to return to Nogales victorious. Then Seth would listen, and perhaps, if Joaquín had proved himself once more a worthy partner, he could convince Seth to come home.

His new shirt was a peon's smock of white cotton, closed with two high buttons and falling in voluminous folds to the middle of his thighs. Magdalena laughed as she perused him. "It doesn't go with boots and spurs," she said with a grin. "Maybe this will help." She reached beneath the shirt, unbuckled his belt and pulled it out, then refastened it around his waist. "That's better," she said, "as long as your trousers don't fall down."

"In such a dress, it hardly matters," he complained.

She laughed. "Come. Fuentes is waiting to meet you."

"Hiraldo Fuentes?" he asked, remembering the bandit whom Seth had cut out of his shipment for making a mistake.

She nodded. "This is his hacienda. He is jefe here."

14

"Where's Escalante?" Joaquín asked, unhappily following Magdalena across the plaza of Fuentes' hacienda.

"He has gone to ambush Calero. It is all arranged. One of the soldiers will be executed for losing the shipment."

Joaquín looked away with disgust. "I do not like this game."

She glanced at him, then asked softly, "What can you do, Joaquín, but play the hand you are dealt, eh?"

"With no weapon, I can do no more than watch," he said, eyeing her rifle.

She stopped and faced him, guessing his thoughts. "I have only two bullets. Even if I gave you my gun, you would gain little. But a woman with a rifle is not such easy prey, so you can understand that I wish to keep it. Maybe Hiraldo will have an extra for you."

"Where is he?"

"This way." Carrying the contested rifle, she continued across the compound and led him down steps into a low dugout lit by tallow candles stuck into the walls. A young man with cheekbones like hooves watched them come in. He sat alone at a table with a bottle of tequila. Magdalena introduced them.

"Mucho gusto," Joaquín said without meaning it.

Fuentes stood up, revealing a fully loaded bandolera above his gunbelt sporting two pistols. Dressed in a black charro suit embroidered with fanciful curlicues of red satin, he walked around the table, his huge spurs jangling. "I have heard of you," he said with menace, looking Joaquín up and down. "You do not seem so big." Fuentes was no taller than Joaquín but his weapons added power. His eyes were black and fierce, and his mouth wore a cruel smile beneath the wings of his dark moustache.

Although his instinctive reaction was to flatten the man who stared at him so rudely, Joaquín remembered his manners and said, "Thank you for your hospitality. I am at your service."

Fuentes laughed. "My home is yours. How is your back?"

"Better," Joaquín said.

"Magdalena is a good nurse, eh?"

"I have no complaints."

Again he laughed. "I doubt that. Would you care for some tequila?"

"Sí, gracias," Joaquín said, not wanting to offend him.

They sat at the table and Fuentes poured two glasses full of the colorless liquor. He raised his. "Salud."

"Salud," Joaquín said, sipping then putting his glass down.

Fuentes drained his and refilled it. He looked at the woman standing by the door with her rifle, then back at Joaquín. "Today I received news from Nogales. Seth's wound festered and perhaps even as we speak he is no longer alive."

A whimper escaped from Magdalena, but Joaquín saw pleasure behind Fuentes' dark eyes. "Seth is strong," Joaquín said. "He will survive."

"Espero que si," Fuentes answered.

"Liar," Magdalena hissed. "You hope he is dead!"

He laughed. "In truth, I would not grieve. But it is different for you, eh, Joaquín?"

"He is my friend," he said.

Fuentes nodded. "Once I felt the same. I helped arrange the deal that is coming down now. Then when it was ready to be played, Seth cut me out. I spent much time and risked my life for this shipment, now I get nothing. Do you think that is fair?"

"Why did he cut you out?"

"I was seen talking with my cousin in Nogales. He is a capitán of the Rurales but I told him nothing. He is the son of my mother's sister, I could not pass him on the street without speaking."

Joaquín made no reply, certain that wasn't the reason.

Fuentes threw down the shot of tequila. As he poured another, he said, "Seth does not understand México."

Again Joaquín kept silent.

Fuentes set the bottle down and leaned closer with a leer. "Do you know what Seth has done to you? I think not. If you did, you would not feel so loyal."

"What has he done to me?" Joaquín asked softly.

"Tomorrow you ride to the camp of the bandidos," Fuentes said. "I do not think they will let a stranger ride out after seeing where they hide. What will you do then, lieutenant of Señor Seth?"

"I will play the hand that is dealt," he answered coldly.

"Ah sí." Fuentes nodded. "But this is not American poker where a man can leave the table at will. México has drawn your blood, it has spilled into the dust of your mother. Perhaps she will demand more, perhaps even all of you to shelter in her earth. If not your body, perhaps your soul, eh? So you will never again forget you are méxicano."

"I have not forgotten it."

"Then why do you live rich while your countrymen starve serving americanos?"

"I do not live rich," he scoffed. "I work hard to feed five women and children. Besides, you have a hacienda."

"Sí, I have a hacienda. In the middle of the desert where nothing grows, hombre. You boast of five people? I feed a hundred! And it is not only the sun and the drought I fight, it is the Rurales and the hacendados who take the good land. Even this hacienda, but I took it back. I am a Fuentes and this water belonged to my father and his father before him. Porfirismo stole it!" He leaned back in his chair, breathing hard. "Now Señor Seth comes to play a little game, to sell a few guns and make a lot of money. He runs no risk delivering his goods. Gringos are protected in México. If Señor Seth had been caught in your place, he would not have been whipped. Calero would have served him supper with fine wine, and they would have laughed together, tickling the breasts of my country for her milk. México is soft for foreigners. It is only méxicanos who suffer here."

"I know nothing of this," Joaquín said.

"Verdad, hombre. Yet you say you have not forgotten you are méxicano. The whip reminded you, no?"

"It reminded me only that men can be beasts."

"Worse than beasts," he hissed, leaning close. "The Devil has his grip on México, and we are all diablos in his service."

"I will not serve the Devil," Joaquín said.

Fuentes laughed. "You will die a saint, then. Maybe someone will put a cross over your grave. Probably not, but who knows?"

"I will not die in México," he said with more certitude than he felt.

Fuentes shrugged. "You did not save yourself from Calero's firing squad. Escalante did. Not even he. It was the power of Señor Seth that saved you. I have a runner in Nogales and I will know in a matter of hours if Seth dies. I will proclaim it in Sonora and his power will not save you again."

"Seth will not die," he said.

"All men die," Fuentes said, emptying his glass. "That is what he has given you, cabron, death in the dust. But you are a gringo and need not worry about the problems of México. When you meet the bandidos, you will be a gringo alone. Unless—" he paused to pour himself more tequila, then slyly met Joaquín's eyes, "you take me with you."

Joaquín decided not to argue. "If Escalante agrees, I will allow you to accompany us."

Fuentes laughed. "If you allow me to accompany you, I will let you live."

"That is not your decision."

"No? I have fifteen armed men outside. Also two pistols in my belt. What do you have? Only a woman with a rifle, and I doubt it is even loaded." He waved his hand. "Get out," he growled. "I am tired of your arrogance."

Joaquín stood up slowly. "Will Escalante be back tonight?"

Fuentes shook his head. "We will meet him at Ojo del Apache tomorrow. You didn't finish your tequila, amigo."

"I have had enough," Joaquín said, turning away.

Magdalena opened the door and preceded him into the cool darkness. But the plaza was not empty. Joaquín felt eyes from everywhere as he and the woman returned to their room. He crossed to the window and looked out at the desert lit only by stars. From behind him, she whispered, "Do you think it is true Seth is dying?"

Joaquín met her eyes in the gloom. "I think Fuentes lied."

She came and stood beside him at the window. "I long to be with him," she murmured.

"Why don't you go?"

She looked up with a sad smile. "He sent me to do a man's job. Do you think he will be pleased if I return and confess my woman's heart made me fail?"

Joaquín sighed, looking across the desolate desert.

"There is something you should know, Joaquíto," she said softly.

"What is it?" he asked with dread.

"The jefe of the bandidos raped Hiraldo's wife. When Hiraldo found out, he shot her. Seth was there and angry with him for doing it, but Hiraldo said the bandido had already killed her and he was only finishing the job. He vowed vengeance on the bandido, and that is why Seth wouldn't let him come."

Joaquín swore beneath his breath, but Magdalena wasn't finished. "If you ride into the bandidos' camp with Hiraldo," she predicted, "the jefe will kill you both."

In the morning they began their return ascent into the mountains. Fuentes took three men, who rode alongside the mules carrying the shipment of rifles. Hiraldo rode in front, and Magdalena rode beside Joaquín in the dust of the packtrain. She had found him a sombrero of pale woven straw. Beneath its high conical crown and wearing the smock of a peon, he felt like a fool. For reassurance he had taken one of the new rifles from the opened crate, but he had no bullets and everyone knew it. Joaquín felt at a definite disadvantage, dressed as a peasant and carrying an empty rifle as he followed an armed charro intent on revenge.

All morning they crossed the hot, parched desert, then in the afternoon began to climb into the foothills. There were no sounds other than the grunting of the mules, the plodding of the many hooves, and the jangle of the charros' huge-roweled spurs. Joaquín hoped Escalante would be at Ojo del Apache when they arrived— if for no other reason, so he could have bullets for his gun.

They ascended a long, narrow canyon and came out on a high plateau covered with scrubby trees. The horses and mules began to snort at the scent of water, and they all picked up the pace into a butt-breaking trot that tore at the scabs on Joaquín's back. He could feel the flow of fresh blood before he spotted the camp. Escalante stood up to greet them. He nodded to Fuentes but came first to speak with Joaquín.

He swung down and shook Escalante's hand. "Did you get the ammunition back?" Joaquín asked.

"Sí, but we cannot go farther with Hiraldo."

"I understand," Joaquín said. "But he has three men and we are only two."

"Three," Escalante said. "You forgot Magdalena."

"Even so, we are outnumbered."

Escalante smiled at Joaquín's rifle. "Is that a pilferage of our profits?"

Joaquín smiled back. "An empty one."

"Ven aca," the Mexican said, leading Joaquín into the camp. From his blankets, Escalante picked up a bandolera loaded with cartridges and tossed it to Joaquín.

He buckled it around his chest, then squatted to take more bullets from the open box on the blanket and load his rifle.

Escalante laughed. "You look like a bandido yourself, amigo."

"Aren't I?" Joaquín asked without humor.

Hiraldo came and stood looking down at them hunkered on the blanket. "How many days from here?"

Escalante stood up and met the charro's eyes. "You cannot go, Hiraldo."

"Who says?" he sneered.

"Seth. You know that."

"Even as we speak he is dying."

Escalante looked at Joaquín, who gave a quick shake of his head. "Until he is dead," Escalante told Fuentes, "I will honor his wishes, and he said you are not to come with us."

"Will you deny me vengeance?" Fuentes growled.

"I deny you nothing except my escort to the bandidos."

Fuentes snarled and walked away.

"How can we get rid of him?" Joaquín asked.

Escalante shrugged. "That is for you to decide. I will go no farther in his company." He, too, walked away, leaving Joaquín alone.

He picked up the box of bullets and took it to Magdalena. "Load your gun," he said softly. "I suspect we will need it before leaving here."

"I will shoot any of them but Hiraldo," she said, sliding bullets into her rifle.

"Why not him?"

Without looking up she said, "He is my brother."

Joaquín spun away in anger, then turned back to meet her eyes. "If I am his killer, will you avenge him?"

"As long as Seth lives, I will follow his orders."

Joaquín took a step closer and whispered hoarsely, "What if he ordered you to kill Hiraldo?"

She snapped the magazine of her rifle closed, then answered, "Seth would not choose someone whose heart is divided."

"My heart is divided!" he said, struggling not to shout. "I have no wish to kill anyone, yet Hiraldo refuses to be left behind and Escalante refuses to take him. What choice do I have?"

She looked at him with disdain. "Seth would not ask counsel from a woman."

He slapped her so hard she fell back on the ground. "I am jefe here," he said between his teeth, "and I will not hear what Seth would or would not do."

She crawled around to lie prostrate before him. "Perdoneme, mí jefe," she pleaded, clutching at his boots. "I beg of you, do not ask me to do this."

Kicking himself free, he carried his rifle into the forest and dropped onto his belly in the carpet of pine needles. As he hid his face in his folded arms, feeling his shirt stick to the fresh blood on his back, Joaquín felt defeated. Already he had been whipped and robbed, and he had yet to meet the bandidos. Though he'd proclaimed himself jefe, he didn't believe it; a jefe was centered in his purpose, and Joaquín felt he had lost all sense of who he was. Neither a gentle lawman who dressed in black like the priests he had once hoped to join, nor the deadly pistolero he had been by the grace of his partner's reputation, he was an orphan, in the shirt and sombrero of a peasant, fighting the powerful diablos of México neither for justice nor mercy, but to aid a gun-running gringo.

That was the truth. Joaquín's wish to save his friend's soul and his own long-standing desire to live with honor were irrelevant now. Any measure of success required survival. Caught in a conflict he hadn't chosen, he must act to prevail. Whatever the consequences, he would at least be alive to ponder their meaning.

He stood up and cocked his rifle in the silence of the forest. Quietly he walked back to camp. Fuentes was talking with his men at the edge of the clearing. Seeing Joaquín raise his rifle, Fuentes reached for his own gun, but Joaquín was already pulling the trigger. He cocked his rifle and fired as the next man wheeled around, cocked and fired again, and again, until four men lay dead amid the screaming of frightened mules. Magdalena ran to her brother and fell sobbing over his corpse.

Joaquín watched her a moment, then shifted his gaze to Escalante standing some distance away. "Vamanos," Joaquín said.

Magdalena looked up with horror. "You will not leave them unburied?"

"You can take them home," he said.

She sat with tears running down her cheeks as he and Escalante loaded the corpses onto their horses. Joaquín saddled Magdalena's and led it over to where she sat in the bloodstained dirt. "Get up," he said.

She rose abruptly, took her reins, and swung into the saddle to stare down at him with eyes of sorrow.

"Qué te vayas bien," he murmured.

"You have found your death," she warned.

"Be glad it is not yours," he said.

Escalante edged between them and handed her the rope to lead the horses. Joaquín took a step back and watched until she disappeared in the forest, then he shifted his attention to Escalante, already loading the guns and ammunition on the mules. Without words, they continued their journey deeper into Mexico.

Joaquín rode behind the mules, tasting the first bitter consequences of what he had done. Magdalena hated him now, and he wondered if she would gather more of Hiraldo's men at the hacienda and come for revenge. Wondered, too, what Escalante was thinking.

Joaquín knew only that they would no longer consider him a lost gringo out of his element. He had proved what he was capable of, and he felt more confidence in his success. All that remained was to trade the merchandise for money and carry it across two hundred miles of enemy territory.

At sundown they camped high in the mountains, unloaded and tethered the mules, then spread their blankets beneath the trees. They ate cold tortillas and jerked beef from Escalante's pack, washing it down with water. No words had passed between them all day. When Joaquín said he would stand guard, Escalante rolled himself in his blankets and fell asleep. Joaquín was determined to stay awake. He needed Escalante to lead him to the bandits, but Escalante did not need him.

Alone in the shroud of darkness, Joaquín doubted the merit of what he had done. Prior to this trip, he had killed only two men, both of them in defense of Seth; now he had jumped that total to six and his motive hadn't been saving Seth's life but his profit. At any point since arriving at Fuentes' hacienda, Joaquín could have abandoned the shipment and ridden north. He hadn't because he wasn't finished with what he'd come here to do. This trip was only an obstacle in the path of his intention to take Seth home. Yet Joaquín could no longer comprehend what home meant.

When he tried to visualize his wife and son, all he could see was Magdalena kneeling over the corpse of her brother. All he could hear above the soft moan of wind in the trees were her wrenching sobs of grief. He compared that sound to the whispered pleasure of her passion when they'd made love, and Joaquín felt stranded between the two poles of himself that had caused both. With his head against his knees, he fell asleep and dreamt of Seth, saw his gray eyes lit with mockery, heard his easy laughter of self-deprecation, and Joaquín jerked awake in the red light of dawn feeling certain Seth was dead. If so, there was no longer any reason for this mission. Yet what was left? If his family's love was lost to his memory, and Seth's redemption was gone from his future, what could sustain Joaquín's honor?

Five thousand American dollars. The price the bandits would pay for one hundred and twenty rifles and two thousand rounds of ammunition. It was a meaningless goal, empty and abstract except for one precious balm: it would provide for the wife and son he had left with the promise of his return, a promise he could no longer imagine keeping. Once more Joaquín understood how Seth had felt, giving money as compensation after love had died.

When he stood up in the sunrise of the new day, Joaquín was the man who had made Magdalena sob with grief; the man who had elicited her tenderness was left behind. Quickly he woke Escalante and helped him ready the packtrain to travel. Joaquín saddled and rode his horse at the rear again, unwilling to turn his back on a man who could profit so handsomely by betraying him.

In the thick light of sunset, the trail dropped into a high valley, and in the falling shadows of dusk, they rode into the bandits' camp. It was like a village: wickiups built of brush, venison drying on racks, a pit built for cockfights, even a shrine to the Virgin of Guadalupe with candles flickering in the breeze. Scanning the faces watching their arrival, Joaquín counted thirty men. He saw their remuda grazing on the lush mountain grass and their women working over smoking fires. He could smell supper cooking in the cauldrons, even hear the innocent laughter of children at play as if this were the best of all possible worlds. He guessed that maybe in Mexico it was.

The bandits wore the clothes of charros, the tight pants with medallions on the legs, the short jackets and huge sombreros decorated with red and gold braid. Bandoleras crossed every chest, pistols were worn on every hip, and many men held rifles, though no guns were raised in threat. The bandits watched impassively, withholding judgment until the jefe spoke.

In the center of the camp, Escalante stopped and studied the men watching him. "¿Donde está Vargas?" he asked.

"Aquí estoy," a hearty voice answered as a man stepped from behind a blanket covering the door of a wickiup. He was thick and squat, dark and dirty, his eyes glittering as coldly as a fighting cock's, vicious and heartless. They gleamed with lust as he looked at the loaded mules, then squinted at Joaquín. "¿Quién es?" the jefe barked.

"Joaquín Ascarate," Escalante answered, turning in his saddle so he, too, was looking at Joaquín. Everyone was. Escalante said, "El es de Seth."

"¿Es méxicano?" the jefe asked.

Escalante shook his head. "Un gringo."

Vargas laughed, a deep rumbling sound echoed by chuckles from his men. "Bueno," he pronounced. "Step down and come into my casita. I have some good tequila."

A boy came up to take the horses' reins. He smiled shyly at Joaquín, who gave him a smile back, which made the boy grin. Realizing he was muy hombre to this child, Joaquín felt the admiration like a sunbeam warming the cold desolation of his soul.

The bandits were already unloading the mules, breaking open the crates and exulting over the weapons. The ammo boxes too were broken open, and hungry hands grabbed fistfuls of bullets. Joaquín looked at the jefe.

Vargas laughed again. "Don't worry. You will get your money." He jerked his head at the wickiup, and Joaquín followed Escalante inside.

It was dark, the only light filtering through the crevices in the thatch. The floor was covered with several thicknesses of blankets, and a woman, lying half naked in a corner, gathered her clothes and left. The jefe sat cross-legged on the floor, yanked a cork from a bottle of tequila, took a swig, and handed the bottle to Joaquín. He sipped politely, then passed it to Escalante.

"How is Seth?" Vargas asked Joaquín.

"Bien," he answered.

The bandit frowned, his dark eyes glimmering. "Why didn't he come?"

"He had other business."

Accepting the bottle from Escalante, Vargas took another drink, then extended the bottle toward Joaquín. When he shook his head, the jefe laughed and reached behind himself for saddlebags he tossed to land between them. "Count it, if you like," the jefe said.

Joaquín opened one of the pockets and saw American money tied neatly in stacks. He wondered where the bandit had found crisp, twenty-dollar bills so deep in Mexico, but they looked real. Each of the five stacks contained fifty bills. He buckled the pocket closed and nestled the saddlebags in his lap. " 'Sta bien," he said.

Vargas smiled. "We will have a fiesta tonight. I will give you a sweet muchacha to keep you warm, eh?"

Joaquín shook his head. "If you will trade me a horse, I'll leave now."

"You think we will steal your money?" Vargas teased.

"I have other business," Joaquín said.

The jefe laughed, looking at Escalante. "He is a gringo, all right." When he turned his eyes back on Joaquín, they were sharp with amusement. "Tell Seth to come for Natividad and we will show him a good time while we discuss future business." Vargas laughed again. "Seth is never too busy for a fiesta, amigo."

"I will him," was all Joaquín said.

The bandit glowered from beneath his bushy brows. "Tell him also to stay away from weddings so maybe he won't get hurt, eh?"

Joaquín jerked with surprise.

Vargas chuckled. "Nothing happens in northern México without my knowing, hombre."

Joaquín nodded. "Is Seth recovering?"

"You yourself told me he is well," Vargas replied.

"Apparently your news is more recent than mine."

"He is recovering," Vargas said, gloating at the power of his spies. "I also know four men died in the forest yesterday. It was a bad loss for the Hacienda de los Fuentes, but for myself, I am pleased at the killings. On your first trip you rid me of a rogue who meant to set himself against me. I am in your debt."

"If that is so," Joaquín said, thinking fast, "can you guarantee my safe passage to the border?"

"No, hombre," Vargas said dolorously. "I know, but I do not control. I could, however, send a man with you. He is young but talented, and he has expressed a special desire to escort you back to Seth."

"Why?"

He shrugged. "I do not ask that question of men, as I forbid them to ask it of me."

"Can I trust him?"

Vargas laughed. "I myself trust no one. But he is also a gringo, so perhaps you will find him sympatico."

"I would like to meet him," Joaquín said.

Vargas yelled out the door for someone to fetch the gringo. He guzzled at the bottle again, then passed it to Escalante, who also drank deeply. After a few minutes, the blanket covering the door of the wickiup opened. As the tall, slender youth ducked inside, Joaquín met the gray eyes of Lobo Madera.

Vargas looked back and forth between them, then grunted. "It is evident you have met before."

Joaquín nodded, not taking his eyes from Seth's son.

"Is he agreeable, then?" Vargas asked.

"If he wishes to come," Joaquín said.

Vargas snickered. "Oye, chico, this gringo wishes company on his long journey home. I have offered him you. Do you wish it?"

"Sí," the kid said without emotion, holding Joaquín's gaze.

"He wishes to leave now," Vargas said. "Saddle him a good horse, eh?"

Lobo nodded and walked out.

The bandit's eyes were dancing with fun, and Joaquín suspected Vargas knew Lobo's connection to Seth, and also that the kid had vowed to kill Joaquín. The jefe grinned. "Perhaps I will see you at Christmas. Perhaps not, too. Qué te vayas bien."

"Adiós," Joaquín said, carrying the saddlebags of money into an early dark.

15

★

 They rode in silence, Joaquín watching Lobo from behind. The kid never once turned to look back. When
they crested the ridge and began the long descent to the desert floor,
Lobo kicked his horse into a trot and kept ahead.

More than two years had elapsed since they last saw each other,
both of them bruised and bloodied from their fight. Lobo had
never forgiven Joaquín for arresting Seth, but the boy had been only
seven then. As the years passed and he approached manhood, his
anger festered into a running sore of constant abuse. That Joaquín
was sheriff made him easy prey for Lobo's taunting, which always
stopped a hair short of flat-out confrontation. Lobo committed no
crimes for which he could be jailed, but the coffers of the township
were enriched by the fines he paid. He brawled in saloons, disturbed
the peace with his six-gun, organized illegal cockfights, and dal-
lied with so many good girls that the sheriff's office sometimes
seemed a salon for irate fathers.

Always when Joaquín confronted him with his latest trans-
gression, Lobo laughed and paid his fine by throwing the money
at Joaquín's feet. As for the girls he came within a breath of ruin-

ing, he denied using force and mocked the fathers for disparaging pleasure. He still lived at the homestead, in the room in the stable where Joaquín had once lived, but Rico only saw Lobo in the middle of the afternoons. Hungover and hungry, he sat at her kitchen table and watched her work with such intimate eyes that she told Joaquín she sometimes felt Seth was there instead of his son. Lobo never touched Rico, however. He flaunted his prowess with prostitutes, honed his seduction on good girls, and tried his hand at cuckolding husbands, but to his father's wife he showed only the courtesy of respect.

Outside that one center of calm in his world, Lobo lived in a cyclone of destruction. At any given time, half the men in town were mad at him. Joaquín was battered with their complaints and accusations of favoritism. He had no defense, readily admitting he cut Lobo slack in hope that the kid would finally expel his rage and be done with it. Yet Lobo grew worse with each passing year. His father could have controlled him, eased the anger in his blood, tempered the cruelty in his fun, and guided him to a productive manhood. But Seth was gone. And because Joaquín had allowed that to happen, Lobo hated him.

The showdown came one rowdy Saturday night in the Blue Rivers Saloon. Lobo had been drinking since sunset. He had made three separate trips upstairs with three different women, yet energy catapulted from his eyes as if he were a wild bronc who had thrown three top-hand riders and was ready for more. It was well past midnight when Joaquín stopped by on his rounds.

The instant he walked through the door, their eyes met across the crowded, smoky room. Joaquín stepped up to one end of the bar and ordered a whiskey. Watching Lobo approach in the mirror, Joaquín sipped his drink while he listened to the barkeep whisper that Lobo was in rare form that night. Then the keep moved away as Lobo came near. Joaquín turned around and gave the kid a smile, hoping for peace.

Lobo grinned, leaning heavily on the bar and refilling his glass from Joaquín's bottle, asking belatedly, "Don't mind, do you?"

Joaquín shook his head.

"You can think of it as a remembrance of old times," Lobo mocked. "How many nights did you stand here and bend elbows with Seth?"

"Quite a few," Joaquín answered.

"Don't s'pose he gets any whiskey in prison," Lobo said, his voice playful, his eyes cold. "Nor women, neither. You ever think about that, Joaquín?"

"Yes," he said.

"How's it make you feel? When you're snuggling your wife under the covers and sticking it to her good, you ever think of Seth doing it to his hand?"

Joaquín sighed. "Why don't you go home, Lobo, and sleep it off?"

"Can't sleep," he said. "Haven't had a good night's sleep for ten years now." He leaned close and whispered, "Remember when I stopped Lemonade from killing Seth? You remember that, huh, Joaquín?"

He nodded.

"You think Seth ever remembers it and wishes I hadn't been there?"

"No," Joaquín said gently.

Lobo's eyes were honest now with an earnest yearning. "You think he's glad to be alive, even in prison?"

"I think he's biding his time for the day he's released."

"Death's the only escape from a life sentence," Lobo scoffed.

"Your grandfather has hopes of a pardon."

"A pardon!" Lobo downed his shot of whiskey and poured himself more. "The governor should beg Seth for a pardon. All of Texas should. As well as a few other people in closer places." He sipped at the whiskey, watching Joaquín.

Joaquín said nothing.

"If he comes home," Lobo taunted, "are you gonna tell him Aaron's his son? That Aaron's mother died in prison bringing him into the world just so her sister wouldn't be childless? That the black pickaninny of a murderess was the fruit of our destruction? Or are you gonna claim to have fathered that half-breed in your home?"

"I will tell him the truth," Joaquín answered softly.

"The truth!" Lobo laughed, turning heads down the bar. "How about the truth that you collected the reward on Seth and it's sitting in your bank account getting fatter every day? How about the truth that he trained you, picked you up out of the gutter and made you a man, then you betrayed him! Or the truth that he's wearing chains while you wear a star! A no-account despicable excuse for a banty rooster strutting his stuff. That's what you are, Sheriff Ascarate. A self-righteous fool so quick to do your duty you arrested your innocent friend for a murder he didn't commit."

The saloon was silent. Quietly Joaquín said, "Seth is not in prison for the crime I arrested him for."

"So what?" Lobo shouted. "You delivered him to the law!"

"He surrendered himself to my custody," Joaquín answered.

Lobo stared at him incredulously. "Is that how you ease your conscience while fucking your wife in the house built with Seth's money?"

Joaquín hit him. Lobo staggered against the wall, started to go down but held his feet and wiped blood from his mouth with the back of his hand. He stepped forward, feinted, swung his right then his left into Joaquín's arms covering his face. Lobo dropped his fists and struck lower, again hitting Joaquín's arms, and then retreated, watching the sheriff hunched in on himself, not hitting back.

"Pinche pendejo!" Lobo jeered. "Did you send your balls to prison with Seth?"

Joaquín's right flung Lobo against the wall again. Lobo was

wide open and Joaquín plowed into him with both fists, slamming the kid's head against the wall, then Joaquín retreated. Lobo shook his head and waded back into the fight, swinging hard and connecting with Joaquín's jaw. The sheriff stood his ground and his fists powered low, pounding the kid's stomach until Lobo staggered a few steps away and puked whiskey on the floor. He leaned with his hands on his knees and spit blood, looked up at Joaquín, then lunged back for more.

Joaquín slammed the kid into the wall again. Lobo tried to cover himself but Joaquín's fists hammered through the kid's tardy defense until Lobo could do nothing but shelter himself from the blows. Joaquín aimed one final punch at the kid's jaw and Lobo slid onto the floor, out cold. For one brief moment, Joaquín wished Seth could have seen his performance. Then he realized he had just beaten the sand out of Seth's son and his victory was empty.

Blue Rivers came across the room and looked down at Lobo, then gave Joaquín a commiserating smile. "I'll see he gets home," Blue said.

Joaquín nodded and walked out on the dark street of Tejoe, down a dark alley to the back of the jail, where he leaned against the door and cried. Lobo had spoken only the truth, and Joaquín had beaten him for it. He wondered when he had lost his integrity, whether it had been the moment he locked Seth in a cell, or way back in El Paso when he'd abandoned the priesthood to follow an outlaw. In either case, the loss had penetrated his soul like a lead bullet, poisoning every vein of honor in his body.

In the morning, he rode out to the homestead to talk to Lobo, to try and reestablish the common ground of their love for Seth in the hope that he could keep the kid from following in his father's bloody footsteps. But Lobo was gone.

Two years had elapsed since then, time in which Lobo had gained strength and cunning. Now he and Joaquín were riding together across the vast, empty wilderness of Mexico.

In the first light of dawn, they stopped in a small forest clearing around a tiny pool of water. Lobo swung down and swept the green moss from the surface of the pool, then lay on his belly and drank with his horse. Joaquín's horse nickered with thirst, but only after Lobo had moved away did Joaquín swing down and do as Lobo had, tasting the sweetness of high mountain water.

When Joaquín stood up, Lobo had unsaddled and was sitting in the shade of a broad tree. Joaquín studied the kid, noting the expensive quality of his clothes. Lobo obviously hadn't suffered from poverty in the years on his own. Only his gunbelt was well-worn, the bone handle of his Colt's .44 darkened from years of use. Unhappily Joaquín recognized that it was Seth's gun, taken from the headboard of Rico's bed on Lobo's last night at home.

Joaquín unsaddled and hobbled his horse to graze with the other, then carried his gear to the edge of the shade. He stretched out with his rifle beside him, settling his sombrero over his eyes in a pretense of sleep.

"You look like a Mexican," Lobo said.

"I am," Joaquín answered, listening for any sound of movement.

Finally the kid asked, "Was Seth hurt bad?"

"When?"

There was no answer and Joaquín tossed the sombrero on the grass and turned on his side to look at the kid. "What are you doing in México?"

"Looking for Seth."

"He's in Nogales."

"I know that now."

"Where have you been?"

"Texas."

"Doing what?"

"Robbing banks and killing lawmen," the kid jibed. "Are you still sheriff?"

"Not here," Joaquín said.

In a softer voice, Lobo asked, "Did you see Seth?"

"Yes."

"Is he all right?"

"He was badly shot."

"That isn't what I meant."

"I was with him only a few minutes," Joaquín said.

Lobo's eyes were sharp, boring into his. "You must have been able to tell something."

"He is the same outlaw I met in El Paso," Joaquín answered sadly, "only older."

"Not the man he was in Tejoe?"

Joaquín shook his head. "He refused to come home."

"Did he know I wasn't there?"

"He asked only of my wife and her sister."

Lobo's eyes were hot with pain. "I thought when he was pardoned, things would be like before. I knew he'd be different. I am, and so are you. But he's free now. I thought we could be happy."

Joaquín sighed. "I don't think that's what he wants."

"What *does* he want?"

"I don't know."

Lobo looked away. "I visited Abraham and Johanna in Austin. Jeremiah's fifteen now. He studies bugs." His voice was baffled. "I went out with him one day and he was catching butterflies in a net."

Joaquín chuckled to think that somewhere in the world boys occupied themselves with such harmless hobbies.

"Johanna's remarried," Lobo said. "Some big-shot lawyer who works for the governor."

"Maybe he helped with Seth's pardon."

Lobo nodded. "Seth wrote them after he got out. Abraham let me read the letter."

"What did it say?"

"That he'll always be grateful for how hard they worked to get him released, but he wasn't ever coming back and they should consider him dead."

Joaquín grunted. "I think it was good advice."

"Why won't he come home?" Lobo demanded.

"I don't know."

"You don't know much, do you," Lobo stated.

"No," he answered, settling the sombrero over his eyes again.

"I could kill you," Lobo said. "Take the money to Seth and be in good with him."

"I don't think you need the money for that."

"What do I need?"

"Nothing. You have it all already."

Lobo laughed. "Think he'll be glad to see me?"

"Yes."

"Was he glad to see you?"

"No."

Softly Lobo said, "That must've hurt a lot."

Surprised at the sudden solicitude, Joaquín wondered if Lobo now understood how a man could sometimes find his worst failure while striving hardest to be right.

"How's Esperanza?" Lobo asked.

Pushing the sombrero back again, Joaquín met Lobo's eyes and said gently, "We had an epidemic of smallpox last year. She helped to nurse the poor, and died."

Lobo got up and walked away. Watching the kid lean on his horse, Joaquín felt for him. Esperanza had been like a mother to Lobo, and Joaquín well knew the weight of that grief. He wondered if the kid would ever get a break, or if his life would be one long trail of sorrow. After a while Lobo walked into the forest, and Joaquín let himself sleep.

He woke up sweating in the sun. Lobo was sitting in the shade several yards away, watching him sullenly. The six-gun and bowie knife on Lobo's belt, and the Winchester at his side, spoke of a prowess made more lethal by the bitter anger in his gray eyes. Joaquín sighed wearily, though he had just woken up.

By the time he returned from the bushes, Lobo was holding his reins, ready to go. Joaquín carried his rifle, saddle, and blanket over to his horse, leaving the saddlebags of money on the ground. He was no closer to them than Lobo, but Joaquín didn't care. As he smoothed the blanket on the back of his horse, tossed the saddle on and leaned under the belly for the cinch, he knew he wouldn't fight Lobo again. If he wanted to take the money to Seth, Joaquín wouldn't stop him short of defending his own life.

Without looking at Lobo, Joaquín retrieved the bags and secured them in place, then swung onto the roan. It was a tall, sturdy gelding, a bandit's horse, which would attract attention among the scruffy mounts common in Mexico. Lobo's horse, too, showed good breeding in the sheen of its dark coat and the prance of its gait.

As they rode down the mountain, Joaquín realized there was no way they would pass through Sonora unnoticed. If they didn't inspire challenge from ambitious pobres, they would no doubt draw the attention of the Rurales. He knew Lobo to be adept with guns, so they had a good chance of winning any fair fight, but Joaquín hadn't experienced much fairness in Mexico. And he wasn't entirely confident of Lobo's help.

They stopped in midafternoon to rest the horses, finding a bank of shade along a final ridge of rocks. Below them stretched the desert, pale pink and chalky yellow, miles of flat, crusted sand. Joaquín sipped from his canteen, noting it was half empty. They had no food and he didn't know where they could find more water. He looked at the kid. "You know this country, amigo?"

"Some." He shrugged. "There's a town out there. Sort of."

Joaquín looked into the distance, shimmering with heat waves. "How far?"

"Four, five hours. If I can find it." He drew his knee up and draped his wrist across it. Joaquín had seen Seth do that many times when he was thinking, as if he had to put his gun hand out of action to use his mind. "There's a notch in the mountains in front of us," Lobo said, "and a peak in the ones behind us that you gotta line yourself up between. I've learned it's real important to check landmarks going as well as coming."

"A good lesson," Joaquín said. "How did you come to be with the bandits?"

"Just something that happened," the kid answered evasively, again reminding Joaquín of Seth.

They waited half an hour more, giving the horses time to rest, then Joaquín followed Seth's son into the desert. They had been riding for hours when finally a notch appeared through the shimmering haze obscuring the low ridge of mountains far ahead. When Lobo twisted in his saddle to look behind them, Joaquín did too. Gradually, watching Lobo adjust their course, Joaquín was able to pick out the peak the kid was using as a guide. The sun was bumping against the horizon when they came upon the scars of wagon tracks gouged into the hard soil. Lobo followed the road north through the long shadows of dusk. The first stars prickled in the darkening sky, then suddenly a yellow light appeared in the distance.

"¡Qué bueno, hombre!" Joaquín said.

Lobo grinned. "The town's called Salsipuedes. You know what that means?"

"Get out if you can," Joaquín said. And they both laughed.

When they were only a few miles from the pueblo, Joaquín saw a distorted cactus looming against the stars. One side of the organ pipe had been slashed off as if by a machete, so it grew ponderously heavy on the opposite side. He dismounted behind the cactus, dug a hole with his hands, and dropped the saddlebags into the pit. At the last moment, he took a few bills off one bundle and put them in his pocket, then buried the stash, tamped the earth, and scattered sand to cover the disturbance. He swung onto his horse and rejoined Lobo on the road. Without a word, they rode the last miles into the pueblo.

Adobe hovels ranged around a plaza whose main attraction was a stone well. Letting their horses drink from the trough, Joaquín and Lobo studied the town, which consisted of little more than a cantina, an empty corral, and a few humble homes. A boy came out of the cantina and offered to tend their horses for five centavos. Lobo paid him, then walked with Joaquín into the cantina.

The room was set down into the earth with wooden steps descending to the dirt floor. Four men watched them come in, three customers and the keep, none of them armed. Joaquín nodded at the men and gave the keep a smile, then asked in Spanish if it was possible to get dinner.

"Ah sí," the man said. "We have caldillo hot in the kitchen, señor. Please, take a chair, my home is yours. Would you like something to drink?"

"Whiskey," Lobo said, before Joaquín had a chance to answer.

"I'm sorry," the keep said. "We have tequila."

" 'Sta bien," Lobo answered.

Joaquín looked at the kid, then at the barkeep. "Café, por favor."

"Como no," the man said, disappearing behind a curtain.

Choosing a table in the corner, they both sat with their backs to the wall, looking down the length of the room dimly lit with tallow candles. The men leaning against the bar chatted softly among themselves. Joaquín guessed them to be farmers.

The keep returned with bowls of caldillo, a mug of black coffee, two glasses, and a bottle of tequila. Lobo pulled a five-peso coin from his pocket, tossed it to the keep, and asked, "Is Felicidad still here?"

The keep scrutinized the coin before carefully saying, "Who is asking, señor?"

"Lobo Madera."

Joaquín watched the keep's eyes brighten with recognition and noted that the men at the bar had suddenly perked up with interest.

"What about you, señor?" the keep asked. "Would you like a woman, too?"

Joaquín shook his head.

"My treat." Lobo laughed. "Go on," he said to the keep. "Tell them to hurry." He grinned at Joaquín and said in English, "Loosen up. Spreading our money around builds good will."

"It also encourages thieves," Joaquín replied.

Lobo laughed again. "Nothing we can't handle," he said, sounding exactly like Seth.

Joaquín sighed. He hadn't forgotten that he'd killed four citizens since riding south, and he wasn't eager to face Mexican justice. "I think we should try not to attract attention," he said softly.

"That ain't my style," Lobo said, turning to watch the girls come in.

They were both younger than Lobo, tiny, delicate creatures with black hair almost as long as they were tall. Their slender bodies were covered only by white cotton dresses that left their shoulders bare and stopped just below their knees. Lobo grabbed one by the waist and pulled her into his lap. "Ain't you gonna say you're glad to see me?" he asked, nuzzling her neck.

"Maybe I am glad," she pouted.

Joaquín looked at the other one. "Siéntese," he said.

She sat next to him, folding her hands in her lap and studying them as if they were new to her.

"What's your name?" he asked.

"Lourdes," she said, giving him a shy smile.

"Are you hungry?"

Her eyes widened and she nodded.

"Patrón," he called to the keep behind the bar. "Bring another bowl for the muchacha, eh?"

"Gracias," she whispered.

He shrugged with a smile.

Lobo didn't offer Felicidad any supper, saying he liked his women skinny. Felicidad answered she wasn't hungry anyway and sat sipping at the tequila, but several times Joaquín saw her look with envy at Lourdes as she cleaned her bowl. When Lobo finished, he washed his meal down with several shots of tequila, then pulled Felicidad close and began kissing her. Joaquín tried to ignore it but when Lobo's hand disappeared under the girl's skirt, he suggested they take it outside.

Lobo glared, then rose and led Felicidad through the back door. Joaquín watched them go, wondering if he shouldn't stand guard outside their room.

"There is no danger here, señor," Lourdes murmured, as if reading his thoughts. "Vargas protects us."

He looked back, admiring her doe eyes in her smooth face. "Many travelers must use this spring."

"At their own risk, señor. The water is not healthy for enemies of Vargas."

"How do you know I'm not one?"

"You travel with Lobo Madera," she answered.

"I am glad," Joaquín replied, "that I travel with so honored a chico."

"Ah sí," she said. "He is muy hombre for one so young."

"What do you know of him?"

"Only what I hear, señor," she answered cautiously.

He smiled, pouring himself a smidgeon of tequila. "I'm new to this country and haven't yet heard the stories."

"Vargas sent him to attack Calero," she whispered, "to retrieve ammunition stolen in shipment. Lobo Madera snuck into the camp and knifed the guard, then loaded the mules and escaped in silence. It proved great cunning, señor."

Joaquín remembered Magdalena had told him a soldier would be sacrificed to cover Calero's complicity. Suspecting Lobo was ignorant of how he had been used to murder a scapegoat, Joaquín sighed deeply.

The girl continued, "Vargas says Lobo Madera will be a great jefe of bandidos someday."

"And Lobo believes it," Joaquín muttered.

"The people believe it, señor," she answered softly. "That is what makes a great jefe."

"There are better things to be than a bandit," he said.

Lourdes shook her head. "A man cannot become a hacendado, he must be born to such power. And to be a Rurale is less than a bandit. To work on the haciendas or in the mines is to be a slave. What is left, señor, if a man wishes to feed his family?"

"He could have a ranch or a farm," he said.

"The hacendados own the land. Pobres must pay rent, and when they cannot pay because of bad harvest, they become indebted to the hacendado and must work for him. Their debt increases and is inherited by their children. Only the families of bandidos are able to buy their freedom, but the hacendados know that, and they suspect anyone who is able to pay. It is a dangerous world, señor, and people need a strong jefe to protect them."

Her eyes were darkly earnest, the lines of her young face set in determination. "How old are you, Lourdes?" he asked.

"Fifteen," she answered. "They say there is revolution coming. I will fight, because the gachupínes have ruled too long. The blue-eyed chocolate-drinkers who own the haciendas but live in the capital and care nothing for our suffering. Porfirismo defends them and also the americanos who own the railroads, but Díaz will not live forever. With his death, México will be at war. I will fight with the men."

Joaquín studied her a moment, then asked, "Do you think the pobres can win against an army?"

"The army is made up of men arrested for stealing bread or raising their voices in complaint. They do not serve with valor."

"And you will fight?"

"Sí. I will be a soldadera," she said proudly.

He smiled sadly. "I wish you luck, Lourdes."

"You should fight, too," she said.

"This is not my home," he answered.

She blinked with surprise. "Are you not méxicano?"

"I was born here, but I am an American now."

"Your clothes mark you for a peon," she said. "The Rurales will assume you have escaped from a hacienda. They will shoot you on sight and you will be buried here, señor. I think then you will be méxicano."

"My clothes mark me for an escaped peon?" he whispered. She nodded.

"Can you get me others?"

She smiled slyly. "For a price, señor."

"I will pay it," he said without hesitation.

"Ven aca," she said, standing up and leading him out the back door.

In the courtyard, she led him across the hard-packed dirt to another door. When she knocked, a woman's voice bid her enter. A crone sat by the hearth sewing from the light of a fire, though it was warm in the room. Her face was cragged, and she stared blindly at the two people in the doorway. "Who is it?" she croaked.

"Soy yo, Lourdes, y un gringo," she said, putting a sarcastic twist on the last word. "He needs those clothes."

"Ah sí?" the crone answered eagerly, setting her sewing aside and shuffling across the room to a leather trunk. She opened it and took out a complete set of American clothes, from long johns to boots and spurs.

Joaquín walked over and looked at them. "Where did they come from?"

"A month ago," Lourdes answered, "Vargas killed a gringo in the cantina. Fortunately he shot him in the eye, so there are no holes in the clothes. They have been laundered since we took them off the corpse."

He watched her young face as she calmly made such a statement, then shook his head and chuckled with despair. "How much for the shirt and hat?" he asked the old woman.

Squinting to see from even so close, she looked at Lourdes.

"Ten pesos," Lourdes said.

The old woman's reaction told him the price was high, but all he had were three twenty-dollar American bills. Wryly he reached into his pocket, pulled one out, and handed it to Lourdes. She stared down at it for a long time. Finally she scoffed, "This cannot be real!"

"It was given to me by Vargas," he said. "I assume it is real."

Her eyes flashed with delight as she laughed. "It is enough," she said.

"Espero que si," he answered, taking off the bandolera, unbuckling his belt and pulling off the peon's tunic, then putting on the dead gringo's shirt. It was dark blue with mother-of-pearl buttons. Joaquín tucked it in and relaced his belt through the loops in his pants, then compensated for his lack of a gunbelt by buckling the bandolera around his waist. The hat was black with a rattlesnake headband, and Joaquín was pleased to discover it fit well. "Hope he didn't have lice," he said.

Both women laughed at his joke.

When they were back in the courtyard, Lourdes led him through another door. From the light of a candle, he saw the small room was furnished with only a woven mat on the dirt floor, and that the door latched with a small piece of wood pivoting on a nail. When he turned around again, Lourdes was pulling her dress over her head. He waited a moment longer than he should have before saying, "You don't have to do this."

She shrugged, tossing her dress aside. "You must sleep somewhere."

He looked at the door again, knowing a child's kick could open it.

"You are safe here," she reassured him. "This is a Vargas estación."

On the mat was a folded blanket. She shook it out and crawled naked beneath it. Removing only his boots and hat, he lay down on top of the blanket.

She whispered, "They say Señor Seth has been shot. Have you heard this?"

"Yes," he answered cautiously. "But he is recovering."

"I hope it is quick," she said. "I do not like to think of him suffering."

"Have you met him?"

"Ah sí. He came once with Vargas, who says even the Apaches honor Señor Seth. They call him Man Who Walks with Death."

"Do you think that a good name?" Joaquín asked.

"Since death is always near, it is wise to be its friend." She turned on her side and touched his cheek. "It is also wise to enjoy pleasure when it is before you."

He pulled her close. "You smell sweet," he murmured into the fullness of her dark hair.

She laughed. "I like you, too."

Joaquín surrendered to her willingness, enjoying himself. Soon afterward, weary from his journey, he fell deeply asleep. When he awoke in the morning, Lobo was gone.

16

★

 Joaquín wasn't surprised to discover that the saddlebags of money had been taken. He didn't even need to dismount to see that the hole was empty. Muttering a curse, he scanned the vast stretch of desert, knowing it would be impossible to track anyone across the rocky soil constantly buffeted by wind. For a moment, he worried about Lobo, doubting the kid had much chance of making it alone to Nogales; then he decided maybe Lobo had a better chance than he did. Since the kid obviously wasn't worried about him, turnabout seemed fair play. Deciding that without the money he wouldn't be in a position to convince Seth of anything, Joaquín wearily headed north, determined to put Mexico behind him.

He followed the road, keeping a sharp eye for the telltale dust that would signal company. At noon, he stopped to rest his horse without the benefit of shade. He loosened the cinch and poured water into his hat, letting the horse drink half his supply. After the two of them had stood for what he gauged to be half an hour, he tightened the cinch and rode on.

The sun was hot and his dark shirt clung to his body with sweat.

He could feel the horse tiring and knew it was thirsty, but he had no choice except to keep moving. The road must lead somewhere. He could only hope that between Salsipuedes and the border he would come across another well. Remembering the Fuentes hacienda, he doubted he could find it or that he'd be welcome if he could. That made him wonder if Magdalena was there or back in Nogales, and if Seth were truly recovering.

Joaquín shook his head, trying to dislodge his concern for his friend. It nagged at him, though, that because of Lobo he had failed. Joaquín also remembered how Fierro and Ryan had threatened to kill him if he didn't return with the money. That revived his anger at Seth, and Joaquín reasserted his resolve to leave both Mexico and Seth behind.

At sunset, the mountains appeared as distant as when he had started, the desert as empty in all directions. A lessening of heat was the only change. Again he stopped and let his horse drink, leaving himself barely a swallow. After resting a while, he tightened his cinch and rode on.

By midnight the horse was beginning to stumble. Joaquín stopped and gave it the last of the water, then had to snatch his hat back lest the animal eat it. When he settled the hat on his head, the cool damp revived him somewhat, but he knew he had no remedy for the fatigue of the horse. Far in the distance he caught one fluttering blaze of a campfire.

He studied the spot for a long time and was rewarded by another flame licking high into the sky before disappearing. Joaquín led his horse forward. He had no idea what breed of men he would find at the fire. Knowing they could be Rurales or bandits, he hoped to see vaqueros or some other peaceful group. As he neared the camp, he saw many horses tethered to a picket. He pinched the nose of his own horse to keep it quiet, then edged closer. With a sinking heart, he saw Rurales around the fire.

Remembering what Fuentes had said about Americans being protected in Mexico, Joaquín reminded himself he was dressed as a gringo now and perhaps could ask for food and water from the army. Still, he hesitated. There was a chance he could sneak over to the picket line, swap horses, and keep going on a fresh mount, perhaps even with a full canteen. As he watched, however, the sentry spotted him. Joaquín barely had time to pull his rifle from the scabbard before he was surrounded by armed soldiers.

He decided his best chance was to pretend ignorance of Spanish. "Evenin'," he said, trying to imitate Seth's Texas drawl. "I sure am glad to find some comp'ny way out here."

"Are you?" an officer asked, stepping through the circle of soldiers.

Joaquín felt caught, recognizing Colonel Gonzalo. But since the colonel hadn't come close to him before and didn't appear to recognize him, Joaquín thought the best course was to continue his charade. "I'm Bob Smith, an American down here to check out some minin' claims in the mountains. I lost the road to Nogales. Could you point me the right direction?"

Gonzalo sneered. "If you are truly Señor Smith, I am Porfirio Díaz."

The soldiers chuckled at his joke. Joaquín smiled awkwardly. "If I ain't Bob Smith, who am I?"

"Hector Thorp, if I am not mistaken," Gonzalo answered with a snide smile.

"You are," Joaquín said, not smiling. "I never heard of Hector Thorp."

"I find that odd, señor, since you are wearing his shirt and hat. Did you perhaps murder him to take his clothes?"

"I bought 'em," Joaquín said, thinking fast. "From some peons a ways back. My bronc threw me and my shirt got tore. By the time I caught my horse, my hat was gone. So I bought these in the next pueblo I come to."

Gonzalo nodded. "Salsipuedes, perhaps?"

"Reckon," he said. "It had one of them long Spanish names."

"Do I not detect a hint of Spanish in your voice, señor?"

"Maybe." He shrugged. "My mother was Mexican."

"And your father was a lying dog," Gonzalo said.

"You have no call to insult me," Joaquín replied testily. "I just rode over to ask for some friendly directions. Since you ain't friendly, I'll ride on."

"I'm afraid that is impossible, señor. You are under arrest."

"For what?"

"The murder of Hector Thorp. Unless, of course, you wish to admit you are he."

Quickly Joaquín calculated. Since Gonzalo seemed to be concerned about Thorp's fate, he figured it might be best to go along with it. "All right, I'm him," he said.

"Then I arrest you for the murder of Muniz Garcia." Gonzalo ordered his men to take the prisoner's weapon.

Surrounded by a dozen guns, Joaquín surrendered his rifle to one soldier while another took his bandolera. Roughly they pushed him into the camp, then told him to lie down. His hands were tied behind his back and jerked tight as the rope was bound around his ankles. Hog-tied like a steer about to be branded, Joaquín watched the soldiers resume their meal as if they had forgotten him.

Wryly he told himself he apparently couldn't imitate Seth's drawl any more than Seth's success. Reasoning that maybe his continual insistence that he was a gringo made his countrymen treat him like an enemy, Joaquín decided that if he finally admitted he was méxicano, someone might help him. "Oye, chico," he called softly in Spanish to a young soldier nearby. "Can you not loosen the ropes so the blood won't be cut from my hands?"

The youth nudged an older man beside him. "El gringo habla español," the boy said with an amused smile.

The man laughed, then called across the fire, "Oye, Colonel, el gringo habla español."

All the soldiers laughed, destroying Joaquín's hope. After a moment the colonel was towering over him. "So, Señor Thorp," Gonzalo said in Spanish, "have you something to tell me?"

"Yo soy Joaquín Ascarate."

"That is the third name you have given. What do you think I should do with a man who lies so easily?"

"I have committed no crime," he said.

"If you are Bob Smith, perhaps you are right." Gonzalo shrugged. "But I do not believe you are Bob Smith. Are you?"

"No," Joaquín said.

"Then you have committed murder, señor. In México, that is a crime."

"Who have I killed?"

"If you are Hector Thorp, I have already told you. If you are Joaquín Ascarate, you killed Hiraldo Fuentes and three of his bandidos. Ordinarily, to kill such men would earn you the gratitude of México, but I have information you did it in the service of another bandido, Rafael Vargas. Is this true?"

"I have never heard of any of those men."

"Have you heard of Lobo Madera?"

"No."

"That is strange, since you were with him in Salsipuedes last night."

"I traveled a short ways with a man. I didn't ask his name."

Gonzalo said nothing.

"Ask Capitán Calero. He will tell you who I am."

"Calero is dead," Gonzalo replied with amusement.

"Are you going to say I killed him too?" Joaquín asked angrily.

"No. He was executed for dealing with bandidos. Perhaps since you knew him, I should assume you are also a bandido, eh?"

"No," Joaquín said.

"It doesn't matter who you are, señor. Tomorrow you, too, will be dead."

"Will you shoot me?" he asked in disbelief.

"I think so, yes." Gonzalo smiled. "Unless, of course, you could lead us to one of the men we have mentioned who is not dead."

"And if I do, then what?"

"You will be alive until we get there. After that, who knows?"

"I can take you to Vargas," he said.

"Not Madera?"

"I don't know where he went."

"That is too bad. I would rather chase one man than ride into a nest of a hundred bandidos, wouldn't you?"

"Yes," he said.

"Well, you think about it, señor. Perhaps by morning you will have remembered the destination of Lobo Madera."

"I cannot remember what I never knew."

Gonzalo smiled. "You have done quite well so far."

"My mind works better when I am not so thirsty."

Gonzalo pretended to ponder. "In my dealings with men," he finally said, "I have found thirst and hunger a great aid to the restoration of memory." Laughing softly, he walked away.

The soldiers sat around their fire, drinking tequila and chatting, sometimes singing along with the gentle music from a guitar. Joaquín couldn't catch anyone's eye. He chided himself for hoping he would receive mercy merely by finally admitting he was a countryman. Apparently, in Mexico, mercy was in short supply. But then again, he *had* lied.

If their positions were reversed and Joaquín, as the sheriff of Tejoe, were striving to stop an outlaw active in his jurisdiction and had caught Gonzalo, who then so obviously lied about what he knew, Joaquín wouldn't cut Gonzalo any slack. In the same circumstances, out in the country without a jail, he would tie his captive as Gonzalo had. Joaquín wouldn't, however, refuse to feed a captive or threaten him with death if he didn't cooperate. He remembered telling Calero that in Mexico the Rurales were bandits. At the time, it had been merely an insult, but now he suspected there truly was no difference between them.

All night Joaquín lay in the dirt listening to the soldiers sleep, though he was always guarded by two who neither slept nor put down their weapons. His back and legs ached and his hands were numb, his tongue thick with thirst and his stomach growling in hunger. By morning he was in agony, and the aromas of coffee and cooking tortillas tortured him further. Finally the young soldier came over and cut him free. Joaquín sat up, rubbing his wrists, unable to feel his hands or feet. The youth returned with a cup of coffee and two tortillas fresh from the fire. Joaquín drank the coffee so fast it burned his tongue, then he ate the tortillas more slowly, watching the soldiers saddle their horses in preparation for departure.

Finally he asked the youth, "¿Como se llama?"

"Jaime Corrales," he answered.

"What will be done with me, Jaime?"

"We will take you to Cabeza de Vaca."

"What is there?" Joaquín asked, dreading the answer.

The young soldier smiled. "Death."

Joaquín remembered what Lourdes had told him about the soldiers being criminals impressed as punishment. Quietly he asked, "Is there no chance, chico, you could help me escape?"

"If I did such a thing," he scoffed, "I would be shot in your place."

"I could take you with me."

"To the United States?"

He nodded. "And reward you for your trouble."

The youth frowned with suspicion. "You have money?"

"Some," Joaquín answered guardedly.

The boy shrugged. "Tal vez. It will take us all day to reach Cabeza de Vaca, traveling north the whole way. I will think about it and let you know."

"Tell no one," Joaquín warned.

The boy laughed as he walked away.

Joaquín's hands were retied behind him before he was helped onto his horse, which had recovered with feed and rest. The horse was led by the chico, but they traveled in the middle of the file of soldiers and so had no opportunity to talk again. All morning they crossed the flat, barren desert. Eventually Joaquín saw a spot of green in the distance, and by midafternoon they reached an oasis where a single cottonwood tree had sunk its roots beside a rocky pool.

He was sequestered under guard in the sun, the meager shade barely sheltering Gonzalo and his chosen favorites. Joaquín noted that Jaime stayed near the colonel, and that Gonzalo often teased the boy in ways which made him blush, though Joaquín was too far away to hear their words. Finally the soldiers rose to depart, but this time Jamie didn't come near. Joaquín decided the youth would help him but was taking care not to arouse suspicion. On this slender thread, he kept his hope alive.

In the thick light of sunset, the troop approached a barren hill of brown dirt crowned with an adobe presidio. Joaquín guessed it must be Cabeza de Vaca. Outside its wall stood a long gallows from which dangled the corpses of four severely decayed men. Joaquín looked away from their gaping wounds torn by vultures who now rested on the crossbeam supporting the remains.

The troop climbed the shoulder of the hill. When a wooden gate in the adobe wall swung open, the soldiers rode into the presidio. Watching Jaime dismount and hurry away, Joaquín felt a sinking certainty that the youth would not help him after all.

Two soldiers took Joaquín off his horse, led him to a cell, and pushed him in. As they cut the rope off his hands, Joaquín could see that the room was five feet square and all dirt. Then the soldiers left and closed the door, shutting out light and air. Flexing his hands to restore circulation, Joaquín sat down to wait. Occasionally he could hear a horse whinny from the yard, but no other sound reached his ears.

In his mind, he saw again the corpses hanging on the gallows, the same number of men he had killed in the mountains, and he wondered if it wasn't justice that he join them. Though the prospect of being left to vultures was not comforting, what he would have to go through before dying disturbed him more. Since he'd first made his decision to follow Seth and live by the gun, Joaquín had thought his death would come quickly with a bullet. He had not anticipated being tortured into submission, and he knew from having been whipped that he would not suffer in silence.

But screaming was one thing, naming names altogether more shameful. Despite the fact that it was Seth's fault he was here, to protect his friend Joaquín now faced hours, perhaps days or even weeks, of agony until death appeared as a blessing. Yet Seth had endured twelve years of torture in prison because of Joaquín. He doubted that at any time in those years of humiliation Seth had ever wished for death. Escape, no doubt, perhaps even retribution for the scars left by the whip, but not death. It was not in him, no matter how vicious life became.

Joaquín felt defeated to be thinking of death as a blessing even before the torture began. He wondered if Seth had survived by nurturing hatred for the man who had finally delivered him to the law, if he himself could survive by nurturing hatred for Seth. By betraying his friend, Joaquín could set himself free. He could lead Gonzalo not only to the bandits' camp in the mountains but also to the cantina in Nogales where the gringo jefe resided. Why shouldn't he? It was his duty as a lawman to cooperate with the law wherever he was. Since Seth had chosen this game, why shouldn't Joaquín play the hand he was dealt?

He remembered his vow to bring Seth to God. Seth had said that was Joaquín's problem, and in truth it was. He had come to Mexico to take Seth home, not to return him to prison or worse. Just as with the trip into the Sierra Madre, what lay before Joaquín now was merely an obstacle to completing his purpose. He must escape Cabeza de Vaca so he could go back to Nogales and try again to save his friend.

For hours, Joaquín sat in the darkness, knowing that by now it was dark outside too. He could neither hear nor see anything in the black void around him. For brief, fitful moments he slept.

Then his hunger and thirst would wake him to a renewal of dread, which he combated with a reassertion of his purpose.

When the door finally opened, he was blinded by bright sunlight. Unable to tell how many soldiers had come for him, he was lifted to his feet and a rope was tied around his wrists again, though this time his hands were in front of him. As the soldiers led him out of the cell and across the glaring white dust of the parade ground, Joaquín blinked his eyes and shook his head, trying to regain his vision.

In the softer light of a room, he was dropped on the floor. When he tried to sit up and focus on his surroundings, a hand came out of nowhere and slapped him back down. He saw only darkness exploding with stars. As he struggled to gather his wits, he felt his boots and socks tugged off, then he heard the men chuckle with pleasure as they found the money in his pocket. When his vision returned, he saw Colonel Gonzalo holding the money as he sat in a chair. Jaime hunkered beside the colonel. They were both smiling. Four other soldiers with grim faces stood between Joaquín and the open door. Joaquín pulled himself to his feet, wavered a moment, then managed to stand erect.

"Do you know where this money comes from?" Gonzalo asked him in a teasing manner.

Joaquín shook his head.

"It is part of a loan from your government to mine. How is it, Señor Thorp, that you carry money belonging to México?"

"Yo soy Joaquín Ascarate," he answered.

Gonzalo nodded at the soldiers. They took hold of Joaquín, one at each arm and one at each foot, and lifted him to sit on a table. As three held him down, the fourth secured his ankles into shackles attached to the table. The man took a key from a nail on the wall and locked the shackles closed, replaced the key, then picked up a club four feet long and three inches thick. Without hesitation he swung the club hard onto the soles of Joaquín's bare feet. The blow convulsed up his spine, knocking the wind from his lungs. Then the pain hit, throbbing with the heat of bruises already swelling with broken vessels. Joaquín groaned and fell back on the table.

After a moment, Gonzalo asked, "Where is the rest of the money?"

"I don't know," Joaquín mumbled. Seeing the soldier raise the club again, he cried, "On the grave of my mother, I am telling the truth!"

The club struck anyway, and this time he grunted with the impact, then shuddered as it reverberated up his spine. When he could listen again, Gonzalo asked calmly, "Who gave you the money?"

"I stole it," Joaquín whispered.

"Obviously," the colonel agreed. "From the people of México."

Joaquín shook his head. "From a man in the mountains."

"What was his name?"

"I don't know."

The club struck again, and this time he screamed as the shock hit his brain.

When he was quiet, Gonzalo said, "We have other, more severe methods, Señor Thorp."

He answered between clenched teeth, "Yo soy Joaquín Ascarate."

"I don't care who you are," Gonzalo replied. "I want to know only one thing: where is the rest of the money?"

"I cannot help you," Joaquín said.

"You should help yourself," Gonzalo replied. He stood up and told the soldiers to light the fire, then he smiled at Joaquín. "When the coals are hot, we will cut off one foot with a machete and burn the stub so you will not bleed to death. After you have regained consciousness, we will ask our questions again. If you still do not answer, we will cut off your other foot." He paused to give time for contemplation. "I will return when the fire is ready."

Joaquín watched him walk out, then looked at Jaime. The youth's eyes were glazed with shock. Though Joaquín said nothing, Jaime whispered, "Who are you to me, señor?" Then he hurried after the colonel.

Joaquín looked at the four soldiers and asked, "Will none of you help me?"

"If we were to do so," one of them said sadly, "your punishment would be done to us."

Joaquín looked at the man laying wood in the oven. "Build the fire slowly, amigo," he said.

The soldiers all laughed.

Encouraged, Joaquín asked, "May I not have some water?"

The man building the fire stood up. "I will ask," he said, walking out and leaving the door open.

The three other soldiers left too, escaping the smoke from the smoldering fire. Joaquín could hear them chatting as they stood nearby but out of sight. They were discussing a baile that had been held the night before in a pueblo called Cuervo. One of the soldiers was teased about losing his horse and having to walk the two miles to the presidio, and how, being so drunk, it was a wonder he could find his way back. The man took the ribbing good-naturedly, saying that by then it was dawn and he merely followed the sun. Joaquín tucked away the information that there was a town two miles west of the presidio.

He sat up, his spine aching with the effort. Uselessly he tugged at the shackles. The bottoms of his feet were bruised black and throbbing with pain. He looked at the key on the nail. It was too far, yet he must try. Bracing his fall as much as he could, he dropped to the floor. His ankles burned as they twisted in the shackles, his feet pulsing with so much pain that he felt himself passing out. He clung to consciousness as he stretched toward the wall, but he could barely touch it with both of his hands still tied together.

The club leaned in a corner. He tried but couldn't reach it. Retreating back close to the table, he flung himself toward the club, again fighting the black edges of unconsciousness as the pain shot through his ankles and ricocheted up his spine. When he had recovered to the point where he could think again, he saw he was a scant increment closer. Again he flung himself at the wall and stretched the full length of his body. This time he was rewarded by the brush of his fingertips against the wood, enough to make the club topple toward him. Hungrily he grasped it, then dragged himself back to the wall, reaching up with the tip of the club to catch the bottom of the key. Gently he pushed until the key fell free of the nail. He let go of the club and caught the key.

Jerking into a sitting position, he fumbled to unlock the shackles. His hands were shaking so badly from the stress on his body that he was clumsy and slow. When he had one foot free, he lifted it carefully to the floor, then let it lay like a seemingly useless stump as he unlocked the other. Now he faced the agony of standing up. He knew he must achieve it in silence or the guards would return. Once on his feet, he must make it out the door and far enough ahead of them that they would shoot rather than chase him. Even shot, he must keep moving so they would shoot again to kill rather than return him to torture.

With his hands on the table, Joaquín pulled himself to stand up. Steeling himself, he shifted his full weight onto his legs, commanding his mind to ignore the pain. It was enough that his feet were still there. However much they complained, they must carry him. He picked up the club and used it for a crutch as he hobbled as quietly as he could toward the door.

Still concealed in the shadowed room, he looked through the doorway to the bright glare of the parade ground. Soldiers were moving toward the gate, which was slowly swinging open. Even his guards walked languidly into the sun to see who had arrived. Joaquín hobbled out the door, watching the soldiers who were watching the gate. He eased around the corner of the building, then dropped the club and ran for the wall.

Each stride was like stepping on fire, like a rack wrenching the length of his spine, a hammer pounding the nape of his neck. The wall was adobe, the mortar between the bricks providing a ladder of crevices dug by weather. Using his toes and his fingers, he crawled up and swung his leg in an arc of agony over the top.

Glancing back, Joaquín saw another prisoner being led through the gate to the torture of Cabeza de Vaca. His hands were tied behind his back and he was hatless beneath the pitiless sun, his mouth already bloodied. Across the field of glaring dust and heedless soldiers, the captive on the horse saw the escapee on the wall. In the gray eyes of Lobo Madera, Joaquín read a just demand for freedom.

17

★

Joaquín dropped down the far side of the wall, nearly passing out as his feet hit the ground. But he had no time for such weakness. In moments the soldiers would discover him gone. He ran, without even the aid of the club now, torturing his wounded feet.

Heading west toward the pueblo of Cuervo, he didn't look back. At each stride he expected a bullet to stop him, but none came. When he crested a slight rise in the earth, he slid down the other side and waited, straining his ears for sounds of pursuit. Hearing nothing, he crawled on, sparing his feet at the expense of his hands and knees accumulating cactus barbs. Now he was six points of agony connected by a throbbing chain of spine, every link of which shrieked with complaint. He kept moving, not bothering to avoid the cactus in his way as he scurried toward the pueblo of Cuervo.

The soldier had said it was two miles to the west, but whether straight, north or southwest, Joaquín didn't know. He dropped onto his belly to catch his breath and calm his heart as he surveyed the sky ahead, searching for a telltale wisp of chimney smoke. The desert was hot in midafternoon. No one was cooking, and the sky was clear.

The ground was cut by shallow depressions between low hills, and he could see nothing except more desert. Even if he found the town, he would have to steal what he needed. Water for certain. If he was extremely lucky, a horse. He could not ask anyone for help. The town existed because of the garrison and would not betray its provider. It would also be the first place searched by the soldiers. Joaquín had no desire to repeat his mistake with Jaime; he had been a fool to think the boy would commit treason to help a stranger.

Joaquín crawled on. As the hours passed and his agony increased, he began looking back over his life for the wrong he had committed that led to this punishment. Had it been when he surrendered Seth to the Texas Rangers, or when he accepted the job as sheriff, a position he was only qualified for because of the skills Seth had taught him? Or the moment he severed their partnership and decided to stand on his own? Or way back when he'd abandoned the priesthood to follow Seth in the first place?

Joaquín longed to return to that moment. If he hadn't stopped in El Paso on his journey north, he would never have met Seth. Joaquín's intention had been to follow the river north to Santa Fe. In the city named Holy Faith, he could have found his life in the church and would not now be facing death in the desert without even the comfort of absolution from a priest. He wouldn't be crawling on his hands and knees with his tongue hanging out like a dog's, his body weak from hunger, wracked by torture, knowing if he made good his escape it would be only to return to save the son of the man who was responsible for his being here at all. In the destitution of such thoughts, Joaquín collapsed with despair and fell into the oblivion of sleep.

When he awoke it was dark and there was no reflection of firelight anywhere in the sky. He had missed the pueblo. Thirty-six hours had passed since he tasted water, another twelve since he had eaten two tortillas with coffee. The thought of that meager meal was like a dream of a banquet.

His hands were covered with the stubs of thorns whose points were driven deep into his flesh. His knees were the same, both protected and aggravated by his trousers, which were snagged with invisible barbs. He decided to walk, the torture between the two methods of movement being equal. When the moon rose, he found a road. Its hard-packed surface was free of cactus and his suffering was slightly alleviated as he followed the long ribbon of distance stretching north. He knew he must find shelter before the sun rose; without help, he would die of thirst or hunger. But he carried neither money to buy assistance nor weapons to demand it, and he had learned that to beg mercy from his countrymen was to ask for betrayal.

Suddenly in the distance he heard the bawl of a cow, long and plaintive. He stopped and listened, trying to pinpoint its location. When he heard the bawl again, he turned toward the east, back toward the presidio and danger. Yet also life. A cow meant blood to drink and flesh to eat, if he could kill it. He staggered off the road and into the cactus again, following the sound. In a moment he heard another cow, then several more, and he realized he was approaching a herd. A herd meant vaqueros. Food and water. Horses. Guns. Survival. He stumbled on until he crested a low rise in the land. In the light of the moon he saw maybe fifty cows bedded down around a windmill, a vaquero riding circle, a chuck wagon off to one side, and beyond it, in a corral of lariats laced between cactus: a remuda of horses.

Joaquín felt too weak to catch a horse or even have the cunning to pilfer food or water. There remained nothing but to surrender himself to the good will of the vaqueros. If they betrayed him, he would die rather than return as a prisoner to the presidio. Stumbling toward the wagon, he wondered who he should say he was. Since lies had gained him nothing, he decided to tell the truth.

An old man was just lighting his lantern to begin breakfast. On the ground were several soogans of the sleeping crew.

"Perdoneme," Joaquín whispered.

The old man looked over his shoulder, then slowly turned and asked in a low voice, "¿Quién es?"

"Soy Joaquín Ascarate. I am americano and have escaped from the Rurales who whipped and beat me. Ayudame, por favor."

"Valgame Dios," the old man answered. "Come into the wagon."

Joaquín approached, hobbling on his swollen feet.

Seeing Joaquín's condition, the old man stepped forward and assisted him into the wagon. "I will bring you some milk," the viejo said, walking away.

Joaquín fell back on the blankets. He waited and listened, hearing only the cattle and a clank of a bucket. After a while, the old man returned and extended a cup. "Gracias," Joaquín said, sitting up and drinking the thick, warm milk.

"Later I will bring more," the viejo said. "Now you should sleep. Try to be quiet and no one will discover you. But even if they do, none of us will send you back."

"Gracias," Joaquín said again. "I will be quiet."

The old man smiled sadly. "It is sometimes difficult after being the guest of Rurales to sleep quietly, mí hijo." He dropped down and went back to work.

Joaquín took comfort from the old man having called him his son. That was a tie of kinship Joaquín had never known. Once there had been a time he wished he were Seth's son. He'd even gone so far as to ask Seth if he'd ever been in Mexico City. Seth hadn't. He was only fourteen years older than Joaquín, and at fourteen Seth had still been living with his family in Texas. So the connection between them had nothing to do with blood, yet its strength couldn't be denied.

Now Seth's son was held prisoner at Cabeza de Vaca, and it fell on Joaquín to free him. The justice of that went beyond Joaquín's responsibility for Seth's imprisonment. In truth, he had been merely the instrument of that happening; Seth had been imprisoned for crimes committed before they met. But the future of their friendship depended on Lobo's release. Maybe for no other reason than that Seth had only taken Lobo from his mother because of Joaquín's promise to help raise the boy. Abandoning him to the Rurales certainly wasn't doing that. As he listened to the viejo building the fire outside the wagon, the smell of burning wood made Joaquín moan as he drifted off to sleep.

He awoke to the soft strums of a guitar. The sky was dark again, and through the canvas he could see the glow of the campfire a short distance away. He started to crawl to the end of the wagon, but the cactus barbs in his hands and knees made him jerk his weight off them. As he sat in the wagon, looking out at the bleak desert illuminated so beautifully by the starlight, he heard the guitarist begin to sing.

His melody was sad, the lyrics heartrending with loss and longing. Sheltered inside the wagon, Joaquín surrendered to the grief of the song, which was so sweet it drained all bitterness from mourning, leaving only a profound melancholy. He thought of his wife and child waiting for his return, and of Seth's wife and children who also waited with hope, while he listened to the vaquero sing of yearning for all those things that made life beautiful. It was a song Joaquín had heard in his youth, an ancient ballad once sung by the conquistadores of Cortez when they longed for home. Joaquín remembered his mother strumming a guitar and singing the song softly as he lay in the bed of his childhood, her voice coming through the open window, carried on the breeze of innocence. When she had sung that song, she was only twenty and he six. Ten years later she died from a disease earned in a brothel. By then she was no longer beautiful, and he had not been a child.

Hearing the song again, Joaquín longed for a power to subsume himself beneath: a jefe to follow without question, a monsignor to obey without doubt. He had neither. "How far I am from my dreams," the vaquero sang. "I live without light or love, wishing for the death of my feelings." As the chords of the song died into a silence broken only by the fire fluttering in the wind, Joaquín remembered that Lobo was imprisoned at Cabeza de Vaca. Though there was no one to command or assist him, Joaquín knew it was a compensation he must make.

He heard the vaqueros talking around the fire. One of them said, "I will guide him to the border. We can do that much for him."

"Sí," the viejo answered. "He has been whipped and his feet beaten. I think he has had enough of Mexico."

"You should go tonight, Jesús," another man said. "Tomorrow the Rurales will come looking for him."

Joaquín slid down from the back of the wagon, feeling the shock as his feet hit the dirt. He hobbled toward the fire and looked at the three men watching him. Managing a smile, he said, "Buenas noches."

"Come, sit down," the viejo said, laying his leatherwork aside and rising to help.

"You are good to me," Joaquín murmured as he let himself be assisted onto the ground, where he sat with his aching feet extended toward the fire.

"Ay, cabrón," the guitarist growled. "The Rurales blacked your feet good, hombre."

Joaquín nodded, then smiled at the old man offering him a plate of supper. The viejo also gave him a goatskin bag of water, and Joaquín drank deeply, then wiped his mouth with the back of his hand, meeting the eyes of the viejo's companions. They were in their early twenties, lean and bronzed by the sun, wearing humble clothes. "You are all good," Joaquín said, "to take me into your camp."

The guitarist shrugged. "Terrazas owns our labor but not our hearts, señor."

"Who is Terrazas?" Joaquín asked, carefully lifting the spoon with his prickly fingers.

"This is his ranch," the viejo answered. He had resumed his work and was stitching thick pieces of leather together with a huge needle, pushing it through with his calloused thumb.

"Sparse land on which to raise cattle," Joaquín said around a mouthful of shredded beef.

"He has much land," the viejo replied. "And other ventures besides ranching. He also owns Cabeza de Vaca and allows the Rurales to use it in exchange for protection."

"He would not like you helping me," Joaquín said.

The viejo smiled. "Since he will never know, it will worry neither him nor us, and should not concern you."

"Muchas gracias," Joaquín said, looking at each of them again. "I am in your debt."

"Perhaps someday we will come to your home fleeing your law, and you will help us," one of the young men said with a laugh.

Joaquín decided against telling them that at home he was the law. Laying his empty plate aside, he asked, "Which of you is Jesús?"

"I am," the one who had laughed said.

Joaquín smiled with melancholy. "I heard you say you would take me to the border. I am honored that you would risk an act against Terrazas for my sake, but I must go back to Cabeza de Vaca for a friend."

The silence was broken only by the crackling of the fire.

"Is it possible, amigos," Joaquín requested humbly, "that you loan me two horses? I will repay you. I have no money now, but when I am home I will send two fine horses in return."

"No one escapes Cabeza de Vaca," Jesús scoffed.

"I have already done so," Joaquín said.

The old man smiled. "You must have been blessed with a miracle from God."

"Then I will hope for another miracle. I cannot abandon my friend."

"You will succeed only in joining him on the gallows," Jesús warned.

Joaquín shrugged. "I would prefer that to letting him face it alone. He is young, and the son of a man to whom I owe much."

The musician picked up his guitar again and began to strum soft, sad chords. No one spoke for a long time. Finally Joaquín asked the old man, "What are you making?"

"Boots," he said, "so you won't return across the desert barefoot."

Joaquín was astounded at their generosity. "How can I repay your kindness?"

"You already have," the viejo answered. "You have given us an opportunity to defy the hacendado who keeps us in poverty. Only at such times can we know what it is to be a man. We are the ones in your debt."

"Why is everyone in México enslaved?" Joaquín complained impatiently. "Can you not rise up and take the power for yourselves?"

"We have no weapons," the viejo explained. "And no money to buy them. They have an army. But revolution is stirring in the countryside, and before long we will drive the gachupínes back to Spain. Then México will belong to the pobres."

Joaquín remembered Lourdes, the girl in the cantina, and how her eyes had shone with dreams of such justice. The old man's eyes gleamed with the same hope. "I wish you the grace of God," Joaquín said.

"And we wish it for you," he replied. "Though I doubt that even God would risk the dangers of Cabeza de Vaca."

"He would do so for his Son," Joaquín said.

Jesús laughed. "He did not save my namesake from crucifixion. Why do you think he will save you?"

"I have no reason to think so," Joaquín said. "But I must try."

"Tomorrow we stay by the water," Jesús said with a smile. "The next day we drive the herd south. If you should succeed in escaping a second time, you can follow our trail back here and the soldiers will be unable to track you. If you ride hard, four hours straight north is the town of Palomas. The border is unguarded at night."

"Gracias," Joaquín answered, again touched by their generosity. "I should go now. My friend has probably already suffered much."

"Wait until I finish," the old man said. "I have always heard that desperados like to die with their boots on."

"You should let me go with you," Jesús said. "I can enter the presidio without question and learn where they are keeping your friend."

Joaquín studied him. "Is it not dangerous for you?"

Jesús shook his head. "Terrazas owns all this land, and I work for Terrazas. There are many reasons I would visit la Cabeza."

"Such as?" Joaquín asked.

Jesús grinned at the old man. "He is suspicious, no?" Then he laughed. "I could deliver a beef for the soldiers to eat. Usually we would do it as we move south, but they will not mind that I bring it early." He looked at the old man again. "Perhaps that is a good plan, eh, Sebastiano? They will butcher the steer and drink much tequila while they smell it cooking." Jesús smiled at Joaquín. "It is perhaps your best chance to go in and out undetected, though la Cabeza is never unguarded."

Joaquín considered the plan as he watched the old man diligently sewing, then he studied Jesús a long moment before asking, "What happens if they make the connection between your early delivery and the escape of the prisoner?"

Now it was Jesús who studied Joaquín. "Is your friend the son of a gringo?"

"Sí," he said.

"Will he not reward me for helping his son?"

"Handsomely," Joaquín said.

"I will go to the United States, Sebastiano," Jesús announced. "With this reward, I will pay your debt to Terrazas. Then we both will be free."

"That sounds like a good plan," the old man predicted, "except that you will be supper for the buzzards at la Cabeza."

Jesús laughed. "We will have a miracle on our side." He stood up, smiling at Joaquín. "Will you accept my help?"

Joaquín pulled himself painfully to his feet. "With honor, amigo," he said, extending his hand. They shook solemnly.

"I will ready the horses," Jesús said, "while Sebastiano finishes your boots."

Joaquín watched him walk toward the remuda, then he looked at the musician gently strumming his guitar. "You will not betray us?" he asked the man.

He shook his head. "The day after tomorrow, when we drive the herd past la Cabeza and I see you and Jesús hanging from the gallows, I will say a prayer for your souls."

Joaquín sat back down, watching the old man working his needle. Softly he asked, "Am I wrong to accept the help of Jesús?"

Sebastiano sighed. "If by the grace of God you succeed, you will have saved not only the son of your friend, but also Jesús. However, if you fail, the death of Jesús will be on your soul. I am close to the end of my life and would not want the death of another on my soul. Perhaps your soul is clean enough, and your purpose pure enough, that such a stain will not tarnish you before God. I do not know you and cannot say, therefore I will not advise you to attempt something which requires a miracle."

"Will you pray for us?" Joaquín asked.

The old man's eyes were bright with fervor. "Sí," he answered. "I will pray for your success, and also, failing such grace, I will pray that your death be quick." He tossed the boot across to Joaquín. "Try it on, mí hijo. The leather is thin and will not last long, but perhaps long enough, eh?"

More a moccasin than a boot, it was only ankle high, a soft piece of leather sewn to four thicknesses of sole. Joaquín tugged it over his swollen foot, grimacing at the pain. "Perfecto," he said to the old man.

"I measured your feet while you were sleeping," he answered modestly.

Jesús returned leading three horses. One was saddled, the other two had only bridles. "If we are caught," he said with a grin, "we will be flogged as horse thieves."

"I will not be taken alive," Joaquín warned, tugging on the other boot. "If I had not escaped, they would have cut off my feet. There is no life for a man without feet."

"Es cierto," Sebastiano agreed, "but they would not have left you alive to worry about it."

"In such a case," Joaquín said, standing up. "I would prefer to die not only wearing boots, but also with feet." He leaned down to shake the viejo's hand. "Gracias por todo," he said.

"De nada." Sebastiano smiled. "Vaya con Dios."

Jesús swung onto the saddled horse, then caught the reins of another. "Expect your freedom within a month, viejo."

He shrugged. "To hear you have escaped will be reward enough."

"Then for once in your life," Jesús said, "you will have more than enough."

The musician played a song from the corrida, a triumphal march heralding the entrance of the picadors into the arena. Joaquín and Jesús laughed as they rode into the darkness accompanied by such a grandiose serenade.

18

The steer bawled as it was driven along, unhappy at being separated from the herd. Its complaints became more melancholy as the distance increased, and Joaquín suspected the animal knew it was being driven to slaughter.

He looked across at Jesús. "Have we no guns?"

Jesús shook his head. "They are very expensive. I have a friend who owns one and would loan it to me, but he lives far from here."

"At least you have a knife," Joaquín said, looking with envy at the sheath on the vaquero's belt.

"I also have a machete." Jesús grinned. "Which would you prefer?"

"The knife," Joaquín answered.

Jesús handed it over with a smile. "A machete is more deadly."

"If you know how to use it," Joaquín agreed. "I am experienced with a knife but have never held a machete."

"Never held a machete? What kind of méxicano are you?"

"A soft one," Joaquín admitted. "Compared to what I have gone through here, my life in the United States was easy."

"Then you will go home much more brave, no?" Jesús teased. "And much more man also. So your visit will have been worthwhile, verdad?"

"If I live to look back on it, perhaps I will be able to think so. Now I would rather not answer that question."

Jesús laughed with understanding. "How did you come to be here?"

"I was sent by a friend to do an errand," Joaquín said dryly.

"Did you do it?"

"Half of it." He hesitated, then decided Jesús had a right to know. "I delivered guns to bandits in the mountains. I was to return the money to the border, but I lost it to this boy we are going to rescue."

Jesús thought about that, watching the steer on the trail ahead. Finally he said, "If the boy had the money when he was arrested, you will not retrieve it, amigo."

"I no longer care about the money," Joaquín said.

Jesús smiled. "Only saving a boy who robbed you?"

"It is a debt I owe his father."

"If I am to discover where they are keeping him, it would help to know his name."

"Lobo Madera."

Jesús stared at him hard. "The gringo who rides with Vargas?"

"You have heard of him?"

"Ah sí. Everyone in el norte de México has heard of him. His father is——" He stopped and looked at Joaquín, then smiled shyly. "But you know his father."

Joaquín nodded.

Jesús laughed softly. "Ay, Madre de Dios. In one moment I have ceased to be a humble vaquero and become a bandit with the best. This is good, Joaquín. Even if I die, I will be remembered as muy macho."

"And that pleases you?" he asked sadly.

"It is everything," Jesús announced.

They rode on in silence, each contemplating what lay before them. In the rosy light of dawn, Jesús stopped and pointed out a jacal in the distance. "No one lives there, hombre. Stay in the shade and wait for me."

"What if the Rurales come and search it?" Joaquín asked, not liking his chances of escaping the small hut in the middle of a flat plain.

"If they were looking for you, they would already have searched it." Jesús unwound the strap of a goatskin waterbag from his saddlehorn and handed it over along with the reins to the extra horse. "La Cabeza is only a short way ahead. I will return as soon as I've learned where our friend is."

Joaquín watched him ride away, herding the now submissive steer. He waited until Jesús was only a speck in the distance, then he reined around and searched the terrain for any pocket of concealment. Finding a depression in the land, he tied the horses to a creosote bush and walked into the desert, making a circle all around to be certain his hideout was secure. Then he returned to the horses and squatted in their shade to wait.

Joaquín wanted to trust Jesús, but experience told him it was unlikely the vaquero would take a risk to help a stranger. Perhaps now that Jesús knew who he was helping and could guess the amount of money involved, he would choose to help the Rurales instead. If so, they wouldn't come looking but would wait for Jesús to deliver Joaquín to the presidio. Even if Jesús didn't betray him, Joaquín knew the Rurales could stumble across his hideout, and he was taking no chances at being captured alive. Inside the jacal, flight would be impossible. In the open, he could run.

So he waited, following the shade of the horses who stood with lowered heads, enduring the heat. He sipped at the water, reserving as much as he could for later. The wind rustled the leaves on the creosote bush, flies buzzed, ravens cried from far away; otherwise there were only the sounds of the two horses sighing, shifting their weight, shuffling their bits. Slowly the sun moved across the white sky. It was bumping against the western mountains when he heard a horse near the jacal.

Carefully he eased up over the rise in the land and stared across the distance. Jesús was there. They saw each other at the same moment, and the Mexican gave such a spontaneous grin that Joaquín's trust in him increased. Jesús was a young man of honor who wished to die muy macho. Knowing that could not be achieved by betraying a friend, Joaquín let himself smile back.

Jesús trotted his horse over, reined up and studied the horses below, then laughed as he met Joaquín's eyes. "You are wary as a coyote, amigo. I will try to remember the thousand ways you anticipate trouble so that I myself will always be ready."

Joaquín shrugged. "I have learned to dislike surprises. What of Lobo?"

Jesús' face saddened. "He is tied at the flogging post, Joaquín. His back is bloody and they give him no water. When he is lucky, he is unconscious."

Joaquín remembered too well how that felt, but all he said was, "He will be no help to us then."

Jesús smiled. "His boots are still on. At least he can walk."

"Will they put him inside tonight?"

"I think not. Colonel Gonzalo left orders to keep him there until he returned. He was called to Tonichi in pursuit of Vargas, who raided the Terrazas cattle. Gonzalo took twenty Rurales with him, but there are still twenty at la Cabeza. They will have a fiesta tonight and barbecue the steer. Already they have started drinking. You should come back with me."

"Just ride in through the gate?" Joaquín asked, suspicious again.

"Sí. No one will recognize you."

"Four men helped torture me," he scoffed.

"They are dead, amigo," Jesús said sadly. "Gonzalo executed them for failing their duty."

Joaquín stared at him, not wanting to believe it.

"You will see them on the gallows as we pass," Jesús said. "The soldiers who were with Gonzalo when you were captured have all ridden out again. He deliberately took men who could recognize you, promising if you are not recaptured, they will all be flogged."

Joaquín turned away. Now he had killed not only the bandits in the mountains but had also caused the execution of four soldiers who were merely doing their duty. Nearly every act he took in Mexico resulted in death, and he was beginning to understand why his countrymen treated it so disrespectfully. Remembering Magdalena's joke—the bull is driven into the arena and tortured to death. Such is life, no? —he realized it wasn't the matador who stood for man in the minds of Mexicans, it was the bull who could never win. Even if he killed the matador, the bull would still be slaughtered for meat.

Hearing again the guitar's fanfare as he and Jesús left on their mission, Joaquín untied his reins and leapt to the back of his horse. "I am ready," he said.

"We will leave the extra horse in the jacal," Jesús said, reining toward it. "I will say you are my cousin who now works for Terrazas, and that you slipped away from the herd to join the fiesta. You must pretend to be happy, Joaquín. To a vaquero, a fiesta is a treat he would risk flogging to enjoy."

"We are risking more than that," he answered.

Jesús grinned. "All the more reason to laugh. This may be our last fiesta."

At the jacal, Joaquín let the extra horse drink from his hat, gave the goatskin to Jesús to tie to his saddle again, then left the horse inside the hut as they rode away.

"When we cross that rise," Jesús said, pointing with his chin, "the sentry will see us. We should joke and laugh or they will suspect we have come for a more serious purpose."

"I understand," Joaquín said.

Upon cresting the hill, however, the first thing he saw was the gallows. Four fresh corpses dangled from the crossbeam, each missing a foot. Joaquín felt a surge of vomit fill his throat. He turned his head and spat violently into the dirt.

As if he'd told a joke, Jesús laughed. When they stopped outside the gate, he laughed again, looking at the gallows, and said, "They will not be walking far, eh?"

"Not unless they have powerful third legs," Joaquín managed to quip.

Jesús guffawed at the joke. "Sí, hombre, they will walk at least in bed, no?"

"I would hate to see the woman who would invite them into her bed," Joaquín said, studying the sentries.

"I hope not too much," Jesús said as the gate slowly swung open. "There will be such women at the fiesta. All they see is a man's money, and for most of them I doubt if they would care if the man was alive or not."

Joaquín watched the sentries laugh as he and Jesús rode into the presidio.

The courtyard was already shadowed with dusk, the steer butchered and broiling over a pit. Across the yard, in the corner near where Joaquín had climbed the wall, was the flogging post holding Lobo. His shirt hung in tatters from the bloody welts on his back crawling with flies, and his weight was supported by his shackled wrists, his feet crooked on the ground. Unless something could be done to revive him, he would have to be helped not only from the post but onto the horse and as well. Joaquín quickly jerked his eyes away, lest someone notice his interest in the prisoner.

Jesús led Joaquín into the stable and introduced him as José Salvador, his cousin from Tamaulipas. Tending the horses, the newly christened José listened to Jesús and the hostler discuss which of the whores from Cuervo would be best, and whether the pleasure of enjoying her charms was worth standing in line. Jesús held out for the quick move and a speedy return to the company of men. When the hostler argued that only men were in line, Jesús replied that their thoughts were on the woman so it was the same as if she were with them. Looking at Joaquín, the hostler asked, "What does your cousin say, eh?"

"I am married," Joaquín said without thinking, "and true to my wife."

The hostler's smile was snide. "Are you certain she's true to you?"

"Verdad," Joaquín said, taking affront.

Jesús clapped him on the shoulder and grinned at the hostler. "He is recently married. Do not shake his faith."

The hostler snickered. "He will lose it soon enough. What is your wife's name? Probably I have heard of her."

"Cielo Tapia," he said.

"From what pueblo?"

"Tejos," he said, not mentioning that it was in Arizona.

The hostler frowned. "I have never heard of it."

"It is a pueblito in Tamaulipas," Jesús was quick to say. "The people who live over the next hill have never heard of it."

The hostler laughed. "Hasta luego, eh?"

Joaquín followed Jesús onto the parade ground. Torches had been lit at intervals along the roof of the portal. The flames fluttered in the wind to light the ground between weirdly dancing bat wings of shadow. Glancing at Lobo, Joaquín saw that the kid was standing on his feet now.

Two soldiers called greetings to Jesús. He led Joaquín over and accepted the tequila one offered. As they passed the bottle around the circle, the discussion again revolved around which whore was best. Joaquín swallowed only small sips of the tequila. Even so the raw liquor burned his stomach and lightened his head. Watching the soldiers quickly empty the bottle, he thought with any luck the entire presidio would be in a drunken stupor by midnight.

He scanned the portal for officers. Though he saw none, he didn't suppose Cabeza de Vaca went ungoverned without Colonel Gonzalo. The soldier tossed the empty bottle into the dust and pro-

duced another from his pocket. As Joaquín was lifting the new one
to his mouth, he casually asked, "Who is jefe here in Gonzalo's absence?"

"Capitán Robles," the soldier said.

Joaquín passed the bottle to Jesús. "Perhaps the capitán would
like some tequila," Joaquín said.

"Robles doesn't drink," the soldier answered. "But I know who
would: the unfortunate hombre at the post, eh?"

"No doubt," Joaquín said, following the man's gaze to Lobo
tugging uselessly at his shackles.

"See how he struggles," the soldier said sadly. "But it is right
that he do so. Tomorrow he dies."

Jesús laughed. "To live is to struggle, eh?"

The second soldier frowned as he stared at Lobo, then he handed
the bottle to his friend and announced, "I will take him some
water."

"It is against orders," the first soldier said quickly.

"I will do it," Joaquín said. "I am under no one's orders."

The first soldier grunted. "You will be if you take him water."

Joaquín met the first soldier's eyes, then the eyes of the second.
"Is that why you are Rurales, because you disobeyed an order unknown to you?"

They both stood up straighter and adjusted their uniforms.
"We are Rurales so we may eat," the first one said. "And our families eat, and their families also. All of our cousins and the children
of our cousins eat because we are Rurales."

Jesús snickered. "When were you last paid?"

They both looked at him harshly. "When we are paid," the second soldier said, "it is five times what you are paid as a vaquero."

Jesús shrugged. "This is true, but I am still paying the debt of
my grandfather, so I work for nothing. Do you work for five times
nothing, amigos?"

They stared at him, then both laughed. "Seguro," one said. "We
work for exactly that." They all laughed, even Joaquín.

A few minutes later, the women arrived. They came in a two-wheeled cart, the wheels solid disks of wood painted in gaily colored concentric circles. Their dresses were no less vibrant. Tiered skirts of fiery orange, lime green, magenta, scarlet, and royal blue, off-the-shoulder blouses over naked bosoms, their long dark hair shining like obsidian in the torchlight. As the soldiers all walked to the middle of the compound to greet them, the women danced on the cart, swirling their skirts high as they laughed insults to the soldiers' manhood.

Joaquín looked down at the empty tequila bottle lying in the dust. Glancing around, he saw that all eyes were on the women, so he retrieved the bottle and carried it over to the water trough, immersed the bottle and listened to its gurgling as he studied the perimeter of the compound. Only one room was lit from within, probably the office of Capitán Robles. Apparently the jefe was content to let his soldiers enjoy their revelry; no doubt the post was a difficult duty and pleasure scarce. Joaquín carried the bottle of water as he walked beneath the shadowed portals toward the prisoner.

As he passed the room where he had been tortured, Joaquín shuddered. Then he remembered the four soldiers on the gallows, all missing a foot. Even the one who had gone to request permission to give him water had been blamed for his escape. The cruelty of Colonel Gonzalo to sever the feet of men he intended to execute was beyond Joaquín's comprehension. He could understand that a government built on slavery would elevate sadists to leadership, but he could not understand what allowed a man to betray his own humanity so severely. It was as if Gonzalo lusted for death. More than death: for a long lament of dying, as if each cry torn from his victim's throat fed his pleasure.

Joaquín remembered Rico saying Seth killed to keep death away from himself, as if by dealing it he could control it. Even as Joaquín felt astonished at her statement, he had recognized its truth, and also that Seth's setting himself up as an equal of death was what gave him the potency Joaquín had admired since they first met. To suffer beneath Seth was to wrestle with the core of what it meant to be a man. To suffer beneath Colonel Gonzalo was to be a helpless creature in the hands of a brute.

Seeing the mangled flesh of Lobo's back, Joaquín was struck with a sudden understanding of what Seth felt when taking revenge on men who had wronged him. During one of their many discussions, Seth had justified having killed a man because the man was evil. At the time, Joaquín thought Seth was absolving himself with an arrogant assumption of superiority. But now, seeing the humiliation in Lobo's eyes, Joaquín understood that Seth may have been right. Colonel Gonzalo not only wronged his prisoners by torturing them and his soldiers by commanding their participation, he wronged every shred of decency humanity could claim. That made him evil and deserving of vengeance.

Holding the water to Lobo's mouth and helping him drink, Joaquín tried to give the kid an encouraging smile.

Lobo spat the water back out. "I was expecting tequila," he accused.

Joaquín laughed. "Drink it, cabrón," he said, proffering the bottle again. "You will need your strength."

Lobo swallowed huge mouthfuls and would have drained the bottle, but Joaquín took it away from him, then surveyed the soldiers still watching the women dance on the wagon. A band had come with them, two guitarists and a fiddler. They sat on the seat of the wagon while the driver held the heads of the horses within the frenzy of shouting men. After a few discordant tuning chords, the musicians broke into a lively fandango for the women to dance to. A cheer went up from the crowd, and the men began bidding for the privilege of being first with each woman.

Joaquín looked back at Lobo and said, "When everyone is well fucked, well fed, and well drunk, we will cut you down."

"Better find an axe," Lobo mumbled.

Joaquín looked at the steel shackles. "Who has the key?"

"One of them." Lobo sighed, resting his forehead against the post.

"Hold yourself together," Joaquín whispered. "Only a few more hours and we will be free or dead."

"I'll take either one," Lobo answered.

"Tomorrow," Joaquín said, "you will be glad you are alive."

Lobo's gray eyes were more humble than Joaquín cared to see. "I'm sorry I took the money," Lobo said.

Joaquín shrugged. "I suppose the Rurales have it now."

Lobo shook his head. "I waited until you left, then went back to Salsipuedes and gave it to Lourdes."

"Why not Felicidad?" Joaquín asked with surprise.

Lobo managed to smile. "She's a whore. Lourdes is a revolutionary."

From the distance, the soldiers laughed, shouting insults at the women, who returned them with vigor. "Do you mean," Joaquín asked, "that you really gave it to her, not left it with her?"

"I'm not sure," Lobo answered with a wry smile, "but if I get out of this, I ain't going back for it. Are you?"

Joaquín shook his head. "I will feel fortunate to cross the border in one piece."

Lobo nodded. "Guess that's why they call it Salsipuedes, huh?"

Joaquín grunted. "This whole country should be called that. I cannot understand it, Lobo. México is my country, in some sense all these men are my kin, yet I cannot understand how they tolerate this life. If I lived here, I would rise up against the gachupínes and kill them all, even if I myself died doing it." He sighed. "No, I would not. I would be like Jesús, working hard and finding fun where I could, maybe taking a chance for freedom when it came, maybe waiting like Sebastiano for someone to find it for me. You don't know them. Sebastiano is an old man who took me in and made these boots." He chuckled. "They are not much, but then again they are the best boots I have ever owned. Jesús is here with me now. He promised to buy Sebastiano's freedom with the reward

Seth will pay for your return." Joaquín sighed again. "When we go back without the money, I wonder what Seth will say to me. Can you imagine his eyes, Lobo? How cold they will be, how they will judge me short for having failed. Perhaps they will glimmer with a remnant of the love we once shared, and perhaps because of that he will stop Fierro and Ryan from killing me, but Seth will never again honor me with his friendship. I know now why he sent me here. He did the same as I to him, he sent me home to pay the price. The price is high, Lobo. It hurts too much even to look at it." Joaquín turned to meet the eyes of the kid at the whipping post, who would surely understand, but Lobo had fainted.

Returning to the trough, Joaquín filled the empty tequila bottle with water again. The men who had won the bidding for the women lifted their prizes to the ground, led them toward the barracks, and disappeared. Outside each of their doors, a cue formed. Tequila passed up and down the lines, the beef sizzled over the coals, the moon rose and moved slowly across the sky.

Joaquín sat under the portal watching the comandante's office, intending to try to steal the key to Lobo's shackles when the light was extinguished. Jesús had disappeared, and that worried Joaquín until he saw the vaquero come out of the barracks. He had been one of the winners of the women. Joaquín shook his head in amazement as Jesús walked over grinning.

Joaquín laughed. "How much did she cost you?"

"I offered great wealth and delivered only promises," Jesús answered. "She was content."

Joaquín smiled. "You must have power in bed."

"Nothing is sweeter to a woman than words," Jesús gloated, dropping onto the bench beside Joaquín. "But, in truth, she is my cousin and fond of me. Have you made a plan for freeing Lobo?"

"I was hoping to get the key to the shackles from the comandante's oficina," Joaquín said.

Jesús looked at the lighted window. "Robles sleeps there. It is impossible." Watching the soldiers dance among themselves to the music, he said, "Pass me the bottle." He accepted it and took a deep swig of the water, then spat it back out, turning offended eyes on Joaquín. "I thought it was tequila."

Joaquín smiled. "Perhaps we can break the chain on the shackles with an axe."

Jesús took another sip and passed the bottle back. "I can do that," he said.

"Are you certain?"

"I've done it before." He smiled. "You are not the first desperado who stumbled across us in the desert. One man was wearing shackles, and I broke them."

"Do you know where to find an axe?"

Jesús nodded. "The woodpile."

" 'Sta bien," Joaquín said. "Once we have Lobo free, we can push him over the wall, though I hope he doesn't break his neck when he falls on the other side."

"We should take him through the gate on our horses," Jesús said. "We can wait until the women leave, then go out with the cart."

"Do you think no one will notice that I have the prisoner on my horse?"

"You can stay behind. I will make a great joking about my cousin who cannot handle tequila. You should trade shirts and give Lobo your hat, then no one will think nothing. As soon as we're gone, you can go over the wall and meet us at the jacal."

Joaquín considered, then said, " 'Sta bien. When will the women leave?"

"Not for hours yet, amigo." Jesús stood up. "Enjoy the fiesta, no?"

"The fewer who see me," Joaquín answered, "the better chance we have of no one noticing that Lobo and I do not look much alike."

"The soldiers will be so drunk they will see nothing." Jesús smiled. "But if you want to sit here and sip your water, I won't argue. Myself, I am going to dance."

Joaquín watched him walk toward the soldiers cavorting in the square. Jesús joined them and began dancing as they did, their hands clasped behind their backs held ramrod straight, their eyes on the ground between themselves and their partners. Only their feet moved, stomping with mincing steps, shuffling in a circle then stomping again with an erotic flamenco rhythm. Those who wore hats doffed them with exaggerated flourishes, then dropped them in the dust and stomped around them.

The dancers were syncopated motion, supercilious and arrogant, matadors flaunting the cape in front of the bull. Hidden inside the cape was a sword; waiting behind the bull's horns were eight hundred pounds of mortal hatred. The dance was the space between the two weapons, the moment before attack. Occasionally a man would release tension with an exuberant yell of defiant joy, mocking death only one step away.

A mockery of death, that was life in Mexico. Whether it came fast or slow, from disease, hunger, humiliation, or violence, death was always there to laugh at the earnestness of men. The four soldiers who swung footless from the gallows hovered above the dancers, above Joaquín motionless in the shadows, Lobo on the whipping post, the commandante behind his curtained window, the lines of lovers still waiting their turn at pleasure. Crowning them all on the crossbeam of the gallows, vultures, satiated on human flesh, slept above the remains of their feast, silhouetted against the star-studded sky. The men danced on as the moon moved across the heavens. The beef was eaten, more tequila consumed. The musicians began to weary, the women to come out from the barracks and exchange tired insults with soldiers too drunk to stand, much less make love. Finally the music stopped, and the women crawled back onto the cart.

Joaquín searched for Jesús, then saw him carrying an axe

through the shadows. Hurrying to join him at the flogging post, Joaquín saw that Lobo was unconscious. "What of the horses?"

"They are ready," Jesús said, taking the axe in both hands and swinging it so far behind himself that Joaquín thought he would topple. He wondered how much tequila Jesús had drunk, if he wouldn't miss the post and send the blade into Lobo's skull. Just as Joaquín opened his mouth to offer to do it himself, the axe swung through the moonlight and severed the chain. Lobo crumpled to the ground as the blade bit deep into the wood.

"Eso," Jesús grunted with satisfaction. "Trade shirts with him. I will get the horses." He walked quickly toward the stable.

Joaquín looked at the soldiers, but no one seemed to notice what was happening in the darkest corner of the presidio. He knelt beside Lobo and shook him by the shoulders. "Wake up. Be quiet," Joaquín said softly. Pulling the kid into a sitting position, Joaquín unbuttoned Lobo's shirt and eased the shreds of cloth off the lashed back, then dropped the shirt, and hurried to unbutton his own.

Lobo was awake now, watching but not helping. Joaquín had to lift the kid's arms into the sleeves of the shirt and button it for him. As he shrugged into the tattered shirt, Joaquín spoke with fierce command. "Our success depends on the next few minutes. Jesús will say you are his cousin José. You are drunk, slumped over the horse. Go where he leads you. Two hours from here is water. Four hours from there is the border. With luck, I will meet you at the jacal. If I'm not there, don't wait."

"You're not coming with us?" Lobo whispered.

"I will go another way," Joaquín said, buttoning the tattered shirt.

Lobo clutched at his arm. "What way, Joaquín?"

"Over the wall," he said. "Then on foot to the jacal where there is another horse."

Lobo's eyes were confused. "Don't leave me," he pleaded.

"You are leaving me," Joaquín argued, taking off his hat and tugging it tightly onto Lobo's blond hair. "Trust Jesús. He is a friend."

"But what about you?" Lobo asked, his eyes brimming with tears. "It's my fault you're here."

"It's Seth's," Joaquín said.

Hearing the horses approach, he yanked the axe free and tossed it aside, then took his place at the post, holding his hands as if they were shackled. He watched over his shoulder as Jesús led the horses near and helped Lobo to his feet.

"I won't go without you," Lobo said stubbornly.

"You must!" Joaquín insisted. "If Seth loses you now, my life will be for nothing."

"Is he everything?" Lobo whispered. "Can't we do anything that doesn't touch him?"

Joaquín shrugged, feeling the tattered shirt tickle the scabs on his back. "Apparently not," he said.

The gate was whining open, the wheels of the cart complaining in their tight turn. Jesús helped Lobo onto the saddled horse, leapt onto the bare back of the other and leaned to catch the reins of Lobo's, then met Joaquín's eye. "Buena suerte," Jesús whispered just before kicking his horse into a quick trot.

Lobo looked back, then remembered to slump forward onto the neck of the horse, hiding the shackles on his wrists beneath his chest. Joaquín watched over his shoulder as they followed the cart through the gate. It had been closed only a moment before it swung open again and Colonel Gonzalo rode in with his troop.

Joaquín ducked his head, trying to hide his black hair, so unlike Lobo's, which caught light even in the dark. Across the yard, he heard the colonel laugh and say he was glad to see his captive still tied to the post.

Joaquín huddled his head between his lifted arms, hoping Gonzalo wouldn't check his condition before retiring for the night. In the commotion of dismounting soldiers and drunken ones trying to present an orderly appearance, Joaquín could have run for the wall. But that would sound the alarm, so and he waited, giving Lobo and Jesús time to escape.

Joaquín's arms ached from being held up so long, the wind moved the tattered shirt across his barely healed back, making it itch, his beaten feet throbbed as his mind swirled with visions of the four footless men executed in his place. If Gonzalo came now, Joaquín didn't think any amount of prudence could prevent him from killing the colonel with his bare hands. But Gonzalo didn't come. Gradually the soldiers dispersed to their barracks until only a few were left, too drunk to move.

Joaquín dropped his arms and rubbed his hands to restore their feeling as he looked around. Now seemed the best chance he was likely to get, and he ran for the wall. It was easy to climb, the seams between the adobe bricks offering a ladder of support. He swung over the top with much more agility than before, and dropped to the ground with much less pain. Keeping within the wall's shadow, he jogged toward the corner and the wide open desert leading to the jacal. Before sprinting into freedom, he peered around the corner and saw Colonel Gonzalo taking a leisurely evening stroll.

19

★

 The officer was alone, smoking a cheroot as he walked.

Behind him, towering into the starlit sky, the four footless soldiers twisted on the gallows in the midnight wind. Joaquín shifted his knife to the back of his belt as he watched the colonel come closer.

Seeing Joaquín, Gonzalo stopped. He inhaled deeply on his cigar, illuminating his face with the glow of the coal, then he smiled. "So, Señor Ascarate, you have come back for more."

"I have come back," Joaquín agreed.

Gonzalo chuckled. "I find that amusing. You are the only man to ever escape la Cabeza, yet you could not stay away. May I ask why you returned?"

"To kill you," Joaquín said softly.

The colonel's eyebrows rose inquisitively. "Without a weapon? As you can see, I am armed. Do you think I wouldn't shoot you?"

"I think there is nothing you wouldn't do," Joaquín answered, restraining his hand.

Gonzalo smiled, puffing on his cigar. "Why is it you wish to kill me so much that you would attempt it with your bare hands?"

"There are four reasons on the gallows behind you."

Gonzalo turned and studied the corpses as if he hadn't seen them before. When he looked around again, his face was puzzled. "They beat you. It seems to me it should give you pleasure to see them dead."

"You ordered the beating."

"In the service of my country. It was nothing personal."

"Did you also execute those soldiers in the service of your country?"

"Yes. They failed their duty." An idea lit his eyes. "But perhaps I was too hasty. Is it possible you were hiding in the presidio all this time and are just now making your escape?"

Joaquín shook his head. "I have escaped twice."

Gonzalo chuckled. "Did you come back to visit your friend, Lobo Madera?"

"I spoke with him," Joaquín said.

"Did you promise to help him, too, escape?"

"I no longer make promises," he said.

This time Gonzalo laughed with admiration. "It is a pity you have chosen to be an enemy of México. You would have done well aligned with the power in this country."

"My experience forces me to doubt that," Joaquín replied.

"But that is because you sided with bandits." Gonzalo shook his head with pity. "They cannot win against an army, and any man who chooses the losing side lacks integrity."

"What do you know of integrity?" Joaquín scoffed.

"Do you think your friend, Lobo Madera, has any?" Again Gonzalo shook his head. "He betrayed you. Under the whip, he screamed your name."

"Perhaps it was a prayer for help."

"No, it was in answer to a question. Would you like to know what it was? I will tell you anyway: who has the money?" The colonel sucked on his cigar but the fire was out. He tossed the cigar away. "*Do* you have the money?"

"No," Joaquín said.

"Then Madera not only betrayed you, he lied. The world is better off without such a man."

"So you intend to kill him?"

"Señor," Gonzalo explained with overblown patience, "this is a place of execution. No prisoner leaves here alive."

"Neither will you."

The colonel laughed. "I like you, Joaquín Ascarate. There is a threat behind your smile I find invigorating. For a small concession I could offer you a position of no mean worth. To be an officer in the federal army is to be seated in the shade at the corrida of México bleeding for Porfirismo. It is we who hide the knife in the scarlet cape, and we who choose which bull will die on which afternoon. It is also to us that the ears are offered in tribute." He chuckled. "All you must do is swear allegiance to Díaz."

"And learn to torture men with pleasure," Joaquín said.

"I have always believed," Gonzalo replied, "that a man should enjoy his work."

"I will enjoy killing you."

Gonzalo looked at Joaquín's empty hands. "Have you a weapon in your belt? What is it, a stick? A gun, even? One shot and the entire presidio will be upon us."

"The entire presidio is drunk."

Gonzalo frowned. "You will not escape again. For a great distance in all directions there is nothing but desert. Where will you go?"

"If I do no more than accompany you to hell, I will be content."

"Ah. I will make a trade, Joaquín Ascarate. I will return inside the presidio and go to sleep. As you say, the soldiers are drunk. In the morning, however, we will track you, and perhaps, depending on my mood, we will kill you quickly. I think a night of running across the desert without water will be punishment enough. It is an especially piquant torture, the hope of impossible escape." Gonzalo laughed. "Hasta mañana, señor," he said, turning and walking away.

Joaquín watched until Gonzalo was nearly at the corner of the presidio. Then, gripping his knife, he sprinted after the colonel, running nearly silently in his moccasins. Catching Gonzalo with a hand over his mouth, Joaquín jerked the colonel's head back and thrust the blade into his throat. Blood spurted in an arc in front of them, glimmering with starlight as it fell. After a moment of quiet struggle, the colonel's body slumped lifeless to the ground. Quickly Joaquín cleaned his blade on the dead man's coat, then replaced the knife in his belt. Lifting the colonel by his armpits, Joaquín dragged him to the gallows.

Spare ropes dangled from the crossbeam. Joaquín untied one and let the noose fall to the ground. He secured the loop around the colonel's neck, then took hold and hoisted the corpse into the air. Straining against the weight, he grunted with exertion until he caught the rope fast around the pole. The excess length jerked taut as the weight of the corpse took up the slack.

Now there were five cadavers for the buzzards to feed on at dawn, and one would be especially succulent. Fresh blood ran from the wound in its neck, creating a dark river down the length of the pale uniform to drip from the polished black boot and spatter in a circle-eight on the rocky soil. Joaquín smiled at his work, then he ran.

Two riders waited in the darkness beside the jacal. When they saw Joaquín coming, they rode out to meet him. He took the reins of the third horse from Jesús, who grinned. Lobo looked ill, clinging to the saddlehorn to keep his seat. Joaquín leapt onto the bare back of the horse and leaned to catch Lobo's reins. "Just hold on, mí hijo," Joaquín whispered.

Lobo's head jerked up and his eyes brimmed with tears. "You call me your son?" he whispered, his voice full of shame.

"Who else would I do this for?" Joaquín teased. "Vamanos," he called to Jesús.

They reined around and urged their horses into a gallop, cutting distance away from Cabeza de Vaca. Soon they slowed to a trot to give their mounts respite, then picked up speed again, moving north toward the only source of water between them and the border. Even there they tarried only long enough to briefly rest the horses and refill their goatskin; then they left again, cutting a diagonal northwest toward Nogales.

They kept their horses moving fast, stopping occasionally to let them catch their breath but never staying long. Lobo had regained his strength enough that he could mount and dismount without help, but he was quiet and kept his eyes away from the others. Joaquín knew Lobo was ashamed for having broken under the whip, and he wished he could find the words to alleviate the kid's distress, but the words wouldn't come. He told himself that perhaps when he was not so tired he could help Lobo understand that no man could endure Gonzalo's torture. If the soldiers hadn't been distracted, Joaquín may have screamed names to save his feet. He had been spared that by Lobo's arrival, so he held no grudge for the kid's betrayal.

Neither did he grieve for the loss of the money. It belonged to Seth; let him retrieve it if he wished. Joaquín was returning with a gift far more precious. Knowing father and son would be reunited, Joaquín could believe his sojourn into his homeland had achieved something other than death. As for his original purpose of convincing Seth to come home, Joaquín would try once more for the sake of his promise to Rico.

Dawn lurked beyond the horizon when Joaquín spotted the lights of Nogales ahead. By the time he and his companions reached the pueblo, the sun was fierce in the pale sky. Already the shadows of the alleys were a welcome relief from the heat, and the cool shade of the stable revived Joaquín for what lay ahead. As he and Jesús tended the horses, Lobo leaned against the wall, his face buried in his folded arms.

Joaquín walked over and said softly, "Let's go ask after your father."

The kid sighed deeply, then turned around. It was evident he had been crying, yet his face was set in hard lines to hide his emotions. He would have succeeded if he had mastered Seth's ability to control his eyes. But rather than glinting with the stately sheen of indifference Seth used to camouflage his feelings, Lobo's eyes were soft with need. "Joaquín," he pleaded, "I can't face him like this."

"You must face him honestly, however you are," Joaquín replied sternly.

"This ain't the way I wanted it to happen," Lobo whispered. "I don't feel like a man now."

"Seth was whipped in prison," Joaquín argued. "Do you think he suffered in silence? Put it behind you, Lobo. That is what a man does."

Lobo shook his head. "If you knew what I've done, you'd say dif'rent."

"I know," Joaquín said gently. "Gonzalo told me."

Lobo's eyes were hot with shame. "When did he tell you?"

"I met him outside the wall after you left," Joaquín said, shifting his gaze to Jesús. "I killed him with my knife and hung him on the gallows."

"Madre de Dios," Jesús whispered. "You must leave México now, amigo."

"Soon," Joaquín said, looking at Lobo. "I would rather not go alone."

Lobo pulled himself away from the wall and stood up straight. "If you let me, I'll be proud to ride with you, Joaquín."

He smiled. "Andale. Let's see if Seth will say the same."

He led them down the alley, past the warehouse where he had

been held prisoner, and into the cantina. The same skinny, bald man stood behind the bar. He stared at them a long moment, then without being asked, walked across to the private room and knocked on the door. Fierro opened it. He, too, stared at the three men standing in the dimly lit cantina, then brushed past the barkeep and walked toward them, leaving the door open. The room was empty.

"Wait here," Fierro growled, walking out the back door. In a few minutes he returned, stood a moment glowering at Joaquín, then said, "Seth asks to see you alone."

Joaquín looked at Lobo. "Trade shirts with me."

His shackles clanking, Lobo complied. Joaquín buttoned the whole shirt on and tucked in its tails as he followed Fierro out of the cantina. They crossed the alley and entered a two-story adobe building. The ground floor was an empty shell. They walked across the dirt and into a corridor intersecting the center of the building. At the far end was a flight of stairs switchbacking to the second floor. They climbed the steps, their boots loud on the wooden planks, and came out on another corridor. Halfway along its length, Fierro stopped before a door and knocked. Raul opened it. The boy looked at Joaquín, then at Fierro, and said respectfully, "Seth asks that he come alone."

Fierro frowned, turned, and stomped back down the hall as Raul beckoned Joaquín inside.

The room was a parlor, furnished with a black leather settee and a large table with six chairs polished to a shiny gleam, the floor an equally dark and glossy wood, the whitewashed walls bare except for one with shutters of golden oak across its width. Raul opened the shutters section by section, swinging them aside to let sunlight flood the room. The view beyond the windows stretched north across the border, and Joaquín felt a swamp of loneliness as he imagined Seth standing there looking toward home.

Raul nodded at a closed door and said, "Seth was sleeping and asks that you wait. Help yourself to coffee." He gestured at a sideboard where an ornate silver service was set out with delicate china cups, then he left.

Joaquín dropped his hat on the settee. He poured himself a cup of coffee and carried it across to the window, looking toward home as he drank the dark, bitter brew. He finished it and replaced the cup, then returned to the window. When he heard a door open, he turned around and watched Seth crossing the threshold.

He looked the same man Joaquín had always known, tall and lean and in the prime of health, closing the door on a woman asleep in his bed. Joaquín wished Lobo were here so he could see how Seth controlled his eyes. They shone with a metallic indifference, their only emotion a playfulness Joaquín knew could turn cruel as easily as kind.

Seth said, "I heard you had a rough trip."

Joaquín nodded.

Seth smiled, though his eyes remained the same. "You succeeded."

"I don't have the money," Joaquín said.

"I know that," Seth answered, walking across to the silver service. Seeing Joaquín's empty cup, he asked, "More coffee?"

"No thanks," Joaquín said, watching him lift the ornate carafe and fill a cup for himself. The comforting fragrance struck Joaquín like a lashing memory of better times. "You used to have simpler tastes," he said.

Seth laughed, setting the silver down. "A gift from Calero," he said, then watched Joaquín over the rim of the cup as he drank.

"Calero's dead," Joaquín said.

Seth smiled. "I know that, too."

"You're well informed."

Seth nodded. "It's the best way to stay alive in this country. Even then, it doesn't always work, as you witnessed."

"Apparently you have recovered."

"Reckon it ain't my fate to die at a wedding. Esperanza always said it would happen in a saloon, remember?"

Joaquín nodded.

"How is she?"

"She died."

Seth looked down, and Joaquín almost smiled to see the jefe hide his emotions. "She was a great loss to all of us," Joaquín said. "Especially Rico."

Seth chuckled, the metallic glint in his eyes again. "Starting right in on me, ain't you, Joaquín?"

"It's the only reason I'm here, to ask again that you come home."

"If I don't, will you go back alone?"

"Lobo has said he will go with me."

Seth's eyes flashed with a heat immediately doused with ice. "You gonna make him choose between us?"

"The choice is between life and death," Joaquín retorted.

"Which are you offering?"

Joaquín turned away from the cruelty in Seth's eyes, berating himself for expecting anything different. Seth looked the same but his heart had been cut out. Remembering he had been the one to wield the knife, Joaquín felt overwhelmed with remorse.

From behind him, Seth said, "You've got fresh blood on your shirt. Did the Rurales whip you again?"

"No," Joaquín said, facing him. "The blood is Lobo's. He too was whipped for serving your purpose, and he wore the shirt on the journey here."

Incredibly, Seth smiled. "Mexico's a rough country."

"Sí," Joaquín said. "I have killed five men and caused the death of four others. I paid a high price for your profit, which I lost in the end."

Seth emptied his cup, then set it down. "I've got the money. Lourdes brought it."

"Is she here?" Joaquín asked in surprise.

"Asleep," Seth said, nodding toward the closed bedroom door.

"And Magdalena?" Joaquín asked with sarcasm.

"At home," Seth answered with a playful smile. "Mourning the death of her brother."

"How do you feel about his death?"

Seth shrugged. "Fuentes was that sort of man."

"What sort are you?"

"Seems to me you should've figured that out by now."

"You had no right to do what you did."

"In which instance?"

"Any of them. If you keep Lobo, I will know you are truly a lost cause."

Seth chuckled. "I told you that from the start but you were convinced you knew better. Are you ready to give up?"

"Not quite," Joaquín said. "I ask once more that you come home."

"So you can keep working on your vow to that priest?" Seth mocked.

"Yes."

"You always did take your oaths seriously. Even when it meant sending your partner to prison alone."

"I did not commit the crimes you were imprisoned for."

"No, you didn't," Seth admitted. He crossed the room to stand beside Joaquín at the window, both of them looking out at the desert.

"It's over now," Joaquín said softly. "Why can't you put it behind you?"

"Maybe I don't want to."

"That's what I told Lobo."

Seth grunted. "What answer did he give you?"

"He was sad you hadn't asked about him."

"I knew he was with Vargas."

"So you sent me to bring him back?"

"Yes."

"Why didn't you tell me that, instead of sending me to sell guns to bandits?"

Seth shrugged. "It's your country. Are you ashamed of surviving your visit?"

"No," Joaquín said. "But I am ashamed for you."

Seth sighed, still watching out the window. "If that's true, seems you'd be glad to say adiós."

"Believe me, compadre," Joaquín answered. "There have been many times I wished I could."

"Why can't you?"

"We are kin. We belong together."

Seth faced him. "Is that why you turned me over to the law?"

"Yes," Joaquín said.

"Yeah, it prob'ly is," Seth muttered, looking out the window again.

"You paid me back by sending me to México," Joaquín said. "Everything I hold to be wrong I did while acting for your purpose. Now I also have been whipped, starved, tortured, and betrayed. Since we are equally soiled and equally punished, can we not be compadres again?" In the length of Seth's silence, he said, "If you insist on staying, at least send Lobo home. Don't drag him into your death."

"He's a Strummar," Seth said.

"There are three more in Tejoe: Rico, Elena, and your youngest son, Jesse, whom you have yet to meet."

Again, Seth was silent.

"Why stay here and be killed by the Rurales?" Joaquín implored. "Maybe even by those who claim to be your friends?"

Seth shrugged. "One way to die is as good as another."

"If you truly believe that, why did you survive prison only to seek death in freedom?"

"I don't know," Seth said.

As when he first came to Nogales, Joaquín felt appalled at the defeat in Seth's voice. He wanted to shake sense into his friend, but instead he moved a step away. "Will you see Lobo before we leave?"

"Better not," Seth answered without taking his eyes from the horizon.

Joaquín sighed. "There is a man with us named Jesús. He took a great risk to help me free Lobo from the Rurales. Will you reward him?"

"What does he want?"

"Enough money to buy the debt of a friend from the hacendado."

Seth nodded. "Money's easy."

Joaquín waited another moment, then reluctantly turned to go.

"Tell me something," Seth said, still looking out the window.

Joaquín stopped and waited.

Without turning around, Seth asked, "Are Elena's eyes still blue?"

Joaquín smiled. "So you remember her eyes. They are gray, like yours. She has changed in other ways, too. She is almost fifteen now and trains horses. Last year she took first prize in the race at the county fair."

Seth chuckled. "Did she?"

"You would be proud of her. Isn't that worth having?"

Seth was silent a long moment. Finally he turned around and faced Joaquín honestly. "Do you think any of what we had is retrievable?"

Joaquín nodded. "Since we first met, you have spoken of a fresh start. I think it is time."

Seth gave him a gentle smile of forgiveness. "All right. But I ain't making no promises, Joaquín."

"You never did," he said.

Elena's Promise

★ Early Summer 1897 ★

20

★

 Elena was fourteen the summer her father came home from prison. She had been only a little over a year old when he left, but she had heard so many stories she felt she knew him well. So when the three men rode into the yard one May afternoon, she recognized the man in the middle as her father.

His horse was the finest Elena had ever seen: a massive, powerful, charcoal gray with black points. When the stallion shook his head, the silver conchos on his bridle exaggerated the beauty of his arrogance. Her father watched her from eyes nearly the same shade as the silver, a shy smile on his mouth. It surprised Elena that the mythical Seth Strummar would feel shy meeting her.

She had been working Two-Bits in the corral, training her for the races in July. Because their ranch was almost all rocky ground and the filly's tendons were delicate, Elena usually worked Two-Bits in a circle on a long lead. Sometimes she rode her on the trails and sometimes she galloped flat out on the road, but on school days Elena hadn't much time before dark. This had been a school day and she had been home an hour, sweating in the sun as the filly kicked up dust around her.

It was dusk when the three men rode into the yard. One was her Uncle Joaquín, who wasn't her blood uncle but the man who had taken care of them in her father's absence. The other was her older brother, Lobo, whom she hadn't seen in two years. Everyone had always commented on his resemblance to Seth, and she could see it now, though the qualities of the two men were entirely different. Lobo flaunted himself as arrogantly as the stallion, while the man astride such beauty seemed subtle in comparison. The stud caught Two-Bits's scent and snorted possessively, making the filly prance as if showing off, then come to a stop hiding behind Elena. They both watched the men line up on the far side of the fence.

"Hello, Lobo," Elena said solemnly. "Hello, Joaquín." Then she looked at her father again, unsure whether to greet him before they had been introduced.

Lobo laughed as he swung off a good-looking bay that must have cost a pretty penny. "We've come home to plague you, Elena," he said as he tied his reins to the top rail. He was tall and lean and, at twenty-one, moved with the swagger of a desperado.

Joaquín swung down and tied his horse, too. It was a sturdy black Elena had ridden once or twice, a well-mannered horse with stamina. He smiled at her, then walked with Lobo toward the house. Seth still sat the stallion, as if he might leave again as easily as stay.

"That's a fine horse," she said.

He chuckled, a gentle, husky sound. "Is that the filly you're gonna race at the fair?"

So he knew about her racing, probably even that she had taken first prize last year, running against men on the best horses in the county. She nodded.

"She looks fast," he said. "What's her name?"

"Two-Bits. What's your horse's name?"

"Padre," he said, giving a Spanish roll to the *r*. "The ranchero I bought him from had a longer handle but I just kept the first part."

"You gonna stand him at stud?" she asked.

His gray eyes sparkled with amusement. She thought it was because she could tell a stallion from a gelding, which most girls couldn't, and because she would boldly ask such a question.

"Might," he said, finally swinging down. Still holding his reins as if he hadn't yet decided to stay, he folded his arms on the top rail and studied her filly. "You aim to breed her?"

"There wasn't a stud in the county I'd consider," she said.

The stallion stretched his neck and whinnied at Two-Bits, which made her skitter against the rope, backing its full length as if she could escape his intentions. Elena coiled the lead as she walked toward her filly, speaking softly, then stroked the long elegant neck as she looked back at Seth. "She's shy," she said.

He nodded with a teasing smile as he let his gaze slide down her body then up again to meet her eyes. "Girls wear pants now?" he asked.

She felt a moment's shame to be meeting him in her dungarees and an old shirt, both dusty. Her hair was braided down the center of her back, a wiry, brown mass that she habitually tied out of her way. "It's easier," she said. "Working with horses, skirts are a bother."

"Your eyes were blue the last time I saw you," he said.

"Were they?" she asked, pleased at the thought. Then she shrugged. "They're gray as gunmetal now." He nodded again, this time with a smile of acceptance that made her want to hug him, but she kept her distance.

"You surprised to see me?" he asked.

"Some," she said. "When you didn't come home right off, I figured any man doesn't want his family, his family sure don't need him." Seeing his smile fade she quickly said, "Rico never gave up, though."

He looked toward the house with a haunted hurt in his eyes, and suddenly she suspected he was dawdling with her to avoid facing the woman he had come home to. She thought maybe he was afraid Rico would be disappointed, that no man could match the dreams of a decade's worth of longing, and she wanted to reassure him but all she could think to say was, "Will you let me ride Padre sometime?"

When his eyes returned to her, they were playful again. "He's a little rough."

"I know horses," she said.

"Yeah, I believe that," he said. "But he's short on manners."

"That's what I'm good at," she said, "teaching 'em to behave."

He laughed uneasily. "I bet you are," he said. "Will you walk with me up to the house?"

She knew then that he was scared to take that walk by himself. Looking across the hard-packed dirt of the yard, she saw Rico come through the door. Elena smiled at her mother and said, "No need."

Seth followed her smile, and Elena lost him.

"I'll put my horse away," she said. Leading the filly inside the stable, Elena tied her in a stall, then went back and stood in the shadows beside the open door.

Having finally tied his reins to the fence, Seth had turned around to face Rico. They just looked at each other for the longest time, both of them obviously wary. Then he took off his hat and held it in front of him as if he were a drifter seeking work, which Elena guessed maybe he was.

She heard Rico ask, "Have you come home to stay?"

"Thought I'd try it," he said. "If you'll have me."

"I've been watching every day since we read of your release."

"Had to work some things through," he said. "I didn't come out of Huntsville a better man."

Rico impatiently brushed tears from her cheeks. "You're alive, Seth. It's over."

More tears fell, glistening red in the sunset. This time he reached up and wiped them away, his fingers lingering to caress her face. "You're still beautiful," he said.

"Oh," she scoffed. "I'm forty-one now. Far past the age of beauty."

"Not to my eyes," he said.

She laughed, sounding pleased.

"There's my girl," Seth said, pulling her close in a hug.

Elena watched them walk away, their arms around each other's waists as they made that dreaded trip across the yard. Slowly she approached the stallion now tied at the rail. He jerked his head back as she raised her hand to pet him. "I'm going to master you, Padre," she said, then looked up to see Joaquín coming toward her.

He untied the reins of his own horse, giving her a smile. "You best be careful with Padre," he warned. "He's still a little wild."

She looked toward the house. "Is Seth home for good?"

Joaquín swung up and gathered his reins as he pondered what he wanted to say. When he met her eyes, she saw he wasn't as happy as she had expected. "If he feels he belongs here," Joaquín finally said, "he will stay."

She stroked the soft, gray nose of the stallion. "I like his horse," she said.

Joaquín laughed. "See you soon," he said, reining around and loping out of the yard toward town and his own family.

Elena climbed the fence and walked toward the house, wondering if she should change into a frock for supper. She decided against it. Tomorrow Seth would see her dressed for school; tonight she would be herself. When she went in, Rico was working at the stove and Jesse was setting the table, keeping his eyes to himself. Lobo was sitting in Jesse's place, which Elena found odd. Seth was leaning against the wall as if he couldn't bring himself to sit down. Their eyes met and he gave her a smile which told her he felt better now that she was there.

She washed at the sink, then sat down across from Lobo. They had been close as children but now he seemed more of a stranger than Seth. The night Lobo had left home, his face was bruised and his lip bleeding so he licked at it as he talked, sitting on the edge of her bed telling her good-bye. She had pleaded for him to wait until morning, hoping whatever it was that drove him to leave in the dark of midnight wouldn't seem so impelling in the light of day. But he hadn't waited. Holding his head in his hands, his words had been muffled when he asked her to go into Rico's room and bring him Seth's gun.

The Colt's .44 had hung on Rico's bedstead since the day Seth had been taken to Texas for trial. Knowing her mother cherished the gun as a talisman promising his return, Elena thought that was silly. There were weapons for sale all over the world and Seth wouldn't come home just to retrieve his gun. But Elena had been only twelve then; she'd learned a lot in the last two years.

The memories her mother associated with Seth's gun hanging on her headboard were akin to why Lobo wouldn't go into Rico's room when she was in bed. It had to do with the way his eyes had followed her while she worked at the stove. Elena had often puzzled over that. Now, struggling to keep her eyes off her father, she felt a glimmer of understanding.

Everything about their family was wrong. She had recognized that during her first year in school, though it had taken a while to comprehend how different they were. Her father was not only in prison, his crimes had made him famous and people still whispered his name with fear. Her mother wasn't even his wife but the widow of another man. She used Seth's name without any legal right to it. They lived off money he had stolen as a bandit, and even though it was supposedly diminishing fast, they had nicer clothes and far better horses than the other kids in school. Her older brother was a troublemaker, always getting into fights. Her younger brother had converted to Catholicism and attended Mass at Our Lady of Sorrows every day after school. Her whole family was off-kilter, Elena included.

As she approached womanhood, people had started to comment

that she would never be the beauty her mother had been. That made Elena defiant, so she sometimes wore boy's clothes even in town, then visited friends and sat in their parlors tapping her foot to hear her spur jingle, sprinkling her conversation with carefully timed curses just to watch the grownups' eyebrows rise in dismay. She laughed in the face of their criticism, but sometimes at night she cried in her bed, wishing that one solitary thing about her was like anyone else.

When Lobo left home, it seemed their fate not to have a man on the homestead. Jesse was already talking about becoming a priest, which meant he would leave in a few years, too. Elena never contemplated taking a husband. She had grown up with animals so she knew all about procreation, but she didn't want anyone ever doing that to her. Sometimes she tried to imagine doing it with Joaquín or Blue Rivers, simply because they were the men she liked best in the world, but even then she saw it as something she would tolerate to please them.

Now she noticed that Lobo's eyes were the same pale gray as Seth's, a fact Rico had often mentioned. His hair was the same light brown, falling in the same lanky straightness to cover his collar, and his build and height were equal to Seth's. Lobo had become a man in the time he was gone, and his smile said he was thinking she had grown up in the interim, too. When she shyly returned the smile, his laughter was bold with a cocky possession.

"You're getting prettier, Elena," he teased. "In another few years, you'll be the belle of the county."

Uncomfortable beneath his pointed scrutiny, she retorted, "Why don't you just curse me with the pox?"

Seth laughed softly and she looked up at him, but he was watching Rico.

Rico brought a spinach pie and a plate of corn tortillas to the table. "If I'd known you were coming," she said to Seth, "I would've cooked something special."

"Didn't come for the food," he answered, finally moving away from the wall and sitting at the head of the table, a place that had been empty for all of Elena's memory.

Jesse sat down between Lobo and Seth, keeping his eyes away from both of them. Rico took her seat and smiled awkwardly. "We say grace now," she said.

Jesse had already bowed his head. Lobo complied, accustomed to the ritual from before he left home. When Rico looked down, tears fell into her lap. Elena looked at Seth, his gaze moving around his family, then settling on her. They smiled at each other as Jesse said in his thirteen-year-old voice, still as high as a girl's, "Bless us, oh Lord, and these Thy gifts, which we are about to receive from Thy bounty."

"Amen," three voices said.

Rico was on her feet instantly, coming around to serve Seth. He slid his hand down the folds of her skirt, lingering on her bottom a moment, and she looked at him quickly, embarrassed. He dropped his hand and teased, "You never served me before."

She laughed, sounding girlish. "Well, don't get used to it. This is a special occasion, and my pleasure." She turned and lifted a portion of spinach pie onto Jesse's plate, then moved to Lobo. "Goodness," she said. "Must you wear your gun at the table?"

He glanced at Seth, then gave her a taunting smile. "New rules of the house?"

"Times have changed," she said, settling into her chair and passing the pie plate to Elena, then looking at Seth. "Men don't wear guns as a matter of course anymore."

"Some men maybe," he said, his smile cool.

Lobo laughed with derision.

"Please, Seth," Rico pleaded softly.

He stood up and unbuckled his gunbelt. Elena felt herself tremble, watching him bend his will to please her mother. He tossed the gun onto an extra chair against the wall, then sat down giving Rico a smile tinged with threat. "Don't get used to it," he said. "This is a special occasion, and my pleasure."

Rico laughed, pleased at her victory.

Seth shifted his gaze to Lobo, who reluctantly stood up and took his gun off, too, tossing it beside Seth's. Elena could tell her brother didn't like capitulating so easily. Realizing Lobo resented Seth's power over him, Elena suddenly understood that he had taken Jesse's chair to put distance between himself and his father. She thought that was odd since she felt she couldn't get close enough.

21

Seth wasn't up for breakfast the next morning, and Elena was disappointed that he wouldn't see her in her dress after all. She sat at the table watching Rico scramble eggs, wondering what it had felt like to share her bed after sleeping alone for so long. Elena wanted to ask but couldn't think how to phrase it. Anyway, Jesse was there, studying his geography book. She asked him, "What do you think of Seth?"

He looked up with a puzzled frown. "What do you mean?"

Asking a question of Jesse nearly always netted another question. "Do you like him?" she asked impatiently.

"I don't know him yet," he said, glancing at Rico.

"He won't like your ambition to be a priest," Elena said with an edge.

Rico carried their plates over and set them down. "Why don't you let Seth decide that?" she suggested gently.

"You know he ain't gonna like it," Elena argued.

"I don't see how he's got any right," Jesse said, "to criticize anything about us."

"He hasn't criticized you," Rico said sternly. "Elena, give your father a chance. Don't go kicking up dust he has to deal with."

She shrugged, digging into her eggs. "Does he always sleep so late?"

"He didn't before," Rico said, sitting down with a cup of coffee. "We'll have to get used to his ways."

"Like letting him wear his gun at the table?" Elena sassed, then had to turn away from the hurt in her mother's eyes.

"What's the matter, Elena?" she asked. "Are you upset that he's here?"

"No," she said, unable to look at her mother.

"You've already attacked both Jesse and me this morning. It isn't like you."

"I'm sorry," she mumbled.

"We must all try hard to make him feel welcome," Rico said. "His ways may seem strange but we'll get used to them, and he'll accommodate us as much as he can. We have to be careful not to ask too much of him."

Elena gave her mother a smile. "I won't drive him away."

Rico laughed. "I'm sure you won't. On your way home, will you stop at the Last Chance and buy a bottle of whiskey? I don't want him going into town just yet, and I'm afraid he will if we don't have it on hand."

"Seems to me you should've anticipated that," Jesse muttered.

Rico looked flustered. "I was hoping he would have gotten over his want of it."

"Will one be enough?" Elena asked, standing up without finishing her breakfast.

"Aren't you going to eat more than that?" Rico asked with concern.

"I'm not hungry," Elena said. She opened the old sugar bowl where Rico kept her pin money and peered inside. "How much does whiskey cost?"

"Better buy two," she said, "so take three dollars."

"I'll be late," Jesse said, giving his mother a quick kiss on the cheek. "The novena for Señora Alvarez is this afternoon."

"Can't you skip it?" she pleaded. "Is Señora Alvarez more important than your father?"

"She's dead," he answered, walking out.

Rico seemed so distressed, Elena gave her mother a hug with her kiss. "Don't worry," she said. "Everything'll work out."

"I'm sure," Rico said. "Hurry home, won't you?"

"I will," Elena promised. As she crossed the yard toward the stable, she watched Jesse trekking toward the sliver of mountain between the homestead and the road, and Elena wondered what Seth would say about his youngest son walking everywhere he went because he was afraid of horses.

When she rode Rojo into the school yard, Danny Nickles stood up from where he'd been leaning against the fence and held her reins while she dismounted at the block, then unsaddled her horse for her. Elena could have done it easily enough, but it was a rule that one of the older boys always did corral duty for the day, helping the girls as they arrived.

Danny was sixteen and lived on the neighboring ranch. They were best friends, though they worked hard to disguise it from the other kids, who would have teased them unmercifully, as if being friends meant they were sweet on each other. Danny tossed her sidesaddle onto the fence, then grinned and said, "You look different today."

She shrugged.

"It's the ribbon in your hair," he said. "Can't remember you ever wearing one before."

"My father came home last night," she said.

"That's keen!" He laughed, excited for her.

"I wore the ribbon for him, but he wasn't awake when I left."

"He'll see it when you get home, if you don't pull it out," he teased.

"If he's still there," she said.

Danny let Rojo loose in the corral. A tall sorrel that was too old now to do much more than make the trip between school and home, the horse had once belonged to Seth. "Don't you think he'll stay?" Danny asked, leaning on the fence as he watched the other boys play keep-away with someone's satchel.

"Who knows?" she said. "I'm to take some whiskey home. Reckon once he gets good'n drunk we'll see what we're dealing with."

Danny studied her carefully. "You used to say how much you wished he'd come home. Now that he has, you sound like you wish he hadn't."

"He's not what I expected," she said. "If he were like Joaquín or Blue Rivers or even you, someone easy to be around, I wouldn't feel so nervous. But he ain't, Danny. There's an edge to him that don't take hardly nothing to provoke. Last night at supper, one minute his eyes would be warm and friendly, and the next they'd glint like knife blades with a threat that made my stomach feel queasy."

Danny laughed softly. "Well, he *is* Seth Strummar. Not too many men have a more able reputation."

"It's not that," she said.

"What is it, then?"

She shrugged, then struggled to explain. "He rode a stallion home. A huge charcoal gray, sixteen hands if he's a foot, with such powerful, rippling muscles, glossy in the sun. The way he tosses his head makes me feel all trembly inside." She stopped, inexplicably embarrassed.

Danny chuckled. "I reckon you're just not used to having a man in the house."

"What's that got to do with his horse?"

"You're the one brought it up."

She frowned, genuinely puzzled.

"Didn't you say it was a stallion?" he teased.

She caught on and suppressed a blush. "It's got nothing to do with that! I have two brothers!"

"There's a difference between a boy and a man."

"What would you know about it? You're just a boy."

"Barely." He smiled. "And it's changing fast."

She knew it was true, and when it did change he wouldn't go riding with her anymore. Just then the Rivers girls arrived in their buggy, and Danny walked away to help them down.

Matty Rivers came over to the fence near Elena. "I hear your father's home."

"Who told you that?" she asked resentfully.

"He stopped off at my father's saloon before riding out to your place. Mama says you're apt to be upset for a while, that a man like that can't come home without disrupting everything he touches."

"He hasn't disrupted anything," she argued.

"Well, you seem kind of upset," Matty pointed out.

"It's that Danny Nickles," Elena said, "teasing me just 'cause I wore a ribbon in my hair."

Matty turned around and watched him unharnessing their buggy horse. "I wouldn't mind if Danny paid a little attention to me," she said wistfully. Then she gave Elena a dismissive glance. "But you always were an odd one."

Elena watched her walk toward the other girls clustered around the schoolhouse steps. It was a circle Elena had never confessed any desire to join. All they did was giggle about boys and repeat the gossip they heard at home, which often revolved around her family. Because Seth had been an outlaw, everyone related to him was considered a pariah. She had heard that word from Mrs. Rivers, though her husband was a friend of Seth's and had once been an outlaw, too. Elena had long ago given up caring what the Rivers women thought about anything.

At lunch, Jennifer Pardee came over and sat down beside her

with a commiserating smile. "I hear your father's come home," she said sympathetically.

"I guess the whole town's heard by now," Elena answered.

"I hear he's still a good-lookin' man," Jennifer said just before taking a bite of her oatmeal muffin. With her cheek puffed full, she added, "And that prison didn't cut a sliver off his style."

Elena didn't have to ask where Jennifer had heard such a comment since her mother worked in the Blue Rivers Saloon. Jennifer was equal with Elena as far as being pariahs went, and they were good friends.

"When my father came home," Jennifer said, "we didn't have a minute of peace 'til he was gone again."

Elena nodded. "I remember."

Hollister Pardee hadn't stayed more than a month, but before he left, Jennifer was living at the homestead with Elena, and Sassy was laid up, bruised so bad Blue wouldn't let her work. Rico had convinced him to pay Sassy's wages while she recovered. When Blue argued that getting beat up wasn't the same as falling sick, Rico got mad and said the whole godforsaken profession was sickening to body and soul. Blue gave in, but that hadn't been the end of it. Mrs. Nickles raised a hue and cry at the church ladies' sewing circle about throwing the harlots out of town. Back living with Sassy by then, Jennifer quit coming to school for a while. One day she just showed up and nothing more was said. Eating lunch with Elena that day, Jennifer's only comment about the whole commotion was, "So much for motherfuckin' fathers."

"They ain't the same, though," she said now, frisking her palms together to clean them of muffin crumbs. "Sassy says your father's gonna make it work with Rico, so you best get used to having him around."

Elena noticed that the muffin had been Jennifer's entire lunch. A waif of a girl on the cusp of womanhood, she let her auburn hair hang tangled to her waist and wore shapeless skirts and dirty middies for the same reason Elena wore jeans and shirts: as a counterpoint to her mother. Since Sassy sparkled, Jennifer worked at looking drab.

She asked, "You know how Sassy knows Seth's gonna make it work with Rico?"

Elena bit into her apple and shook her head.

" 'Cause he didn't take no doves upstairs last night. She says that's the surest sign there is he means to give Rico his best shot. That most men would've sharpened their rapier 'fore goin' home, but what they'd really be doin' is dilutin' their purpose, and Seth's too wily." She laughed lightly. "Sassy said he looked the doves over, though, and she wouldn't be surprised if he wandered once he got his home life settled in."

Elena spat an apple seed onto the ground. "Sassy said a lot."

Jennifer nodded. "I think if Rico don't mind her p's and q's, Sassy's gonna know which ones she misses."

Elena felt a nudge of resentment but didn't let it show. "You want some goat cheese?" she asked, extending the kerchief-wrapped package.

Jennifer took it eagerly, unwrapped it, and folded a strip into her mouth. "Sassy told me to say you're welcome to come stay with us if things work out that way."

Elena swallowed the last of her apple, then asked, "Which way?"

"Like with Hollister Pardee and me," Jennifer said, taking another strip of cheese. "Don't you want any of this?"

Elena shook her head. "Did he actually try it?" she asked softly.

"He flat-out did it," Jennifer huffed. "I never told Sassy, figured she'd kill him, she was so mad as it was." She shrugged. "Never told nobody 'til you, now. Just want you to know, Elena, life goes on, and our house is open if you need it."

"Thanks," Elena murmured. "I don't think I will, though."

"Me, neither." Jennifer smiled. "Any man who can stay away

from doves can do the same with his daughter." She stood up. "I'm cuttin' out. Want to come?"

Elena shook her head. "I have to take some whiskey home right after school."

Jennifer chuckled sarcastically. "You best make yourself scarce once he gets into it." She glanced at the schoolhouse, then scampered away under the trees.

When Elena arrived home that afternoon, the stallion was tied in the corral and she heard the sounds of blacksmithing coming from the stable. She leaned from the saddle to unlatch the gate and relatch it after herself, then rode Rojo inside. Seth had been shaping a horseshoe on the anvil. His shirt was off and the curves of his muscles gleamed with sweat in the dim light. Watching Elena ride in, he held a hammer in one hand and the red-hot horseshoe with tongs in the other. His gunbelt was hanging from a nail on the wall behind him. Rojo stretched his neck toward Seth and nickered.

He set the hammer down and immersed the shoe in a pail of water. Steam hissed up as he came forward, his eyes on the horse. Elena sat there watching them say hello, feeling pleased that Rojo remembered him. The horse pushed its nose into Seth's bare belly, slobbering on him with its big lips. He laughed as he rubbed the red nose, then he kissed the bony space between Rojo's eyes. Finally he looked up at Elena.

"You're a sight," he said, his voice full of love. "I spent my loneliest days in the company of this horse, running from one lawman or another, and there you sit with your skirt falling over your knee and a ribbon in your hair like a vision I don't deserve."

She felt pleased beyond measure. "I think you deserve it," she said impulsively.

He laughed, reaching up to lift her down. "Lord, you don't weigh more'n a feather," he said, setting her on her feet in front of him.

The top of her head barely reached to the rise of his chest, covered with a thick mat of brown hair funneling into a line that disappeared beneath his belt. She looked up as he bent down to kiss her cheek. Before he could get away, she moved her face to kiss him, too, and accidentally brushed his mouth with her own. Surprised by the taste of whiskey, she touched it with her tongue. He pulled back in surprise, though his eyes were laughing, then he grabbed her close in a hug.

"You're playing with fire, Elena," he whispered against her ear. "You best watch your step." He let go of her and returned to the anvil.

She saw his back then, crisscrossed with scars from what must have been more than one brutal whipping. There wasn't an inch of skin unmarred. She shuddered, though it was hot near the fire. He turned around and gave her a playful smile, telling her he knew what she'd seen, then he picked up the tongs and fished the horseshoe out of the water. "You ever shoe a horse?" he asked.

She shook her head.

"I could use some help. Maybe you best go put on some pants, though, so you won't look so pretty."

"I ain't pretty," she said.

"Who told you that?"

She shrugged. "Everybody."

"Well, they're wrong," he said.

She wanted to laugh, but all she said was, "I brought you some whiskey."

"Did you?" He smiled. "Where is it?"

"In the saddlepockets," she said.

"I'll put Rojo up. You run along and change."

"All right," she said, unwilling to leave him.

He laughed. "Move, girl! I want you back here by the time this shoe's ready to fit."

She laughed too, running from the stable and the hold of his eyes. She climbed the fence, kicking her skirts out of the way with impatience, and ran across the yard into the house. When Rico called her from the kitchen, Elena reluctantly answered her mother's summons.

"I'll need your help," Rico said, not looking up from the pot she was stirring on the stove.

"Seth wants me to help shoe Padre," Elena protested.

Rico frowned, then gave in with a sigh. "Why didn't I have two daughters, if the one I have is only going to be half a girl?"

"Seth seems to like me the way I am," she retorted.

Rico smiled. "So do I. Go along. Maybe Jesse will be finished with his novena in time to help in the kitchen."

Elena spun away, hurrying into her room to change.

Rico came and stood in the door, watching her. "Did you get the whiskey?"

"Yeah. But Seth already had some."

A tremor of worry ran across Rico's face. She walked to the window and looked out at the yard. "I wish Esperanza were here," she murmured, as if talking to herself. "She always had such good advice."

"What do you need advice about?" Elena asked, stepping out of her petticoats.

Rico laughed gently. "Nothing you would understand."

Elena sat down to unbutton her shoes. "I was talking to Jennifer about when *her* father came home."

"I hope you're not putting Seth in the company of Hollister Pardee," Rico admonished.

"No," Elena said, kicking her shoes off and standing up. "It's just that both she and Matty knew Seth was back before I told them."

Rico nodded. "He stopped off at Blue's on his way through town."

Elena stepped into her overalls, tucked in her middy, and pulled the straps onto her shoulders. She remembered Jennifer saying Hollister Pardee had "done it" to her, and on impulse Elena asked, "Did you like having Seth in your bed again?"

"Very much," Rico answered, the color rising to her cheeks.

"What's it like?" Elena asked.

"You'll find out in good time. Why all these questions? Has Danny been putting ideas in your head?"

"No," she said quickly, sitting down again to pull on her boots and tuck her pant legs inside. Staring at a scar on the toe of one boot, she whispered, "Rico, I feel strange with Seth."

Her mother came over and hugged her close. "It'll pass," she said softly. "We have to remember that he feels strange, too, and we all have to help each other."

"I mean," Elena said, her face pressed against the soft warmth of her mother's skirts, "he makes me feel all trembly inside."

Rico stroked Elena's hair. "You have a place in his heart no one else ever will. I envy you."

Elena looked up. "Why?" she asked, incredulous that anyone would envy her.

Rico smiled. "Because in many ways I'm just one more woman in his life, but you're his only daughter."

"Doesn't that mean his feelings for me will always be limited?"

Rico shook her head. "It's married love that's limited, because it's confused with a lot of other things."

"What other things?"

Rico sighed. "Power and remorse, regret and desire."

"I don't understand," Elena said.

Rico laughed. "Neither do I. Run along now and help him all you can."

Elena took her hat from the peg and stepped through the window, as was her habit, then ran across the yard and climbed the fence. When she walked into the stable, she saw that Seth had put his shirt on and that the new bottle of whiskey was a third gone. He grinned at her overalls. "Why don't you put a hay stalk in your mouth and say 'dad-gumit' or something?"

"Something," she said.

He laughed, retrieving the finished shoe from the bucket of water. "Come here," he said, starting for the door. "I want you to keep Padre quiet while I hammer nails into his feet."

She took a firm grip on the rope just beneath the stallion's chin, murmuring comforting sounds while Seth approached the near forefoot. Padre jerked the tether out of her hands, yanking it tight against the fence. She grabbed the rope and pulled his head down again.

"Whoa, there," Seth said, sidling up backward to lift the hoof between his knees.

With one toss of his head, Padre again slipped from Elena's hands, pulled his hoof free, and reared as high as the tether allowed. Seth jumped out of the way, then looked at her as if she were failing him. "Here now," he said gruffly to the stallion, reaching for the hoof again.

"Easy, Padre," she cooed, pulling his head down and rubbing his nose. "You're gonna like having new shoes."

As the first nail struck into the hoof, the horse shuddered. "See, it doesn't hurt," she crooned. "It just feels strange, is all. Sort of like having a father around who nails you to the wall with his eyes."

Seth looked over his shoulder at her. "It's no worse than having a daughter," he said around the nails in his mouth, "who kisses me in ways she shouldn't." He took a nail out, turned away, and lifted the hammer.

Just before it fell she said in a coaxing tone, as if still talking to the horse, "I can't help it. He makes me feel that way."

The hammer came down hard and Padre jerked at his tether, but this time Elena held him.

"I've always believed," Seth said between blows, "that some girls oughta marry young."

"At fourteen?" she asked.

"I thought you were fifteen."

"Next month is my birthday."

He hammered the last nail in, dropped the hoof, and stood up looking almost worried. "You mad at me 'cause I forgot that?"

She shook her head, then smiled impishly. "As long as you give me a present."

He laughed. "What would you like?"

"Padre," she said.

"You're asking for my horse?"

"Just to ride at the races," she pleaded.

"You ain't strong enough to handle him."

"The race isn't until July. I could gentle him in two months."

"Riding around the ranch alone," he conceded, "maybe you could. But in a field of other horses, some of 'em mares, you ain't got the muscle to control him."

"I'll never have much muscle," she retorted angrily, "but there's other ways to accomplish things."

He chuckled at her anger. "I'm beginning to suspect the world was lucky you weren't born a man."

"Some man will be, too," she answered, stroking the sleek neck of the stallion as she wondered what on earth had possessed her to say that.

"I agree," Seth said softly, "but you'll be hard put to find him."

"That's your job, ain't it," she murmured, then bit her tongue, remembering Rico had said they shouldn't ask too much of Seth. Shyly she met his eyes.

They were the pale gray of smoke, camouflaging his thoughts. "Reckon it is," he said. "You think you could give me a little time?"

"You're the one said I should marry young," she pointed out.

He laughed, taking more nails from his shirt pocket. "For

today, let's just finish shoeing this horse. Think you can handle that?"

"I'm ready," she said.

"Ripe is more like it," he muttered, turning to lift the rear hoof.

22

Lobo came loping his horse into the yard just as they finished. The stallion kicked up a ruckus when the gelding entered the corral. Elena stepped back fast, watching the stud take affront that he was tied in place while a eunuch trotted into the stable sheltering four horses, two of them mares. Padre screamed his outrage, kicking his hind feet with enough force to knock a wall out of his way, then rearing as high as the tether allowed, bellowing his frustration that he couldn't attack the gelding flat out.

"Want to try him now?" Seth asked with an amused smile.

"Why not?" she answered, swallowing her fear.

"You sure?"

"Will you come with me?"

He nodded, then turned toward the stable. "Hey, Lobo, let me borrow your horse."

Lobo came back, leading the gelding. "Where you going?"

"Me and Elena are gonna take a ride," Seth said, walking into the stable.

Lobo looked at his sister. "You sure you can handle Randy?"

"I'm riding Padre," she said.

He laughed. "You're shittin' me."

Seth came back carrying his blanket, saddle, and bridle. He gave the bridle to Elena. Like the saddle, it was black and studded with silver conchos. She studied them, thinking Danny's designs were more intricate but these medallions were thick and polished brightly. She looked back at Seth in time to see him yank the cinch tight and tie it. The stallion snorted angrily. Seth glanced at her legs, calculating their length, then adjusted the stirrups. "Reckon that'll do," he said, taking the bridle.

Seth grabbed Padre's forelock, pulled his head down, and forced the bit against his tooth. The stallion reared, lifting Seth off his feet, all hundred and eighty pounds of him. "Here now," he said roughly, jerking the horse down and shoving until the bit was in place, then grabbing an ear and securing the head strap. He unhooked the halter and pulled it out from under the bridle, then flipped the far rein across the stallion's withers and turned to offer her a hand up.

She looked at Lobo, who had forgotten to close his mouth, and his total disbelief in her ability to ride Padre spurred her ambition. She accepted Seth's hand and approached the horse.

"He ain't trained to hold still for a mount," Seth said. "So you best be there quick as you can."

She took the reins, grabbed the horn, and stabbed her foot into the stirrup. Seth put his hand on her bottom to impel her up as Padre skittered sideways. She swung her leg across and caught the other stirrup just as the stallion lowered his head to buck. She yanked him back up and kicked in her heels, thinking to expend his energy circling the corral rather than fighting her, but he broke for the far fence and jumped it before she could catch her wits. Managing only to keep her seat, she clung to the horn as Padre galloped across the yard and around the sliver of mountain.

He was fast! That was all she could think as she leaned low into his whipping mane. He hadn't even hit his stride yet but was still hurtling forward like a bullet. They reached the road and she reined him left, toward the desert instead of town, thinking that at his speed the miles to Tejoe would be covered in an instant and they would go tearing through the streets like an Apache uprising. She laughed in the wind of his power.

He had turned with her rein, so even though she couldn't yet stop him, she could direct him. That was all she needed to win a race. It wouldn't matter if they kept running to the Pacific Ocean: first across the finish line was all that mattered. Padre settled into a rhythm and she rode him like a rocking chair, marveling at the smoothness of his gait as she watched the desert flash by, a glimpse of saguaro, a patch of prickly pear gone before she could anticipate landing in its barbs. Gradually she became aware of a horse following in the distance, and she smiled, knowing no one could catch her. She was free by the grace of the stallion she rode.

When she saw the turnoff to the Nickles ranch, she couldn't believe they had galloped so far. She turned Padre up the trail, thinking to show him off to Danny. Again, from the distance, she heard the horse coming behind. She reined Padre in a tight circle until he stopped, dancing and mincing against the bit. Seth came galloping around the turn on Lobo's lathered gelding, a horse most men would give their eyeteeth to own. Elena laughed, seeing that Padre hadn't even begun to sweat. Seth trotted over to her, smiling his congratulations.

"We'll beat everything in the county," she crowed.

"I believe you're right," he said.

"Come on," she called, giving the stallion his head. "Want you to meet a friend of mine."

Again the other horse was left in Padre's dust. She galloped up the trail and tore into the Nickles's yard, leaning all her weight against the reins and shouting "Whoa, Padre, whoa!" The stallion nearly collided with the veranda, then reared and spun around until she could hold him in place, though he danced with impatience.

Abneth and Danny Nickles had been sitting on the porch waiting for supper. They lurched to their feet at the attack of the horse. Danny left his father behind and came down the steps with a grin, but Abneth was less amused.

"Goldurn, Elena," he shouted. "Where'd you get too much horse?" Seth came galloping into the yard and Abneth Nickles nodded solemnly. "Should've known," Abneth said, walking out to greet him.

Elena watched as Seth swung down and shook hands with his neighbor.

"Good to see you home," Abneth said. "Glad you came by to visit."

"Thanks," Seth said. "It was my daughter's idea."

They turned to look at her just as Danny caught hold of the stallion's bridle. "Won't you step down and sit a spell, Elena?" he asked.

She tore her eyes from Seth and smiled at her friend. "We've galloped the whole way," she said. "Reckon we ought to walk our horses a spell."

"Reckon that's best," he conceded, letting go of her bridle and moving toward Seth. "I'm Danny Nickles," he said, extending his hand. "Pleased to meet'cha, Mr. Strummar."

"Haven't we met before?" Seth asked, shaking with him.

"You're prob'ly thinking of my brothers," Danny said. "Ethan and Abe are away at school. We lost Josh in the smallpox epidemic a coupla years back."

"Sorry to hear it," Seth said to Abneth.

"Had four sons and lost three," the farmer said. "Built up this spread to pass down and none of 'em want it. Even Danny thinks he's too good to work the land."

Danny smiled at Seth and said, "Elena told me at school that you brought a stallion home. He's a beauty."

"Thanks," Seth said.

The men all smiled up at her as Padre pranced. She turned and held him, but just barely.

Abneth said, "Whyn't you stay for supper?"

"Some other time," Seth said, swinging back onto his horse. "We're expected at home."

"Will we see ya in church on Sunday?" Abneth called.

"Is Holcroft still preaching?" Seth asked, gathering his reins as his horse chomped noisily on the bit.

"Yeah. And Miss Gates at the pianer."

Seth laughed. "Nobody's married her yet?"

Abneth shook his head.

"What's wrong with the men in this county?" Seth joked as his horse spun beneath him, making the stallion stomp in disdain.

Abneth grinned. "You've been gone, and the young blades forgot how it was done."

Elena felt a tug on her reins and looked down at Danny, holding the stallion's bridle again.

"I see what you mean," he said, sounding hurt. "Can't hardly anyone else compete."

"I wanted you to see me with Padre," she offered.

"Which one?" he asked with an edge.

She felt a surge of anger. "Let loose!"

Danny dropped the rein and backed away, spreading his hands wide in a mock gesture of apology. She gave him a puzzled frown, then kicked the stallion into a run, hearing Seth follow behind. Out of sight of the house, she reined the stallion to a nervous trot along the trail.

When Seth had caught up, he asked, "Is Danny the one you wanted me to meet?"

"Reckon," she said.

Seth thought a moment. "Seems to me he beat Lobo up once about fifteen years ago."

"You're thinking of his brothers," she said. "They always did everything together."

"Can Danny stand on his own?"

"You tell me."

He chuckled. "If you weren't my daughter, I'd turn you over my knee and spank your bare bottom."

She blushed, unable to look at him as she asked, "You mean you'd spank a woman who wasn't your daughter?"

"Only a troublesome one who kept pestering for what she was gonna get anyway."

Elena couldn't think of an answer to that.

After a moment, Seth said, "You sit that horse mighty well, Miss Strummar."

"Thank you, sir," she answered demurely, finally daring to look at him again. His eyes were like ice.

"Of course any young lady who rides astride," he said, "is putting ideas into the mind of every man who sees her."

"Is that her fault?" she asked defensively.

"Maybe not," he admitted. "But she's gonna have to deal with the consequences."

"Seems to me," she said, "all women ever do is deal with the consequences of loving men."

His eyes warmed until they were almost blue. "You sound like Esperanza."

"I take that as a fine compliment," she murmured.

They shared a painful moment of sorrow before he looked away. "Did she hear I was pardoned before she died?"

"Yes," Elena said.

"I'm sorry I missed her," he said.

Angrily she asked, "What were you doing that was more important than coming home?"

Resentment flared in his eyes. He iced them over with a sheen of indifference as he let his gaze slide down her body and return to her face, but his voice was kind when he said, "The world's more complicated than you prob'ly think, Elena."

She nodded, conceding the truth of that, then asked with more politeness, "Where did you go after prison?"

"To a friend," he said, looking away again. "I was sick and . . . just sick. I needed shelter, that's all. Lourdes gave it to me."

"Where was that?"

"San Antone."

"Did you see your wife before leaving Texas?"

"No," he said with an edge. "She's remarried now anyway, so she ain't my wife anymore." Again he let his gaze drift down Elena's body before meeting her eyes. "Rico's my wife."

"You never married her," Elena pointed out.

"No, I didn't," he agreed.

"Do you intend to?"

Sharply he said, "I never expected so many questions from my daughter."

"What did you expect?" she asked softly.

"That she'd be a child, easy to handle."

"I'm not a child," she said.

His eyes bored into her as if that fact were somehow her fault.

Trying to lighten his anger, she said, "Maybe I just want you to make an honest woman of my mother."

"Is that why you kissed me in the barn?"

She looked away. "I don't know why I did that," she admitted.

"I do," he said. "Look at me, Elena."

Slowly she managed to raise her eyes to his.

"I feel it, too," he said sternly, "but what we share is more important than that."

"My being your daughter, you mean."

He nodded.

"And the other?"

"Will pass if we let it."

She looked ahead toward the road to home. "It feels so strong," she whispered.

"That's why we have to curb it," he said. "If we let it loose, it'll destroy every chance for happiness we have left."

She was silent, thinking he held her only chance of happiness.

"I'm not only old enough to be your father," he said, as if reading her thoughts, "I am your father. And believe it or not, Elena, there are some rules I won't break."

She shrugged. "Can't see why their rules matter when everybody thinks we're pariahs anyway."

He laughed painfully. "I found out they matter a lot."

"Because they put you in prison?" she asked softly.

"Among other things. But the truth is, I've lived my whole life in prison, only instead of being shut in, I was shut out. Most nights I slept in the wilderness with only coyotes for company, and I kept moving so often that sometimes I had to get up and look at the country before I could remember where I was."

She thought about all the explorations she had gone on with Danny, and how they never went so far they couldn't get home for supper. "Some folks would call that freedom," she said.

"You, maybe?" he teased.

She snuck a look at him and saw his eyes were as kind as his smile. "All the stories I heard about you," she said, responding to his warmth, "made a big point of how much fun you had being an outlaw. How you were always laughing in the face of death, telling jokes and making clever remarks in the middle of a showdown, always in command and riding danger like a hawk glides on the wind. Seems to me, living in the wilderness and dropping into towns once in a while to show the good citizens how it's done would be a pretty satisfying life."

"You shouldn't believe tall tales," he said.

"Are you saying they weren't true?"

"How much of what the good citizens of Tejoe say about you is true?"

She thought a minute. "Some of it's partly true."

He laughed.

"There's an oasis on the other side of that bluff," she said. "Want to get down and sit a spell?"

"All right," he said, though his eyes were wary again.

She reined the stallion away from the trail, into a box canyon green with grass fed by a spring. Listening to him coming behind, she shivered with the anticipation of having his undivided attention without even the horses between them. She swung down and stood holding her reins, watching him hobble his horse, then take off its bridle and hang it from the saddlehorn. Without looking at her, he did the same with the stallion. Giving her a guarded smile, he laid his arm on her shoulders as they walked into the broad canopy of shade beneath a cottonwood tree.

He dropped his hat on the grass, then lay on his stomach, hiding his face in his folded arms.

She fell to her knees beside him. "May I touch you?" she whispered.

"Sure," he answered without looking up.

She reached out to slide her palm lightly across the breadth of his shoulders, feeling the tension of his muscles flickering with her touch. "I want us to love each other, Seth," she petitioned.

"I want that, too," he said from within the shelter of his arms.

She watched him a moment, restraining her desire to trace the curve of his ear with her fingertip. Instead she ran her hand down the knobby length of his spine to his gunbelt, studded with cartridges she caressed as if they were him.

"Elena," he said, rolling onto his side and meeting her eyes, "I want you to understand I ain't no hero."

She took his warning as an invitation. Before she could allow herself to hesitate, she moved away from him to sit on the grass and tug off her boots. She could feel his eyes, though she couldn't bring herself to look at him, could feel what she took to be his approval as she stood up and unfastened the clasps on her overalls, let them fall and kicked them free, pulled her middy off over her head, unlaced her camisole and took it off. Feeling sunlight on her breasts for the first time, she pulled her drawers down and stepped out of them, pushed the pile of her clothing away with her foot, then boldly met his eyes, warm with love.

"Is this how your mother brought you up?" he teased.

"I was brought up to go after what I want," she answered.

"I can see that. But do you really think this is right?"

"I don't care about being right."

"I can see that, too. It'll get you in trouble."

"Touch me," she pleaded, dropping to her knees in front of him.

He took hold of her hand and guided it between his legs. "Feel how it's soft?" He laughed. "I can't fuck you, Elena. I love you too much."

She felt her palm pressed into the soft mound held tight by his pants. His genitals were hot and alive, stirring beneath her touch.

"You're better off," he said. Lifting her hand to his mouth, he kissed her fingers. "I tend to hurt the women I fuck."

"Why?" she whispered as his lips gently brushed across her fingertips.

He sighed. "Reckon I've still got a lot of meanness inside me," he said, kissing the palm of her hand. "Most of the time I'm able to keep it under rein, but when my guard's down it tends to break loose."

"I don't believe you'd hurt me."

He dropped her hand and touched his finger to her lips as he said, "I want you to keep on believing that." He stood up. "You go on home, and we'll act like this never happened."

Dismayed, she watched him grab the stallion's forelock and slide the bit into his mouth. The horse raised his head, apparently more interested in savoring his last biteful of grass than in having the bridle secured over his ears. Seth adjusted the stirrups, letting them out full length, then pulled the hobbles free and swung on.

He studied her a moment, sitting naked cross-legged in the grass, then he smiled as if with regret. "I'll always remember you offering me the sweetness of your promise, Elena. I feel it's an honor you did it. I hope you can understand my refusal is one, too." He reined the stallion around and rode away without looking back.

Elena remembered the regret of his smile, the pride in his eyes that she dared do such a thing, and the heat of his sex beneath her hand. She felt certain that in time they would break through the barrier of his reluctance and throw propriety to the wind.

Slowly she stood up and retrieved her clothes, feeling almost as happy as she imagined she would have if he had succumbed to her temptation.

When she rode into the yard, Lobo came out of the house and walked across to meet her. His face of impending ridicule plunged her mood into gloom.

"Did Padre throw you?" he smirked, possessively grabbing the reins of his horse.

"No," she answered, swinging down. "Seth wanted him back, is all."

"Where he'd go?"

She shrugged, turning away.

Lobo caught hold of her arm. "What'd you do to him, Elena?"

"Nothing!" she cried, trying to escape.

"I bet," he accused. "I saw the way you were looking at him last night."

"I don't know what you're talking about," she retorted.

He snickered and said, "The way women look when they'd crawl across hot coals to suck a man's cock."

"What an obscene thing to say," she whispered.

"Not as obscene as doing it with your own father," he answered. Letting her loose, he swung onto his horse, jerked it around so it spun in a rear, then dug in his spurs and galloped out of the yard.

She stood watching the dust of his departure settle around her, feeling stunned that what she felt so deeply could be read on her face. Escaping to the privacy of her room, she smothered her tears in her pillow, hoping Rico wouldn't hear her crying. But her mother came into the room and sat on the bed.

"What's wrong?" Rico asked softly.

Elena turned and nestled her face in her mother's lap. "I made a mistake," she sobbed.

"That's not unusual when you're young," Rico answered, stroking Elena's hair. "It's not even especially difficult when you're older."

Elena sat up and wiped her tears with a sleeve of her shirt. "Seth didn't come back from our ride, did he."

"No," Rico said.

"Where do you think he went?" Elena asked with a sniffle.

"To Blue's saloon. Or maybe to visit Joaquín."

"Will he come home?"

Rico studied her a moment, then asked, "Is there a reason he shouldn't?"

Elena let herself fall back on the pillow. Staring at the ceiling she asked, "Did he make love to you last night?"

Rico took a long moment to answer. Finally she murmured, "No."

Forcing herself to look at her mother, Elena said, "He told me he hurts women he fucks."

Rico smiled sadly. "I've always known that about his past, but he never hurt me. He kept me away from all that."

"Does that mean he loves you?"

"Yes."

"Can he love a woman he doesn't fuck?"

"Don't use that word, Elena. It's not becoming on a girl."

"Will you answer my question?" she demanded impatiently.

Rico studied her another long moment, then asked, "Are you interested for my sake, or your own?"

Elena saw the hurt in Rico's eyes and felt ashamed. "Oh Mama," she sobbed, burying her face in her mother's lap again. "I don't understand what's happening to me."

Rico sighed, stroking Elena's hair in a gentle rhythm. "You're just now discovering what it is to be a woman," she said tenderly, "and you have no experience of Seth as your father. When you put that together with the feelings you've bottled up all these years, the love and yearning you've felt for him all mixed up with anger that he wasn't here for you, it's not surprising you're confused. Seth understands what's happening. He won't hurt you."

Elena thought of everyone understanding what she felt while she alone floundered in ignorance. "I feel like an idiot," she whispered.

"You know something?" Rico asked sadly. "Last night I felt like one too, not knowing how to make him touch me. So I did nothing. The only thing I can figure out to do is wait for him to want me."

Elena sat up. "I thought when he came home, our problems would be over."

"And we'd live happily ever after?" Rico laughed softly. "Is that what you thought?"

Elena felt a flash of insight, discomfiting in its certitude. "That won't ever be true, will it."

Rico shook her head, then stood up and looked out the window. Darkness had fallen across the yard, silent and empty beyond the pane of glass. "I made a special supper tonight," she said. "And now it looks like Seth won't be here."

"Because of me," Elena said, ashamed again.

Rico turned around with a smile. "Don't take it all on yourself. Will you come eat with me?"

"Yes," Elena said, not because she was hungry but because her mother had made a special supper. "Where's Jesse?" she asked, following Rico into the kitchen.

She sighed. "Still at the novena, I suppose."

"So we're alone."

"The men will be back," Rico said without conviction.

23

★

 They ate alone in the silent kitchen. On the table were huge bowls of marinated brisket and gravy, mashed potatoes, snap beans, and a basket of fresh sourdough rolls. An apple pie cooled on the windowsill, filling the room with the scent of hot cinnamon. Between the two of them, they barely made a dent in the feast. They washed the dishes and put the food away, then sat under the portal listening for a horse on the trail.

Jesse came home an hour later, silently walking into the yard. Rico heated him a meal from the leftovers and sat in the kitchen talking with him as he ate. Elena could hear them through the open window, but she wasn't much interested in his geography test or the novena for Señora Alvarez. Afterward, he came out and sat with them a while, the three of them watching the moonlit yard from the shadow of the portal. "It's more peaceful here," he said, "without Seth and Lobo around."

"Give them a chance, Jesse," Rico said patiently. "This is only their second day home."

"They ain't home, though," he answered. "Seems like they're the ones not giving us a chance."

"Some things take time," she said.

"All those years should've been enough," he countered. "Seems to me Seth don't want a family, least not one he has to live with."

"I'm sure it's hard for him after being alone so long," she said. "He'll get used to us, and then he'll stay around more."

"I'd just as soon he decided he didn't want us and went back to Mexico. It'd be better'n always waiting for him to show up."

Rico gave him a gentle smile. "You don't have to wait, sweetheart. Go ahead with whatever you'd be doing if he weren't here."

"Since he ain't, guess I will." After a moment, he said, "This is what we mostly do at night anyway, sit on the porch."

Rico laughed softly. "Yes, it is."

"Only all of a sudden it feels like we're doing it 'cause of him."

"Yes," she said again.

"Think I'll go study," Jesse said, standing up. "That way I won't be waiting."

"Give me a kiss," she said, holding up her arms.

He leaned down and hugged her close as Elena watched. At thirteen, Jesse was just starting to gain his height. His hands and feet seemed too big, and his careful control accentuated his clumsiness. He would probably end up as tall as his father, but Elena couldn't imagine Jesse ever achieving the grace that came from mastering life. When he kissed her cheek on his way by, she kissed him back with more affection than usual.

About nine, Lobo came home. After putting his horse away, he walked across the yard and leaned against a post of the portal. "I remember hearing a motto once," he teased, "about time being a woman waiting. Or in this case, two."

Rico laughed, then asked, "Do you know where he is?"

"Yeah," Lobo said, dropping his gaze. "He's at Blue's."

"Wearing his gun?" she whispered.

He nodded, meeting her eyes again.

Rico sighed. "I wish he could understand that times have changed."

"Times may have," Lobo said, "but Seth never will."

"Did he say anything about coming home?"

"He said he'd see me later." Lobo smiled. "You got anything to eat?"

Elena stood up. "I'll get it," she said, walking into the kitchen. Through the open window she heard Rico ask, "What was he doing when you found him in Nogales?"

Lobo laughed. "Running guns to bandits in the Sierra Madre."

"Was he living with a woman?"

Elena raised the wick on the lamp and quietly set the skillet on the fire before she heard Lobo say, "Not any one in particular."

Rico was silent.

Lobo asked gently, "Won't you come in and sit with us?"

"It's cooler out here," she said.

He came into the kitchen through the back door, hung his hat on a peg, and sat down, watching Elena cut the brisket. She lay three thick slices in the skillet and poured gravy on top, listening to it simmer as she began shaping the cold mashed potatoes into cakes. From behind her, Lobo said, "Seth told me you did real good on Padre."

She didn't look up, wary of his friendship. "Is that all he said?"

"What do you want to hear?"

She shrugged, turning away to lay the potato cakes in the bubbling gravy. Moving them around with the spatula, she asked, "He's not mad at me?"

"What for?"

She shrugged again. "I was just wondering, is all."

"I think he likes you a lot, Elena. But then, he always did."

She opened a drawer, took out a knife and fork, and laid them on the table. "What do you mean?"

"When you were a baby," Lobo said, "he used to fuss over you so much I'd get jealous. Used to threaten me, too, saying stuff like he was gonna teach you everything he knew since I was obviously ungrateful for his wisdom."

"I don't remember any of that," she said, moving back to the stove and flipping the potato cakes.

"You were just a baby," Lobo said. "He liked to sit under the portal, where Rico is now, holding you in his lap and playing games with his eyes. You'd laugh and he'd smile. I'd get so jealous I could hardly stand it."

She watched him intensely. "What kind of games?"

"Damn if I could tell. You're gonna burn my supper."

She lifted the skillet off the fire and quickly took the food up on a plate, then carried it to the table. As he began eating, she poured him a glass of milk from the pitcher in the icebox, put the pitcher back, and set the glass by his plate. "If he'd never left," she said wistfully, "everything would be so different."

"If he hadn't gone to prison," Lobo said around a mouthful of brisket, "somebody would've killed him by now. You ever think of that?"

She sat down across from him and shook her head.

"There was a thousand-dollar bounty on him, dead or alive. We lived like we were at war." Lobo cut a hunk of potato cake and sopped it full of gravy. "I had a standing order that if anyone rode into the yard I was to come inside and stay away from the windows." He finished off the potato cake, drank some milk, then wiped the moustache off with his thumb. "You missed all that, Elena. And, looking back on it, I don't see how he could have survived with so much money on his head. Now he's got a pardon and not much to worry about in that area."

"Not much? What?"

"There's always a chance," Lobo said, moving another potato cake into the puddle of gravy, "that some hotshot kid'll come along and try to make his reputation killing Seth. That's why Rico doesn't want him to wear a gun."

Appalled, Elena said, "He couldn't defend himself without a gun!"

"Wouldn't have to," Lobo said. "Can't make a reputation shooting an unarmed man." He finished off the brisket and sopped up the juice with the last cake. "That's what Rico means too: times have changed and men don't wear guns like they did. Seth's wearing one is telling everybody he's still in action. Which he was in Nogales. But he don't need to be here."

"You wear a gun," she pointed out.

He nodded, swallowing the last of his dinner. "Yeah, but I'm in my prime and ain't nobody could beat me. Seth's forty-eight, and though it's hard to tell, twelve years in prison must've taken something out of him."

She stood up and carried the dirty dishes to the sink, then leaned against the counter. "What are you gonna do, Lobo, now that you're home?"

"I'm thinking of going into business with Blue. We were talking about it tonight."

"Doing what?"

"Partners in his saloon. New blood, younger generation. Seth set him up, you know."

She shook her head.

"Well, he did. And all Blue's kids are girls. Women have been known to run saloons, a'course, but the Rivers girls like to pretend their money's cleaner'n that."

"Owning a saloon isn't such a disreputable thing," she said.

He grinned. "Sassy's running a whorehouse upstairs. That shades it a little darker in the eyes of the good citizens."

Elena shrugged, sick to death of what the good citizens thought of her and her family. "What do you think Seth'll do for money?"

"Nothing!" Lobo laughed. "I found out tonight he came home with ten thousand dollars."

"Where'd he get it?"

"Loot from his bank-robbing days." Lobo grinned. "Him and Allister stashed it and never got a chance to go back. After his pardon, though, Seth just rode up pretty as you please and found it where they'd left it, in a gully south of Goliad."

"Allister," she scoffed. "The very name makes me cringe."

"Does it?" Lobo asked curiously. "I wish I'd had the chance to meet him."

"Why?"

"He must've been one tough hombre."

"I'm glad he's dead." She shivered. "Imagine if he rode in here and asked Seth to put him up for old times' sake."

"That'd be something, huh? A pensionnaire for retired outlaws." Lobo laughed again. "Yeah, I can see it."

"I can't," she huffed. "They'd be smoking and spitting tobacco juice everywhere, prob'ly drunk most of the time."

"Seth don't use any kind of tobacco," Lobo mused. "And I've never seen him drunk. I mean I guess I have. If I put away as much whiskey as he does, I'd have trouble standing up. With Seth, nothing seems to happen except the bottle gets emptied."

"Do you think he'll be home tonight?"

Lobo shrugged, then lowered his voice when he said, "Sassy was coming onto him pretty strong when I left."

Feeling herself blush, Elena turned away to scrape the scraps out of the skillet into the coffee can they used for garbage.

Lobo came over and kissed her cheek with unexpected gentleness. "Thanks for supper," he said, lightly slapping her bottom before leaving her alone.

As she washed the dishes, Elena tried to imagine how it would feel to be Seth's son rather than his daughter. Lobo strutted through life like a walking challenge, wearing the gun Seth had worn as an outlaw. Jesse went to Mass every day seeking expiation for sins he was incapable of committing. Plenty of boys were aggressive, and most attended church, but she didn't know any who were as excessive about those things as her brothers, so Elena guessed it was being Seth's sons that pushed them to extremes.

All the members of her family were pariahs because of Seth, even Rico, who shone with virtue. Though everyone in town called her Mrs. Strummar, they all knew she wasn't his wife. Elena had once heard some church ladies clucking with pity over the fact that Seth had never married Rico. Elena had pounced on the old biddies, reminding them of what they already knew: that Seth had a wife in Texas who refused to divorce him. When they'd looked at her as if she had the pox, Elena had realized she couldn't defend her mother's honor by making a spectacle of herself in public.

But it seemed nearly everything she did created a public spectacle. Within hours of the race at last year's county fair, Mrs. Rivers had told Rico the churchwomen were scandalized that she'd allowed Elena to ride in the race—not only competing against men, but wearing pants and sitting astride. Rico had defended her, saying she was only thirteen and still a child, then teased Mrs. Rivers by saying, "Amy, you're just jealous because Elena doesn't have to wear a merry widow in this heat." When Mrs. Rivers got huffy and said she wasn't the only one raising eyebrows, Blue told her to shush, arguing that Elena had won and that's all anybody should care about. She *had* won, but the tumult in town over her audacity took away the glory of it.

Suddenly she sympathized with Lobo, in an inside-out kind of way. He wanted the world to be as it was in Seth's past, wide open and wild with danger, and she wanted the world as she imagined it would be in the future, with girls having the same opportunities as boys across the board. Both she and Lobo were out of step with their times, and for both of them their oddity was more noticed because they were the children of a famous outlaw. Jesse was different, but she suspected he spent so much time in church because he was trying to hide from his father's fame.

Having finished the dishes, Elena turned down the wick on the lantern, then walked across the parlor to stand in the open front doorway.

Rico looked up and gave her a smile. "Going to bed, sweetheart?"

Elena nodded. She wanted to comfort her mother, but couldn't think of anything more to say than, "Good night."

"Good night, Elena," Rico said.

The sadness in her mother's voice made Elena feel like crying. She went to her room and changed into her nightgown, then lay on top of her covers beneath the open window and fell asleep, wishing Seth would come home.

Waking up to the jingle of silver outside her window, she sat up and saw Seth tying Padre to the portal. Her father's face was lit by the dim lamp in the kitchen, and she thought Lobo was right: if Seth had been drinking all these hours, she couldn't tell. He looked handsome, giving Rico a smile, then he moved out of Elena's vision as he sat down.

"Thought you'd be asleep," he said.

"I was getting ready to go in," Rico answered. "Are you hungry?"

"Not for food," he said.

"Wait, Seth," Rico murmured. "Talk to me a while, won't you?"

He sighed and Elena could hear the clink of his spurs as she watched his boots appear on the railing. "Reckon that's why I stayed in town so long, hoping I wouldn't have to do that."

"And to get drunk enough to fuck me?" Rico asked with an edge in her voice that Elena had never heard before.

After a moment, Seth said, "I can get drunk here."

"Did you go upstairs at Blue's?"

"Don't push me, Rico," he warned.

"I'm merely asking a question."

"All right," he said with measured calm. "No, I didn't. Why should I when I have two beautiful women at home?"

"That's what I want to talk to you about, Seth," Rico said, suddenly pleading. "Be careful with Elena. She's at a vulnerable age."

He laughed softly. "I'd say she's prime to get married."

"She's only fourteen."

"Almost fifteen," he said. "You know what she wants for her birthday?"

"No," she said.

"To ride Padre in the race."

"Don't let her, Seth. He's too strong for her."

"She handled him all right today."

"He ran away with her! I saw it. You shouldn't have let her anywhere near him."

Seth chuckled. "Too late now. She's had the feel of a stud between her legs and won't be satisfied with that little filly you bought her."

"You make it sound dirty," Rico protested, but there was laughter in her voice.

"Power is, ain't it?"

"Yes," she whispered.

His boots disappeared and Elena could hear the rustle of her mother's skirts, but the two people under the portal didn't stand up. Elena's cheeks burned as she imagined what they were doing.

After a moment, he said, "About last night——"

"You don't have to explain," Rico said.

"I was afraid I'd hurt you," he said anyway.

"And tonight you're not?"

He sighed, propping one boot on the rail again, the silver rowel of his spur shining in the lamplight. "Elena told me something today. She said most of women's lives are spent dealing with the consequences of loving men."

"Elena said that?"

"She's a lot older'n fourteen," he said.

"Yes," she said.

"That's all your life's been these last years, Rico—paying the price of loving me. I'd like to try'n make it up in the time we have left."

"We could have lots of time, Seth."

"Maybe. We got tonight, I'm pretty sure of that."

Rico laughed.

Elena listened to them walk into the house and close the front door, then the door to their bedroom. She lay alone, trembling with a need she could neither deny nor explain.

After a while, Seth came out of Rico's bedroom, crossed the parlor, and went outside again, then she heard him leading the stallion toward the barn. On impulse, she climbed out the window and ran after him.

The stallion shied, snorting and sidestepping away. Seth quieted his horse, then turned to look at her wearing only her nightgown. He smiled. "You're apt to step on a scorpion going around barefoot, Elena."

"I'm sorry for what I did today," she blurted out. "I'd take it back if I could."

He pulled her close in a hug. "I wouldn't," he said, his voice soft by her ear. "Don't ever tell your mother I said so, but I was proud of you for doing that. It took a lot of sand." He pulled her around to his side, away from his gun and the hand that held the reins, leaving his arm on her shoulders as they walked toward the corral. "I was also proud of myself for how I handled it," he said, smiling down at her. "You think I handled it okay?"

"Yes," she said, sliding her arm around his waist, her fingertips touching the cartridges in his gunbelt, round and hard and snug in their leather loops. She fondled them, gaining a sense of security from the perfection of the enclosure.

"Good," he said. " 'Cause I ain't felt proud of myself for a while."

"When was the last time?" she asked, loving the sound of the stallion clomping along behind them.

"I can't hardly remember," Seth said.

"Try," she coaxed.

He unlatched the gate and let her walk in ahead of him, then led the stallion through. "Let's see," he said, relatching the gate. "Guess it was when Joaquín got married."

"Why did that make you feel proud?" she asked, puzzled.

"I always felt bad for taking him on as my partner," he said, holding her hand as they crossed the soft dust of the corral. "I needed him, but he sure as hell didn't need me. Reckon I was proud of keeping him alive long enough to reach the point where he felt he could handle the responsibility of a wife. And then he'd stood up for me when I got married and it was like closing the circle, doing that for him." He let go of her hand to open the stable door. "I felt I'd done something right. Course, it didn't take me long to mess it up."

"How did you mess it up?" she asked, standing isolated in the dark until he lit the lamp. As she watched him tie Padre then unknot the cinch, she wondered if Seth would answer her.

He tossed the saddle on the rack, led the stallion into a stall and took off the bridle, then came out and hung it on a peg. "It's a long story," he said, his eyes warm but sad.

"I'd like to hear it."

Lifting her by the waist, he set her on the half-wall of Rojo's stall, then leaned against the pillar and studied her a moment. Finally he said, "I played with a woman I shouldn't have, and she killed a man thinking she was protecting me, so I let myself be arrested to protect her."

"You're talking about Hekuba, aren't you?"

"So you know about it."

"Some. I know she was sent to prison for killing a man. I never knew exactly what happened, but I've heard stories about it. She died in childbirth, and Heaven and Joaquín went to Yuma to bring the child home." She stared at him with sudden understanding. "Aaron's your son?"

Seth nodded.

"Life is sure complicated. All these years I've been thinking of him as my cousin even though I knew he wasn't, and now it turns out he's my brother."

Seth chuckled. "I haven't met him yet. What's he like?"

She bit her lip, trying to think of the words to describe Aaron. "He's pretty tall for his age, taller'n me even though he's younger, and he's not afraid of anything, it doesn't seem. He goes hunting in the mountains a lot, sleeps out like an Apache all by himself. He's good with his rifle and brings home plenty of game." She shrugged. "He's quiet, but I like him."

Seth asked softly, "You got anything on under that night-gown?"

The door at the end of the aisle opened, flooding them with light, and Lobo stepped out. He stared at the two of them, then finally said, "I heard voices."

Seth smiled. "Must've been us."

"So you came home," Lobo said.

Seth looked at Elena. "Yeah," he said, lifting her down. "And now I'm going to sleep. See you tomorrow."

He laid his arm on her shoulders as they walked out, and she could feel her brother's eyes until Seth closed the door. As they crossed the corral, she said, "He's always felt jealous of us. He told me so tonight."

Seth opened the gate, let her go through, then latched it behind himself. "Lobo's jealous of a mirage," he said, laying his arm on her shoulders again and guiding her toward the house. "I wish he could see that and stop chasing what might have been."

"I wish we could run away together, just the two of us," she whispered, snuggling close as they walked, inhaling the faint scents of sweat and barroom smoke off his shirt.

He stopped and looked over her head at something else. "Wouldn't you miss your mother?" he asked, almost absently.

"Yes," she admitted, raising her face to watch him.

"So would I," he said, his eyes on the dark casita where Esperanza had slept. "I miss her, too."

"Me, too," Elena said.

He let loose of her and walked across to the casita, opened the door, and stepped in. She followed him and watched him look around the room, barely lit by the moonlight. In the corner was the bed with Esperanza's flowered quilt still on it, though Elena knew the mattress beneath it was bare. Seth walked across and touched the quilt with his fingertips, then looked at the mantel and the cedar box holding Esperanza's tarot cards. "I used to give her hell about those cards," he said.

"She told me," Elena said softly. "She told me lots of things about you."

"I can imagine," he answered.

"Everything she said was about how fine a man you are."

"She was a fine lady," he said, taking Elena's hand and leading her back out, closing the door, and starting across the yard again. "You never answered my question."

"Which one?"

He chuckled. "Never mind. I can see Esperanza shaking her head at me for asking." He opened the door to the house, then followed Elena inside and closed them in darkness. They stood apart but so close she could catch the scent of whiskey on his breath.

"Is Rico asleep?" she whispered.

"I don't know, but you should be. Ain't you got school tomorrow?"

"It's Saturday."

"You mean I'm gonna have to put up with you all day?"

"Let's do something grand, Seth."

He laughed deep in his throat. "We could work with Padre. Would you like that?"

"Do you mean it?"

"Don't see why not, if I ever get any sleep tonight."

The door to Rico's bedroom opened and she stood there silhouetted against the candlelight. "I heard voices," she said.

Seth smiled and leaned low to kiss Elena's cheek. "Good night," he said. Then he walked into Rico's room and closed the door, leaving Elena alone in the dark.

24

★

 The next morning, Elena was the first one awake. She hurried to dress, pulling on a pair of clean dungarees and a mended white shirt. When she tugged on her boots, she saw the scar across the toe of the left one, and again she wondered when it had happened. Lacing her belt through the loops on her jeans, she watched herself in the mirror as she closed the buckle, a brass filigree butterfly.

It had been a birthday present from Danny last year. As she ran her fingertips around its smooth curves, she remembered tearing her boot when she and Danny were exploring an old mine. The tunnel had been long and dark, its earthen walls damp with melting snow. Unsure of her footing in the pitch blackness, she'd abruptly turned to retreat and collided with Danny. His arms clasped her waist as he kissed her. More than that, his tongue came inside her mouth, warm and wet and moving sinuously as a snake. She jerked away with repulsion and ran back toward the safety of sunlight. Halfway out of the tunnel, however, she tripped on a stretch of old wire hidden in the dust. Falling, she struck her knee on a stone. Instantly Danny was at her side, helping her to her feet.

"Keep away from me!" she yelled, shaking off his hands and limping back to where they'd left their horses. She sat down on a rock and cried.

He followed her, his face solemn with apology. "I'm sorry, Elena," he petitioned. "I didn't mean to scare you."

"You didn't!" she retorted. "I tore my boot, is all."

He kept his distance, awkward as a half-grown colt.

"Don't you ever try that again," she accused.

"Guess you didn't like it," he said miserably.

"I know all about it," she cried, "and I'll tell you right now, Danny Nickles, no man's ever putting anything in any part of me. Is that plain enough?"

He nodded, then gave her a maddening smile. "Reckon you'll change your mind when you get a little older."

"Reckon I won't!" She jumped to her feet and untied her reins, then stepped into the saddle so she was looking down at him. "Ain't no better way to ruin a friendship, Danny Nickles," she'd said. Yanking Rojo around, she had galloped away.

Neither of them mentioned it again, and she was surprised at how completely she had forgotten it, though all that had happened only last winter. Yet his prediction came true. On Seth's first day home, she had kissed him like that, and in every waking moment since, she thought of doing even more. With a shrug of impatience, she turned away from the mirror and climbed out the window onto the portal.

Inside the stable, Lobo was feeding the horses, wearing only his trousers and boots as he filled a wooden bucket at the bin. He gave her a smile and the other horses nickered when the grain slid with a whoosh into Rojo's manger, sending a small dust cloud into Lobo's face. She marveled at how much he looked like Seth.

Yet the resemblance was a matter of appearance only. When he dumped grain into Padre's trough, the stallion's rear hoofs struck the gate like a pop of thunder, cracking the wood, then he whinnied and half-reared to the stretch of his tether. Lobo backed away, eyeing the horse warily. "I'd cut him if he was mine," he said. "He'll never be a decent mount as a stud."

"Seth's gonna let me gentle him," she said.

Lobo looked at her with disbelief, then laughed with derision. "You can't even get on him without Seth's help."

"Reckon I'm gonna have his help," she answered.

Lobo studied her harshly a moment, then said, "You shouldn't be around him in your nightgown like you were last night."

She let her gaze slide down Lobo's body, the way Seth used his eyes on her. "You're half-naked right now. What's the difference?"

"I'm your brother. We grew up together."

She shrugged. "He's my father."

"Seth doesn't honor obligations of kinship."

"That's a terrible thing to say," she chided. "Anyway, if that's true, why did he come home?"

"Beats me," Lobo said. "You should've seen him at Blue's. He looked over every tart in there as if she were a horse he was thinking of buying."

"Did he buy one?" she whispered.

"Not yet. But he'll have 'em all 'fore he's done. Blue and I made a bet on which one Seth's gonna choose first. I put my money on Sassy, but Blue's going for Carmelita."

"That's mean!" she cried. "You should be ashamed of yourself, Lobo, betting on your father falling into sin."

Lobo laughed, then walked down the aisle to his room.

She saw his back was marked as Seth's was. Not as badly, but crisscrossed with thin red lines obviously left by a whip. That they were red meant they were new and not completely healed. Wanting to ask him about it, she followed him into his room, but he was already buttoning his shirt, and something in his eyes made her keep quiet. He turned his back to open his trousers and tuck in his shirttails, then faced her again as he buckled on his gunbelt. Softly she asked, "Ain't you glad Seth's home?"

"Doesn't make much difference to me one way or the other,"

Lobo said, pulling the gun and popping the cylinder open to check the rounds, as if he needed ammunition to go to breakfast.

"When we were kids," she said, "we used to talk about what it would be like if he came back. Remember that?"

Lobo shrugged, snapping the cylinder closed and dropping the gun in his holster. "It ain't like that, is it?"

"No," she said, thinking that for her it was better. But obviously it wasn't for Lobo. As a child, he had dreamed of being Seth's partner in the same way Ben Allister was, and then later Joaquín. But Seth wasn't an outlaw now and she didn't guess he needed a partner like that anymore. "You're gonna be partners with Blue," she said gently. "Isn't that what you told me last night?"

"Yeah," he muttered. "If I want to spend my life in a gloomy saloon listening to old men spin tales of glory." Suddenly he grinned. "Maybe I'll go back to Mexico and ride with Vargas."

"Who's he?"

"A bandit."

"Don't go away again, Lobo."

"Would you miss me?" he jibed.

"We all would," she said, not sure she wasn't lying. Then she remembered what Seth had said about Lobo being jealous of a mirage, and the longing in his voice when he'd wished Lobo would get over it. "Things might not be like you wanted," she said, "but Seth needs you with him."

"Seth doesn't need anybody," he bit off.

"I think you're wrong," she said softly. "Maybe 'cause you're such a hothead, he has a hard time telling you how he feels. Maybe he needs you to help him, did you ever think of that?"

"Elena, you don't know what you're talking about. All I ever wanted was to help Seth. I killed a man when I was seven in defense of him. You never knew that, did you? Joaquín had broken loose and I'd already proved myself worthy of being Seth's partner. Then he went to prison and that was stole from me! Now he acts like he hardly remembers who I am."

"Maybe that's it, Lobo," she suggested carefully. "Maybe he doesn't want you following in his footsteps."

"He raised me to it," he said.

"A person doesn't have to be what he was raised for. Look at Danny. His father wants him to be a pig farmer but he ain't gonna do it."

"It ain't hard to turn down being a pig farmer," Lobo scoffed.

"All I'm saying is, you can be whatever you want, even an out-law if you think you have to, but I hope you don't. I think that's the worst thing you could do to Seth—get yourself in the kinda trouble he's finally free of."

"I can't help noticing, Elena, that all your advice is aimed at helping him more'n me." He grabbed his hat and stalked out, leaving the door open behind him.

By the time she walked into the kitchen, Lobo was sitting at the table with Jesse, who was reading a book. Elena moved across the room to help Rico at the stove. She thought her mother had a new smoothness to her cheeks and a softness in her eyes that made her look younger. When Seth came in, he hesitated on the threshold a moment, watching his family all look at him, then he gave Rico an uncertain smile and said, "Mornin'."

She walked across to hug him. Looking up from within his arms, she smiled radiantly. "Good morning, Seth," she said, her voice rich with love.

He chuckled, that husky sound of pleasure Elena loved to hear. Lobo snorted from the table, and Elena met his eyes, bright with ridicule.

"Mornin', Elena," Seth said, taking his place at the head of the table. She murmured a response, but he was appraising his sons, his eyes noncommittal. Yet when Rico took him a cup of coffee, his expression warmed again as he smiled at her. Elena looked at Lobo, his face hard as he stared out the open door, then at Jesse between them, who kept his eyes on his book.

Rico brought the coffee back to the stove and smiled at Elena.

"Watch the sausage, will you?" Rico asked, pouring buttermilk into the hotcake batter.

Elena glanced at the sizzling links in the skillet, then looked at the men again.

Seth blew on his coffee to cool it. "What're you reading, Jesse?"

He didn't look up as he answered, *"The Confessions of St. Augustine."*

Seth sipped his coffee, then set the cup down. "What's a saint have to confess?"

Jesse gave his father a long look before saying, "He was a rogue as a young man. After he became a Christian, he gave up his wild ways and became a leader of the church."

"So his book is about how much he regrets the sins of his youth?"

"Not so much regret," Jesse said, obviously pleased with Seth's response. "More a testimony of how empty their pleasures were, and about how Christianity gave him relief from his suffering. The great beauty of Christ is His power to absolve even the worst sins and make men clean again."

Seth smiled playfully. "What kind of sins you got that need absolving?"

Looking down, Jesse murmured, "We all inherit the sins of our fathers."

Elena wanted to give Seth a smile, but he stared at Jesse. At Rico's nudge, she picked up the fork and moved the sausage around the skillet as her mother poured the first hotcakes on the griddle. Their toasty aroma hit the air with a hint of comfort belied by the tension at the table. Elena looked over her shoulder and saw Seth watching Lobo now, who was slouched down in his chair. Sunshine from the window reflected off the butt of his pistol, throwing slivers of light to tremble on the ceiling with his breath.

In a falsely cheerful voice Elena asked, "Does it bother you, Seth, that Lobo wears your old gun?" She saw Lobo stiffen, but he didn't look up.

Seth's eyes chilled with warning. "It's his now."

"I don't see why either one of you needs a gun," Rico said, flipping the pancakes so their raw sides sizzled on the heat.

Seth looked away from the women to study his sons again, both of whom were avoiding his eyes. "I thought I'd take a ride around the ranch this morning," he said, glancing back and forth between them. "Would you like to come with me, Jess?"

Jesse kept his nose in his book and said, "No thanks."

Seth nodded, then lifted his cup and drank deeply.

Elena hurried to amend the misunderstanding. "Jesse doesn't ride," she said.

Seth flicked his gaze at her then looked back at Jesse. "Don't you ride to school?"

"I walk," Jesse said, still hiding his eyes.

"The whole five miles?"

"It gives me time alone for meditation."

Seth was quiet a moment, then said, "I've often felt that way about riding."

Jesse looked up with surprise. "All I can think about when I'm on a horse is getting thrown."

Seth smiled. "Well, you can ride Rojo. He won't throw you."

"He's awful big," Jesse answered cautiously.

Seth studied him a moment. "I'd like you to come, and I'll take you on the back of Padre if that's the only way you'll do it, but I can't promise both of us won't be thrown."

Jesse laughed with delight. "I bet you've *never* been thrown from a horse!"

"Padre threw me on the ride here. Didn't he, Lobo?"

"Yeah," he mumbled, his eyes on the cactus garden outside the door.

"I'll ride Rojo," Jesse said.

"Good," Seth said. "How about you, Lobo? Will you come?"

He shrugged. "If you want me to."

"I do," Seth said. "Between me and Jesse, we're apt to get lost."

Jesse laughed. "How many times have you been lost?"

"More times than I've been thrown," Seth said.

"Can I go?" Elena asked, holding her breath.

Seth shook his head as he met her eyes, then he smiled slyly. "You and I went riding yesterday. I'd rather take it easy today."

She blushed, marveling that even his rejection felt sweet.

"You're burning the sausage, Elena!" Rico scolded.

"I'm sorry," she said, taking the skillet off the fire. The links were blackened and shriveled to half their size. She sighed as she carried the platter to the table. When she sat down across from Lobo, he gave her a smirk.

"Elena likes to think she's all grown up," he taunted, "but most women I've met know how to cook."

Rico sat the platter of hotcakes on the table, sat down, and smiled at Jesse. "Shall we say grace?"

Again the three of them bowed their heads. Elena and Seth watched each other, but she couldn't read anything in the gray sheen of his eyes. As soon as the amens had sounded, he reached for the sausage and took half a dozen.

"Kind of burnt, ain't they?" Lobo muttered, accepting the platter.

"I've gotten sicker'n a dog eating undercooked pork," Seth said, forking a stack of hotcakes onto his plate. "This is just the way I like it."

"Do you want maple syrup or honey?" Elena offered happily.

His eyes dancing in fun, he asked, "Which one is sweeter?"

"Honey," she said.

"I'll take the syrup." He smiled, accepting the pitcher, then winked at Rico.

Lobo snickered as if at a joke, but Elena couldn't see anything funny.

The men cleaned their plates in a few minutes of unconversational eating, then Seth stood up. "Ready?" he asked his sons. They both followed him out the kitchen door.

The women stacked the dishes in the sink before walking out under the portal to watch the men leave. Lobo and Jesse were already mounted as Seth led Padre out of the corral, his silver conchos flashing in the sun.

Seth spoke quietly to the horse, then stabbed his boot in the stirrup and gained his seat as Padre tried to sidestep out from under him. When Seth kept Padre's head up to prevent him from bucking, Padre reared instead, then came down in a hard twist with his forelegs braced to jar against the earth while he kicked behind as if the Devil himself were there. Seth lost his hat with the impact. He reined into the twist and the stallion spun, gave another quick buck and half-rear, then stood and whinnied his mastery of all he surveyed. Seth nudged the horse over to where his hat lay in the dust. Leaning from the saddle, he grabbed the hat out from beneath the danger of the prancing hoofs. Padre skittered sideways as Seth regained his seat. When he slapped the dust out of his hat against the horse's ears, Padre snorted and stomped at the affront. Seth laughed, then settled his hat on his head.

"Lord have mercy," Rico murmured. "All that just to get on the beast."

"Yeah, but he runs like the wind once you're there," Elena said.

Seth tipped his hat to the women, then reined around and the three men rode out of the yard. Elena felt forlorn at being left behind.

All morning she worked with Two-Bits in the corral, building the strength of her legs. She was sleek and fast, but there would be no contest if Padre ran. Other people would see it, too, and though Padre would earn the purse, that was only a hundred dollars. The real money came from the betting and the odds wouldn't be advantageous to such an obvious winner.

Last year, Blue Rivers had handled the betting for Elena. She had ridden a horse of Blue's too, a bay colt named Dusty she had gentled from a foal. Blue had split fifty-fifty with her, the wagers as well as the purse, but that night when they were all gathered around the Rivers's kitchen table, he announced her share was two bits. She'd known he was teasing but she didn't care about the money; she was hoping he'd give her Dusty. So she was disappointed when he started counting bills onto the table in front of her. Elena had gone to bed that night fifteen hundred dollars richer, and she had spent part of that money on the yearling filly she named Two-Bits.

Two-Bits was long-legged and delicate compared to the strong horses the cowboys rode. Because she didn't look like a winner in most men's eyes, she'd carry better odds than Dusty had. Whether Two-Bits won or not, however, Elena would never race her again. The filly's legs would be damaged by just the one race, as they would be if Elena ran Two-Bits on the rocky ground of the homestead. After the race, she intended to breed the filly to a stud with power, and drop a foal with the agility of its dam and the strength of its sire. Then she would show the people of Tejoe what a racehorse was meant to be.

Padre was exactly the stud Elena had in mind, but she hadn't contemplated such a horse being a challenger in the race. Now, watching the sun shimmer off the filly's sleek muscles as she lifted her feet so precisely in her circles around the corral, Elena regretted asking Seth if she could run Padre. Two-Bits deserved her one chance at glory before spending her life as a brood mare.

But there was no help for it now. Seth had said they would work with the stallion today, and Elena knew she couldn't confess a change of heart. It would make her seem frivolous to Seth, so he'd doubt that she knew her own mind. Just as when she'd asked him to consider Danny as her eventual husband, though it wasn't Danny she wanted.

Suddenly Elena felt dizzy. She commanded Two-Bits to stop, then led the filly into the cool shadows of the stable. Elena's knees were trembling as she tied the horse in a stall. She walked down to Lobo's room and fell on her stomach across his bed, hiding her face in her folded arms. Her brother's scent permeated the pillow, and

she thought of him and Jesse riding with Seth, allowed to go because they were sons. She thought, too, of Seth pulling her hand
between his legs as he said he couldn't fuck her because he loved
her too much. She had never touched a man there before, had never
seen a man naked, though she'd seen Jesse when he was a baby. She
had once watched a stallion service a mare, however, and the memory made her moan into the masculine scent of her brother's bed.

She rolled over with impatience and stared at the ceiling. Suddenly her life had been turned upside down. Her greatest satisfac-
tions had been relegated to insignificance while her mind was
consumed with doing something she never suspected she'd want.
Worst of all, she knew it was wrong that she wanted to do it with
Seth, and she squirmed with shame that she had so boldly made
him aware of her desire.

Not only him. Lobo had seen how she felt. If Lobo saw it,
surely Rico did too. Elena wondered if even Jesse was aware of her
lust for their father. She felt helpless naming it that. Angry, too,
because it was nothing she had chosen to feel, yet her desire refused
to be denied.

She reached down and touched herself. Feeling the pleasure so
easily aroused, she imagined Seth's hand caressing her cheek and
sliding down her neck to fondle her breasts, going lower to penetrate the crevice between her legs. The softness she had felt in his
pants became hard in her fantasy, thrusting into her as his eyes
mocked her need even while he filled it, then the palm of his hand
slapped her as he laughed, giving her punishment instead of pleasure, and she writhed beneath his scorn in her first orgasm.

For a long moment she lay breathing hard with her eyes shut
tight. Then she forced herself to open them and admit she was
alone on her brother's bed, that the door was wide open but the
stable was empty. Slowly she stood up and walked out to the
trough in the corral. She worked the pump handle a long time,
watching the fresh water shine as it fell through the sunlight. Leaning with both hands on the edge of the trough, she hung her head

and listened as the flow from the spout thinned to a trickle and then to large drops falling one by one, shimmering her reflection in the water. Suddenly she slapped her image, shattering the reflection, then dipped deep into the trough and lifted handfuls of water to her face, scrubbing hard, as if she could rid herself of guilt as easily as dust.

She went back to the house and helped Rico fix lunch. They said little. When she caught her mother looking at her oddly, Elena merely smiled and went on with her work. The only sounds were the whack of Rico's knife chopping the brisket on the cutting board, the clink of the spoon as Elena mixed the batter, then the hiss of the grease as they fried the gorditas. Once Rico said, "It feels good cooking for men again." Elena smiled but gave no answer.

When the men rode into the yard, she went to the window and watched them dismount by the corral. Seeing Padre was crusted with sweat, Elena knew the stallion had been run hard to cut his energy before their afternoon workout. Angrily thinking Seth meant to coddle her like a child, Elena intended to prove to him that she wasn't.

From behind her Rico said, "You've ripped your boot, Elena. How'd you do that?"

She turned around and leaned her back against the counter. "I tripped over some wire," she said.

Rico smiled. "We'll have to buy you a new pair. If you insist on dressing like a boy, at least you don't have to look like a ragamuffin."

Elena glanced down at her dungarees and mended white shirt, then watched her mother take the pitcher of milk from the icebox.

As she set it on the table, she said, "I think you've outgrown those jeans, too. They fit awfully snug."

"I like 'em this way," Elena said defensively. "Besides, no boy'd wear a butterfly on his belt."

Rico laughed. "Thank goodness for Danny. If it wasn't for him around, reminding us you're a girl, we might've started calling you Elias instead of Elena."

"Elias!" She laughed. "What a funny name."

"It was my father's," Rico said softly, arranging the crisp gorditas on a platter.

Elena watched her carefully. "You never mentioned him before except to say your parents are dead."

Rico sighed. "I suppose watching you with Seth reminded me of him, is all."

"I thought you didn't like your father," Elena prodded, not seeing the connection.

"I didn't," Rico said with a melancholy smile, then Seth came in and her face brightened.

He walked over and leaned down to kiss her mouth. "Sure smells good in here," he said.

"We've made gorditas," Elena offered proudly. "We're gonna make you fat so nobody else'll want you."

He laughed, looking down at Rico again. "Think that'll do it?"

"No," she said.

Elena watched unhappily as they shared another, longer kiss. Jesse and Lobo came in and crossed the room to wash their hands. "Careful, little sister," Lobo whispered, "your petticoat's showing."

She looked down instinctively, remembering the instant before she saw them that she was wearing dungarees.

Lobo chuckled as he dried his hands, then he tossed her the towel. "What's to eat?" he asked Rico. "Or did you make enough for me?"

She laughed. "Sit down. Hurry up and wash, Jesse."

Elena had nothing to do but sit at the table, too. Lobo was directly across from her, his eyes still teasing. Thankfully, he kept quiet. She felt Seth's gaze but couldn't bring herself to look at him again, afraid of what everyone would see in her face. Rico sat down, and Jesse intoned: "Bless us, oh Lord, and these Thy gifts, which we are about to receive from Thy bounty."

During the prayer, Elena snuck a glance at Seth. He was watching Lobo, who had his head bowed and his eyes closed. Seth felt her gaze and gave her a brief smile before everyone else said, "Amen."

After lunch, Seth stood up and announced he and Rico were taking a siesta. Their three children sat at the table avoiding each other's eyes as they listened to the bedroom door close. Before Lobo could make any remark, Elena got up and started washing the dishes.

As she watched him cross the yard and disappear inside the stable, she wished they could be friends as they had been in childhood. But Lobo had come back with a sharp edge. She supposed he'd had it before; certainly he'd been known around town as a troublemaker, but he'd never shown that side to his family. These days he was cutting them all down, and that made her feel bad for Rico, who only wanted everyone to be happy now that they were together again.

Suddenly Elena felt swamped with fresh guilt. She tried not to think of her parents in bed at that very moment, tried to push Seth from her mind. Yet when Jesse stayed in the kitchen and dried the dishes for her, recounting the pleasures of their morning ride, Elena listened eagerly.

"We rode clear to Apache Summit," Jesse boasted. "When we were sitting our horses on top, admiring the view, Seth moved Padre over just a foot or two and spooked a rattler that must've been there all along. Padre reared. When he was still in the air, Seth pulled his gun and shot the rattler's head off!"

"Pretty good shot," Elena said, impressed.

"I'll say," Jesse agreed. "Seth calmed Padre down, then holstered his gun and looked at Lobo." Jesse lowered his voice and asked, "You know what Seth said?"

She shook her head.

" 'Where were you?' " Jesse whispered.

"Seth said that to Lobo?"

Jesse nodded. "Don't make sense, does it? I mean, Seth was so fast nobody could've beaten him to that snake. Then with a few quick words he calmed a horse I wouldn't get near, let alone ride. If I'd done either one of those things, I would've felt so proud you'd have to knock me down to get me to see straight, but all he felt was mad at Lobo."

"What'd Lobo say?" she asked softly.

"He got mad, too, and said it seemed to him that Seth had already handled it. Seth asked what if he'd missed, and Lobo said he'd like to see the day. Seth's eyes got real cold—you know how they can, like ice, over?—and he asked Lobo if maybe he wouldn't enjoy seeing that so much he wouldn't be there to fill the gap. Lobo said he guessed they'd have to wait and find out, and then they just stared at each other for such a long time I expected 'em to shoot each other. I said maybe it was time to go home, and Seth laughed and everything was okay again."

Elena smiled. "He has a way of doing that, doesn't he."

"He's not like I thought he'd be," Jesse whispered.

She looked across at his puzzled face. "What did you expect?"

Jesse took a long time to answer, drying and stacking three plates in the cupboard before saying, "I believed all the stories about him until I turned seven. Then one night I really thought about them and knew they were lies." He snuck a glance at her from under his lashes, as if testing her sympathy. Apparently satisfied, he said, "I cried."

She gave him a sad smile of understanding, having gone through a similar realization that her father couldn't be as good as the stories made him out to be. That was before she met him, however.

"It ain't that the things they talk about didn't necessarily happen," Jesse said, "maybe even like the stories say. I believe they could've since meeting him and seeing things like this morning. But that's not the way they're lies."

Carefully she lay the platter in the dishwater, looking at him over her shoulder. "How are they lies then?"

" 'Cause he ain't a good man, Elena. He was a bandit who killed anyone who got in his way, lawmen who chased him, lots of men, any sort it seems. None of the acts that built Seth's fame were right, and I can't understand how folks can admire a man who's broken every law they hold sacred. When I remember the songs written about him, and how often I've heard men sound envious when they're talking about the things he did, I feel like the whole world's a lie. It's an awful feeling." Jesse sighed, taking the clean platter from her hands, dunking it in the rinse water, then holding it dripping over the sink. "Not too long after I realized all this, I accidentally wound up at Joaquín's on Sunday morning, and I went to Mass with him and Heaven and Aaron. You know my Spanish ain't all that good, but when Padre Mathias gave his sermon, I felt like he was talking straight to me. I found him afterwards and told him I wanted to be a Catholic."

Elena watched him meticulously drying the platter. "What did you think the sermon was about?"

He set the platter on the shelf, then closed the cupboard and met her eyes. "That our true Father is in heaven," he answered, as if speaking words memorized by rote, "and just like Jesus denied having brothers, sometimes we have to deny our blood kin 'cause we all face God alone."

She shivered in the chill of his piety. "Don't you feel any kinship with Seth?"

Jesse shook his head.

Elena scrubbed the skillet, rinsed it in the second basin, and laid it on the wooden drain rack. With her hands dangling over the dirty water, she looked across the yard to the isolated casita. "I wish Esperanza was still alive."

"Yeah," Jesse agreed. "She was the only one who didn't hold it against me when I converted."

"I didn't," Elena protested with surprise.

He simply looked at her, his eyes the same smoky gray as Seth's in a guarded moment.

"I didn't understand it," she admitted, watching them soften to a color approaching blue. "You have his eyes, Jesse," she whispered in awe. "Much more than Lobo does."

"Do I?" he asked, flirting with pride.

She nodded with a congratulatory grin. "It's proof of kinship beyond doubt."

"He's killed more'n twenty men," Jesse objected. "That's nothing I want in my blood."

"I don't think that part is," she said, looking across the dusty yard to the stable, "but I think it's in Lobo's."

25

★

When she walked into the stable, Lobo was practicing his draw with his back to the door. She watched him a moment, thinking he looked fast but any decent gunfighter would have detected her presence. Reaching behind herself, she pushed the door further open until it whined. He spun around, aiming his pistol at her and looking so surprised she halfway expected him to pull the trigger. Her heart leapt to her throat as she stared down the barrel of Seth's outlaw gun.

Lobo grinned, twirled the pistol on his finger a few times, and dropped it back in the holster.

"Life with you ain't never dull," she said, swallowing her fright as she walked across to look in at the stallion. He had been rubbed down and his coat shone like moonlit smoke. "You gonna enter the sharpshooting contest at the fair?"

"Might," he said.

She turned around and studied her brother. "Would you compete against Seth?"

"He won't compete," Lobo scoffed.

"Why not?"

"Seth makes a man run a risk to take his cut," Lobo said, then laughed. "That's the code of an outlaw. The Rangers' code is to never draw your gun unless you mean to use it, and never use it without shooting to kill. They both boil down to the same principle though, that a gun is a weapon, not a toy."

"I like Joaquín's code," she countered. "Don't use a gun unless there's no other way."

"Yeah, but he's sheriff of a podunk town. All he deals with are cocky kids and drunks."

"I can think of one cocky kid he used to spend a lot of time dealing with," she teased.

Lobo frowned. "That's over. He saved my life in Mexico and I owe him now."

"How did he save your life?" she asked, curious about what had happened in Mexico.

Lobo seemed on the verge of telling her, but just then Seth walked into the barn.

"Ready, Elena?" he asked with an easy smile.

She turned eagerly toward the glow of his smile, her curiosity about Mexico paling in comparison. Seth led Padre out of his stall and saddled him while she watched, admiring the grace of the man as much as the horse. Then she followed them both into the sunlight of the corral, where she practiced getting on and off the stallion.

As she prepared her mount, Seth held the horse, then guided her by the elbow to impel her into the saddle before Padre sidled out from under her. The lesson was aimed at teaching him to stand still, but the goal was to achieve her mount no matter what he did so he would learn that escape was impossible.

Seth was always near, holding the bridle the moment her feet left or found the ground, and she was as keenly aware of his body as of the stallion's. One time she would have missed the mount and fallen if Seth hadn't caught her at the last instant and pushed her up with his palm flat against her bottom. After that she felt tempted to fail so he would touch her there again, and the contradiction twisted inside her.

Once when she stood ready to mount, contemplating her jump to the stirrup, Padre suddenly reared, lifting Seth off his feet. With his free arm he pulled Elena close to him and away from the stallion's hooves. Seth jerked the reins hard, then dragged the horse's head down and leaned close to murmur in his ear, "Stop fighting me, Padre. I guarantee you're gonna lose."

The horse pricked his ears toward the honeyed threat in Seth's voice, then nickered. Still holding her close, Seth laughed softly as he looked down at Elena and said, "I think something finally sunk in."

Looking into his face so full of confidence and pride, Elena would have done anything to please him. But when he let her go, she felt diminished.

"Try it again," he said.

Making her plan in motion, she leapt for the stirrup and caught it, then deliberately fell back toward the touch of Seth's hand. Padre stood motionless, however, and she grabbed for the horn to achieve the mount unassisted.

"Not exactly graceful but you got there," Seth said, watching the horse. Padre's legs were stiff as he trembled in place, his eye on Seth, knowing the man was in command, not the featherweight girl in the saddle.

"Go ahead, take him around," Seth said, letting go of the bridle and stepping back, still watching the horse.

Elena turned Padre's head and held him at a walk along the fence. As they rounded the corner, he danced against her tight rein but she held him, delighted at the spring of his gait and hoping her control now made up for her clumsy mount. As they made the last turn and were facing the barn again, she saw Lobo talking with Seth. When Seth laughed and looked at the ground, tugging his hat lower over his eyes, Elena felt angry enough to shoot Lobo.

She reined up in front of them just as Lobo walked into the stable without looking at her. Seth took hold of Padre's bridle and said, "That's all for today, Elena."

She jumped down, waiting to hear him praise her performance. He stepped close to the horse and let the stirrup out full length, walked around and fixed the other one, then came back and swung on just as Lobo rode out of the stable. "See you later," was all Seth said. He touched his spurs to Padre's flanks and the stallion galloped the length of the corral and sailed over the fence. With a yell of challenge, Lobo leapt after him. Elena stood watching their dust cloud disappear, then she sank to sit cross-legged in the dirt and hold her head in her hands, fighting tears.

After a while, she stood up, climbed the fence, and walked across the yard to Esperanza's casita. The one-room adobe was cool and dim. She sat down, then lay back on the bed, letting her boots dangle over the edge as she stared at the latillaed ceiling. Many times as a child she had lain there with Esperanza, listening to stories about Seth. But now when Elena needed advice so badly, Esperanza was irrevocably gone.

Elena had confessed her deepest feelings into the soft, commodious bosom of the old woman, and no matter how ashamed or confused Elena felt, Esperanza always knew the words to make it better. She had been a bottomless well of comfort and had spoken fervently of the time when Seth would come home. Elena searched her memory for something Esperanza had said that could remotely apply to what she was feeling, but finally had to concede that not even Esperanza had anticipated how Seth's return would affect his daughter.

When Seth and Lobo didn't come home for supper again, Elena felt it was her fault. The meal was served at its usual time, and no one mentioned the two empty plates on the table. Rico kept the conversation going by questioning Jesse about their morning ride. He talked about the country and riding Rojo and how impressive the stallion was, but never mentioned the shooting of the rattlesnake. Elena kept stealing glances at Rico, realizing for the first time that everyone sheltered her. None of her children ever confided in Rico as they had in Esperanza, because they strove not to add to her burden. Elena now realized Rico's burden was Seth, as if loving him carried a debilitating disease.

Remembering how she had deliberately slipped when mounting the stallion because she wanted Seth to catch her, Elena wondered if Rico's fragility didn't stem from the same source. She was rarely ill and had enough strength to hitch the team to the wagon and carry the supplies in when she got home. She kept the windmill in working order and supervised the tending of a milk cow and chickens as well as half a dozen horses. She cultivated a garden every spring and harvested it in the fall so her family could eat vegetables and fruit all winter, and she kept that family clothed in the latest fashions available from the catalogs. Her best friends were the sheriff and the owner of the bawdiest saloon in town, and she sometimes sat with them under the portal until late in the night, sipping whiskey and talking in the comfortable banter of equals.

There was nothing weak about Rico, yet everyone treated her like a delicate wildflower that would wither at a cold glance. They did it because, for as long as Elena could remember, Rico had been mourning the absence of Seth. If he had been dead, they could have buried and missed him like they did Esperanza. But he was in prison in Texas, kept from them against his will, and Rico pined all those years for his return.

His absence was a misfortune Joaquín had caused, though no one except Lobo held it against him. Because of his love for Seth, Joaquín stood between them and poverty. That was the truth Elena knew, and the other was a tragic accident no one discussed because it hurt Joaquín and grieved Rico.

As she helped her mother with the dishes that night, Elena remembered what had happened the morning after Lobo left home. When she found Rico crying at the kitchen table, Elena sat down feeling guilty. Rico looked up and said Lobo was gone, and that she knew he wouldn't be back because he had taken Seth's gun.

"When I think of him coming into my room and taking the gunbelt off the bedstead," she said forlornly, "I feel as if a ghost of Seth did it, like he won't be back now. I know it doesn't make sense, Elena, but I feel so abandoned, having lost his son."

Rico's sorrow was almost more than Elena could bear, knowing she'd been the one to go into her mother's room. She'd done it to save Lobo from his fear of Rico's bedroom, though she hadn't understood his fear. Neither had she anticipated how the loss of Seth's gun would strike at Rico's courage. In desperation Elena reminded her mother they still had Jesse, who was also Seth's son.

Rico shook her head. "Jesse's mine," she said. "Lobo's pure Strummar."

"What am I?" Elena asked, feeling very much the thief at that moment.

Rico had smiled. "You're my salvation, sweetheart. I don't think I could bear being the only woman among such men."

Such absent men, Elena thought as she dried the dishes. Back then, as now, the only male in the house was Jesse kneeling below the crucifix in his room to say his prayers. Now, however, Elena understood the longing her mother had lived with all those years.

They worked quietly together, their ears honed to every nuance of sound from beyond the open window, hoping to hear hoofbeats heralding the men's return. But the silence outside was broken only by the rasp of cicada in the cottonwoods.

When the dishes were done, Elena excused herself to her room. She sat in the darkness on her narrow bed, staring out the window at the moonlit yard as she remembered that night two years before. By stealing the gun to please Lobo, Elena had betrayed Rico. Despite all her efforts to shield her mother, Elena had dealt a blow into the pit of Rico's survival. Yet Rico had survived. Elena no longer felt certain she herself could without Seth. She undressed in the dark, then stood before the mirror naked in the moonlight.

Her body was thin and boyish, her legs hard and firm, her waist practically nonexistent, her breasts almost flat. She unbraided her hair and fanned it across her shoulders so it fell like a cape down her back to the rise of her hips. Thick and wiry, her hair was an unmanageable mass as brambly as rabbitbrush. She was a freak, all right: an elfin creature with a head of hair half as big as she was. Certainly there wasn't much else feminine about her.

On an impulse, she dug into her chiffonnier and came out with a corset her Aunt Heaven had given her the year before. The garment was white satin, skintight, and fitted with stays that pushed her breasts up so they looked bigger, cinched her waist so it was smaller, and ended with a flounce over her thighs. In the corset, Elena didn't think she looked so boyish after all.

Surveying the white hourglass of her figure silhouetted against the dark cape of her hair, she smiled, wishing Seth could see her. She stood before the mirror a long time, brushing her hair in the moonlight, until finally she lay down on top of her covers and fell asleep.

The creak of the corral gate awoke her. Then she heard the deeper moan of the stable door. After a while she heard the metallic song of Seth's spurs as he crossed the yard, his footsteps through the kitchen and parlor, then the quiet closing of her mother's bedroom door. Yearning for his presence even from a distance, Elena pulled a wrapper on and climbed out under the portal, sneaked around the corner of the house, and knelt below her parents' open window. The moon had set and only stars lit the desert before her eyes.

She heard the clink of a belt buckle first, then a mumbled inarticulate murmur from Rico.

"You awake?" Seth asked softly.

"Umm," Rico answered. "Did you have a good time in town?"

"Fair," he said, the bed sighing under his weight. Elena heard the thud and jingle of first one bespurred boot, then the other, as he dropped them. The springs creaked and she heard his stocking feet cross the floor, then his voice from farther away, "Wish you could come with me. Why is it ladies ain't allowed in saloons?"

There was a rustle of bedcovers before Rico said, "No respectable woman drinks in public."

Seth laughed. "But it's okay at home?"

Elena heard water being poured into the basin, then Rico asked, "Shall I light the lamp?"

"No," he said. "It's seven and a half steps between me and you. I counted 'em often enough in prison."

"Did you?" She sounded pleased.

There was a splash of water, then his bare feet crossed the floor again. "And all the things I'm about to do to you," he said as the bed sighed under his weight.

Elena listened in agony through the ensuing silence. Then Seth laughed and said, "You know what Blue and Lobo did?"

"No," Rico murmured, her voice muffled.

"They made a bet on which of Blue's girls I'd take upstairs first. Sassy told me about it, trying to enlist my help over Carmelita."

"That's a terrible thing to do," Rico replied indignantly. "Especially Lobo, your own son."

Seth chuckled. "I cut myself into the action. I bet 'em I'd stay true to you."

"Did you?" she purred.

"Yeah. What I'd *like* to do, though, is take both Sassy and Carmelita upstairs and give them a good spanking for going along with it."

"Then you'd all lose your bets," Rico said.

"Reckon so. And I plan on winning this one."

Elena hugged herself, hearing the covers slither to the floor.

"That's more like it," Seth said. "It ain't exactly cold in here, you know."

"Summer in the desert is usually hot," Rico said breathlessly.

"I've noticed," he whispered back.

The bed moaned, and Elena began to cry. She rested her head on her drawn-up knees as she wept silently. When Rico whimpered, the sound struck Elena like a fist, and she sobbed.

The room fell silent behind her. She heard him get up and Rico whisper his name; then she heard his spurs as he pulled on his boots. Elena told herself she shouldn't let him find her there, but the knowledge he was coming compelled her to stay.

He didn't hesitate as he rounded the corner. He strode straight to her, bare-chested beneath the starlight, his eyes as cold as death. Lifting her by one arm, he half-dragged her beneath the portal, through the parlor, and into her room where he shoved her onto the bed and locked the door.

She lay frozen, seeing his anger coil in the tautness of his muscles. In a low voice he said, "I can't let you get away with that, Elena."

"I want you," she whispered helplessly.

He nodded. "I'm gonna give you a taste of what you're asking for. Get up."

As she warily obeyed him, her wrapper fell open. Astonishment flashed on his face. He took a step closer and pushed the wrapper off her shoulders so it fell to the floor, revealing her body clothed only in the seductive corset.

"Sonofabitch," he muttered, his eyes hot now meeting hers. "It doesn't change anything," he said. "This ain't that." He sat down on her bed and pulled her belly-down across his lap.

The corset didn't close at the bottom, and stretched across his knees, she was naked nearly to her waist. She felt his hand caress her with a loving touch, so delicate she raised her hips to entice his fingers deeper, and he slapped her hard.

She gasped at the pain, then screamed as he spanked her with the force of a strong man not holding himself back. Though she fought with all she had, he easily held her down with one arm. She kicked and flailed with her fists, howling with outrage that he would hurt her. Gradually she became aware of Rico pounding on the door, shouting for Seth to stop, but he kept hitting Elena as if he meant to break her spine across his knees. She fell slack to appease him, hoping that without opposition his anger would subside. Rico pleaded through the door, her fists frantic, until finally he stopped.

He stood up abruptly, dumping Elena on the floor and towering over her as she lay crying, meeting his eyes. They were so full of hurt she wanted to comfort him, to pull him down beside her and soothe away the pain of his violence with love. She stopped crying and sat up to throw the mass of her hair out of her way, across her shoulders to fall down her back, exposing her breasts in the tight garment designed for seduction.

"Jesus, God," he said under his breath. "Ain't I ever gonna get any mercy?"

"Seth!" Rico sobbed.

Without a backward glance he strode across the room, unlocked the door, and flung it open so hard it banged against the wall. Elena stayed where he'd dropped her, watching her mother as Seth brushed past and abandoned them both. They stared at each other, stunned beyond words at the sudden turn, then the footsteps of the man yanked Rico around.

"Where are you going?" she cried, planting herself in his path.

Elena watched in silence, aching with pain.

"Town," he muttered, wearing a shirt already tucked in, concentrating on buttoning the cuffs as he stood before her. "I'll sleep at Blue's."

"No!" Rico cried. "She deserved to be punished. It's over. I'm sure it won't happen again."

"I'm sure it won't, too," he said, his face set against her.

"Because you won't be here?" she accused. "Because you'll leave every time it gets difficult? Make a joke, walk out, refuse to stick it because it takes a toll on your precious sense of command?" She slid to the floor, holding his knees as she bowed her head. "God in heaven, Seth, don't leave me. It's hard for all of us, but don't leave me again. Please," she begged, clinging to his knees.

He looked in at Elena, silent on the floor. With his eyes on his daughter he said, "You know me, Rico."

"We can handle it together," she answered, then raised her head and saw his gaze riveted on Elena. Rico looked at her, too. "Tell him, daughter," she commanded. "Tell your father we need him."

Slowly Elena pulled herself to her feet and walked painfully to the threshold, keenly aware of the scanty corset testifying to her complicity. "I'm sorry," she whispered, meeting his eyes for one brief moment of mutual agony. "Please don't leave, Seth." Then she closed the door and crossed to her bed, burying her head beneath her pillow so she couldn't hear their words.

She couldn't escape their faces, however. Seth's eyes had seared into her as if he felt tortured, and Rico's had been devastated with such a horrified sorrow it was evident she knew exactly what was going on. If not for her interruption, the spanking would have ended differently, Elena felt certain of that. When she remembered the pain in his eyes as he pleaded for mercy, she knew he had been a sliver away from succumbing. The marvel was that, knowing everything, Rico had pleaded with him to stay. Even now she had enticed him back into her bedroom. When Elena thought of what they were doing right then, she agonized over what he felt for his daughter as he listened to her mother in the dark.

The first light of dawn found Elena awake. She buried the corset deep in her chiffonnier again, then dressed quickly in yesterday's clothes, climbed out the window, and walked across the empty yard to the stable. Going in through the small door, she lit the lantern in the still-dark cavern of the barn and set about feeding the horses. Besides Padre and Two-Bits, there was Rojo and Rico's palomino, Nugget, nearly as old; and her chestnut buggy team, Bonnet and Barley; and Randy, the dark bay Lobo had brought home from Mexico. She fed them all and was wondering what else she could do to avoid going back to the house when Lobo opened his door. "Want some coffee?" he asked with a friendly smile.

Following him into his room, where a coffeepot simmered over a small fire in the potbelly stove, she sat down on the wooden box.

He filled two cups and gave her one, then moved across the room to stand looking out the window as he blew on his coffee to cool it. Finally he turned around and asked, "What happened up at the house last night?"

She stared into the blackness of her coffee. "Seth spanked me," she whispered.

Lobo chuckled. "You must have loved that."

"It hurt!" she complained.

"I bet it did." He smiled. "That's pretty good, Elena. I lived with him three years before I made him mad enough to hit me. How'd you accomplish it so fast?"

She stared into her cup.

"What'd you do to make him mad?" Lobo coaxed.

He sounded like a friend again, so she looked up when she said, "I spied on him and Rico in bed."

Lobo smiled. "You should've known Seth has sharp ears for anyone nosing around his vicinity. It's funny, though, he'd punish you for that."

"I shouldn't have done it," she admitted contritely.

He shrugged. "When I was first traveling with him, he'd bring a different woman to our hotel room every night. I could hear 'em plain, but I could never figure out what they were doing, and I pestered him about it until finally he gave me a demonstration." Lobo grinned. "That's a far cry from what he did to you for having the same curiosity, ain't it."

"It's not fair," she protested.

"Cheer up," he said. "Things'll be better between you now."

"Why do you say that?" she asked unhappily.

"He's only at ease with people he's proved he can beat. You watch and you'll see that most everything he does is a contest and he always wins. Half the time it's 'cause few people'll risk making him mad. I've seen grown men cringe away just 'cause Seth looked at 'em hard." Lobo shook his head, then gave her a smile. "It's how an outlaw stays alive and he ain't lost none of it, but I bet he's feeling real paltry this morning for having to impress it on you."

"You think he regrets punishing me?" she asked.

Lobo laughed. "I think he loved it. And I think he hates that he loved it. What you have to do now is make a big deal out of forgiving him. Not in gushy words but by going out of your way to do things for him, like keeping his cup full at breakfast and stuff like that. I've seen other women make up to him after something like this, so you oughta heed my advice. The way women get Seth to stop hurting 'em is to prove they can take it. I know it don't make sense, but somehow that shames him into treating 'em decent." He shrugged at the astonishment on her face. "Tell me, where was Rico in the middle of all this?"

"On her knees begging him not to leave," Elena whispered.

Lobo laughed. "If you want to please Seth, study your mama. She's the only woman he ever came home to."

When they walked into the kitchen, Seth and Jesse were at the table. Rico was working alone at the stove, but Elena sat down and stared sullenly straight ahead, unable to heed Lobo's advice enough even to look at Seth. Jesse had obviously listened to the event of the night before from behind his closed door, and he, too, was wary of meeting his father's eyes. No one spoke until Rico brought the food and asked Jesse to say grace.

"Bless us, oh Lord," he prayed, "and these Thy gifts which we are about to receive from Thy bounty."

"Amen," everyone but Elena said.

Seth helped himself to the scrambled eggs, then passed the bowl to Elena. Their eyes held for a minute, his softly teasing, but she looked away fast. She'd be damned if she'd crawl and beg, unable to believe he really wanted that. Giving herself a smidgeon of eggs, she passed the bowl to her mother. Rico's eyes were pleading, but Elena looked away from them, too, and met the brashly amused eyes of her older brother. She was beginning to understand why Lobo carried such a chip on his shoulder: being Seth's child brought it out in a person.

Not in Jesse, however. She watched him eat, keeping his eyes to himself, not taking sides. As soon as they were finished, he stood up and announced, "I'm going to Mass now. Do you think it'll be all right if I ride Rojo to church, Seth?"

"He's yours," Seth answered.

Jesse looked at his sister and said, "Elena always rides him to school."

"I want you to have him," Seth said.

"Thank you," Jesse said. "I trust him."

Seth smiled. "He's a good horse."

Jesse looked awkwardly at Elena again, then kissed Rico on the cheek. "Will you help me saddle him, Lobo?"

"Sure," he said, standing up. "Reckon I'll go to Sunday services, too." He kissed Rico's cheek on his way by.

"You?" she teased.

He laughed, taking his hat from the peg. "Blue offers first communion at eight o'clock. I aim to be there for it."

Rico watched him go, then stood up and began clearing the table. She scraped the garbage onto one plate and carried it out to the chickens, leaving Seth and Elena alone in the kitchen. Elena wanted to get up and walk out, too, but thought she should make some flippant remark as she did it, and she couldn't think of one.

Softly Seth asked, "You mad at me, Elena?"

She shook her head, keeping her eyes on her lap. "It was wrong, what I did."

"Well, I was wrong, too," he said. "I'll never hurt you again. I promise that."

"You just gave away my horse!" she retorted, meeting his eyes with indignation.

He smiled playfully. "I know I left Rojo here, but I always considered him mine."

"You left your gun here, too," she sassed. "Lobo took that and you didn't take it back."

"Do you need it?" he asked, calm in the face of her fury.

"No," she said.

"That's the difference. Jesse needs a horse he can trust."

She relented. "I don't mind his having Rojo. I'm glad he's finally stopped walking everywhere like a penitent, but what am I gonna ride to school?"

"What about your filly?"

"I'm saving her legs for the race," she said.

"I thought you wanted to race Padre."

She was silent, unable to look at him.

"Did you change your mind?"

"Yes," she said, her eyes on her lap. "He's too much horse for me."

"I thought you did real well on him yesterday," Seth said.

She jerked her head up so fast tears splashed across her cheeks. "Why didn't you say so then? Or is it easier for you to talk with the flat of your hand?"

Seth studied her a moment. "If you weren't my daughter," he finally said, "I could fuck that spit outta you. As it is, I don't know what to do with it. Think you could give me some advice?"

"What's wrong with a girl having spit?"

"It's a ploy to catch a man's attention. And since yours is tangled up inside a little girl wearing a woman's underwear, a man's apt to respond by gaining your submission. If you act like this with anyone else, I doubt you'll like the results."

"Do you think I liked them last night?"

"I was hoping you wouldn't."

"Did you?"

He leaned back away from her, his eyes smoky with camouflage. "I ain't your run-of-the-mill father, Elena, and like I tried to tell you before, you're playing with fire." He stood up. "So maybe it's a good thing you've decided Padre is too much horse. Now we can avoid each other's company and stay outta trouble."

She listened to him leave the house, numb with the realization that she had handled everything wrong again. Yet her response to him was beyond her control, and she suspected he knew that and could help her but chose to refuse.

Rico came back and sat down with a sigh. "Seth's going into town again," she said forlornly. "He'll spend the day drinking at Blue's. Why is it you feel compelled to drive him away?"

"It's not what I want!" Elena answered defensively.

"Tell me what you want," Rico said, "and I'll do everything in my power to help you."

Meeting her mother's earnest blue eyes, Elena whispered, "I want him to make love to me."

"Thank you for being honest," Rico said calmly. "I knew it without being told, of course." She took a deep breath, then said, "I think it's a good idea that you stay with Blue's family for a while. Amy and the girls will be glad to have you."

Elena stared at her incredulously. "You said you'd help me!"

"I'm trying to do that," Rico answered. "Eventually these feelings will pass and we can live together as a family again. Perhaps by spending more time in the company of girls, you might learn the finer points of decorum I have obviously failed to teach you."

"This isn't fair!" Elena cried. "How can I train Two-Bits if I'm living in town?"

"I'm afraid I'm going to forbid you to enter the race. I know this is hard, Elena, but I've obviously been much too lax raising you. You are not to wear dungarees again. I want you always in a skirt, and I want you to learn to comport yourself as a lady. Believe me, this is a remedy long overdue."

"I can't believe it!" she wailed.

"Think, Elena!" Rico retorted, losing patience. "What will happen if you get what you want? Do you think Seth would stay here, living in this house with both of us? Or that you and I could remain friends? Or that you would have any friends? All you can see is what you want, not what it would do to everyone involved. I'm acting to save you from that."

"It isn't fair!" she cried again. "I can't help what I feel."

"Sweetheart, I know that," Rico said firmly. "But I didn't go far past the door when I left the kitchen. I listened to you and your father, hoping and praying you could make peace with him. Instead, you taunted him with challenge. Seth has spent his life controlling people through violence, and you're begging to be hurt, Elena. If I don't get you away from him, what happens will be far worse than last night."

"Does he hurt you?"

Rico shook her head. "I don't fight him."

"That's right," Elena sassed. "I saw you on your knees begging him to stay."

"I never realized you were so impudent! Seth is trying hard to be gentle. Do you think that's easy after living the way he has? He and Allister ran roughshod over every hellhole on the border. Do you think they did it with kindness? Do you think he learned more kindness under the whip in prison? It's to his credit he's trying to catch hold of himself and become a decent man. I won't let his own daughter destroy him."

"But you'll destroy me to save him," Elena accused.

"You won't be destroyed by living in town. Now go pack your clothes. I'm taking you to Amy's this morning."

"Give me another chance," she pleaded. "I won't do anything wrong again, I promise."

Rico shook her head. "Someday you'll thank me for this."

"Never!" Elena cried, jumping to her feet and running from the room.

26

★

Amy Rivers was small and plump with dark blonde braids wound above normally laughing blue eyes and pink cheeks. Today, however, she had a cold, making her eyes look tired and her cheeks pale. Her daughters had gone to church, and her husband to work, though even she smiled when referring to Blue's showing up at the saloon on a Sunday morning as work.

Her smile never wavered while she listened to Rico explain that she wanted Elena to live in town for a while and mingle with the other girls at the church socials. Amy beamed a welcome on Elena, and Rico departed with a final admonishment that she hoped her daughter wouldn't embarrass the family.

Left alone with Elena in the parlor, Mrs. Rivers gloated. "I knew Seth's coming home would cause a few readjustments," she crowed, then clucked with sympathy. "You must feel as though you've been banished, Elena, but your mother is only acting to protect you."

"Do you think I need protection from my own father?" Elena asked archly, wondering if the two women had spoken in some secret language known only to mothers.

"Given the man in question, yes," Mrs. Rivers said without hesitation. "I wasn't happy to hear he'd come home. I know Rico was pining for him but I doubt if even she will be better off." Amy sighed wearily, pushing herself to her feet. "Come along, Elena. You can stay with Matty."

Elena hefted her valises and followed the plump woman up the stairs and down the carpeted hallway to a back bedroom. The room was frilly, cluttered with such absurd things as a vase of peacock feathers on the mantel. One bed sported a collection of dolls, the other had been arranged as a day bed with a plethora of pillows. She sat down on the edge of it and stared at the carpet woven with a pattern of pink cabbage roses.

"The girls'll be home in an hour," Amy said. "I think I'll lie down. Lunch is at one." She went out and closed the door.

Elena stood up and stared out the window at the manicured backyard, a tiny patch of grass surrounded by desert. Beyond it was the stable where Blue kept his horses, the feisty Dusty she had raced at the fair, and two for harness because the Rivers girls didn't ride horseback, which also meant there was no sidesaddle in Blue's stable. Although Elena felt tempted to steal Dusty and escape, her valises contained no dungarees and she wasn't so immodest as to sit astride wearing a skirt. Her frock was nearly her best, a soft gray with a scalloped red velvet belt, but she felt as forlorn as if she were dressed in mourning.

Weeks, maybe months stretched ahead of her filled with the company of silly girls talking nothing but clothes and curling irons and everybody else's business. Girls who couldn't tell a stud from a mule and went to the county fair only to giggle over boys. Elena didn't think she could bear it, not even the first moments of Matty crowing about her exile. Elena waited until she thought Mrs. Rivers was soundly asleep, then she slipped quietly from the house and walked toward the shabbiest section of town.

She had only one friend she could expect not to be in church on Sunday morning, and that was Jennifer Pardee, who lived with her mother in a small frame house of three rooms. Knowing Sassy slept most of the day, Elena walked around back to Jennifer's window and tossed a pebble against the pane. Her friend opened the kitchen door and beckoned her in.

"I was just makin' coffee," Jennifer said, speaking quietly so as not to wake her mother. "Want some?"

"Reckon." Elena sat down at the table in the long, narrow kitchen. It was hot from the stove, and she was glad Jennifer had left the door open.

"Did you ditch church?" she asked.

Elena shook her head. "Rico brought me in to stay with the Rivers girls for a while."

Jennifer nodded, folding her arms beneath her breasts as she leaned against the counter. She was wearing a shapeless blue skirt and a man's white shirt hanging like a smock nearly to her knees. Her bare feet were dirty, and her long, auburn hair looked uncombed from bed. Softly she asked, "Did Seth make a move on you?"

Elena shook her head again. "I made a move on him."

Jennifer stared, then asked in a near whisper, "What're you talkin' about, Elena?"

She recounted the event of the night before, watching her friend's face for any hint of judgment. "Then this morning," Elena finished, "I sassed him at the breakfast table and he rode into town. Rico got mad at me, saying he'd spend the day drinking at Blue's and it was my fault."

"So she brought you to stay with Mrs. Rivers," Jennifer said.

Elena nodded.

Jennifer took the coffee off the fire, filled two cups, and brought them to the table. She sat down and spooned sugar into hers, then slurped noisily, not lifting the cup. Leaning back, she shook the tangled length of her hair out of her face and shrugged with a grimace. "It'll blow over," she predicted.

Elena thought of her friend saying her father had "flat-out done it" to her. "What's it feel like," she asked in a whisper, "to, you know, do it with a man?"

Spooning more sugar into her coffee, Jennifer didn't answer right away. Finally she said, "Not like you'd think."

"I don't know what to think," Elena said. "I never would've guessed I'd want it."

Jennifer emptied her cup. She got up and refilled it, looked at Elena's untouched, then put the pot back on the stove.

"Did you want to do it?" Elena asked.

"Not the first time," Jennifer said, flopping into her chair. "But it grows on a person." She smiled. "Hollister Pardee was good at it. Course I didn't know that then, but I've done it with others now, and I can see he had a knack to how he went about it."

"Who else've you done it with?" Elena asked with surprise.

"Sam Little and Charlie Two Horns," Jennifer said, spooning sugar into her fresh cup of coffee.

"Charlie's half Apache," Elena said.

"They're built the same as white men, take my word on it."

Elena squirmed in her chair, looking away from her friend to stare out the open door at the barren yard stretching into the desert. "Does it hurt?" she asked, watching a raven land on a saguaro in the distance.

"Sometimes, especially at first," Jennifer said. "After that, it mostly feels good."

Elena met her eyes. "Better'n doing it to yourself?"

"I thought you never did that," Jennifer teased.

"I have now," Elena admitted.

Jennifer laughed. "I'm lookin' forward to meetin' Seth. He must be something to turn you around so fast."

"You'll prob'ly see him before I do," Elena complained, "since I've been banished to town."

Jennifer sipped her coffee, then said, "That's where he is, ain't it?"

Elena stared at her.

"Go petition his help, silly! If he's hot for you, too, seems to me he'll take you home."

"He doesn't want to be," Elena protested.

"But he is, or Rico wouldn't have sent you away."

Elena sighed. "I feel so confused. Ever since Seth came home, I can't stay away from him. Yet every time I go near, he hurts me in one way or another, and that's not what I want. I guess I feel if I could break through something, he wouldn't hurt me anymore."

"Most men hurt women," Jennifer said. "Sometimes Sassy comes home with bruises from the men she took upstairs. Reckon it's our instinct to want it."

Elena thought about that, then said, "Rico told me Seth doesn't hurt her."

Jennifer shrugged. "Maybe she's lyin'. I mean, it ain't exactly something to tell your daughter."

"She says if I get what I want it'll hurt everybody."

"She's just lookin' to protect her own," Jennifer argued. "I lost my cherry to my father and can't see I'm any the worse for it. The worst would be if you got pregnant, but there's remedies for that."

"There are?" Elena asked.

"Sure. Do you think doves carry every seed planted in their womb? Hell, no. They get rid of it 'fore it interferes with their work."

"How?" Elena whispered.

"There's stuff you take."

"Have you ever taken it?"

Jennifer shook her head. "I ain't been caught yet. After I lay with a man, I jump up and down a lotta times to shake his seed loose. It's worked so far." She shrugged. "Another year or so, I'll be workin' saloons and gettin' paid for what I'm givin' away now. Sassy'll cry, tryin' to stop me from followin' in her footsteps. Funny, ain't it, how mothers always tell you what not to do but never exactly how you're s'posed not to do it. Reckon if they knew, they wouldn't've done it themselves."

"Reckon," Elena said.

"Damn straight. Sassy went with Hollister Pardee 'fore they got married. I know 'cause their wedding certificate's dated only six months 'fore I was born. And Rico *still* ain't married to Seth, is she?"

Elena shook her head.

"So if you want to fuck him, I say do it. There's no reason why the two of you can't sneak around behind Rico's back without anyone ever catchin' on."

"It isn't right," Elena argued weakly.

Jennifer laughed. "Who gives a shit? He's an outlaw, remember? I bet if you go see him right now he'll admire your spunk."

Elena smiled nervously. "I'm not even sure I can find the saloon."

"I'll take you," Jennifer said. "Come on. You can change your mind on the way there if you want."

Elena followed her friend down the alley toward the center of town. It seemed everyone was in church. The streets were deserted, and even when they turned the corner into the tenderloin, the hitching rails were empty. Elena had never been in this part of town. The entire block was saloons, and the broad, dusty street was littered with dung, evidence that the district had done a good business the night before.

"There it is," Jennifer said, stopping and nodding toward the door of the Blue Rivers Saloon.

Elena hesitated.

Jennifer smiled with encouragement. "You look wholesome as strawberries'n cream. Inside that den of sin, you'll shine in Seth's eyes. I think it's your best chance."

Elena nodded. "Thanks," she said.

Jennifer laughed, turning and walking away, leaving Elena alone in the middle of the street.

She squared her shoulders and approached the door, then stepped through it as if the saloon were no different than an emporium. The room was cavernous and dark, nearly empty so early on a Sunday. A man stood behind the bar, still washing glasses from the night before, and Lobo stood talking with him, drinking a cup of coffee, Elena noted, so his boast of first communion hadn't been whiskey after all. When she had crossed the room and stood before them, Lobo seemed amused but the bartender didn't.

"See here, Miss," he said gruffly. "This ain't no place for a lady."

Lobo laughed. "This is my sister, Elena Strummar. This is Gus Willis, Elena."

"Pleased to meet you," she murmured, giving him a brave smile.

"I'm pleased to meet'cha, too, Miss Strummar," Gus said. "But I wish it'd been someplace else."

"I need to see Seth," she told Lobo.

His laughter mocked her.

"Is he here?" she demanded.

Lobo shrugged. "I'll take you up. Come on, I'm gonna enjoy this."

She followed him across the wooden floor, their footsteps echoing in the huge barroom. Beyond the sweeping staircase was a room reserved for gambling, its roulette wheel idle, a woman looking bored sitting alone at a table. Her eyes weren't kind as she watched Elena climb the stairs. On top was a long balcony only dimly lit from below. Lobo walked over to one of the many closed doors and knocked, then opened it and gestured for Elena to precede him.

The room was an office. Blue and Seth sat on opposite sides of a desk, their feet up on its cluttered surface. Seth's boots were on a corner so his spurs hung off the edge. Blue's, free of spurs, were in the middle of his blotter. A half-empty bottle sat midway between them, and both men held glasses of whiskey. Blue winced as he watched Elena come in. Seth slowly lowered his feet and stood up, setting his glass aside as he studied her. "What is it?" he asked gently, though his eyes were cool.

"I need to talk to you," she said.

"Couldn't it wait?"

She shook her head.

"I'll be downstairs," Blue said, coming out from behind the desk. As he passed Elena, he gave her a curious smile tinged with warning.

Seth looked at Lobo and he left too, closing the door quietly. "Have a seat," Seth said, gesturing toward a black leather settee against the far wall.

Its window was covered with wooden shutters. She walked across the thick, dark carpet and sat down, smoothing her skirts as she looked around the masculine sanctuary. At the opposite end from the desk were four straight-backed chairs tucked under a felt-covered table sporting a deck of cards; against the far wall, a mahogany sideboard held assorted liquor bottles and a tray of clean glasses. Above them hung a painting of a nude woman in a rumpled bed. She held her head in her hand propped up by her elbow, and her mouth wore a wicked smile of invitation. Elena tore her gaze away from the naughty painting and looked at her father.

He was watching her as he finished his whiskey, then he set the glass aside again, pulled a chair away from the table, and straddled it backward. His smile was noncommittal as she struggled to find the words to begin.

"I need your help," she finally said.

He kept quiet, though his smile became more playful.

"Rico sent me away," she said. "To live here in town with Mrs. Rivers." In his continued silence, she said, "She also told me I can't ride in the race, and that I have to wear skirts all the time and go to church socials with Matty and Sarah and Beth."

"Maybe she wants you to be a girl," he pointed out, "instead of the half-breed you are."

"Why can't I be how I am?" Elena cried, fighting tears.

His gaze slid down her dress, lingered a moment on her red

belt, then met her eyes again, his smile warm with a gentle humor. "That touch of velvet is mighty fetching."

She laughed in desperation. "That doesn't make sense, Seth. Rico's forcing this change to keep us apart, and now you say you find me fetching in a skirt!"

"Don't reckon she thought you'd come inside a saloon to petition my help."

"Will you help me?"

He chuckled. "What do you want me to do?"

"Take me home. Rico won't argue if you insist it's what you want. She told me herself she never fights you."

He laughed, standing up and walking back to the desk to pour himself more whiskey. "She opposes me, though. And I'm pretty sure she'll stand solid on this."

"Won't you at least try?"

He sipped his whiskey, then said, "I did that this morning. Rico told me her plan before we got up, and I argued to let me try one more time to find some peaceful ground between us. Guess she doesn't think we found it."

"Only because you left."

"I left so I wouldn't have to tell you good-bye."

"If you'd stayed, she wouldn't have done this."

He stared into his whiskey a moment, then shook his head. "I've been gone more'n ten years," he said, giving her a melancholy smile. "I ain't got the right to tell her how to raise her children."

"I'm your daughter, too."

"You don't act like a daughter."

She stood up, though her knees trembled. "I can't help what I feel. You've admitted you feel it, too. It isn't fair that I'm the one to be punished."

"You want me to leave?"

"No! I want us to live together."

"And go to bed together?"

"If we could do it secretly," she answered, struggling to control her voice, "what harm would be done?"

"You'd get pregnant, Elena. You ain't so innocent you don't know that."

"There are remedies," she said.

He snorted as if amazed at her knowledge, then said, "I think you best stay in town."

"No, Seth," she pleaded. "I've lived without a father all my life. Maybe I don't know how to act right, but all I want is to please you. Whatever you want, I'll do. Just don't let us be separated."

He studied her a long moment, and she raised her head bravely beneath his scrutiny. "Goddamn if you ain't mine," he said with a sigh. Then he set his glass down and held out his hand. "Come on, I'll take you home."

She ran to him, slipping her hand within his and letting him lead her toward the stairs, seeing Blue and Lobo and Gus and the harlot watching from below. At the turn of the landing Seth muttered, "I want you to remember you promised to obey me."

"I will," she answered.

"We'll see," he said, his eyes icy with threat.

Lobo stood up straight, looking back and forth between them. Seth gave Blue a whimsical smile, but when he looked at his son the playfulness evaporated. "I need your help," he stated flatly.

"Anything, Seth," Lobo said, and Elena was impressed with his loyalty away from home.

"Come outside with us," Seth said, nodding his farewell to the others then leading Elena out the back door. The harlot watched them, her eyes dark with what Elena thought was envy.

Padre and Randy were tied to the pillars of the back porch. As Seth lifted Elena to sit sideways in his saddle, the stallion tossed his head until Seth untied the reins and threw the far one over, then Padre stood quivering, waiting for command. Seth told Lobo, "Go by Blue's and pick up Elena's things. Take them home and help

Rico move her bedroom into Esperanza's casita. Tell her we'll be home directly. Can you do that?"

"Sure," Lobo said, glancing quickly at Elena. She caught a gleam of admiration in his eyes.

Seth put his foot in the stirrup and swung up behind her. She slid her arms around his waist, her fingertips lingering on the leather ridges of bullets held snug in his gunbelt. "See you later," he said to Lobo.

Seth held the stallion to a lope around the edge of town, then reined up in front of Joaquín's house. Walking Padre through the open gate into the yard, Seth asked with a smile, "Feel like paying a visit?"

"Whatever you say," she answered.

He laughed, swung down and lifted her to her feet beside him, then turned away to tie the horse just as the door opened. Joaquín stood there, looking pleased to see them. For an uneasy moment, Seth stared at the sheriff's star on Joaquín's jacket, then smiled awkwardly. "Just came by to say hello," he said.

"Come in," Joaquín replied, opening the door wider and stepping back to let them pass. "Heaven and Aaron went to church."

"Why didn't you?" Seth asked, holding Elena's elbow as they walked into the parlor.

"I haven't been to confession since I returned from México," Joaquín answered. "I'm not looking forward to it."

Seth laughed softly. He let go of Elena and dropped his hat on a table, then sat down on the settee as he looked around the room. "You got any whiskey?"

Joaquín smiled at her. "Sit down, Elena."

She, too, sat on the settee, watching Joaquín cross to the sideboard, take out a bottle, and fill two small glasses. He handed one to Seth. "Salud," Joaquín said, raising his glass to sip at the liquor.

"Salud," Seth muttered, draining his glass and setting it aside.

Joaquín looked at it a moment, then asked, "Would you like more?"

"That'll hold me for now. Are you gonna sit down or stand there staring at us?"

"Like the wrath of Jehovah?" Joaquín teased.

"Pretty damn close. Think you could take your jacket off so I don't have to look at that badge while we talk?"

Joaquín removed the silver star instead and slid it into his pocket. "Is that better?"

"Thanks." Seth smiled, then reached out and put his arm around Elena's shoulders, pulling her close. "What do you think of my daughter in a skirt?"

"She's pretty," Joaquín answered, finally sitting down on a needlepoint chair. "But she doesn't need fancy dresses for that."

"Rico thinks she does," Seth said.

As Joaquín looked back and forth between them, Elena could see he didn't approve of how Seth was holding her. Finally Joaquín asked, "Did you go to church this morning?"

"No," Seth said. "We had a family fight."

"About what?"

"Elena's skirts."

Joaquín's eyes sharpened. "Shall I assume Rico won?"

"I don't think she'll see it that way," Seth said, "but I'm hoping to change her mind. I came by to ask if you know anyone who could live with us and help her with the work."

Joaquín nodded. "I can think of several people in need of employment."

"Tell me about 'em," Seth said.

"Well, there's Anamaría Contreras. She's recently orphaned and living off charity, which won't last long. She's sixteen and a good worker."

"Too young," Seth said. "I don't want to tempt Lobo."

Joaquín smiled. "How about Sebastiano de Terrazas? He can cook and sew as well as most women. And since you bought his freedom from the hacendado in Sonora, his loyalty is beyond doubt."

Seth stood up and carried his glass across to the sideboard, poured himself more whiskey, then sipped at it as he stared through the open door into the patio. Elena caught Joaquín watching her, though he immediately dropped his gaze.

Seth drained his glass and turned around. "All right. Where can I find him?"

"I'll be seeing him today," Joaquín said. "If he's interested, I'll send him out to talk over the arrangement."

"Make it tomorrow," Seth said.

"Okay."

Looking around the room, Seth smiled painfully. "Been a long time, Joaquín."

He nodded. "Why don't you and Rico come for supper tomorrow night? Heaven and Aaron have been looking forward to seeing you."

"I bet," Seth scoffed.

"Well, Aaron at least," Joaquín admitted.

"Does Heaven hate me?" Seth asked, his voice low.

Joaquín shook his head. "She misses her sister, is all."

"So do I," Seth said.

Anger flashed in Joaquín's eyes, but his voice was gentle when he said, "Aaron has a lot of his mother in him."

Seth nodded thoughtfully. "What happened to the house she was renting?"

"It's still yours. I paid the taxes and boarded up the window after vandals broke it. Would you like the key?"

"Reckon," he said.

Joaquín walked across to the desk, slid open a drawer, and found the key. He stared down at it a moment, then tossed it over. "What will you do with the house?"

"I don't know," Seth said, pocketing the key without looking at it. "Maybe I'll burn it."

"Adobe is difficult to burn," Joaquín replied.

Seth nodded. "See you tomorrow night?"

"Espero que si, compadre."

Seth retrieved his hat and Elena stood up.

"How do you like having your father home?" Joaquín asked with a playful smile.

She looked up at Seth as she said, "He makes everything different."

Joaquín chuckled, meeting his eyes. "He's not one to pass through unnoticed."

Seth laughed too, but Elena heard little pleasure in the sound. She followed the two men into the yard. As Seth lifted her onto Padre then swung up behind her, she knew Joaquín was wondering why they hadn't brought two horses, but he didn't ask.

Seth turned northeast, crossing the empty desert as they circled Tejoe. Padre's power surged beneath the tight rein, his hooves pounding the stony ground with suppressed energy. Elena felt she would be content to ride forever listening to the stallion dance beneath them as she was held in Seth's arms. In too short a time, he reined up in front of an adobe casita no larger than Esperanza's. This one, however, was situated forlornly alone on the farthest edge of town.

Seth reined the restless stallion to pace back and forth in front of the house. Elena watched Seth, feeling hurt at the pain in his eyes. Finally he swung down, leaving her in the saddle as he tied the reins to a pillar, then walked under the portal. He stood immobile a moment before reaching into his pocket for the key and turning the lock. Gingerly he pushed the door open with his fingertips. The hinges whined, making Padre jerk at the reins. Seth stepped across the threshold and disappeared.

Elena knew the history of the abandoned house. It had been pointed out to her more than once by kids with a ghoulish sense of humor. She slid down and followed Seth inside. He watched her come in, his eyes soft with grief. Looking around the simple, one-room home, she saw a table and chairs, bare shelves, and an empty stove, all covered with a thick accumulation of dust. In the corner was a tarnished brass bed, its mattress adorned with a moth-eaten quilt of faded blue decorated with a once-white star yellowed with age. On the single, boarded-up window were tattered curtains barely showing a pattern of bluebonnets, a flower that grew only in Texas. She looked at her father as she whispered, "This is where you were arrested."

He nodded. "I was standing about where you are when I surrendered my gun."

"Do you regret it?" she asked.

He lifted his hand and let it fall in a gesture of acquiescence. "I regret the crimes that sent me to prison, the years I wasted there, Hekuba's death, and the stain I left on Joaquín's marriage, but being brought to account for all I'd done was what I was angling for."

She stared at him in puzzled silence, trying to follow his thinking. "So you don't hold it against Joaquín at all?"

Seth shook his head. "When Allister and I split company, he wanted me to kill him. Only after a coupla years in prison could I understand why, and how taking on Joaquín as my partner was the way I avoided wanting that for myself."

"Why did Allister want you to kill him?"

"He needed mercy," Seth said, "and his partner was the only one he could expect it from."

"So you think Joaquín was merciful in sending you to prison?" she asked, confused.

Seth nodded. "He could've killed me."

"Could he, really?"

"He was mad enough. And he was right, I was wrong. I'm not sure I could've mustered an effective defense against him."

She smiled. "It's a good thing you chose an ex-priest for your partner."

"He chose me."

"What do you mean?"

"I was the biggest challenge he could find."

"The baddest bad man?" she teased.

"It's the truth, Elena. I used to like sprouts your age 'cause of the stars in your eyes, but after kicking the stars out a few times, I got weary of the hurt that replaced 'em. Now I'm just weary of hurt."

"I would never do anything to hurt you," she said.

His laughter mocked her. "You know who else said that to me?"

She shook her head.

"Lobo's mother. Esther was about your age when she came crawling into my blankets one night announcing she'd never hurt me. But everything we shared was full of pain; Lobo's proof of that."

Elena thought of her troublesome brother, then of the long string of women Seth had left behind. "Are you sorry you loved Hekuba?"

"Yes," he said, his voice warm again. "Not for the pleasure we shared, but because I used her to force Joaquín's hand."

"To do what?" she asked, still confused.

"Punish me," he said.

"I don't understand," she murmured.

"I know you don't, but I'm counting on you, Elena, to deliver something you don't understand."

"What?" she whispered.

"Mercy," he said.

"How can I do that?"

"By doing something I never did: put my wife's happiness above everything else." He studied her a moment. "Rico's your mother. You think you can help me make up for all the hurt I've dealt her?"

"If that's what you want," she said.

"It is." He smiled. "Let's go home."

She preceded him out, then watched him lock the door. Pocketing the key, he kept his head down so the brim of his hat hid his face while he untied the reins. She took a step forward as he threw the far rein over the withers. "Easy, Padre," he murmured, then took hold of her waist and lifted her into the saddle. She was looking down on Seth now, and their eyes met in a brief moment of mutual assessment, as if they had just gone through a test and were reading the results. He glanced away to catch the stirrup, and the leather creaked as he swung up behind her. Holding the prancing stallion in place, Seth looked at the house again, then abruptly reined the horse into a sharp spin and touched his spurs so Padre surged to a gallop.

Elena clung to Seth as the stallion rampaged across the earth, sand and stones flying from his hooves as he leapt the tangles of barbed mesquite and sashayed around spiny ocotillos or towering saguaros. Seth deftly maneuvered him between the sharp points of attack, sheltering Elena as they both bent low over the whipping mane. When they reached the road, he touched his spurs again, and Padre opened up in a dead run, flying like an arrow of destruction.

They galloped past the turnoff to their homestead without a second's hesitation, past the trail to the Nickles ranch without breaking stride, and kept going until the road became only a faint scar of wagon ruts and the wilderness stretched empty to the ledge of mountains jagged on the horizon. Suddenly Seth pulled Padre in, shouting "Whoa!" The horse reared, then came down with a sharp retort and stood heaving in place. " 'Attaboy," Seth said, turning the stallion and holding him to a walk as they headed back.

Elena was breathing almost as hard as Padre, her heart pounding as fast, but Seth seemed relaxed as he smiled down at her, his eyes dancing with fun. Padre heaved a huge sigh and blew dust from his nostrils, then tossed his head and whinnied as if in triumph. Seth laughed and said, "I love this horse."

"He's the best I've ever seen," she agreed.

"You didn't see Rojo as a stud. He was the same before I cut him."

"Why'd you do it then?"

Seth looked down at her with amazement, then laughed again. "If Rojo had made a run like Padre just did, the last thing I'd want is him crowing about it." He gave her a playful smile. "Being quiet's the easiest way to get away with something."

She thought he was talking about them, and impulsively she stretched to kiss his mouth.

His eyes cooled with the sheen of indifference she was learning to recognize as camouflage. "First rule of our arrangement," he said. "You don't kiss me without an invitation. Agreed?"

"Yes," she answered, hoping he would ask her often.

He turned Padre up the trail to the Nickles ranch. "Want to pay another visit?"

"Whatever you wish," she said.

He laughed. "Somehow I never believe a woman when she says that."

Abneth Nickles was alone on the porch. He stood up and walked across his yard as Seth swung down to shake hands.

"Good to see you both," Abneth said, looking up at her on the horse. "Can you stay for dinner?"

"No thanks," Seth said. "But I'd accept a drink if you offered it."

Abneth smiled. "Come on up to the porch and sit a spell."

Seth lifted Elena down and the three of them crossed the yard to the long, shady veranda. As Seth tied Padre to the rail, Abneth hollered through the open door, "Lucy, come say hello to Seth and Elena."

Mrs. Nickles came out drying her hands on her apron. She had iron-gray hair tied in a tight bun, and sharp black eyes. "My you look pretty, Elena," she said, her tone belying her words. "Pleased to see you home, Mr. Strummar. We missed you in church this morning."

"We're still settling in," Seth said.

"Maybe we'll see you next Sunday, then," she answered.

Seth looked at Abneth, who laughed. "Run fetch us some whiskey, Lucy," he said. "Sit down, folks, and rest a spell."

Lucy Nickles looked unhappy to be serving whiskey on the

Lord's Day, but she disappeared inside and returned with a tray holding a new bottle and two glasses. She set them down and left. As Abneth poured the liquor, he said, "Danny's down at the barn unhooking the team, Elena."

She was surprised that Mr. Nickles thought she would squander this occasion with Danny, but Seth said, "Leave us be a while."

She started to protest, then remembered she'd promised to obey him. He smiled as if reading her mind, and she left reluctantly. At the corral, she glanced back but he wasn't even looking at her. She opened the gate and walked on into the barn.

Danny was just hanging the harness on the wall. His face lit up with a smile. "Hey, Elena! Missed you in church today."

"We're still settling in," she answered.

He laughed. "I heard your horse and wondered who it was. How come you're riding alone all dressed up?"

"I'm with Seth," she said.

"Oh," he said, puzzled. "I only heard one horse."

"He picked me up in town," she said.

Danny nodded, obviously curious but too polite to pry. "You want to sit down?" he asked, gesturing toward a plank bench along the wall.

She shrugged and sat down. Smoothing her skirts as she watched him sit at the far end, she smiled, remembering how Seth had pulled her close on the settee in Joaquín's parlor.

"How're things going?" Danny asked.

She considered her answer, then admitted, "Rico kicked me out this morning."

"Why?" he asked with concern.

"She decided I was impudent, and what I need is to live in town and wear frocks all the time. So she carted me to the Rivers's house and left me there. Fortunately the girls were at church and Mrs. Rivers was feeling poorly, so she went to bed. I snuck out and ran down to Blue's saloon to find Seth. When I told him what happened, he said he'd take me home, but we've been riding all over the county ever since."

Danny stared in astonishment. "You went inside Blue's saloon?"

She shrugged. "Lobo was there. He took me upstairs."

"You went upstairs?" Danny asked with dismay.

She laughed. "What's wrong with that?"

"Those rooms are for whores, Elena," he said indignantly. "Lobo had no business taking you up there."

"We went to Blue's office," she said, chastened. "I was with my father and brother the whole time."

"I can't believe Lobo did that." Danny shook his head, then managed a smile. "I'm glad Seth got you out of there."

"Me, too," she said. "I don't think I'll do it again. This was an emergency situation."

He nodded. "I think Rico should keep you home. Any girl who'd walk boldfaced into a saloon shouldn't live in town."

"Haven't you ever walked bold-faced into a saloon?" she teased.

"Once or twice," he said, angry again. "It's all right for a man, but they're pitiful places for women."

She remembered the harlot sitting alone by the roulette wheel, apparently at the beck and call of any man who came through the door. "Have you ever gone upstairs?"

"No!" he retorted. "You got me beat on that one, Elena."

"I don't have you beat on anything," she answered haughtily. "I'm still a virgin."

"That's good news," he said, jerking to his feet and walking a few steps away. "I've always defended you to my mother, saying just 'cause you wear pants don't mean you're loose. I'd hate to have to eat my words and admit she's right."

"Have you really defended me?"

"Are you kidding?" He stared at her sullenly. "I defend you against pretty near everyone we know. They all say you're a wildcat, that blood can't be denied and you're an outlaw's daughter and carry his sins." He stopped, appalled at his words. "I'm sorry, Elena. I'd hoped you would never hear that."

"I've heard it before," she lied, tossing her head with feigned indifference. "I'm proud of my father, I don't care what people say."

Danny gave her a tentative smile. "I would be, too, if he was mine."

She laughed, relieved to see him smile again. "That surprises me since I've never seen you shoot a gun."

He shrugged. "I can do it, though. And a lot of other things you prob'ly wouldn't suspect."

"Like what?" she teased.

He smiled shyly. "Why don't you come to the dance with me on Saturday and find out?"

Seth called her name and she jerked to her feet. "I have to go," she said.

Danny caught her arm as she passed. "What about the dance, Elena?"

"I'll let you know tomorrow," she said, shaking his hand off and running lest Seth leave her behind.

He stood holding the stallion's reins. Mr. and Mrs. Nickles were on the porch, already having said their good-byes. As Seth lifted her into the saddle, Elena heard Danny's mother "tch" in disapproval. Seth swung up behind, tipped his hat at Mrs. Nickles, then trotted over to the corral where Danny sat on the top rail. Seth extended his hand with a smile. "Good to see you again, Danny."

He laughed with pleasure, shaking Seth's hand. "Same here, Mr. Strummar. I asked Elena to the dance. There ain't any reason she can't go, is there?"

Seth looked down at her, then back at Danny. "Not that I know of, long as she wears a skirt." He and Danny laughed.

As Seth nudged the stallion into a lope, Elena felt angry with the men for making a joke about her wearing skirts. As much as she enjoyed being close to Seth, she resented the confining garments that necessitated being lifted on and off his horse. The constant weight of three petticoats alone was debilitating, to say nothing of the continual bother of keeping her hem out of the muck, and she warranted if men had to wear skirts they wouldn't laugh about it. She also felt puzzled that Rico had been the one to make an issue of it, then remembered thinking Rico's love for Seth was a kind of debilitating disease. Suddenly Elena felt melancholy, contemplating what it meant to be a woman when men were around.

Seth turned the stallion onto the road, then slowed to a walk and said softly, "Seems to me an invitation to a dance ought to perk a girl up."

"Do you think I should accept it?" she asked with indifference.

"Sure." He smiled. "I'll take Rico so I can keep an eye on your beau and discourage him from crossing any lines."

"Danny Nickles wouldn't do anything like that," she scoffed.

"Don't underestimate him," Seth said. "Him and his father both got a lot of sand for pig farmers."

"It's a hog ranch," she corrected him.

He laughed. "Is Danny any good on a horse?"

"If it's been gentled." She shrugged. "He won't use a whip or spurs, and I've seen him thrown from broncs."

"I'll have to gentle you well, then, Elena," Seth said.

She stared at him with sudden understanding. "Are you thinking you're gonna marry me off?"

He grinned. "Ain't that what you asked me to do?"

"That was before!" she exclaimed, amazed he hadn't understood. "I was only trying to get you to see I'm a woman."

"I see it plain." He laughed. "Anyway, it's too late now. I've just spoken with Abneth and he's amenable."

"I won't do it," she said.

"You promised to obey me," he reminded her sternly, though his eyes were lively with fun.

"You're not being fair!" she exploded. "What good will it do if you take me home only to ship me off to live on a pig farm?"

"Hog ranch," he said.

"You're mean!" she shouted, twisting to jump free.

He held her close though she struck with her fists. Padre didn't like the commotion. He lowered his head and bucked, sending them both catapulting through the air to land on the road. Elena sat tangled in her petticoats, watching Seth spring up and grab the trailing reins before the stallion escaped. She pulled herself to her feet and batted the dust from her skirts with an angry hand, then looked at Seth. They both laughed.

"Come here," he said, opening his arms. She ran to him, and he held her tight, saying softly into her hair, "I thought Danny could come live with us."

She looked up at her father, trying to imagine the reality of what he was proposing.

"Ain't that what you asked, Elena, that we not be separated? This is the only way I can see to achieve it without a lot of grief."

"I'll do it," she whispered, "if you kiss me now."

His eyes cooled with warning.

"Please," she begged.

With a soulful sigh, he leaned down and kissed her, his mouth tasting of whiskey, his body hard and lean against hers. His hand slid down and cupped her bottom, pulling her into his loins, and she wanted to drop to her knees in submission, to drag him down in the dirt of the road and satiate the hunger she tasted on his tongue. Too soon he broke the kiss and drew back, the glee in his eyes barely concealing the desire that reflected her own. "When you belong to another man," he said, "I'll owe it to him to stay away from you."

"I'll always be yours," she whispered.

"I know that."

She hid her face in his shirt. "Help me, Seth," she pleaded.

"Will you help me, Elena?"

"Yes," she said.

He took hold of her shoulders and set her away from him. "I

want you to promise not to ask for a kiss in the middle of a public road on a Sunday afternoon ever again," he said in his stern-father voice, though his eyes were laughing.

"I promise," she answered.

"Or anywhere else or any other time," he said, his smile playful now but his eyes iced with warning.

"All right," she whispered.

"All right," he said. Clasping her waist, he lifted her onto his horse, then swung up behind her and turned toward home.

27

★

Rico was waiting under the portal. Seth walked Padre
straight across the yard and swung down in front of her,
holding his reins. Elena stayed on the horse, thinking she had never
seen her mother so angry.

"You had no right to overrule me, Seth," Rico bit off, standing to confront him.

"I know it," he answered. "Figured we could talk about it once
more. I didn't come home to break up your family."

"It wouldn't have been forever," she said, unrelenting.

Seth lifted Elena down, warning her with his eyes to keep
quiet. He let loose of her and held out his hand for his wife. "Come
talk to me while I put Padre away?"

She stared with fury a moment, then accepted Seth's hand.
Elena watched them walk across the yard, both of them silent as
the horse clomped along behind them; then she sat down where her
mother had been, unhappy at being excluded.

After a minute, Lobo came through the parlor and stood leaning against the doorjamb. He grinned down at her and said, "Rico
was fit to be tied when she heard you'd gone into Blue's."

"You had to tell her, of course," Elena snapped.

Lobo shrugged. "I wasn't gonna lie. When I gave her Seth's message, she wanted to know whether you'd gone to him or he'd gone to you."

"Did she do it?" Elena asked.

"Do what?"

"Move her bedroom into Esperanza's?"

He nodded. She turned away and they both watched Seth and Rico come out of the stable. Without even looking at their children, they walked across the yard with their arms around each other's waists and disappeared inside the casita.

Lobo chuckled. "Guess they're gonna baptize the bed."

"You're crude," Elena said, jerking to her feet.

"You're jealous," he retorted, blocking the door.

"Get out of my way, Lobo."

He stepped aside to let her pass, but followed her to her room and leaned against the open door as he watched her unpack. "You know it's funny," he said.

She looked up from the petticoat she was unfolding to see his eyes glint with a barb of cruelty.

"I've lusted after Rico since I was twelve years old," he said, "but I never acted on it. You don't have the integrity to admit that what you want would betray your mother."

"You think you have integrity?" she accused. "If you do it's 'cause I saved it for you. I'm the one stole Seth's gun from her bed. That betrayed her, and you knew it would before you sent me to do it!"

"Better for you to lose a little honor," he said, "than for me to fuck my father's wife."

She stared at him. "You make everything so ugly, Lobo."

"What about you?" he mocked. "Lusting after your mother's husband?"

"What I feel has nothing to do with her!" Elena cried in frustration.

He nodded superciliously. "That's what I mean. Do you think if I fucked Seth's wife, he wouldn't take it as a personal insult?"

"They're not married," she argued.

He snorted with scorn. "And you're a bastard, Elena." He turned around and walked out.

"So are you!" she yelled after him, but he was already gone.

She looked down at the petticoat crumpled in her hands. Unable to see how any of it was her fault, she sank onto her bed and buried her face in the garment, remembering Danny saying people thought she carried her father's sins. Even if they were right and she was wicked, it still wasn't her fault.

She sat up and looked down at the tiny pink bows sewn along the petticoat's final flounce. She could remember Rico sitting in front of the fire last winter with the petticoat spread on her lap as she carefully attached each bow an equal distance around the seam. Elena had been struck with a compassionate pity for her mother, trying so hard to make her pretty when she couldn't care less.

That was the winter between Seth's release and when he finally came home, a year they had lived in suspension. Elena remembered her mother looking up from the petticoat spread in the firelight and saying she wanted Seth to be proud of his daughter when he saw her for the first time as a young lady. When it finally happened, Elena had been wearing dungarees covered with dust from working Two-Bits.

She felt a sudden surge of anger that everyone expected too much from her. Kicking her valises out of her way, she changed into the worst clothes she could find, climbed out her window, and walked across the yard to the stable. Angrily she strode into Two-Bits's stall and yanked the filly's head down to catch the lead in the halter. The horse reared and shied away, unaccustomed to Elena's sudden ferocity. She lashed at the filly's flanks with the rope until Two-Bits backed into a corner and stood nickering nervously.

In the reflection of the horse's frightened eyes, Elena saw her own image. Her dungarees were dirty, and her shirt was a throw-away of her older brother's, with bloodstains down the front. Her scuffed, bespurred boots were spread wide to straddle more ground, her face wore a scowl, and her fists gripped a length of rope she had used for punishment when no wrong had been done. For the first time, Elena saw how aggressive she was, and she sank to her knees with apprehension.

Seth had been kind to call her a half-breed. In truth, she was a freak, like a two-headed critter who couldn't make up its mind which way to turn. She wanted to be a woman to please him, but not to be under anyone's command. She wanted to master the world as she did horses, to move freely without the drag of petticoats, to act on her own judgment and go wherever and whenever she chose. To accept being a woman was to confine her very breath inside the lace stays of a corset called propriety; to elect to be a man was absurd since she hadn't been born one. So she was stuck being neither, which anyone would say made her a freak.

A flash of sunlight lit the inside of the stable. The small door thudded closed and she heard the rustle of Rico's skirts. Elena drew up her knees and hid her face as the stall door opened. She could see the hem of her mother's dress, a soft, indigo blue that matched her eyes, though Elena couldn't bring herself to meet them.

Rico sat down in the straw beside her. "Look at you," she crooned. "You couldn't look worse if you tried, Elena."

"Can't see how it matters," she said, her face still hidden against her knees. "Everybody hates me anyway."

"No one hates you, sweetheart," Rico said. "We all love you very much."

"Couldn't prove it by me," she said.

Rico sighed and leaned against the wall beside her. "I remember being fourteen. It's hell, isn't it."

Elena turned her head just enough that she could see her mother's face over the sleeve of her brother's shirt.

Rico smiled. "In two more weeks you'll be fifteen. Maybe that'll feel better."

"Did it for you?"

"Oh well," she answered with a scoffing laugh, "your life doesn't have to be like mine."

"What happened when you were fifteen?"

Rico picked up a piece of straw and beat it against her knees a few times, then tossed it aside. "I left home."

Elena studied her mother for a long moment. "Why?"

"Oh," she said with an embarrassed smile, "I had a similar situation with what we're going through now, only it was turned around: my daddy was after me. I didn't like him as much as you do Seth and I found the idea quite repellent. So I ran away with a young man who promised to make me happy." She laughed at her girlish foolishness. "You can imagine my dismay when I discovered he wanted the same thing my daddy did. I gave it to him, of course, counting on his giving me happiness in return."

"Did he?" Elena asked.

Rico shook her head. "He took me to Santa Fe. All the way there I thought any city called Holy Faith must be a grand place to live. But he was a gambler, and you know how superstitious they are. He decided I was the cause of Lady Luck turning against him, so he left me in a hovel close by the Pecos Trail. I sat there for three days watching the wagon trains roll into the plaza. At the end of those three days I was out of food. All I owned was a fancy red dress he'd bought me, so I put that dress to work." She smiled at her daughter. "My gambler wasn't cheap and that dress lasted a long time. It was made out of a fine satin that never lost its sheen. I met your father while wearing that dress. It was old then, but I can still remember his eyes when he told me how nice he thought it fit." She laughed. "I finally threw it away because I couldn't get the smoky smell of saloons out of it."

Elena had never considered what her mother looked like when she'd first caught Seth's eye. "Did you meet him in Santa Fe?"

Rico shook her head. "I first met Seth in Pinos Altos in 'seventy-five. We had a brief romance, one of those flings that happen between drifters and saloon girls. A few days of delirious happiness, that's all." She laughed softly. "Seth was trying to go straight, riding shotgun on the ore wagons. So many gunmen came to challenge him, though, that his boss finally said he was paying Seth to defend his own life more than the ore. He fired him and Seth left for Colorado. Me and another girl, Melinda, went down to Tombstone. After we'd been there six months or so, one night Seth walked into the saloon where I was singing. As soon as our eyes met, it was on between us again. We lasted a little longer that time. I wanted it to last forever but one day he was gone." She snorted delicately. "Said good-bye sitting his horse in the yard of the boardinghouse where I lived. Just stopped by on his way out of town. Someone was after him, of course, but I didn't want him to go. I felt so forlorn, I tried to kill myself."

She nodded at her daughter's dismay. "That was silly, I know, but I simply didn't believe I could survive without him. I did, of course. Melinda took care of me until I was back on my feet, and it was after that I married Henry Lessen. But I didn't love him and he knew it. We were unhappy. One day we went to town and my husband got into a fight and was killed. I turned away from his death and saw Seth standing in the crowd. He drove me home. On the way there he told me he'd killed a Texas Ranger who was tracking him, and that he needed a place to disappear for a while. So we sold my husband's property near Tombstone and moved here. You were born a year and a half later." She reached across and tucked a strand of Elena's hair behind her ear. "He loved you so when you were a baby. He used to call you Elita and hold you on his lap as we sat under the portal after supper, and I felt so full of happiness I thought nothing was strong enough to break it."

"But you were wrong," Elena whispered.

Rico nodded. "I think I knew all along he wasn't yet mine to keep. Too many men had staked prior claims on him." She paused, then said, "All those claims are paid now, Elena. Seth has owned me from the moment we met, but this is the first time he doesn't have an excuse not to meet the responsibilities of ownership. He's trying hard to be a good husband and father."

"If that's true," Elena asked, "why doesn't he marry you?"

Rico smiled with indulgence. "He's never had much respect for the law. And he married Johanna in a church and that didn't last, so he can't see as how sacred vows mean much, either. He's a man of action, not words, and his being here is all I ask."

"It's not all you ask of me," Elena said.

"That's different. I'm your mother and my expectations are your education."

"What if I don't agree with them?"

"You must bow to my experience. The world can be a treacherous place, Elena. Not everyone is as fortunate as you."

"I don't feel fortunate," she answered.

"But you are." Rico smiled, gently smoothing Elena's hair. "I want you to know that whatever you do, you'll always be my daughter, and I will never send you away again."

Elena considered all the implications of that before asking, "What did Seth say to change your mind?"

Rico stood up and brushed straw from her skirts. "I've already told you, Elena, he's a man of action, not words." She met her eyes with a teasing smile. "Will you come help me with supper? We have the privilege of three men to feed."

"I guess," she said, standing too. "Did you know Seth's gonna hire a man to help you with the work?"

"Goodness, Elena!" she exclaimed. "Did you have to wear that shirt?"

Elena looked down at the bloodstains and shrugged. "Did you hear what I said?" she asked, coming out of the stall and hanging the rope on a nail, giving Two-Bits an apologetic smile.

"Yes, someone named Sebastiano," Rico said. "He's to stay in Lobo's room and your brother's to move into the house."

"What about the race?" Elena asked, listening to the rustle of her mother's skirts as they walked down the aisle. "Will you let me run it?"

"I don't like you riding Padre. He's too strong for you."

"What if I ride Two-Bits?"

Rico smiled but shook her head. "We'll see."

As an act of defiance, Elena didn't change clothes before supper. She could feel the three men she had the "privilege to feed" watching her as she helped Rico prepare their food, but only Jesse said anything. As she set the platter of pork chops on the table, he mumbled, "Did you come straight from a fistfight, Elena?"

Lobo laughed and said, "That's the shirt I wore when Joaquín clobbered me in Blue's saloon."

"What were you fighting about?" Seth asked.

Lobo looked at Elena carrying the applesauce to the table and said pointedly, "I insulted his wife."

Seth smiled. "The only surer way to make a Mexican mad is to bad-mouth his mother."

"What about his daughter?" Elena asked, going back for the basket of bread. "Will a Mexican fight to defend her honor?"

"Depends on the daughter," Seth said, giving her a sardonic smile.

Lobo snickered, "I've met some daughters no man would defend."

"Hush," Rico said as she brought a bowl of potatoes and a small cauldron of gravy to the table. "There's no need to brag about living in the gutter." She sat down and unfolded her napkin, waited until Elena was settled, then smiled at Jesse.

Jesse bowed his head. "Bless us, oh Lord, and these Thy gifts, which we are about to receive from Thy bounty."

"Amen," five voices said.

Elena watched the men passing the food, then looked at her mother and asked, "Did you know Lobo's gonna work for Blue in his saloon?"

"Seth mentioned it." Rico smiled, her eyes on Lobo.

"It doesn't bother you?" Elena asked.

"I'm pleased he's decided to stay in Tejoe," she said, giving him another smile.

"It would bother you if I worked there, though, wouldn't it," Elena said.

"Yes, it would," Rico replied, suddenly stern.

"You worked in saloons," Elena said.

Seth laughed softly. "She's got you on that one, Rico."

She huffed. "If people can't share with their children the hard lessons they've paid dearly to learn, what's the point of our suffering?"

"Maybe there ain't one," Seth teased.

"Yes, there is," Jesse said. "It's to pay for our sins."

"What about newborn babies?" Lobo argued. "I've heard stories about soldiers knocking Indian papooses up against rocks and bashing their brains out. Are you saying those babies deserved to be hurt?"

"We all pay for the sins of our fathers," Jesse said.

"I'm getting tired of hearing that," Seth said.

Jesse met his father's eyes without flinching. "It's in the Bible."

Seth dropped his knife and fork so they clattered on his plate. "I don't give a good goddamn what's in the Bible. If you want to preach, open a church. But don't expect to see me there 'cause I've had twelve years of preachers quoting scripture about sin. I don't need to hear it from my son. Do you understand me?"

Jesse nodded, slowly standing up.

"Where you going?" Seth asked.

"I don't care to eat with you," Jesse said.

"Eat with your mother, then, and your sister, and this half-lunatic you're stuck with for a brother."

Jesse just stared at him.

"Sit down," Seth said.

Jesse sat back down.

"Jesus Christ," Seth said to Rico. "Did you deliberately raise them to torment me?"

She shook her head, trying to laugh at the notion.

"Well, they're doing a damn good job," he said, glaring unhappily at his children.

They were all silent, their eyes on their plates, Rico's meal growing cold. Finally Jesse said, "I'm sorry, Seth. It's unchristian of me to keep bringing up your past. I'll try not to do it again."

"Thanks," he said with sarcasm. "I'll try never to mention that you're scared of horses and most of the rest of the world."

Jesse gave him a shy smile. "I'd appreciate it," he said.

Lobo laughed. "Now that's settled, can we eat?"

"Who's stopping you?" Seth asked.

Hatred flashed from Lobo's eyes as he looked down the table at his father. "Nobody," Lobo said, picking up his silverware.

Jesse ate too, and so did Rico. Elena joined the effort and they all cleaned their plates while Seth sat with his food untouched. Finally Rico asked softly, "Aren't you going to eat, Seth?"

"Doesn't look like it," he said.

"Aren't you hungry?" she coaxed.

"Apparently not."

"Is there something else you'd like? I have some chicken in the icebox."

"You got any whiskey?"

"It's in the casita."

"Good place for it," he said, standing up. "Let's go keep it company."

Their children sat in silence listening to them leave the house. When they heard the door across the yard close, Lobo laughed and said, "Good work, Jess. You got him going that time."

"You're mean," Elena said, standing up and stacking the dirty dishes.

Jesse looked puzzled. "Seth believes it, or it wouldn't rile him so bad."

"Oh yeah, he believes it." Lobo laughed. "And you're like a picador stabbing el toro every time he forgets he's still in the ring."

"That isn't what I mean to do," Jesse said. Then his eyes caught with a glint like steel and he stood up. "That's just the way you're seeing it, Lobo, 'cause you see everything as a fight. I'm trying to love him. I may be clumsy at it, and I don't think he's doing real well, either, but we'll find a path and it won't be yours." He turned around and walked out.

Lobo shook his head with mock concern. "Poor Jess. He's so buffaloed by Seth he'll *never* have any backbone."

"I could say the same of you," Elena muttered.

He snorted. "I suppose you think you're the only one of his children with any sand."

"At least I'm not attacking him all the time," she argued.

"No, you're seducing him." Lobo grabbed her as she walked by on her way to the sink, slid his arms around her waist from behind, and stole a kiss off her cheek. "If you're so hot to fuck a relative, won't I do?"

She dropped the plates on the floor, whirled around, and slapped his face.

He took a step back. "Someone's gonna knock that spit out of you real hard, Elena."

"It'll take more man than you'll ever be," she retorted.

"No, it won't." He grinned. "I figure when you lose the race, you'll be humbled right proper."

"Want to make a bet on my losing?" she asked with disdain.

"I wouldn't take your money," he boasted. "I'm gonna race Padre. You and Two-Bits ain't got a chance."

"You'd run against me?" she whispered.

"What do you think we've been doing since we were born?" he scoffed, sauntering out.

She stood staring at the empty door until Jesse came in behind her. He brought the broom and dustpan to sweep up the broken plates, then dumped them in the trash barrel outside the door. When he came back, she began washing the dishes, and they worked together to set the kitchen right again.

When they finished, Jesse went to his room. Elena walked out and sat under the portal. The casita across the yard was dark, though it wasn't yet nine o'clock. She thought of Rico meeting Seth in a saloon, and wondered if it had looked anything like the Blue Rivers. Remembering the naughty painting in Blue's office, Elena thought of all the other doors off that hallway, and of what went on behind them.

After a time, she saw a flickering light through the window of the casita and knew one of her parents had lit a candle. In a few minutes, Rico came out and walked toward the house. Not seeing her daughter sitting in the shadows under the portal, she walked in the back door.

Elena followed her and saw Rico take the chicken from the icebox. Her mother smiled and said, "I thought you were asleep."

Elena shook her head and sat down at the table, watching her mother make a sandwich. "Is that for Seth?"

"Yes," she said. "He's hungry after all."

"For food, you mean," Elena said.

Rico looked up sharply, then returned her attention to her task.

"Why is it all right," Elena asked, "for Lobo to work in Blue's saloon but I'm not even supposed to go there?"

"I think you know why," Rico said. She placed the sandwich on a plate and covered it with a tea towel.

"I don't understand it, though. Danny told me saloons were okay places for men but pitiful places for women. Why is that?"

Rico opened the icebox and took out the pitcher of milk, poured a glass full, and replaced the pitcher. She set the glass and plate on a tray, then faced her daughter. "Most of the women in saloons are prostitutes. Danny's right in thinking they're pitiful."

"Were you one?"

Rico shook her head. "I was a singer."

"But you've been to bed with a lot of men, haven't you?"

"A few," she admitted.

"Is it different with Seth than it was with the others?"

"Yes, because we love each other."

"Those two times you knew him before, was it different then?"

"Yes."

"Did he hurt you?"

Rico sighed. "I wish you'd stop thinking about this, Elena. It isn't healthy for a young girl to be so preoccupied with it."

"It keeps coming to mind," she said.

Rico smiled. "Maybe Seth is right and it is time you were married."

Elena looked away.

"Do you know Seth has spoken to Danny's father?"

She nodded.

"How do you feel about marrying Danny?"

"I don't think I should marry anybody until I get all this straight in my mind."

"All what?" Rico asked softly.

Elena met her mother's eyes. "Jennifer told me Sassy sometimes comes home with bruises from what the men do to her. Seth said he hurts women, and you told me it didn't matter 'cause he doesn't hurt you. All the men we know spend a lot of time in Blue's saloon, yet because of what they do there, we aren't even allowed to step foot inside the door. None of that seems right."

"It isn't," Rico said.

"Then why does it happen?"

Rico sighed. "All I can say is it's a man's world, and life being what it is, when they're hurt they sometimes take it out on us. That's not right, it's just the way it is."

"Do all men hurt women?"

"Joaquín doesn't. I don't think Jesse ever will. And I'm sure Danny won't."

"Does Lobo?"

"I don't know."

"Does Blue?"

"I don't think so."

"Jennifer told me Blue takes Sassy to bed."

"I wish you wouldn't spend so much time with Jennifer," Rico said.

"How can Blue run a whorehouse and still love his daughters?"

"He doesn't run it. Sassy does. He only rents her space."

"He's still making money from it, though, isn't he?"

They both heard the door to the casita open and close, then the soft jangle of Seth's spurs coming closer.

"Let's finish this talk tomorrow," Rico said. "Seth's had a hard enough time tonight."

He walked into the kitchen, then stopped just inside the door. "Am I interrupting something?" he asked warily.

"I was just coming," Rico said.

"I'll eat at the table since I'm here." He sat down and smiled at Elena. "What're you doing awake?"

"Trying to figure things out," she answered, ignoring her mother's frown.

"What kind of things?"

"Men," she said.

He looked regretfully at Rico setting the sandwich and milk in front of him. "Wish I'd stayed in the casita," he said.

"Yes," Rico murmured.

Seth leaned back with a sigh. "Well, go ahead and spit it out, Elena. What's bothering you?"

"I can't understand," she said, unable to look at him, "why men want to hurt women."

He chuckled. "Women hurt men, too. Did you ever consider that?"

She looked at him, amazed he could laugh about it.

"It's true," he said. "I've seen plenty of men torn up 'cause some woman broke his heart."

"That's not what I mean," she said. "I was talking about what happens upstairs at Blue's."

He studied her a moment before asking, "What do you think happens?"

"Women get hurt, don't they?"

"Reckon sometimes they do."

"I don't understand it. Blue's got daughters. You have one, too. Don't you think what happens there affects us?"

"Not if you stay out of there."

"Did you know Sassy's daughter is my friend?"

"I didn't even know she had a daughter."

"Well, she does. And she's my friend."

Seth sighed. "I can't change the world, Elena. I'm having a hard enough time with myself."

She looked at her mother, whose pleading smile made her relent. "Reckon I just feel confused right now."

"Growing up tends to do that," Seth said.

"Do you think that's what's wrong with Lobo?" she asked. "That he hasn't grown up yet?"

"How's Lobo figure into this?"

"He kissed me tonight," she said, then felt ashamed for having told on him.

"I'll speak to him," Seth said, his voice cold.

She shook her head. "I slapped him for it. Reckon that was punishment enough."

Seth laughed. "I bet you pack a wallop, Elena."

"You should know," she said. "I've hit you."

"Yeah, but I'm a little more thick-skinned than Lobo," he said, giving her a wink.

Elena wanted to snuggle up close to him. She would have if her mother hadn't been there. "Guess I'll go to bed," she said, standing up and walking out.

"Good night, sweetheart," Rico called after her.

Just before closing her bedroom door, Elena heard Seth say, "I get the feeling I didn't handle that right."

"I'll handle Elena," Rico answered. "You keep a rein on Lobo."

28

★

When Elena went in for breakfast the next morning, Jesse sat alone at the table studying his arithmetic. Rico was working at the stove. "Good morning, Elena," she said brightly. "How did you sleep?"

Elena shrugged and sat down, watching her mother carry two plates of eggs and biscuits to the table. She returned with the coffeepot and filled all their cups. Setting the pot on its trivet, Rico sat down and said, "I hear Danny invited you to the dance on Saturday. Would you like a new dress?"

"I'm not going," Elena answered, working her way through the eggs.

"I thought you liked Danny," Rico said softly.

"I don't know how to dance," Elena mumbled.

"I could give you a lesson this week. Would you like that?"

Elena shrugged.

Rico sipped her coffee, then said, "You look pretty this morning with that blue ribbon in your braid."

"It matches the dress, is all," Elena said.

"Very nicely, too," Rico agreed. She stood up and carried the dirty plates to the sink. Looking out the window, she said, "Here comes Lobo with your horses."

Jesse shoved his book into his satchel, kissed his mother's cheek, and hurried out. The sound of her brothers laughing beyond the open door made Elena feel angry, as if they were laughing at her the way Seth had the night before. She stood up and started out.

"Don't I get a kiss?" Rico called.

Elena turned back. "Do you want one I don't feel?"

Rico smiled, though her eyes were hurt. "Maybe by doing it, you'll feel it again."

"Can't see any sense in that," Elena said, walking out.

Jesse was already on Rojo. Lobo held the reins to Nugget, Rico's palomino. Of all the horses on the homestead, Elena would have chosen her mother's mare last, but she took the reins, led the horse to the mounting block, and settled herself in the sidesaddle. As Jesse turned Rojo, she reined Nugget alongside, feeling Lobo's eyes follow them out of the yard.

When they were beyond the sliver of mountain that cut off their view of home, Jesse looked across at her and said, "I'm sorry I took Rojo from you."

Elena shrugged. "He was Seth's to give." Her brother still looked doubtful, so she said, "I'm glad you have him, Jesse. It'll be fun riding to school together instead of alone all the time."

"Do you mean it?" he asked.

She nodded, though she felt unhappy contemplating the five miles covered at a snail's pace. Then she wondered why she was in such a hurry since Danny would be waiting to hear her answer about the dance. If not for Seth, she would probably go. She liked Danny's company better than any boy's, but everything was different now.

When they finally rode into the schoolyard, Danny was waiting. He walked over and smiled up at Jesse. "Good to see you on a horse," Danny said, then turned to hold Nugget as Elena jumped down. As soon as she was on the ground, he asked softly, "Have you decided about the dance, Elena?"

She thought he could have waited until lunch, and his impatience made her angry all over again. "I don't think I can go," she said, starting away.

He caught hold of her arm. "Ain't you even gonna thank me for asking?" he demanded, his eyes angry now, too.

"I'll put the horses up," Jesse said from behind them, tugging Nugget's reins out of Danny's hand.

He glanced at Jesse, then looked back at Elena. "Did Seth tell you what he and my father talked about yesterday?"

"Yes," she said, staring down at his hand still holding her arm.

He let go. "Don't guess you like the idea," he said, "if you won't even go to the dance with me."

She sighed, relenting at the hurt in his voice. "Ever since Seth came home, everything's been upside down. I'm just confused right now."

Danny nodded, then gave her a playful smile. "Well, he got Jesse on a horse and you with a ribbon in your hair. Seems maybe things were upside down before."

"You're just like the rest!" she accused. "Wanting to make me into a silly girl!"

"Nobody thinks you're silly, Elena," he answered. "But then again, it might be easier'n dealing with a riled hen all the time."

"You're the one who was mad yesterday," she reminded him.

"Because I care for you," he said, his voice softer.

Though she couldn't understand why, she preferred his anger. "Did you have to defend me from your mother last night?" she asked tartly.

He nodded, obviously puzzled by her tone. "She said the way Seth was riding you around, it appeared something unnatural was going on."

She looked down to hide her eyes.

"Goddamn, Elena," he whispered. "Is it?"

The school bell began to ring and the younger children ran laughing and shouting to line up outside the door. Elena started away but again Danny caught her arm and held her beside him. "Tell me the truth," he demanded.

"Nothing's going on," she said.

He studied her a long moment. "That's good," he finally said, " 'cause I'd kill Seth if he did that."

She stared in astonishment, then laughed with ridicule. "You think you could?"

"I think he'd help me."

"You're loco," she retorted, pulling herself free.

Without looking back, she took her place in the line of girls. Their softly whispered secrets and soprano giggles filled Elena with hatred. She looked at the boys noisily shoving each other, their line scraggly next to the smoothly scalloped skirts all in a row, and she didn't want to be in either line, didn't want to go into the schoolhouse and sit all day watching the prim teacher drone on about King Lear and the Boston Tea Party. Elena had promised to obey Seth, however, and knew he wouldn't look lightly on truancy. In another two weeks, school would be over and she would have the whole summer at home. She would also be fifteen, which apparently was old enough to get married. She looked for Danny, but he had disappeared.

At the last minute, Jennifer came walking into the school yard wearing a black skirt and a blue middy. She had a man's belt cinched tight around her waist, the extra length dangling like a dead snake. The way her skirt hung limp made it plain she wasn't wearing any petticoats and probably not even a shimmy, and suddenly Elena realized her friend was destined to be a slattern. Feeling bad for her, Elena gave her a smile. Though Jennifer grinned and waved, they didn't get a chance to talk until lunch. Again Elena vainly searched the school yard for Danny, then decided he had ditched school.

Jennifer didn't have any food, so Elena shared hers. When she thought of her mother fixing it and making her breakfast and how she hadn't even given Rico a good-bye kiss, Elena felt bad again, then realized that lately she was always feeling either sad or angry. Nothing seemed fun anymore.

Jennifer bit into the apple and asked, "So how'd things turn out?"

Elena shrugged.

"Are you home or still stayin' with Mrs. Rivers?"

"Home," she said.

Jennifer laughed. "Told you it'd work, didn't I?"

Elena nodded. "Things're different, though."

"How?" Jennifer asked, then spat out a seed.

"Last night I tried to talk to my parents about what goes on upstairs at Blue's. Seth thought it was funny, and Rico just said it wasn't right but that's the way the world is."

"What'd you wanta hear?"

Elena thought a minute. "That it wasn't true, I guess."

"Well, at least they didn't lie to you," Jennifer pointed out.

"Yeah, I reckon that's the best can be said about it."

They sat in silence a moment before Jennifer asked, "You still hot for Seth?"

Elena shrugged. "His laughing at me kinda put a damper on it. Seems everything I do with him hurts one way or another."

Jennifer wiped her mouth with the back of her hand. "Outlaws ain't known for bein' gentle."

Elena remembered Rico telling her nearly the same thing. "They want me to marry Danny Nickles. Seth's already spoken to his father about it."

"No kiddin'?" Jennifer whispered, her voice full of envy.

"You think it's a good idea?" Elena asked with surprise.

"Shoot! I'd do it in a second. But I'd marry jus' about anybody to keep from followin' in Sassy's footsteps."

"You should've kept your chastity then," Elena said. "Men want their brides to be virgins."

"That wasn't exactly my choice," Jennifer retorted. "My father didn't come home and find *me* a husband, did he?"

"I'm sorry," Elena answered. "I know it wasn't your fault."

Jennifer tossed her hair out of her eyes. "Don't matter," she said. "Most daughters of doves end up bein' doves, too. Guess I shouldn't expect any dif'rent."

"Your mother does, though," Elena said gently. "Rico told me her expectations are my education."

"Yeah, well, Rico fell in love with Seth. For all his hurtful ways, he took her out of saloons and set her up respectable. Sassy fell in love with Hollister Pardee and he drug her down lower, so I reckon expectations come out of what happens to a person."

"I reckon," Elena said. "It's funny, ain't it, that Seth never married Rico yet did better by her than Sassy got from being Hollister Pardee's wife?"

"Seth's doin' better by you, too," Jennifer said.

Elena looked away. "But why does he have to hurt me to do it?"

"Maybe he's just tryin' to keep his distance," Jennifer suggested, "so he won't be tempted to give in to his baser instincts. All men have 'em, you know. That's what keeps whorehouses in business." She sighed. "I'm cuttin' out again. Wanta come?"

Elena shook her head. "Where're you going?"

"To meet Charlie Two Horns." Jennifer grinned. "Figure when I start sellin' my favors it'll be work and I won't enjoy it as much. So I'm gonna get my fun while I can."

Elena felt melancholy all afternoon, thinking about Jennifer with Charlie Two Horns. On the way home, Jesse sensed her mood and kept quiet, then took the south fork toward afternoon Mass at Our

Lady of Sorrows, so Elena rode into the yard alone. She tied Nugget to the portal, intending to put the horse away after she changed clothes, then walked into the kitchen and saw an old Mexican man working at the stove. She stopped dead still.

He looked up and smiled. "You are Señorita Elena, no?"

She nodded.

"I am Sebastiano de Terrazas."

She nodded again.

"You like green chili? I am making some for supper."

They hadn't had green chili since Esperanza died. "Are you making enchiladas?" she asked.

"I could. Is that what you like?"

"Yes," she said. "And the chili real hot."

He laughed. "Señor Seth already told me that."

"Is he here?" she asked.

"I think he is taking a siesta with your mother." The old man smiled, his dark eyes twinkling in his brown, creased face. "Would you like me to put your horse in the stable?"

"I'll do it," she said, starting from the room. She turned back at the door and said, "Thanks anyway, Sebastiano."

"No problem," he said.

She walked into her room to change, thinking a man in the kitchen would make her home a different place. He seemed pleasant enough and willing to be helpful, but it was unnatural to see a man doing women's work. It was almost as if Lobo were getting his wish and the homestead was turning into a haven for old men. She wondered if Sebastiano had been an outlaw, then remembered Joaquín saying Seth had bought the old man's freedom from a hacendado in Mexico.

Wearing clean dungarees and a shirt without any stains, she tugged on her always-bespurred boots, intending to run Two-Bits on the road. As usual, she climbed out her window onto the portal. When she settled her hat on her head, she felt the smooth length of satin still in her hair. Since she didn't want to crumple the rib-

bon into her pocket, she left it there as she led Nugget toward the
stable.

She wondered if Sebastiano would wash their clothes, then
guessed he might for the men but Rico wouldn't let him launder
their undergarments. Elena found that thought slightly reassuring.
Since beginning her monthlies she often found spots on her
bloomers, and she would be horrified if a man ever saw them.
Which was another example of how unfair life was, that men
flaunted their blood as proof of prowess while women hid theirs as
evidence of shame.

When she reached the corral she was angry again, but by the
time she had settled Nugget into a stall, Elena felt only a happy
anticipation at the prospect of running her filly. She saddled Two-
Bits and led her through the corral gate, then leapt to catch the
stirrup and cantered out of the yard toward the road.

The filly was antsy with pent-up energy, and Elena realized she
hadn't thoroughly worked Two-Bits since seeing Padre. She wondered if Seth would really let Lobo run the stallion in the race, guar-
anteeing her defeat. It didn't seem fair, but then nothing did
anymore. She still smarted with indignation when she thought of
Seth giving Rojo to Jesse.

She could see it was right, since the old sorrel was as gentle as
the day was long and Jesse needed that from his mount, but Elena
couldn't deny the resentment she felt. She had proved her compe-
tence to both Rico and Blue by handling the sorrel when he wasn't
gentle, turning him into a mount a child could control. All the
years she'd been doing that, she'd felt bonded with Seth because
she was riding his horse. Yet one of the first things he'd done when
he got home was take Rojo away from her.

Elena listened to Two-Bits's hooves strike the road with equal
force, so she knew the filly wasn't favoring any of them. If Elena
ran her every day between now and the race, her tendons would be
as strong as they were ever going to get. At two, she was in her
prime for speed; another year would add strength, but she would

never top out faster than now. Still, they didn't have a prayer against Padre.

When Elena rode back into the yard and saw Seth handing Rico into the buggy, she remembered they were going to Joaquín's for supper. They were both dressed up, Seth in a dark suit and Rico in the green dress she had ordered when they first learned of his pardon. She hadn't worn the dress until now, and Elena realized this was a celebration for them, their first evening out since his return. She struggled to think of something nice to say as she reined in her filly, well-lathered from their workout.

Seth walked around the team, stepped into the buggy and gathered the reins, then smiled at Elena and asked, "How'd she do?"

"Fine," Elena answered with an edge. "But there's no way she'll ever beat Padre."

Seth frowned. "She won't have to, will she?"

"Lobo told me he's gonna run him in the race."

"First I've heard about it," Seth said.

"Does that mean you won't let him?"

"Let's discuss this another time," Rico said. "We're late, Seth." To Elena she said, "We'll be home by midnight. Help Sebastiano with the dishes, will you?"

"Sure," she said.

Still Seth waited, as if he wanted to say something else. Rico touched his arm and murmured, "We should go, Seth."

"Wish you were coming," he said to Elena.

It dawned on her that he wasn't looking forward to seeing Heaven and meeting Aaron, and she felt pleased he thought she could help him through it. But Rico said, "We haven't time for her to bathe and change."

Seth nodded. "From now on, tell someone where you're going, Elena."

"All right," she said softly. "I didn't know you wanted me along."

"It ain't just that," he said. "I don't like you riding the country alone. Any number of things could happen."

She laughed. "I've been doing it all my life."

"It was different before I got here. From now on I want you to take a gun when you go off by yourself."

"Please, Seth," Rico pleaded. "You'll frighten her."

"Just 'cause I've been pardoned doesn't mean I don't have enemies," he told her. "You want Elena falling prey to some excuse for a man intent on hurting me?"

"I don't want her afraid of the world," Rico said.

Seth smiled. "She ain't got an ounce of fear in her." He winked at Elena. "We'll talk about it another time," he said, slapping the reins so the buggy moved forward.

Watching it disappear around the sliver of mountain, Elena wished Seth was right about her courage, but at that moment she felt very much afraid. Suddenly the world lurked with enemies, and she guessed that was why he had hired Sebastiano instead of a woman: Seth wanted a man at home when he was gone. She looked toward the house and saw Lobo sitting under the portal, and she wondered why he didn't fit the bill.

Jesse came into the stable while she was rubbing down Two-Bits. He unsaddled Rojo and led him into a stall, then came over and watched her tying liniment soaks around the filly's tendons. "I passed Seth and Rico on the road," he said. "Seth told me not to leave home without a gun anymore."

She looked up from where she knelt on the straw. "What'd you say back?"

"That I don't know how to use one. He told me I should learn!"

She stood up and smiled at him. "You'll have a good teacher."

Jesse shook his head. "I told him I didn't ever want to touch a gun, that I'd never shoot anyone no matter what they did. I'd rather be shot myself than go to hell."

"What'd he say to that?"

"He didn't say nothing," Jesse answered, looking away, "just stared at me like I was some sort of freak."

She came out of the stall and pulled him close in a hug. "Well, you kind of are," she said gently. "I guess we all are, except Rico. She ain't got any Strummar blood."

"You should've been his son," Jesse whispered. "Neither Lobo nor I measure up."

She held him out at arm's length. "Why do you say that?"

"I'm gonna be a priest," he said, "and Lobo's a coward."

She stared at him. "What're you talking about? I bet he's picked fights with every man in town."

Jesse shrugged himself free and sat down on a bale of hay, leaning forward with his head in his hands. She waited for him to explain himself. When it looked like he wouldn't, she went over and sat down beside him. "What're you talking about, Jesse?" she coaxed.

"I committed an awful sin today," he whispered.

She ran through the things he could have done since leaving school. One time he'd told her what he said in confession, and his sins seemed like trifles to her. "What'd you do?" she asked, humoring him.

He sighed deeply, then looked at her with tears in his eyes. "I didn't mean to," he said, imploring for understanding. "I meant to go to confession myself. But the church was empty when I got there, so I went on into a booth and just sat and waited. Padre Mathias didn't know I was there, I guess. After a while I heard him come into the sanctuary with someone else. The window was open in my booth and I heard his confession plain. I didn't want to listen, but I couldn't not."

"Whose was it?" she asked.

"Joaquín's," he whispered.

She stared at him, then grinned. "Was it a bad one?"

Jesse nodded solemnly. "He killed nine men in Mexico, five

outright and four he feels responsible for, though they were hung by the Rurales."

"Nine?"

"That wasn't the worst of it," Jesse said.

"What else?" she asked, astounded he would consider anything worse than murder.

"He committed carnal sin with women, too. But what he really talked about was Seth and Lobo."

"What about them?" she whispered, pricked with sudden dread.

Jesse sighed deeply. "All the time Joaquín was in Mexico, he was mad at Seth for forcing him to deliver guns to bandits. He said Seth's men held him prisoner, and Seth made it a condition of Joaquín's freedom that he agree to help them, and he was so mad about that, he did things he's sorry for now. He killed the first four men taking the guns to the bandits, then when he had the money and was getting ready to leave their camp, the jefe sent Lobo with him. They stopped overnight someplace, and when Joaquín got up the next morning, Lobo had taken the money and left him behind. Joaquín was caught by the soldiers, but he escaped. Just as he was climbing over the wall, he saw Lobo brought into the fort as a prisoner, and Joaquín knew he had to rescue Lobo. Before he did, though, Lobo was whipped by the soldiers. They were trying to make him tell who had the money, and Lobo not only betrayed Joaquín but he lied too, saying Joaquín had it even though Lobo knew he didn't. When Joaquín went back for Lobo, the captain of the soldiers told him what Lobo said. Joaquín killed the captain 'cause he'd executed the four soldiers who'd let Joaquín escape. When he and Lobo got to Nogales, Lobo cried. He said he couldn't face Seth after having broken under torture, but Joaquín convinced him he had to face Seth like a man, so Lobo did it. Neither of 'em told Seth what happened, but somehow he knew. He cursed Lobo for breaking under torture, saying the one thing a man never does is betray his partner, no matter what. Joaquín told Padre Mathias he thinks it's his fault 'cause he was the one who sent Seth to prison and took him away from Lobo when he was growing up."

Elena stared at Jesse in stunned silence.

"I shouldn't've told you," he said. "I don't want to know any of those things but I don't guess I'll ever forget 'em, and now you won't either, will you?"

She shook her head.

"What're we gonna do, Elena?"

"What *can* we do?"

"I don't know," he said, "but I believe the reason I overheard Joaquín's confession is that I'm s'posed to do something. I couldn't think of anything, that's why I told you. You're smart, Elena, and more like Seth than any of us. If it were his problem, what do you think he'd do?"

"It is his problem," she said.

"It's ours, too. He's our father and Lobo's our brother. We gotta make 'em love each other again."

"You can't make anybody love someone," she scoffed.

"We gotta try, don't we?"

"I don't think there's anything we can do, Jesse."

"Then things'll blow up and one of 'em'll leave. That's what Joaquín said: it's just a matter of time."

"It'll prob'ly be Lobo," she said sadly.

"Can you imagine never seeing him again, Elena? I don't want Seth to leave either, but I don't have any memories of him. I have lots of good ones with Lobo. He's the only brother I have and I don't want to lose him. I feel bad for Joaquín, too, 'cause he thinks it's his fault for sending Seth to prison." Jesse sighed. "Everything would've been so different if that never happened."

"Yeah," she agreed.

"I prob'ly wouldn't be Catholic," he said. "I won't make the same mistake Joaquín did, though: I ain't giving up the priesthood to follow Seth. If Lobo ain't man enough to please him, there's no way I could."

"I think you do please him, even so," she said. "He gave you Rojo, didn't he?"

"Yeah, and he's letting you ride Padre. But what's he given Lobo?"

"His gun," she said.

"Lobo stole it," Jesse argued. "That's prob'ly why it still didn't make him good enough."

Elena leaned back against the wall, thinking she would never escape guilt for complicity in that theft. "We can't let Lobo know we've learned all this," she finally said. "That would make everything worse."

"You think Rico knows?"

She shrugged.

"The way I see it," Jesse said, "nobody can change what happened in Mexico, so we've got to help Seth forgive Lobo."

"How're we gonna do that?"

"Maybe by doing what Rico said. The other night she told me Lobo feels like he's a remnant of Seth's past and not quite family, and we should be gentle with him 'cause he needs help right now."

Elena thought about that. "Sounds like she knows, doesn't it."

"Yeah," he said.

She sighed. "Well, look at it this way. If everyone else knows, it's better we do, too, so we can understand some of what's happening."

"I guess that's right," he said. "It sure felt better not knowing, though. That's what I like about the church: I can forget about myself when I'm reading the Early Fathers and reciting the prayers, knowing just doing all that'll get me to heaven. But since Seth came home, I'm beginning to understand I'm gonna be alive a lotta years 'fore I'm old enough to die, and there're things that need my attention in the meantime."

Elena smiled. "Welcome back to the world."

"It sure is a mess," he said.

They heard the thud of boots and the sharp jangle of spurs as Lobo jumped down from the fence, walked across the corral, then appeared in the door of the stable. He was silhouetted against the red dusk, their tall, lean, handsome kid brother who happened to be the oldest. Elena remembered that when she'd come home he'd been sitting under the portal, and she thought he'd probably been there alone ever since. He was smiling but his eyes were hurt, seeing them so chummy together.

"Sebastiano's got supper ready," he said.

"I'm starved," Elena answered. "We were just about to come see what the holdup was. Weren't we, Jesse?"

"Yeah," he said, shyly looking up at his brother.

"What were you talking about?" Lobo asked.

"The birds and the bees," Elena said before Jesse could open his mouth.

Lobo smiled sinuously. "If you want a real lesson, Jess, you ought to come into town with me tonight."

"No, thanks," he said. "Fornication's a sin."

Lobo laughed. "I'm going to hell anyway. Might as well get there well fucked."

Elena looked back and forth between them. As Rico had said, Jesse was hers; but Lobo had been born to a woman in Colorado named Esther, who had been only fourteen when Seth abandoned her, pregnant. Elena wondered if it was the turmoil of Lobo's conception that made him so difficult, and if it was Seth's love for Rico that made Jesse so sweet. But then Elena guessed Seth had loved Esther, too. It was just that he'd been an outlaw then, with nothing to offer in the way of a home. Only after he was settled here with Rico had he gone back for Lobo, and Elena wondered if Lobo might have been better off if Seth had never done that. Overwhelmed with the complexities handed down from the past, she said sadly to both of her brothers, "Let's go eat."

They walked out of the stable and across the corral to climb the fence. When they reached the top rail, they all perched there a moment, looking at their home rather than each other.

The sunset was fiery, tingeing the yard a soft, dusty rose. In front of them, Esperanza's casita looked plump, its windows reflecting the crimson sky. The big house was shadowed under the cottonwoods. Golden lamplight fell from the kitchen window, and beyond the house the windmill creaked in a sudden breeze, its metal blades flashing silver in the red sky. They could hear the water trickling into the stone cistern, lapping gently as it overflowed into the acequia. The stream reflected the sunset as it flowed into Rico's garden and filled the furrows between rows of earth sprouting with the first growth of spring. Even the nascent leaves were tinged red in the dusk.

Elena cast a quick glance at her brothers. Jesse's face was pious as he soaked in the beauty of their home; Lobo's smile was sarcastic, his eyes bitter with a fierce mockery. Elena looked down at Seth's .44 on Lobo's gunbelt, studded with cartridges catching light. Softly she asked, "Can I hold the gun?"

Lobo lifted his arm out of the way. "Help yourself," he said, then warned, "It's loaded."

Carefully she nudged the keeper strap off and lifted the heavy pistol with both hands. Its grip was bone, darkened with use to the same gray as the metal, its barrel long, reflecting the red of the sky. When she shifted the weapon into one hand, she accidentally touched the trigger. The hammer rose and fell with a click like the ghost of an echo from long ago. With sudden aversion, she dropped the gun. It fired on impact, sending a bullet into oblivion. The explosion ricocheted off the mountains and faded into silence while they all stared at the gun as if expecting it to move.

Sebastiano called from the house across the red dust of the yard. "You okay, niños?" They all looked at him standing in the golden door with a rifle.

"Sí!" Lobo called back. "Es nada, gracias."

They watched Sebastiano disappear inside, then they looked at the gun again.

Finally Lobo boasted, "It's got a hair trigger. I warned you it was loaded."

"Let's leave it there," Jesse whispered.

"You're loco," Lobo said. But no one moved to pick it up.

After a while, Jesse said, "Seth killed twenty men with that gun."

"More'n that," Lobo scoffed.

"Robbed banks and hurt women," Elena agreed.

"Hung Allister's wife," Lobo added smugly.

After a moment, Elena said, "I think we should bury it."

"Yeah," Jesse said, "and say a prayer of absolution."

"Wait a minute," Lobo said.

"It makes sense," Jesse argued. "With that weapon, Seth committed the sins we're all paying for now. Maybe if we bury it, we'll be done with the past."

Lobo dropped to the ground and picked up the gun. He opened the chamber and revolved it slowly, the metallic clicks of its evolution like eternity edging inexorably on, then he snapped the chamber closed and dropped the gun back in his holster. Meeting their eyes, he said, "It's mine now."

29

★

Before supper, Elena went to her room and changed her dungarees for a dress. She wasn't sure why she did it except for a vague notion that because their parents were gone she was in charge, and somehow she felt she had more authority wearing skirts. When she returned to the kitchen, Lobo smirked, but Jesse smiled his approval. Sebastiano set the food on the table and left, picking up his rifle as he went out the back door.

Lobo immediately walked over to look out the window. "Just as I thought, he's standing guard." Lobo laughed, coming back to the table. "Now you're gonna learn what it's really like to live with Seth."

No one answered him. The enchiladas were good and they all ate heartily, keeping their thoughts to themselves. Elena watched her brothers as they ate. Jesse's manners were delicate and he was quickly satisfied; Lobo wolfed down his food, broaching the boundaries of decency.

He burped as he stood up. "Sure you don't want to ride into town with me, Jess?" he teased.

"No, thanks," Jesse said again.

"Adiós." Lobo laughed, sauntering out.

After a few minutes they heard his horse galloping away.

"Is Sebastiano gonna wash the dishes?" Jesse asked.

Elena nodded.

"I'll go read, then," he said, pushing his chair back and walking into the parlor.

She heard his bedroom door close, then the creak of the windmill as the breeze picked up, carrying the smell of rain. Sebastiano walked in. He left his Winchester in the corner and smiled at her as he crossed the room to clear the table. She stood up and began helping.

"Gracias, señorita," he said solemnly, "but there is no need to help me."

"I don't mind," she said, carrying two plates to the sink.

"Andale pues. Is always better to have company, no?"

"What work did you do in Mexico?" she asked, tying on an apron.

"I was a cook for vaqueros," he said proudly.

She set the teakettle on the fire. "How'd you meet Seth?"

"I never did in México," he answered, sliding the leftover food into the icebox.

"Oh, I thought you had."

"I heard much of him," he said, coming back and lifting the washbasin from under the sink, then smiling at her as they waited for the water to boil. "Your padre is a famous man in el norte de México."

"Famous for what?" she asked.

Sebastiano thought a moment. "He is brave and smart, and many people owe him their lives. I myself owe him my freedom. Señor Seth gave the money to pay my debt, and I came here because I wanted to thank him in person. It made me very happy when he offered this job. I hope I can please his family and serve him well."

"As you saw," she said, "we liked your enchiladas."

"Qué bueno," he answered, pouring the hot water from the kettle.

They worked in silence a few minutes, then she asked, "Had you also heard of Lobo in Mexico?"

"Sí," he said, not looking up.

"What did you hear?"

"That he was captured by the Rurales for killing a soldier. My friend Jesús helped Joaquín take him from the presidio. That is why Jesús could buy my freedom."

"Why did Lobo kill a soldier?"

"The Rurales had taken the ammunition from Señor Seth's shipment to the bandidos. Lobo killed one of the soldiers, getting the ammunition back."

"Do you think he's brave and smart?"

"To kill a soldier in México is to flirt with death," Sebastiano said. "That is certainly brave, but not smart, I do not think. But then, I am old and death is too close. When a man is young, it seems far away and he knows only his own power."

"But if his power isn't very strong," she said sadly, "he won't likely live to be old."

"Verdad, señorita. Of all the boys from my village, only I am still alive. That is because I left at a young age. I came north to los Estados Unidos and worked for a while in El Paso. That is where I learned to speak English, and also to shoot a gun. When I went home, I decided it was better to feed men than kill them, so I became a cook instead of a bandido. For me, it was a simple choice. For my compadres, it was more important to live boldly as a young man than to die as an old one."

She thought about that as she dried a plate. Laying it in the cupboard, she boasted, "Seth is doing both."

"He is graced by God," Sebastiano agreed.

"And smart and brave?" she teased.

"Sí, but Señor Seth is . . . ¿Come se dice? English has no word for macho." He paused to think. "It is a man who contains within his heart a force so strong he can change destiny, not only for himself, but for hundreds, sometimes thousands of others." He looked at her quizzically. "Do you understand?"

"I think so," she said. "What do you call a woman who has a power like that?"

"Una bruja!"

Elena felt as if he'd slapped her. "Doesn't that mean witch?" she whispered.

"Sí! Such power is not feminino. If a woman had it, she would have stolen it from a man, and to do such a thing would require great evil in her soul."

"Why is it evil for a woman to have power?" she asked, summoning her indignation.

He looked at her warily. "A woman's power lies in submission to the father of her children. By making herself less, he is made more, and the family survives."

"Why does she have to make herself less?"

"Is it not obvious?"

"Not to me!"

He smiled. "A man puffs himself up like a rooster to win a lady, and she whittles herself down to catch him. If she were already less, it would be the other way around."

Elena laughed with delight.

"That is why I never married," he said. "I had no desire to puff myself up."

"It seems a crazy way to run the world," she said. "Why can't we be who we are?"

He shrugged. "This is who we are. You will see, Señorita Elena. When you love a man, you also will do anything to help him stand tall, take off a notch here, build another there, until he is perfecto."

Thoughtfully she said, "You make it sound like men are blocks of wood women carve to be what they want."

He nodded. "First his mother, then his wife, and finally his daughters and their daughters make a strong man. It is in their happiness that he sees the success or failure of his life."

"More than his sons?" she asked curiously.

"I think so. I have never known a strong man able to live in peace with his sons." He smiled playfully. "Have you?"

"Not yet," she said. "I'm glad you're here, Sebastiano. I think you'll be good for all of us."

"Gracias," he said. "Now the kitchen is clean. Muchas gracias for your help. Hasta mañana, eh?" He walked across the room and retrieved his rifle. At the door he turned back and said, "Sleep well, niña. I will be on guard until your father comes home."

"Did he tell you to stand guard?" she asked.

"He didn't have to. Not long ago he was a bandido, and it is always best to be alert."

She started to argue that Seth had been pardoned, then realized Sebastiano was talking about Mexico. Elena blew out the lamp and stood in the empty kitchen, staring into the darkness outside the window as she pieced together everything she had learned about what happened in Mexico. According to Sebastiano, Seth had saved many lives, but she couldn't understand how he could do that selling guns to bandits. Joaquín had killed five men, and felt responsible for the deaths of four more, serving Seth's purpose. Lobo had killed a soldier and been caught by the Rurales. When whipped, he had betrayed Joaquín, but Joaquín had saved him anyway and taken him to Nogales, where Lobo cried because he couldn't face Seth. Then when he garnered the courage to do it, Seth had torn him apart. Elena trembled with the weight of so much suffering.

Had all that happened so bandits could have guns? Was she now living on the money paid for those guns? Maybe it wasn't true that Seth had come home with ten thousand dollars from his outlaw days in Texas, maybe he had brought the money from Mexico. But then, when she really thought about it, there was no difference.

The livelihood of her family had always been bought with blood, and she felt frightened that nothing good would come to any of them because of it.

Wearily she walked into the parlor and stood there a long time, letting her gaze fondle the familiarity of her home with the melancholy knowledge that she would never see it the same. The settee covered with an old Navajo blanket, a three-legged stool in a corner, the rocking chair and Rico's sewing hutch beside it were the entire furnishings of the room. There were no pictures on the walls, no mementos on the mantel, not even a rug to decorate the scrubbed oak of the wide-plank floor. What had always seemed pleasingly spartan now struck her as monkish, as if her family were paying penance for living well on stolen money.

She walked to the door of Rico's room and pushed it open. Her chiffonnier and cedar chest were gone, her guitar and toiletries. The brass bed was the same but the quilt had been changed. She walked in and sat down on it, seeing Lobo's wooden chest from his room in the stable. Other than that, the only sign of his occupancy was a Winchester leaning behind the door. Then she remembered that the gun wasn't his. Seth had always kept the rifle there, and after he was gone it had stood like a sentry awaiting his return.

The wind moved the shutters on the window, open to catch the breeze. As she looked over her shoulder at the saguaro silhouetted against the starlight, she remembered Rico once telling her how Seth would come home late and stand at that window before joining her in bed, and how she would feel safe with his strength between her and the darkness outside. Then Rico had said, "If I'd known his strength would be what sent him away, I might have tried to take him down a notch. But I loved him so, just the way he was."

Elena lay back on the bed, closing her eyes and falling asleep to a litany of her mother's voice saying, "I loved him so." Curled in a fetal ball on the bed of her conception, Elena dreamt of the act that had given her life. She was a virgin, however, and the only image she owned came from watching the mating of a stallion and a mare: the stallion dominant, powerful, driven; the mare submissive and acquiescent.

Elena's cheeks had burned, witnessing the horses copulate. When the owner of the stallion came to take him back, Elena was unable to look at the man, and secretly she vowed never to succumb to anything so nasty. But that was before she met Seth. Now as she tumbled through the images of her dream, she stomped her delicate hooves and tossed her silken mane, daring the stallion to surrender a part of himself inside her.

She awoke to the gentle cadence of a horse loping across the soft dust of the yard. Opening her eyes, she listened to the whisper of the corral gate swing open, then the heavier moan of the stable door. Elena remembered how often Rico had lain awake in this bed, waiting for Seth to come home from Blue's. How she had listened to that same corral gate and that same stable door, and had heard, as Elena was hearing now, the soft tread of boots accompanied by the silver song of spurs as the man crossed the yard. He came in through the kitchen and laid the crossbar in place, then passed through the parlor and opened the door. She met Lobo's eyes as he stopped on the threshold.

"Hello," she said, not moving.

He closed the door and crossed the room to stand looking down on her. "What're you doing here, Elena?"

"Did you have a good time in town?" she answered.

He unbuckled his gunbelt and hung it on the bedpost, the same gun Seth had taken off in this room, the same bed, the same starlight shining through the window. Lobo sat down and let himself fall back beside her. "No," he said.

"Why not?" she asked.

He turned on his side to face her. "Why are you here?"

"I came in after helping with the dishes, and I guess I fell asleep."

He reached across and pulled the ribbon from her hair. "You're about to lose this." He smiled. "Wouldn't do for Rico to find your ribbon in my bed."

"I guess not," she said, watching him run the length of blue satin through his fingers.

He let it fall on the quilt between them. "You still a virgin, Elena?"

"Yes," she said.

"You won't be for long if you make a habit of falling asleep in men's beds."

"You're my brother."

"Half-brother. The only blood we share is Seth's."

He looked like his father, smiling sardonically in the starlight. When she licked her lips nervously, he leaned close to kiss her. He tasted of whiskey and smelled of smoke. She kissed him back. He withdrew mere inches and laughed softly. "Who taught you to kiss like that?"

"Seth," she whispered.

"Me, too." Lobo laughed again. "I learned it from his whores."

She remembered the harlot she'd seen in Blue's saloon, and she tried to picture her in bed with Seth, then his leaving and Lobo coming in to learn what Seth had taught her.

Lobo said, "If I didn't know you were wishing I was him, I might make love to you, Elena."

"It wouldn't be right," she said.

"So what?" he scoffed. "Do you think he ever once considered being right before he did anything?"

"He considered it before he kissed me," she said.

"But he still did it." Lobo smiled, leaning forward to kiss her again. He pulled her close, his hand cupping her bottom as he pushed hard against her, moaning with hunger.

"Please," she murmured.

"Yeah, please," he mocked, reaching up to unbutton her dress.

"Don't," she pleaded, catching his hand.

He stopped, his eyes laughing at her. "Why not?"

"I love you too much," she said.

He laughed, falling back away from her. "That's a new one."

She felt closer to him than ever before, nestled together on the bed. It reminded her of all the times she had lain out in the country with Danny as they talked over their mutual confusions. Except for that one kiss in the mine, Danny had never touched her, and she wondered how it would feel to be in bed with him. "Have you ever thought about getting married, Lobo?" she asked softly.

"Seth never got married," he said.

She was surprised at his answer, not least of all because she had momentarily forgotten Seth. "Yes, he did," she said. "Her name was Johanna."

"Yeah, I know. But they only lived together seven weeks. A month of that time he was recovering from being shot, and another week of it he was gone, so their marriage lasted all of ten days." He laughed. "Course, that was in El Paso and Seth was wanted in Texas. I still can't figure, the situation he was in, why he got married. That's why I went to Austin, to find out what was so special about her."

"What'd you find out?" Elena asked eagerly.

"Nothing! She's real pretty, a'course, but I'd never choose her over Rico."

"Why not?"

"She was bossy," he said without having to think. "I wasn't there two hours before she started correcting me. Stuff I couldn't understand why she'd bother noticing, like which fork I used at the table. Who cares, for chrissake? And the way she'd do it, like she was being gracious to an outlaw's son who hadn't had the benefits of society, as if she was giving me something when what she was doing was putting me down. Her son Jeremiah minds his p's and q's. I bet he hasn't farted since he got out of diapers."

Elena laughed. "No one would say that of you, Lobo. You burped at the supper table tonight."

He grinned. "It ain't exactly the same."

"Who cares?" she teased.

He laughed and pulled her close in a hug. "Ah, Elena," he whispered into her ear. "I wish more girls were like you."

"How like me?" she asked with surprise.

"You're good company," he said, lying back down but keeping his hand on her waist, " 'cause you don't expect a man to be better'n he is."

"Maybe I should," she said, remembering her conversation with Sebastiano.

"Uh-uh," he said. "Your husband's gonna be a lucky man."

"It's likely to be Danny Nickles," she said. "Seth's already spoken to his father."

Lobo sat up in astonishment. "What's the hurry?"

She bit her lip, then told the truth. "Seth said if I belonged to another man, he'd owe it to him to stay away from me."

Lobo dropped onto his back and laughed. "Everything he does is selfish."

"I suppose you could see it that way," she said.

"What is it, Elena," he asked, rolling onto his side and lifting her braid to twist around his hand, "that makes him so irresistible to women?"

"I can't say about the others," she answered thoughtfully. "Whenever he's near me, I feel an overpowering need to be filled, as if I've always been empty but never knew it before."

Lobo chuckled. "Won't another man do?"

"I haven't met anyone else who makes me feel that way."

"Yet you'd marry Danny because Seth wants you to?"

"I promised to obey him so he'd let me come home."

"I had to make the same promise," Lobo said, leaning so close she could feel his breath on her mouth. "Let's break it together."

"He wouldn't like it," she argued.

"What do you think he'd do?"

"I don't want to find out."

"Then make love with me, Elena," he murmured, sliding his

hand up under her skirts, "and I'll never tell that you were waiting in my bed."

She caught hold of his hand. "Stop it, Lobo."

He snickered, pulling her hand out from beneath her petticoats. When she tried to pry it free with her other hand, he caught both of them over her head with one of his, then pinned her waist to the bed with one leg as he tugged her drawers down.

"No, Lobo!" she protested, twisting and kicking in a vain attempt to escape him. "I don't want this."

He laughed with scorn. "You've been wanting nothing else all the time we've been here."

"It's not true!" she cried as he yanked her drawers over her feet. He slid his hand between her naked thighs and touched her, making her shudder.

"You're wet," he gloated. "You want it as much as I do, you're just too chicken to admit it."

"I don't!" she shouted.

"Be quiet," he said, freeing his hand to open his trousers. "You're gonna wake Jesse. You want him to watch you become a whore?"

"Lobo, please!" she begged as he tossed her skirts out of his way. Desperately she said, "You'll never be a man if you do this!"

"Seth raped plenty of women," Lobo said, forcing himself between her legs. "I don't hear anyone saying he's not a man."

She groped for the last weapon she had: "He'll say you're not."

Lobo raised himself above her and slapped her face. She gasped beneath his blow, then moaned in terror at the hatred in his eyes as he leaned back on his heels staring down at her. "God, Lobo," she sobbed. "What's wrong with you?"

He rolled off her, lying on his belly with his head in his hands as he snarled, "Get outta here, Elena."

She leapt to her feet, grabbed her drawers off the floor, and ran out, stopping to close the door and survey the parlor as if she expected someone to be there. It was dark and empty. She ran out of the house into the sultry wind of the approaching storm, then fled through its sweltering humidity across the yard. Half blind with tears, she climbed the fence into the corral. Stumbling onto the ground, she clutched her underwear as she ran into the stable and down the aisle to Rojo's stall. She edged in beside the old sorrel and crumpled onto the straw beneath his manger, whimpering uncontrollably. The horse lowered his head and nickered as he brushed his huge lips across her hair. She sobbed, reaching up to pet his nose. "It's all right, Rojo," she crooned. "I'm all right."

For a long time, she cowered in the corner of the stall, trying to be quiet as she cried. Finally she just sat there, hugging her knees as if she were cold. After a while, she heard the buggy in the yard and knew her parents were home. The corral gate whined open, then the stable door groaned as if with agony. A lantern was lit and she heard Seth say, "Gracias, Sebastiano, hasta mañana."

"Sí, patrón," the old man answered. "Duerme bien, eh?"

"Gracias," Seth said again.

She heard Sebastiano walk down the aisle and close the door to his room, then Seth leading Bonnet and Barley into their stalls. Elena's drawers were on the straw in front of her. Frantically she pulled them on, standing up to fluff her skirts back down, then cautiously she walked into the light.

Seth was just coming out of a stall. He stopped and looked her up and down, then asked softly, "What're you doing here?"

She shrugged. "I couldn't sleep."

He studied her. "You've been crying."

"A little," she admitted.

He glanced toward Sebastiano's door, then held out his hand. "Come here," he said, leading her into the humid, dark night, the stars obscured behind clouds as thunder rumbled above the mountains. He led her to the fence, then lifted her onto the top rail. "What were you crying about?" he asked, standing near her knees, his face shadowed by the brim of his hat.

She reached into the shadow and touched his cheek, rough

with a new growth of whiskers. "I love you so much," she whispered.

"I love you, too," he said, catching her hand and dropping it with impatience. "Is that why you were crying?"

"Isn't it enough?" she asked.

He sighed, looking toward the lamp in the window of Esperanza's casita. When he looked back at her, the light glinted cold on the metallic gray of his eyes. "I gave you credit for more sand, Elena. Is that all you were crying about?"

"Not entirely," she admitted.

"What else?" he asked sharply.

She couldn't lie to him, any more than she could deny his power over her, so she said, "Because of Lobo."

A shutter of ice fell across Seth's eyes. "What about him?"

"Jesse told me things this afternoon," she answered, suppressing a chill as the wind shifted. "He didn't want to, but he had to get it off his chest."

"What things?" Seth asked, his voice flat.

"He went by Our Lady of Sorrows on his way home from school, and he accidentally overheard Joaquín's confession."

Seth frowned. "So?"

She studied him standing with his boots spread and his shoulders back as if he were poised for a fight. He even had his jacket tucked behind the butt of his pistol, ready to draw the weapon with no interference. Suddenly she saw him for who he was—a man adept at wielding violence—and the reality of his crimes came clear to her. She stifled her fear by reminding herself that he needed help.

Speaking slowly, feeling her way in an effort to penetrate the sheen of indifference in his eyes, she said carefully, "When Lobo was afraid to see you after what he'd done in Mexico, Joaquín said if he faced you as a man, you would forgive him. But when he did, you cursed him, and that's what broke Lobo, not what happened between him and Joaquín."

Seth swept his hat off and threw it on the ground. "Were you crying for your brother," he demanded angrily, "or because you'd lost your adulation of me?"

"Maybe I was crying for all of us," she answered, hugging herself in the chill of the storm, "because we waited too long for you to come home."

"Jesus Christ! Maybe I should've waited a while longer."

"We would've shriveled up and died without you, Seth."

"Well, you're killing me! I swear, Elena, you kids are more deadly than any desperados I ever dealt with."

"We're your children," she said.

"And the sins of the father are forever reborn? Is that what you're saying?"

"Maybe," she said, quivering before his anger. "Unless we find something to break the cycle."

"And what would that be?"

"I don't know," she said. "You have to find it."

"Thanks," he muttered.

She took a deep breath. "Sebastiano was telling me tonight how smart and brave you are. He said something else, too, though. He said men see the success of their lives in their daughters' happiness, but that he's never known a strong man who can live at peace with his sons. I don't think that can work, though, 'cause we're all tied together."

"So what do you suggest?" Seth asked with sarcasm.

She rubbed her hands up and down her arms, wishing she had a shawl, the wind had grown so cold. "I think you broke Lobo 'cause you can't face up to being responsible for who he is. Even before Mexico, you took him from his mother and trained him to be an outlaw, then you left him alone while you went to prison to pay for your sins. But your biggest sin is what you did to Lobo. Now you're making it worse by refusing to help him out of the fix you got him into."

"You little bitch! You ain't earned the right to criticize me."

Repelled by his curse, she summoned all of her courage to ask, "Who has? Allister? He's the only one I ever heard of who's shed more blood than you."

"Mother of God," Seth moaned, sinking to the ground and leaning low.

Astounded that she had the power to drop him to his knees, she murmured, "Have mercy on us sinners now and at the hour of our death."

Seth was silent, folded in on himself beneath her.

"That's a prayer," she said. "Jesse recites it every night before he goes to sleep."

"It's a good one," Seth mumbled.

Lightning flickered across the sky quick as a whip. She watched him from the fence, wanting to comfort him but wary of climbing down to meet him on equal ground. "I just thought of a joke," she said. "Want to hear it?"

"I could use one," he said.

She cleared her throat. "Growing up is like tracking someone across the desert: you never suspect the man you're following doesn't know where he's going."

Seth straightened up to meet her eyes. Bravely she gave him a smile, and he laughed. Rain began to fall, huge drops that speckled the dust around him.

Elena lifted her face to the sky. "Rain!" she exulted.

As if her voice had slashed them open, the clouds burst, drenching the parched land with an excess of abundance. Seth stood up, found his hat, and settled it low above his eyes, watching her still on the fence.

"You're apt to get hit by lightning," he said, lifting her down beside him.

Rico opened the door to Esperanza's casita, shining a pathway of light through the darkness. He opened the gate, guided Elena into the shallow lake already accumulating in the yard, then watched her over his shoulder as he latched the gate. "I'll see what

I can do," he said, facing her again, "about the fix you think I put Lobo in. You go on to bed or you're apt to catch your death in this storm, and I don't think I could carry being responsible for that." When he leaned to kiss her cheek, she clung to him, both of them drenched in the downpour of rain. Leaving her alone, he joined Rico in the casita of light.

Elena watched until the light was extinguished. Then she looked at the dark house at the end of the lake the yard had become. Slowly she walked through the mud, dragging the weight of her skirts to find shelter with her brothers.

30

★

Elena overslept the next morning. When she walked into the kitchen everyone else was at the table, breakfast already over. She hesitated on the threshold a moment, seeing her parents smile at her as if the three of them shared a secret from the night before. The storm was gone, the door open, and the muddy yard glistening in the bright sun. For a moment Elena felt a cusp had been passed and their peace finally achieved. Then Lobo stood up with a smirk and gave her a silent bow, as if he were a gentleman who always stood when a lady entered the room.

She stared at him, wary of the cruel glint in his eyes. Seth stared, too, his eyes cool with suspicion.

Lobo said, "Reckon I owe you an apology, Elena."

"It's not necessary," she murmured, taking her place at the table.

"Oh, well then." Lobo chuckled. "You left this in my bed last night."

She looked up to see her blue ribbon flutter onto the table in front of her, then ducked her head and whimpered at her brother's betrayal.

Lobo sat back down. "Can I have some more coffee, Sebastiano?" he asked lightly, as if the silence weren't lethal with threat. No one moved.

Finally Rico said, "Go saddle the horses for school, Jesse."

"I can't yet," he argued, sounding hurt at being dismissed. "I ain't strong enough to tie the cinch."

"I will help you," Sebastiano said, his voice low. "Come, chico." He pulled Jesse's chair out and led him from the house.

Elena gathered her courage to look at Seth. He was watching Rico, his eyes unreadable. Elena looked at her mother, but she was staring at Lobo, her eyes fierce with accusation. Struck with pity to see her brother gloating, Elena asked again, "What's wrong with you, Lobo?"

He laughed. "I'm healthy as a bull. Reckon I proved that last night."

"You're proving you're an ass now!" she retorted.

He shrugged. "And you're a whore. Did you think we could keep it a secret?"

Seth asked, "Is this why you were crying last night, Elena?"

"Nothing happened," she said, but she could see he didn't believe her.

He looked at Rico. "Go find out."

Rico didn't move, her face agonized with disbelief.

"You want me to do it?" he asked.

She shook her head, then slowly stood up. "Come with me, Elena," she said, walking from the room.

Elena stood up, too, staring at her brother. "Tell them the truth, Lobo," she pleaded. "Why make them hate you for nothing?"

Lobo just smiled, as if he were enjoying the slow twist of the knife.

"Go with your mother," Seth told Elena, but he was watching Lobo, their enmity now mutual.

She fled from her failure. Rico was standing in the door to her bedroom, but Elena didn't stop. She ran from the house and across the yard, unlatching the corral gate and leaving it open as she ran into the stable. Grabbing Rojo's reins from Jesse, she leapt into the saddle, bunching her skirts immodestly high on her thighs as she kicked the sorrel hard and galloped out of the barn, through the open gate, and around the sliver of mountain beyond sight of her home.

The road was muddy but the sorrel never floundered. She leaned low into his whipping mane, feeling it sting her face with a hurt that was welcome compared to what she felt inside. In one instant of false accusation, her parents had shunned her. Neither of them believed her denial. Both of them believed Lobo's lie. She shuddered to remember him smiling like an assassin as he dropped the evidence on the table, but the outrage she felt at his betrayal was nothing against the pain of her parents' condemnation.

Lobo would tell them he had come home and found her waiting in his bed. He would probably say he'd tried to resist, but he was drunk and she persistent. Seth had found her crying in the stable. Would he remember how she'd argued for him to help Lobo? Could he think she would do that if Lobo had raped her? But then, no one was calling it rape. Because she had flaunted herself so boldly in front of Seth, it would be easy for him to believe she had merely shifted her attentions to Lobo.

She moaned under the weight of his betrayal. She had stopped him from committing incest, then tempted Seth's wrath hoping to find peace between father and son. Last night she thought she had achieved something; even for that brief moment when she first walked into the kitchen this morning it had seemed as if more than the storm had passed. But Lobo had destroyed her victory with the delicate flutter of a ribbon. She couldn't understand why.

If only he had stayed home until Seth's return, and Mexico had never happened. If only the one man who could have helped Lobo hadn't been the sheriff who delivered Seth to the law. If only she hadn't crept into Rico's room that long-ago night and stolen Seth's gun for Lobo to wear in his attempt to become his father's equal.

She decided that theft was the source of Lobo's failure, so every-thing that followed was her fault. Just as what was happening now was her fault because she'd left her ribbon in his bed, allowing him to use it as a weapon against Seth and, coincidentally, Rico.

Rojo slackened his pace, breathing hard, and she let him fall back into a lope, then a trot, and finally an ambling walk. When he heaved a weary sigh, she felt bad for him. The horse was old. He had done good service in his lifetime and she had no right to run him so hard. Reining him onto the trail to the Nickles ranch, she turned off into the arroyo leading to the oasis.

The spring was gushing with the aftermath of the storm, swamping the grass so the mud underneath sucked at Rojo's hooves. She swung her leg over and stood in the stirrup a moment, sur-veying the white rush of water, the desert beyond, tawny against a brilliantly blue sky. She was alone. In all the world, there wasn't anyone she could turn to for help.

Rojo tugged at the reins. She let herself slide down his side, feeling water seep into her shoes as she reached up to his ears, pulled off the bridle, and hung it on the saddlehorn. He nickered with gratitude, ambled to the edge of the stream, and lowered his head to drink. She watched until he was grazing on the lush grass, flicking his tail in idle contentment, then she walked away to sit on a boulder at the edge of the desert.

A black hawk circled high overhead, its wings motionless as it rode the wind. White butterflies bounced across the meadow. The red horse tore mouthfuls of green grass and munched without hurry. A lizard crept close to the stream and drank deeply, then dis-appeared in the rocks of the desert again. It seemed the whole world was at peace outside her family.

Rojo lifted his head and pricked his ears toward the trail. He swallowed his last biteful of grass and whinnied a welcome as Elena saw Joaquín ride into view on his black horse. Dressed all in black, as he always was, the silver star of his badge flashed in the sun as she watched him come.

He reined his horse close by the rock and smiled up at her. "It's a good day for playing hooky," he said.

She couldn't muster a return smile, and his dark eyes softened with compassion. He swung down, pulled the bridle off his horse and hung it on the saddlehorn as she had done, then climbed onto the rock and sat beside her. Neither of them spoke for a long time.

Finally he asked, his voice gentle with humor, "How's Seth?"

"Mad," she said.

"At you?"

"And Lobo."

He lifted her braid from where it fell over her shoulder, straightened it down her back, his touch warm with comfort, and coaxed softly, "Why?"

"Do you really want to hear it?"

"Yes," he said.

She sighed, then told him everything, beginning with how she had stolen Seth's gun for Lobo so long ago, encouraging him to emulate Seth's violence. How she had been changed from the first moment Seth rode into the yard, had felt so overpowered with a need to be close to him that she'd offered herself shamelessly right here in this meadow, and how Lobo had seen what she felt and tried to substitute himself for his father. How she had stopped Lobo and then argued with Seth to help him, but Lobo had destroyed any chance of that with his lie. Now they were all doomed to unhappiness because her mistakes had ricocheted with such irrevocable destruction.

Joaquín listened without watching her, granting her the privacy of hearing only with his ears. After she had been silent a moment, he said, "I wish Esperanza were here. She would know how to advise you."

"What do you think she'd say?" Elena asked.

He leaned back on his elbows, so his voice caressed her from behind. "First, she would find the words to convince you that none of what has happened is your fault. This fight between Seth and

Lobo has been building since before you were born. It's because Seth loves you so deeply that Lobo has used you against him. Lobo loves you, too, though he's having trouble showing it right now." Joaquín thought a moment. "Esperanza once said Seth was striving to redeem himself through Lobo, but Lobo only wanted to be another Seth, and both of them would fail. None of that is your fault, Elena, but perhaps the strength of your love can prevent their failure."

She turned around and met his black eyes beneath the brim of his black hat. "How?"

He smiled. "Lobo has gone into battle with an empty gun, which is what he always does, and someone always rescues him. In this case it falls on you. Are you willing to go home and save him from his lie?"

"I already told the truth," she scoffed, "and they didn't believe me."

"They didn't believe him, either. They sought proof, but you ran away rather than offer it. Running away achieves nothing."

"You're telling me to fight Lobo," she argued, pounding her fist on the rock, "when what I want is for my family to stop fighting."

"Then you must defeat him, Elena. Lobo doesn't need to win, he needs to learn to live with the loss of Seth's past. If he doesn't learn how to do this, he will repeat Seth's mistakes and lose not only his life but also his soul." Joaquín waited a moment, then asked, "Will you let me take you home?"

"Yes," she said, hugging her knees to hide her face in her skirt. When she heard the horses come close, she looked up to meet Joaquín's dark eyes, and she felt a hint of what her father must have felt meeting those eyes as he wiped blood from the blade of yet another killing, knowing he could never live up to Joaquín's expectations.

She whispered, "I don't feel strong enough, Joaquín, to stand between them."

He smiled. "You are between them, though. It is your challenge to be true to your sex and prove a woman's love is stronger than men's destruction."

She remembered the morning after she'd stolen the gun, when Rico had said, "You're my salvation, sweetheart. I don't think I could bear to be the only woman among such men." Thinking of her mother alone now, Elena sighed. "All right. I'll try."

Joaquín lifted her from the rock to sit sideways on Rojo. "In all those years I rode with Seth," he said, "if I had known this moment was coming, I would have followed him with more hope."

"Why do you say that?" she asked in astonishment.

He handed her the reins with a smile. "Because a child ran away this morning, and a woman is going home."

She watched him swing onto his black horse. "Will it always feel this bad to be grown up?" she asked petulantly.

He laughed. "Only half the time."

She laughed, too. As they ambled in a comfortable silence along the muddy road, she tried to anticipate what awaited her at home. She felt certain nothing would ever be the same, but she couldn't predict how things would be different. When they reached the trail, Joaquín suggested it might be better if she went on alone. She stared at the mountain between her and her family, doubting her courage.

"I will come if you wish," he said softly.

She did wish it, but when she turned to tell him that, she saw the silver star of his badge and knew Seth and Lobo both would see the law accompanying her into their home. "I'm a Strummar," she said. "I can handle it."

Joaquín smiled with approval. "Qué te vayas bien, Elita."

She nudged Rojo forward without looking back, feeling Joaquín's love follow her. As she rounded the mountain and rode into the yard, she saw the stallion tied in the corral. Padre tossed his head, and the silver conchos on his bridle flashed in the sun as he whinnied his ownership of all he surveyed with the arrogance of an outlaw. From inside the stable, the mares answered the stud, but Rojo shook his ears as if with superior wisdom.

No one came to greet Elena. She sat watching the house until finally Sebastiano came out the front door, walked across the yard, and solicitously took hold of her reins. "I will put Rojo away, eh, señorita?" he offered.

"Why is Padre tied in the corral?" she asked.

"Señor Seth left him there," the old man answered, meeting her eyes cautiously.

"Is he going somewhere?"

"I don't know, señorita."

"What happened after I left?"

Sebastiano hesitated, then said, "Harsh words were spoken in the house. Then Señor Seth came for his horse. Lobo followed and attacked him from behind with more words. Your father turned to face him in silence, and in the quiet of that moment, Jesse asked them to walk with him to the camposanto. They are there now, all of them together."

"Gracias," she said, reining Rojo away. She guided him around the house, beneath the newly leafed cottonwoods shading the cow and the chickens, along a rocky trail ascending into the foothills. When she reached a small plateau overlooking the homestead, she stopped at the edge of the camposanto.

The cemetery was stark, a stretch of pale, rocky soil, dry in the sun. A single juniper shaded the lone grave marked with a pink marble headstone. Though she couldn't read it from that distance, Elena knew well the etching on the stone: Esperanza Ochoa, Beloved Friend, 1839–1896.

Rico sat in the dust near the stone, her knees drawn up beneath her skirts, her face hidden within her folded arms. Jesse knelt at the foot of the grave with his head bowed and his hands clasped in prayer. Seth sat on the cedar bench, his elbows on his knees as he shifted his hat in his hands. Lobo stood with his back to the others, staring off the precipice.

Seth saw her first. He stood up and settled his hat on his head, so she couldn't read his eyes. Rojo nickered across the distance, moving toward him without urging. She draped the reins and let the horse stretch for Seth's touch, nickering again as Seth ran his hand the length of Rojo's long, sleek neck. Elena could see only the brim of her father's hat, a fine, gray felt. He reached up to clasp her waist and lift her to the ground, and then she was looking up into his smiling eyes.

"Did you go to the oasis?" he asked. She nodded and he chuckled with the deep, throaty sound of pleasure she loved to hear. "I almost went after you," he said. "Least I would've found you."

"What would you have said?" she asked.

"I hadn't figured that out yet," he answered, sliding his arm around her waist and turning her to face their family.

Lobo was staring at her, his eyes glimmering with resentment. Rico raised a hand to tidy her hair, as if an unexpected guest had arrived. Jesse, sitting cross-legged on the ground now, smiled shyly at his sister as if she were someone he had just met.

Elena felt like an interloper disrupting a moment of mourning. If not for Seth holding her close, she would have fled. He guided her firmly to the bench, then sat down beside her, took off his hat again, and tossed it to land on the grave. From the valley below, the stallion complained with unhappiness at being held on a short tether, then was quiet.

Lobo took a few steps closer, the jangle of his spurs discordant. They all looked up at him holding his hat. It was white, the crown ringed with a thick braid of liquid silver that caught sun as he turned the brim in his hands. His belt buckle was silver, too, as were his spurs, flashy with exaggeration.

Elena remembered Sebastiano saying men puff themselves up to find equal ground, and she decided she could lower herself to meet Lobo halfway. "What happened last night was my fault," she said. "I shouldn't have been there."

Lobo shifted his gaze to their father, and she looked at him, too.

Watching Lobo, Seth's eyes were cold with apparent indifference. She realized if Seth could learn to reveal his feelings, Lobo wouldn't think himself disregarded. But Seth had spent a lifetime camouflaging his thoughts, and she didn't guess he was likely to change. The mystery was why Lobo couldn't sense what Seth felt. Elena looked back at her brother and tried to help him. Gently she asked, "Did you tell them the truth?"

"Yeah," he said belligerently. "You want me to say it again? I was a prick taking advantage of your innocence, and if you hadn't stopped me, it would've been true."

"Is that an apology?" Seth asked.

Elena looked back and forth between them, anger glinting in the equal ice of their eyes. Quickly she said, "I ran into Joaquín when I was gone. He told me something Esperanza used to say about the two of you. Would you like to hear it?"

"I would," Rico said.

Elena shared a smile with her mother, and looked at her as she spoke. "Esperanza said Seth is trying to redeem himself through Lobo, but that Lobo only wants to be another Seth."

Rico smiled again. "She knew them well."

"You don't have to talk about us as if we ain't here," Seth said.

"Maybe it's the only way you'll listen," Rico teased.

"Do you think it's true?" Elena asked him.

He looked at Lobo. "My part was, then. Reckon I've given up on Lobo redeeming anybody, including himself."

"And I used to want to be like you," Lobo retorted. "But I ain't, am I?"

"You both get mad just as easy," Jesse said.

Seth looked down at him and laughed, then smiled at Lobo. "Reckon we got something in common, after all."

"It's the worst thing about us," Lobo muttered.

"Yeah, it is," Seth agreed.

"It wouldn't be so bad if you didn't both wear guns," Jesse said.

"As it is, every time something happens I expect you to shoot each other."

The stallion bellowed his anger at being forgotten, then there was only the wind sighing through the juniper above Esperanza's grave. Seth looked down at Elena on the bench beside him, then at Rico in the dust, then at the tombstone with the dates circumscribing the life of a woman whose presence they all felt moving on the wind. "Tell you what, Jess," he said, standing up and unbuckling his gunbelt. "I'll let you keep mine for me. Will you do that?"

"Yes," Jesse said hesitantly.

Seth handed the gunbelt down with a smile. "Take good care of it. I may ask for it back someday."

"Yes, sir," Jesse said, accepting it gingerly. "Is it loaded?"

Seth laughed. "What's the answer to that, Lobo?"

"A gun that ain't isn't worth much," he said, a smile flickering on his mouth.

"And a gun that is?" Seth asked.

"Is only worth the man behind it," Lobo said.

Seth nodded, then looked at his wife. "Reckon we're gonna find out what I'm worth without one," he said. "Come on, Rico, I feel weary after all this family combat. It's time for siesta."

She rose to take his hand and let him lead her away. As their three children watched, Seth slid his arm around Rico's waist and leaned low to steal a kiss just before they disappeared beneath the hill.

Lobo said, "He never quits."

"Neither do you," Jesse said, standing up and walking after them, the gunbelt slung on his shoulder.

Elena looked at Lobo. "Why did you do it?"

He settled his hat on his head, tugging the brim low. "Maybe I just wanted to raise a little ruckus," he answered with a teasing smile.

"Was it worth it?"

"Least we ain't bored." He winked, then sauntered away.

She picked up a stone and threw it square in the middle of his back. When he whirled with his gun in his hand, they stared at each other a long moment. "Are you gonna shoot me?" she taunted.

He looked behind her as if someone were there. "Not in front of Esperanza," he said. Then he holstered his gun and left Elena alone.

She turned around and saw Seth's hat still on the grave. Kneeling to pick it up, she stayed on her knees to be close to Esperanza as she ran her fingers around the curve of gray felt. Then, for the first time, she noticed the ornament Seth had chosen for the crown.

It was a knotted cord of thin leather, aged to a dusty gray. The knots were stained with something dark. She touched one and it felt hard and brittle. A tiny flake came off on her finger. When she lifted it to the sun, the flake glimmered red against the pink of her flesh. She studied the cord again, recognizing that the souvenir Seth kept from his past was the remnant of a whip once used to draw blood in expiation of sin. Elena settled the hat over the ribbon in her hair, and led Rojo to follow her family down the trail.

31

★

Every summer Saturday night, Tejoe held a community
dance at the schoolhouse. It was the only social event
that included all the residents, bringing the Catholics and the
Protestants, the faithful and the infidels together in a celebration
of the town's survival. People began gathering in the soft shadows
of dusk, sharing a potluck supper set on long tables in the yard. By
the time stars were twinkling in the black sky, the food had been
put away and colored lanterns hung on every tree, viga, and post
to light the dance floor.

In May, the wooden platform was decorated with ribbons in
the colors of spring, pastel pinks and blues and yellows. On Independence Day it was festooned with red, white, and blue bunting
and the mayor gave a political speech at the start of festivities. On
Halloween, the last dance of the year, the stage was draped with
orange and black, and the children of Tejoe frolicked around jack-
o'-lanterns glowing from its corners.

Early June marked no special event on the calendar, and the
decorations were remnants of other celebrations, a hodgepodge of
colorful bows fluttering long sashes in the breeze. The music was

lively, and the people sashaying across the wooden dance floor added the rhythm of their feet to the guitars and fiddles of the band. When a pair of matched chestnuts pulled a buggy into the light, ladies missed their step, men turned their heads to peer from beneath hat brims, and children who a moment before had run giggling through the spectators now stopped and stared. Illuminated by the brightly colored lanterns, all the faces glimmered with curiosity as the people turned away from their fun to watch the Strummars arrive.

Elena felt uncomfortable being the focus of everyone's attention, but she guessed all johnny-come-latelies had to suffer it equally. She wore her best dress, a yellow frock with short, puffy sleeves and a neckline scooped low enough to show her collarbones. A yellow ribbon was entwined in her braid, and on her left wrist she wore a gold bracelet that belonged to her mother.

Rico wore pale blue. The sleeves of her dress ended in tapered points over the backs of her hands, the neck was high and closed with a sapphire brooch. Her slender waist was accentuated by a wide belt sewn from dark blue suede, while her pale skirt fit snug across her hips then flared beneath her knees. It was the latest fashion, as was her coiffure, a smooth bouffant framing her face and crowning her head with a thick, golden braid. Watching Seth hand Rico down from the buggy, Elena thought her mother was as beautiful and graceful as a queen.

Seth wore a gray suit over a white shirt with a black four-in-hand tie. His boots were black, too, as was his belt, a thin leather strap closed with a discreet silver buckle. Just before they'd left home, he slid a Winchester under the front seat of the buggy, but he wore no gun as he faced the collected citizens of Tejoe for the first time since his return.

Jesse was dressed in a solemn black suit and a white shirt with a black four-in-hand tie. They had been late, as usual, and Seth had tied it for him. Elena and Rico, despite their hurry, had shared a moment of proud happiness watching Seth do it. Now Seth turned and offered Elena his hand, and she laughed, pleased at being so close to him even for the brief moment he helped her from the buggy. Jesse jumped down behind her as she stood smoothing her skirts with her palm and wondering what she was supposed to do next.

Hearing Danny's voice, she looked up to watch him shake hands with Seth and then Jesse. He said hello to Rico before turning to Elena. "You look as pretty as always," he said.

She smiled shyly, and Seth laughed. "Where's the whiskey?" he asked.

"Around back," Danny said.

"Let's go," he said to Rico, taking her hand and starting away.

"I can't go there," she protested, not moving.

Seth stared at her, their clasped hands extended between them. "Why not?"

"It isn't proper," she answered.

"Bullshit," he said, catching her around the waist and leading her away.

Elena stood between Danny and Jesse as they all watched Seth and Rico leave. Then Danny murmured, "Seth ain't one for following custom, is he?"

Elena shook her head.

"You want to dance?" he asked.

"I'd rather just sit and watch," she said. "Rico was supposed to give me a lesson this week but somehow we never got around to it."

He nodded, then looked at Jesse. "See you later, Jess," Danny said, taking Elena's elbow and guiding her to one of the circular benches built around the trees. They had eaten lunch together on those benches many times as children, sitting close in the uninhibited candor of innocence as they shared their perceptions of the world; but now they sat properly with a stretch of emptiness between them. After an awkward moment he said, "I've quit school, did you know that?"

"Miss Emory told me," she said, watching Matty Rivers dance with Frank Engle. His father owned the biggest mercantile firm in the county, and Elena guessed a merchant would be a good match for a girl who thought about clothes all the time. "You would've graduated in two more weeks, Danny," Elena said, giving him a puzzled smile.

He shrugged. "Can't see I'd learn much in two weeks."

"You'd have a diploma," she pointed out.

"If a man don't believe I know what I say I do, a piece of paper ain't gonna convince him."

"No, I suppose not," she said, looking away to watch the dancers again. They were mostly young people she and Danny knew from school, a few older couples moving more sedately. The platform was ringed with spectators, and the yard crowded with people laughing in conversation. A string of bachelors lounged against the corral fence, and small circles of maidens hovered near the schoolhouse door. The younger children ran in packs, weaving their shrill screams through the general noise of festivity. Elena hadn't seen so many people in one place since the county fair. "Are these dances always so popular?" she asked.

"Tonight's an especially big turnout," Danny said. "Reckon a lot of folks're here to see Seth."

When she jerked around with surprise, Danny grinned. "I noticed he ain't wearing a gun," he said. "I heard some men making bets on whether he would."

"What's it to them?" she demanded.

Danny laughed gently. "It's against the rules, Elena, and the sheriff enforces that rule. I think some of these folks were hoping to witness a repeat of history."

"That's ghoulish," she said, looking at the crowd again, not seeing them as quite so pretty and gay.

After a minute, he said, "So Lobo's working for Blue now."

"Yeah," she said, still feeling a nudge of misgiving every time she thought of Lobo.

"I've opened a silver shop across the street," Danny said.

She turned around again to stare at him. "That's not the nicest part of town, Danny."

He shrugged. "The rent's cheap, and Seth said I'm apt to get my best business from cowboys wanting some flash on their bridles or a pretty to take home to their sweethearts."

"When did he say that?" she asked, uncomfortable with the thought of Seth and Danny having conversations she didn't know about.

"We've gotten in the habit of sharing a beer at Blue's in the afternoon," he answered, watching her closely.

She turned away again to see her parents coming back from behind the schoolhouse as the band began a waltz. Seth guided Rico up the steps to the dance floor. The other couples parted to allow them entry, then gave them so much room the circle constantly opened and closed with their passing.

Elena watched her parents with a breathless awe, seeing how gracefully Rico followed Seth, how adeptly he led her, how masterfully they both bore the scrutiny of everyone there. When they shared a smile, flaunting their enjoyment of life, Elena felt proud to be a child of their love. Studying the faces of the crowd, she saw envy and admiration, leniency and generosity, even ridicule and resentment, but nowhere did she see indifference. The good citizens called him the outlaw and stigmatized his family in society, yet it was evident the people of Tejoe claimed him as their very own pariah. Elena felt overwhelmed with love for the man who had come home to endure that for the sake of his family.

Danny asked softly, "Do you think you could ever look at me the way you're looking at him?"

She turned around and really looked at Danny Nickles. He was neither tall nor physically strong, would never be a man who could drop the world to its knees with the ice of his eyes. Danny's eyes were the color of honey held to the sun, as warm and sweet as the best memories of childhood.

In response to her silence, he murmured, "I think you're beautiful, Elena."

She laughed in denial. "No, I'm not."

"To my eyes you are," he said stubbornly. "But if you want to laugh when I say it, reckon that answers my question."

"I haven't answered your question," she said.

His eyes softened. "I'm living on the edge of town now. The house has ten acres with it, so there's room for a stable and corral, if we want to build one."

Helpless to prevent what she knew was coming, she kept quiet.

"The house is kinda small," he said, "but big enough for two. We could add a room when the baby comes."

"What baby?" she whispered.

"The one that always comes," he said, "when a woman sleeps with a man she can look at in the way I was asking about."

The music stopped, and she turned away to watch her parents descend from the dance floor. At the foot of the steps, the Ascarate family waited to greet them. The men shook hands with ironic smiles, then Seth leaned down and kissed Heaven's cheek as Joaquín bestowed a kiss on Rico. A hush had fallen over the crowd, and Elena suddenly realized they were all watching the public spectacle of the outlaw forgiving the sheriff who had arrested him.

The fiddler struck up a gay fandango, and the moment was gone, the people again swirling on the dance floor and laughing between themselves in private pleasures. Elena watched Aaron. He was standing behind his parents, waiting for Seth to grant him recognition. When Seth did, the boy stepped forward and solemnly shook his hand, and Elena saw a light of love in her father's eyes that brought home what house Danny was talking about. "Do the curtains have bluebonnets on them?" she whispered.

"Yeah," he said, "but they're old and faded. I was hoping you'd help me put up new ones."

She watched Lobo arrive, tying his horse at the fence and greeting the line of bachelors by name, then walking across and saying hello to Seth and Rico and Jesse, who had joined them now, then Joaquín and Heaven and Aaron. When Lobo said something that made them all laugh, Seth threw his arm across Lobo's shoulders and pulled him close in a quick hug. From her place in the shadows beneath the trees, Elena saw that her brother wasn't wearing the gun. She turned around to smile at Danny. "Lobo's running the stallion in the race. Did you know that?"

Danny shook his head. "What about you and Two-Bits?"

In the back of her mind, Elena knew she had been sacrificed, for Lobo's sake and in the name of peace, but she was striving to accept her fate with grace. "Reckon we'll both be pregnant by then," she said with a mischievous smile.

"The race is only a month away, Elena."

"So?" she teased.

"Are you sure?" he asked, sternly solemn.

She fell in love with his fatherly voice. "If we're getting married anyway," she said, "why not jump the gun?"

He stood up and offered his hand to help her. As Danny led her away from the lights, Elena looked back at her family, intent on a story Lobo was telling. Seth looked up and gave her a smile. With his blessing, she followed her best friend across the moonlit desert, and found her husband in a lonely casita that hadn't sheltered love in many years.